Praise for *True Spies*

"Engaging plot, snappy dialogue, and likable characters...a charmer."

—*RT Book Reviews,* 4 Stars

"Lively pace, likable characters, and espionage-laced plot come together to create the perfect escapist read."

—*Booklist*

"This lighthearted, fast-paced cloak-and-dagger romp will amuse even the most discerning Regency reader."

—*Publishers Weekly*

"A laugh-out-loud, yet sensual, historical romance that is sure to become a favorite."

—*Romance Junkies*

"[Galen's] use of verbal imagery is cinematic, action scenes are well thought out, and Galen's ability to build character and relationship while moving the story along at a quick pace is what keeps me captivated and anticipating her books."

—*Gourmande Girl*

"I so love a good spy book and Shana Galen doesn't disappoint... Brilliant."

—*The Royal Reviews*

"Moving at a brisk pace, the novel is a mix of adventure, snappy dialogue, and spicy love scenes between husband and wife."

—*Historical Novel Review*

"A spy caper and a romantic romp… *True Spies* is a treat."

—*New York Journal of Books*

"Entertaining, humorous, witty, and just well done."

—BookLoons.com

"A thrilling, fast-paced historical romance that I absolutely loved…delightful."

—*Imagine a World*

"Once again, Ms. Galen has thrilled her readers with a love story that is not only filled with secrets, deception, but with dangerous intrigue and sexy romance."

—*My Book Addiction Reviews*

"Gorgeous…electric and vibrant."

—*My Written Romance*

"The subtle humor that permeates scary scenes, love scenes, social scenes, and more makes *True Spies* a delight."

—*Long and Short Reviews*

"Takes readers on a fast-paced romp… Very well written."

—*Debbie's Book Bag*

Praise for *If You Give a Rake a Ruby*

"Galen expertly entwines espionage-flavored intrigue with sizzling passion."

—*Booklist*

"Galen is at the top of her game… Galen is a grand mistress of the action/adventure subgenre."

—*RT Book Reviews*, 4½ Stars, Top Pick of the Month

"Engrossing and fun. Shana Galen is known for her fast-pasted Regencies, and she scores again with *If You Give a Rake a Ruby*."

—*Historical Novel Review*

"Sensual and sexy…"

—*Publishers Weekly*

"Passionate, exciting, and dazzling… A lighthearted read that is plenty of fun, but it is also an emotional journey that will captivate you completely."

—*The Romance Reviews*

"The writing is excellent and the characters are captivating. Ms. Galen delivers a steamy romance."

—*Night Owl Reviews*, 5 Stars, Reviewer Top Pick

"Full of daring and danger, this Regency romance sizzles with sexual tension, brims with subtle humor, and entertains with characters that sweep the reader into a whirlwind of high-risk action and euphoric love."

—*Long and Short Reviews*

Also by Shana Galen

Sons of the Revolution

The Making of a Duchess
The Making of a Gentleman
The Rogue Pirate's Bride

Lord and Lady Spy

Lord and Lady Spy
True Spies
The Spy Wore Blue (novella)

Jewels of the Ton

When You Give a Duke a Diamond
If You Give a Rake a Ruby
Sapphires Are an Earl's Best Friend

LOVE AND LET SPY

SHANA GALEN

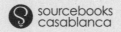
sourcebooks
casablanca

Published by Sourcebooks Casablanca, an imprint of Sourcebooks, Inc.
P.O. Box 4410, Naperville, Illinois 60567-4410
(630) 961-3900
Fax: (630) 961-2168
www.sourcebooks.com

Printed and bound in Canada.
MBP 10 9 8 7 6 5 4 3 2 1

For my daughter. I hope you grow up as smart, savvy, and strong as Bonde, and I hope all of your dreams come true.

One

Somewhere in Europe, 1816

SHE CREPT DOWN THE CORRIDOR, BACK TO THE WALL, straining to place the voices of the men. Somewhere a woman was crying, a dog barked, and a horse-drawn cart rattled by. The stench of urine and blood burned her nostrils, but she moved forward.

Two men. French-speakers, though only one was a native speaker. The other…the accent sounded Turkish? She turned her head to locate the voices.

Closed door.

Room at the end of the hall.

Three steps. Two. One.

She paused outside, drawing her knife. She didn't want to risk her pistol misfiring and left it tucked inside her coat, along with a stash of ball and powder. She was dressed as a man because the clothing was more practical and attracted less attention. She didn't think she'd fool anyone who looked closely. And she didn't care.

A man inside the room—the Frenchman—spoke again, and her hand stilled on the door's latch.

"Reaper is dead," she translated silently. "He took his life in prison."

News traveled quickly, though not accurately. The report she'd seen claimed Foncé had gained access to Reaper and slit his throat. The leader of the Maîtriser group didn't tolerate failure. When Foncé realized she, an agent of his hated Barbican group, had tracked two of his men to this ramshackle flash ken, their lives would be forfeit as well. Perhaps that cold fact would be incentive for them to assist her in locating their leader.

Or perhaps it would only make them more eager to kill her.

Either way, the games were about to begin.

She pulled her hand away from the door, stepped back, raised a booted foot, and kicked. The thin wooden door splintered and shot open with a loud *crack*. The men jumped up, but they didn't move quickly enough. Her knife flew from her fingers, catching one man in the shoulder and pinning him to the wall behind him. He screamed while the other man fumbled for his pistol. She obligingly reached for hers. "I'll kill you before you even pack your powder," she said in French. "Do us both a favor and lower your pistol before I'm forced to shoot you."

"I don't owe you any favors, Bonde." The man holding the pistol sneered. He was called Tueur, and he was an assassin—one of Foncé's best now that Reaper was dead. She wished she'd thrown the knife at him. They'd met before and, since he had been trying to kill her at the time, had not parted amicably. But she could let bygones...and all of that rubbish. "That's *Miss* Bonde to you. Shall we have a little chat?"

"No time today," he said and threw the pistol. Bonde ducked, and the weapon clattered to the floor behind her. She reached for it, tucked it in her waistband, then whirled back around. Tueur had wasted no time. He waved as he raced across the room and climbed out the window.

She uttered a most unladylike expletive, her body pulled between Tueur and the Turk. She couldn't split in half—that was the disadvantage of working alone. Working with another agent—that was the disadvantage of a partner.

She headed for the window, glancing at the Turk over her shoulder. A knife protruded from his neck. Tueur had made certain the other man wouldn't talk. He'd also made her decision easy. She leaned out the window and spotted Tueur hanging from the faded awning of the shop below. He dropped to the ground and made a rude gesture.

Bygones were, apparently, not bygone in Tueur's opinion.

She did a quick calculation then dove out the window, pulling her knees in so when she landed on the awning she would roll easily to the edge. She held her breath for the free fall and felt the air whoosh out of her when she hit the fabric.

But she didn't roll.

She heard an awful ripping sound and reached out just in time to catch the edge of the awning before she fell through. Her feet dangled above the hard cobblestones as the material slipped through her fingers.

With a sigh, she let go, dropped, and tumbled. The ground was hard, bruising her hip and shoulder. She hobbled to her feet and wiped her bloody hands on her trousers. Where was the dashed man? She glared left and then right.

Unfortunately, he'd seen her and took off at a fast clip.

She went after him, her hip protesting the movement. Red clouded her vision, and she realized her forehead was bleeding. She swiped the blood away and rounded a corner, emerging onto a busy avenue lined with carts and vendors. Men and women walked leisurely along the avenue, shopping on the lovely spring day. Bollocks! Again she'd lost him. And on a crowded street, no less.

Bonde noted a statue and raised fountain standing in a nearby esplanade, and she dodged horses and carriages to reach the monument. She climbed up, hanging on by one arm, and peered down the busy street. He was gone…no—wait.

There! He'd climbed into a Bath chair, which two men were hastily pulling away. She jumped down, searching for another chair for hire and realized Tueur had taken the last. She glanced about, her attention landing on a sporty gig. A footman waited beside the horse, presumably while the vehicle's owner shopped for produce. Bonde ran for it, hopping up before the footman could protest. He stared at her dumbly for a moment, but when she snapped the reins, he grabbed for the horse's bridle.

"Sorry!" she said, straining to control the skittish animal. The horse tried to rear and then shot off.

Fortunately, the beast chose the direction she wanted. Unfortunately, he was going much too fast for the crowded avenue. Men and women jumped out of the way as she struggled to gain the upper hand. The Bath chair was just ahead, but the horse bolted to the side before she could jerk him back. The gig's wheel caught on the edge of a fruit stand, sending the vendor's cart toppling over. Oranges and lemons tumbled into the street, and apples bounced in every direction. One bounced into the conveyance, and she caught it with a hand, took a bite, and snapped the reins.

She was grinning. She had Tueur now. He yelled furiously for the men pulling his chair to go faster, but they couldn't compete in a race with a horse. She gained ground until she finally pulled alongside the chair. "Ready for our chat now?" she yelled.

"Go to the devil, Bonde!"

"You first," she muttered, steering the horse closer to the chair so the men pulling it were forced to move aside. Tueur didn't wait for the inevitable. He rose and jumped from the chair, smashing onto the ground. She reined in the horse and jumped nimbly down, landing on her feet and running to grab Tueur before he could rise. She all but collided with a woman carrying an armful of flowers, and the woman tripped and went sprawling to the ground. Bonde spit a daffodil from her mouth and kept running. But the delay cost her. Tueur was up again and moving quickly toward a busy alleyway, where artists sold jewelry, paintings, and mementos. She pictured the city map in her mind. At the end of the alley was a canal. If Tueur reached the canal, he could jump on a vessel and she'd never catch him.

She pushed two men out of the way and raced forward. Tueur saw her coming and began to jog. Some of the crowd saw them approach and parted, but others had to be thrust out of the way. Bonde jumped lithely over a stack of crates, wobbled, and regained her balance.

Tueur was definitely headed for the canal. If she lost him, M would have her head. She sped up just as a young mother holding a little girl's hand stepped out from behind a stall. With a yell, Bonde narrowly avoided them and crashed into a flower cart. Everything went dark and floral for a moment, and when she surfaced, this time spitting tulip petals from her mouth, the flower girl screamed obscenities. At least Bonde thought they were obscenities. Amidst the haze of petals and stems, she'd forgotten in which country she'd landed and the native language spoken. She pulled a rose from her hair, handed it to the woman, and arrowed for the canal.

Tueur was already there, and she saw his dilemma immediately. No vessels. Bonde reached for her pistol. She had him.

He saw her coming then looked back at the water. Then back at her. He took a step forward.

"No!"

But it was already too late. He took two steps back and ran. She reached the edge of the canal as the water splashed back down, mud from below churning up and darkening the already filthy waterway.

"Come up. Swim, damn you," she muttered. The ripples grew larger, and the water stilled. She stared at the place he'd gone under for a long moment, her gaze scanning the rest of the canal.

Nothing moved.

"Bollocks," she said.

"Hey!"

Bonde turned to see a crowd of angry merchants and shoppers approaching. Some waved damaged goods, some waved fists, some didn't have the courtesy to wave.

"Bollocks," she said again. There was nothing for it. She pulled off her cap, allowing her golden hair to spill down her back, and smiled prettily.

Two

London Season, 1816

"I DON'T CARE HOW BEAUTIFUL OR RICH OR BLOODY socially acceptable she is," Dominic said, turning fiercely from the drawing-room mantel. "I am not marrying her."

"Sir, need I remind you that your mother is present?"

The marchioness waved a hand. In her pale blue muslin morning gown, she seemed almost one of the furnishings in the drawing room, which had been done in blue and cream and a panoply of gilt and ormolu. "I have heard it all before," his mother said. "One does not raise four sons without hearing a bit of the vulgar tongue."

Dominic gestured as if to say, *See?*

"I do not give a bloody farthing," the marquess said, standing and pointing at Dominic. "You *will* show your mother some respect."

Dominic refrained, just barely, from mentioning the contradiction inherent in his stepfather's curse. The man had no sense of humor and would not appreciate the irony. He also had a selective memory. At the moment, he chose to forget that his wife possessed a somewhat less than savory past.

Dominic wished he could forget.

"My lord," Dominic said, tamping down his fury from long habit, "I do not wish to marry. I have no obligation to produce an heir, as I have no lands or titles to pass on. There is no need—"

"There is every need!" Lord Edgeberry boomed. Dominic clenched his fists to keep from using them. He was a grown man and did not enjoy being treated like a child. But he would tolerate it for his mother. "Your behavior is scandalous, and I'll be damned if I stand by while you produce a passel of bastards who show up on my door, begging for money."

Dominic cut his gaze to his mother, and the marchioness hissed in a breath and shook her head at her eldest son, her eyes pleading for forbearance. "My lord," she said, rising and taking her husband's arm. "Might we speak in private for a moment?"

Dominic turned his back on the room and faced the mantel, staring at the figure of a small porcelain shepherdess. She was a typical English beauty with flaxen hair, rosy cheeks, and huge blue eyes. Dominic hated the type. Behind him he heard his mother's rapid whispers. Every few moments, he was able to discern one of her words. "Fatherless...Pride...Careful."

The door opened, and Carlisle, one of Dominic's half brothers, entered. "Oops! Sorry." He stepped back out just as quickly, but not before catching Dominic's eye and giving his older brother a grimace.

"No, no, Carlisle," their mother said. "Your father

and I will speak in the parlor. You go ahead." And she tugged the marquess out of the room, leaving Carlisle little choice but to enter.

"I'm not going to ask what that was about," Carlisle said, "so you'll have to volunteer the information."

Dominic couldn't stop a smile. Carlisle was his youngest half brother and just out of school. At nineteen, he was not yet jaded by the world. But then again, why should he be? He was the son of a marquess, he was handsome with his blond hair and brown eyes, and he was wealthy. Nothing could touch him.

"I'll give you one guess," Dominic said, lifting his teacup from the drawing-room side table. He'd always liked his youngest brother. With thirteen years between them, they were too far apart to be rivals.

"The woman who showed up with the babe last week?"

"Your father wants me to marry before I bring more shame on the family name." He sipped the tepid tea. He'd not even had a chance to taste it before his stepfather launched into his tirade.

Carlisle popped a tea cake into his mouth and reached for another. "Is marriage so bad?"

"I don't see you rushing into the parson's mousetrap."

Carlisle held the tea cake in front of his chest like a shield. "I'm far too young. You're an old man."

"Charming to the last," Dominic retorted.

"Was the babe yours?" Carlisle asked, his mouth full. Dominic rolled his eyes. The boy had no sense of decorum.

"No."

"Whom do they want you to marry?"

"Does it matter?"

He seemed to consider as he reached for a dainty sandwich. "It might."

"A Miss Jane Bonde."

Carlisle dropped the sandwich, and it rolled under a chair. The boy ignored it. "And you refused?"

"I don't want to marry, and I certainly won't marry some chit I haven't even met."

"But you've seen her?"

"I don't think so." Dominic avoided social events. He had nothing to say to the *ton*. He was well aware they looked down on him. He did not need to be reminded of it nightly.

"That explains it then." Carlisle reached for another sandwich.

Dominic drank his tea. "You imply that if I laid eyes on her, I would change my mind."

"Probably not," Carlisle mumbled around the bread. "But you'd think twice."

Dominic set his teacup down. He was beginning to think it a good idea to escape while he had the chance. "I doubt we have the same taste in women."

"She is every man's taste, I assure you. Are you leaving?"

Dominic was halfway across the room. "Yes, but I must say, Carlisle, you have intrigued me. I might have to see this Miss Bonde for myself."

"There is a long line of men ahead of you."

Dominic opened the door. "Give Lord Edgeberry my regards."

"That ought to be a pleasant task," Carlisle muttered. Dominic closed the door and started for the stairs. He hadn't made it far before his mother stepped in front of him. She was petite, dark, and exotic with her Gypsy coloring. As far as Dominic knew, she was not of Gypsy blood, but she did nothing to dispel the rumors. He was a great deal taller than she. His father must have been a man of some height, for Dominic was a head taller than his stepfather and his three half brothers. But woe to the man or woman who equated height with power. Titania Griffyn—now Titania Houghton-Cleveborne, Marchioness of Edgeberry— was a force to be reckoned with.

"A word, my darling son." She gestured toward her boudoir, where she met with her closest friends, and set off, not waiting to see if he would follow.

Dominic sighed and followed.

∜

Elsewhere in Mayfair

It was never a simple matter to descend the facade of an edifice with no more assistance than that of the occasional ledge or outcropping that might be used in place of a hand- or foothold. Trying to accomplish such a feat while wearing a ball gown and the accompanying silk slippers made the task even more difficult. And, in Bonde's opinion, it was an all but impossible commission when one was wearing gloves.

But she was determined. And besides, she had to make a good showing. Poor Lady Keating—code name Butterfly—was expecting her to act as an example. Bonde lowered a foot, searching for purchase, found it, and moved down the wall of the gray stone mansion.

"Tell me again why we must attempt this," Butterfly said.

"Because," Bonde answered, trying to secure a handhold and floundering slightly. *Show no fear. Show no fear.* Her glove slipped, and she flailed, but she managed to regain her balance by grasping a hole in the limestone with her other hand. "At some crucial juncture you might need to make a quick exit, and there are times when a window is more accessible than a door." She glanced down at the ground, still a good distance below her. Baron stood in the shadows under them, keeping watch and occasionally glancing up and frowning. "Baron, do I have the right of it?"

"Of course," he called up. "Talk later. Concentrate now."

Bonde did not think chitchat much of a distraction. Having someone shoot a pistol in one's general direction or dump a pot of hot water down the side of a building, those were credible distractions. But, she reminded herself, Butterfly was still learning. Bonde descended the next few feet in silence, listening instead to the sounds of the orchestra playing at the ball taking place inside the Grosvenor Square mansion. The low rumble of voices and the clink of champagne glasses rose above the music at times, as did the tittering laugh of some woman or other. She decided that for all the exertion of the climb down, she much preferred it here than inside.

"What is taking so long?"

Bonde knew that voice and sighed. She glanced at Butterfly above her. The other spy was still proceeding slowly but surely. Bonde could have drunk a glass of ratafia by now if she'd not moved slowly to make certain Butterfly did not need her. And now here was her uncle, expressing his usual impatience.

"We are trying to concentrate, Uncle," she called down.

"Everyone is asking for you," he answered. "Your aunt, in particular."

That news was rather worrisome. What could her aunt possibly want with her? She'd worn the gown her aunt had chosen, allowed her hair to be styled by her aunt's lady's maid, and promised to dance with no fewer than six eligible gentlemen, none of them more than once, of course. What else did her aunt require?

Her actual appearance, she supposed. Bonde glanced up at Butterfly again and noted the woman seemed to have her footing now. She did not have far to go, and there was a window ledge under her, which made the last few feet child's play. Bonde crawled, spider-like, down the rest of the building and jumped neatly beside Baron and her uncle.

"What the devil was that?" Baron asked. "Are you part ape?"

Bonde smiled. "I assume you meant that as a compliment. Some ladies might take offense."

Baron raised a brow. He was handsome with those green eyes and that unruly brown hair. Not that she cared whether men were handsome or not. She had never been swayed by appearances. She knew well how often they might deceive.

"Some ladies do not descend walls as though they are part monkey."

"Hmm." Bonde inspected her gloves for any traces of dirt. "Another questionable compliment."

"He excels at those," Butterfly added from her perch above the window.

"Will you concentrate?" Baron barked and moved underneath his wife. Bonde glanced at her uncle. The idea of two married spies working together was still a novelty to her. But then, she insisted upon working alone.

"He's a bit overprotective," her uncle murmured. "That's why I called you in. I didn't feel he was challenging her to reach her full potential."

"She's good," Bonde acknowledged. "She has natural instincts."

"I'm pleased you agree."

Baron caught his wife around the waist and set her down, rather than making her descend the last few feet. She looked spent and relieved. Bonde would have flayed him for such presumption. If she started something, she finished it.

Butterfly all but skipped over to them, smiling from ear to ear. "I did it. I really did it!"

"Of course you did," Bonde said. The alternative had been to splat on the stone paving on which they now stood.

"You performed beautifully," Baron said.

"Not as beautifully as Bonde. I don't think she has a hair out of place or a wrinkle in her gown." Butterfly looked down at her own wrinkled gown and her ruined gloves. "You made it appear so completely effortless."

"That is why she is the best," her uncle said.

"You were certainly correct on that account, Lord Melbourne," Butterfly agreed.

"Excuse me," Baron said, frowning, "but I do think a man should be able to rely on his wife championing him, even if no one else does so."

"Oh, poor Winn," Butterfly said, patting his arm. "I was mistaken. You are the best. Now, please take me home."

Bonde felt a sharp jab of surprise. "Oh, but won't you be attending the ball?" Was everyone but her allowed to escape?

"I'm far too fatigued," Butterfly said. "Not to mention, we promised our girls we would be home to tuck them into bed."

She had forgotten they had children. "Oh, I see." As she watched, the spies became less and less Baron and Butterfly, and more and more Lord and Lady Keating.

"Come then." Her uncle took her arm. "I dare not keep Lady Melbourne waiting any longer." He escorted her around the side of the house and into the garden, where several couples were strolling. Spring was in full bloom, and the flowers looked lovely in the moonlight. Not that Bonde had taken any time to look at the flowers, but she imagined if she ever did have time, they would look lovely. Her uncle led her up the steps of the house to the open doors of the ballroom. The cool night air wafted inside, rustling the curtains and relieving a bit of the stifling heat caused by the crush of people.

It took Bonde several moments to adjust to the sounds and the lights and the mass of bodies, but before the first gentleman bowed and said, "Good evening, Miss Bonde," she had become Miss Jane Bonde again and had left Bonde, the spy, outside.

She smiled, her lips curving prettily, and tossed her blond curls back over her shoulder. "Mister Asprey. How good to see you again."

He looked as if he would detain her, but she could not speak to him longer or he might ask her to dance, and her toes would not tolerate another mashing.

"My aunt awaits," she said as she glided away. As a consolation, she tossed him a charming smile. He almost stumbled.

"Jane, darling!" Her aunt clutched her arm and dragged her aside. "Where have you been?"

Jane looked at her uncle for assistance, for she was not certain what he had told his wife as an excuse. But her uncle had suddenly disappeared. He was quite good at disappearing, especially when his wife was nearby. "Aunt, I am so sorry to have kept you waiting."

"It is not I you have kept waiting, but someone very special." As she spoke, Lady Melbourne propelled Jane through the crowds and toward the supper room. Jane did not argue, which would have been pointless at any rate. The supper room would be quieter than the ballroom, and her head was already pounding from the noise of too many voices. Oh, but she hated these affairs. Why could she not turn thirty already and be declared officially on the shelf? At four and twenty, she was unsuitable and elderly, but not yet completely unmarriageable.

More was the pity.

How would she survive six more years of Seasons? She had several sources of hope. One: that her aunt and uncle would run out of discretionary funds and have to forego all social activities. But though Lady Melbourne spent quite extravagantly, Jane's last peek into her uncle's account books revealed he still had enormous funds at his disposal. Since her uncle was a former operative, Jane had suspicions as to where those funds might have originated.

Her second hope was that a crisis requiring her intervention would interrupt her participation in the endless round of balls, musicales, and routs. This was by far the more likely scenario. It had been six months since any new information about Foncé had been reported and four since another agent from the Barbican group had apprehended the assassin for the Maîtriser group, Foncé's criminal organization. But though Jane had questioned this Reaper on many occasions before his untimely death, he had proved less than talkative.

Still, Foncé would not lick his wounds forever...

If he would just make another appearance in London or Europe or anywhere. Here, in the supper room, would have been preferable at the moment. No good could come of anything or anyone her aunt believed was *special*. Heaven forbid any person receive the designation of *very special*.

As soon as they stepped into the supper room, the noise from the ball dimmed. Jane's head throbbed in relief. What she would not give for a night of quiet and a good book on ancient weapons or deadly poisons. Out of habit, Jane scanned the room, taking quick note of her surroundings. Several tables had been laid with delicacies of every sort—cold meats and thick sauces, glossy fruits, savory breads, and sumptuous sweets. The hot dishes would be set out right before the call to supper, but Jane would have been quite happy with the cold dishes alone. She thought she'd eaten a piece of cheese at some point this afternoon, but that might have been yesterday. She'd spent the better part of the day at the Barbican's offices, and there was never anything to eat there.

"Now, Jane," her aunt turned to her and whispered hurriedly, looking back at the door as she did so. Who *was* she expecting? "I want you to be polite."

"I am always polite."

"Yes, but sometimes you are polite in such a way as to actually be insulting. The person to whom you are speaking might not notice, but I do." Her aunt's large hazel eyes fastened on Jane's face and held. Jane did not look away. Instead, she studied her aunt's handsome features—her glossy auburn hair, her high forehead, her pointed nose, and her firm mouth. She was barely forty, several years younger than her husband, and she had obviously been a beauty in her day. She was still a beautiful woman, intelligent as well. Jane felt a little sorry for her, because like most women of her station, there was little for her to do but sip tea, gossip, and marry off her sons and daughters.

But Lord and Lady Melbourne had no sons or daughters. That was a shame, because her aunt would have been a wonderful mother. She had taken in the broken daughter of her husband's brother and raised her with affection and kindness. And even though Jane had been young when she'd come to live with her aunt and uncle, she had never thought of them as mother and father. There was a distance between them, a formality.

Lady Melbourne peered at the door again, and Jane followed her gaze. "Who is it I am to meet?"

"A Mr. Dominic Griffyn. His mother is the Marchioness of Edgeberry."

Edgeberry… Jane had an image of a passel of attractive young men, all with blond hair and brown eyes. They might have been her brothers for all the resemblance they shared.

"I see, and what makes Mr. Griffyn so…" She trailed off as a footman carrying a silver tray with champagne glasses approached.

"Champagne?" he inquired, smiling at her.

"Thank you," Lady Melbourne said, taking a glass.

"Miss?" the footman asked, offering her the tray. Her aunt gave her a stern look, but Jane ignored her. She did not care for champagne, and if she was going to have to meet this Mr. Griffyn, she feared she needed fortification.

"Would you be so kind as to fetch me a glass of ratafia?"

"Of course." The footman nodded. "I would be more than happy to fetch you ratafia—or…or anything at all, miss." He gave her a long, meaningful look, and Jane supposed the *anything at all* might include more than refreshment.

"Cherry, please."

"My pleasure." He began to walk away.

"Shaken, not stirred."

"Certainly, miss. I'll see to it personally."

He moved swiftly to carry out the request, and Lady Melbourne hissed, "Can you not sip champagne?"

"I prefer ratafia."

"You are too particular."

"He did not seem to mind."

"Because he could not stop staring at you. But enamored footmen aside, you are too particular."

Oh, dear God. Jane hoped this would not be another discussion about marriage, and then she narrowed her eyes. "Aunt, what makes this Mr. Griffyn so *special*?"

Her aunt looked away, and Jane's heart began to pound. "You do not intend for me to marry this man, do you? I have not even met him."

"I had hoped to discuss this matter after you met him."

Jane shook her head. Had the orchestra moved closer? All of a sudden, everything was once again too bright and too loud.

"What matter?"

"Jane…"

Jane grabbed her aunt's gloved arm. *"What matter?"*

Her aunt frowned. "Very well." She lowered her voice so that none of the servants or guests passing by might hear. "Your uncle and I have decided. You and Mr. Griffyn will marry."

Jane released her aunt as if she had been burned. "No."

"The issue has been decided on both sides, Jane," her aunt said with a stubborn lift of her chin.

"No." Jane looked about. She would find her uncle. He could not have possibly agreed to this. "Lord Melbourne—"

"—agrees completely. In fact, Mr. Griffyn was his choice."

But why? Jane did not understand. She was an agent,

not a wife. Hadn't her uncle always been pleased with her performance? Why would he want to marry her off and relegate her to a life of utter insignificance? She still had Foncé and the Maîtriser group to defeat. How could she do that if she had a husband demanding she be home to remove his slippers every evening?

"I won't do it," Jane said flatly. "I am sorry to disobey you and my uncle in anything, my lady, but I will not, under any circumstances, marry Mr. Griffyn."

Her aunt's eyes widened into enormous saucers, and there was a long silence. Too long. At some point, the orchestra had finished the reel they'd been playing. Finally, the sound of a man clearing his throat echoed in the quiet supper room. Jane whirled about.

"Shall I return at a more opportune time?" the man standing behind her drawled. Jane gaped at him as warmth unrelated to the stifling ballroom crept from her belly to her cheeks. He was tall, much taller than the average man, and at least a head taller than she. He had broad shoulders, not as broad as Baron's, but broad enough that he filled out his dark green coat quite nicely. His hips were slim, his breeches snug, and his legs muscled.

She glanced back up and looked into his face. He was smiling, looking somewhat amused. She imagined her perusal of him was what caused the smile. She had completely forgotten herself, and now she was about to do so again. He had the most cocky, arrogant smile she had ever witnessed on the most sensual lips she had ever seen on a man. He had obviously not shaved, as he had a dark shadow of stubble on his strong jaw and sculpted cheeks. She knew many women who would have killed for his cheekbones. His eyes were impossibly dark, the eyes of a man one might expect to encounter in a Gypsy camp. His eyebrows were two dark slashes above thick eyelashes, and his hair, straight and windblown, fell carelessly over his forehead. The style was too long, brushing his shoulders, and not at all fashionable, but she could not help thinking it suited him perfectly. It made his already dark, sensual features look even more exotic.

"Mr. Griffyn!" her aunt all but screeched.

Jane shook her head. This could not be Mr. Griffyn. For if it was Mr. Griffyn, she had just completely embarrassed herself and her aunt.

But more importantly, if this was Mr. Griffyn, she was in trouble.

Three

"LADY MELBOURNE," DOMINIC SAID THROUGH HIS clenched jaw. The poor woman was shaking with agitation. He turned his gaze to the girl. "You must be Miss Bonde."

"I must apologize for my earlier statement. I meant no offense."

"No offense taken. I have heard of you as well."

She shook her head. "But—"

"And I must say, the accounts have been exaggerated."

The lovely flush on her face darkened, and her clear blue eyes turned from expressive to stone. He'd wounded her, as was his intent, but he did not feel any triumph. He wished the accounts had been exaggerated, but if anything, his brother had been modest. The girl standing before him was absolutely breathtaking. She was classically beautiful, the English ideal with her blond hair, her blue eyes, and her porcelain skin.

He knew the type. He couldn't count the times he'd seen derision in a pair of blue eyes. The beauties of the *ton* had shown him time and again that he was not worthy of them. This girl was no different.

Except this girl had something else, something more. There was a voluptuousness, a sensuality to this girl that tugged at him. He couldn't look away from her. He couldn't walk away from her. He wanted to rub his thumb over her full bottom lip, wanted to touch her skin to see if it was as soft as it looked, wanted to slide his palm over the full curve of her breast and test its weight.

He wanted her, and she had made it abundantly clear she did not want him. He could hardly blame her, but that did not mean he would forgive the slight.

"I suppose that is that then," she said, turning. "If you'll excuse me…"

"No!" Lady Melbourne looked panicked. "Mr. Griffyn, wait just one moment." Her niece was already moving away, but the older woman moved swiftly to catch her. "Jane, do not walk away, or you will have your uncle to answer to."

The girl stopped at that threat, and Dominic realized she was as trapped as he was. Her aunt and uncle had thrust him upon her, just as she'd been foisted upon him by his mother. But that did not mean he had to forgive her for the snub she'd given him. Why should he not make her suffer?

"You must at least dance with him," Lady Melbourne hissed.

"Yes, Miss Bonde, you owe me a dance at the very least."

She whipped her attention back to him, her mouth slightly agape. "You expect me—"

"Excellent notion, Mr. Griffyn," Lady Melbourne said. "You have my consent to dance. Go ahead. I will return in one moment." She glared at her niece. "I am going to fetch Lord Melbourne." And she hurried back into the ballroom.

"That sounded like a threat," Dominic drawled. He was surprised when she moved quickly to his side and gestured for him to follow her out of view of the ballroom.

"I do not know who you are or what sort of hold you have over my aunt and uncle, but I will find out, and I will take you down."

She actually looked as though she meant it, and Dominic did not know why that should arouse him. Her face was inches from his, her gaze boring into him, and all he could think was he wanted to kiss those pursed lips. Strange thought. He did not kiss. Ever. "I take it you are not overly fond of dancing," he drawled.

"No."

"Good. Let's walk." He moved in the direction of the doors open to the lawns, but just as they reached the exit, a footman rushed through, almost knocking them down. The glass on his tray wavered and then toppled, the dark red contents aiming for Miss Bonde's sapphire-blue gown. She moved rapidly, faster than he'd ever seen anyone move, and caught the glass without spilling a single drop. With her left hand, she steadied the tray and righted it. The footman began to apologize profusely, promising to fetch her another ratafia or a cake or anything she desired.

Miss Bonde sipped the drink and smiled. "This is perfect. Thank you."

"I'll fetch you another, miss. Ratafia. Shaken, not stirred, correct?"

"That's not necessary."

"It's my pleasure." And he rushed away.

"Do all men react to you like that?" Dominic asked.

"What do you mean?"

"That is answer enough. Come." He offered his arm. He would have preferred she not touch him, but in this situation he knew the protocol. Even so, she looked as though she might refuse, but then she narrowed her eyes at something she saw in the ballroom and laid her hand on his sleeve. He waited for the shudder of revulsion at her touch, but it never came.

He was still standing there, looking at her arm on his like an idiot, when she said, "Proceed, Mr. Griffyn. I think I would like a walk."

He led her through the ballroom. A better man would not have noted how many heads turned and how many raised brows accompanied those turned heads. A better man would not have felt a rush of triumph at having the woman every man wanted on his arm.

Dominic was not that man.

They stepped through the doors and into a garden lit by torches and lanterns. The breeze caused the flames to twinkle and flicker, and he could smell the fragrance of summer flowers. The air was cool, but Miss Bonde did not seem to mind it as they made their way past the small crowd of men and women just outside the doors. She paused to sip her beverage once again before setting the glass on a short stone column. He led her down a gravel path, toward the edges of the glow from the ball. Dominic had thought to keep quiet and allow her to speak. In his experience, ladies rarely remained silent for long. But Miss Bonde surprised him, yet again, by keeping her own counsel. She surprised him further by not objecting when he turned down a long aisle enclosed by tall, manicured hedgerows. Most well-bred ladies would have objected, concerned for their virtue. But she seemed…distracted.

Was his company that tedious?

"I have been to far more events this Season than I like to admit," she said. Dominic was relieved. He had actually been contemplating speaking first. "And I have not seen you before. Have you recently returned from abroad?"

"No." He expected some show of annoyance from her for his brief answer, but she was peering up at the hedgerows and seemed not to mind. In fact, she seemed not to notice him. He actually peered at the hedgerows himself to see what intrigued her so.

"Do you live in London?" she asked, dragging his attention away.

"When obliged."

She smiled at that. "You prefer the country?"

"Not necessarily."

"My lord—" she began, looking up at those blasted hedgerows again.

"I'm no lord."

"Of course not. I do believe we have satisfied the requirements of our respective guardians."

"Hardly."

She glanced at him then, giving him her full attention for the first time since they'd stepped outside. Her eyes, he now noted, were so blue as to be almost violet, and the effect of those stunning eyes focused solely on him was a bit unsettling, which must have accounted for why he wanted to kiss her. Again.

Unprecedented.

"No, you are correct. That was poor wording. But you must agree we have at least made a start. If you'd like to return to the ball, or perhaps slip away, I am perfectly capable of finding my own way back inside."

Dominic stared at her. She was trying to rid herself of his company. He should have been offended, but he'd been offended too many times, and this woman was a contradiction. She'd followed him down a dark path in a garden and then tried to persuade him to leave. What was she about?

"I don't even merit a kiss?" he asked. He had no bloody idea why he'd said it. He really did not intend to kiss her.

Her gaze, which had now strayed to some point behind him, snapped back. "Pardon?"

"You heard me."

"I do not desire..." She trailed off and gazed above his head again. Dominic turned quickly, to peer behind him, but saw nothing except the hedgerows and darkness.

"What are you looking at?"

His attention was jerked back to her when she grabbed his shoulders and turned him to face her. He barely had time to sputter a curse before her hands were on opposite sides of his face, and she was pulling him into a kiss.

His first instinct was to push her away, remove her hands from his face. But to his surprise, her touch was actually light and pleasant. Her gloved fingers were warm, her lips silky, and her breath slightly minty. Why push her away if he was enjoying this?

Because she wasn't really kissing him.

She held his face between her hands and pressed her lips to his firmly, and after a few moments of this, Dominic narrowed his eyes at her. Her own eyes were open and staring above his head. "What the devil are you doing?" he mumbled against her rigid lips.

She pushed back, and now she looked annoyed. "You said you wanted a kiss."

"Is that what you call this?"

She gave him a look designed to make ordinary men quake in their boots. But he was not ordinary, and he was not affected by some chit's regal glare. He cocked a brow. "Is that the best you can do?" Not that he had any experience kissing women—not on the lips, at any rate—but he could do better than that.

"You said you wanted a kiss."

"I repeat, is that the best you can do?"

She turned on her heel, throwing her hair over her shoulder in a gesture he found both annoyingly childish and strangely erotic. He wanted to catch that tail of hair and wind it around his hand, pulling her back for a proper kiss. "You'll never know," she tossed back at him, stomping away.

Well, he couldn't let that challenge go unanswered, could he?

It took two long strides before he caught her arm, but when he yanked her against him, she surprised him by thrusting an elbow in his belly. He doubled over, and she caught him in the jaw with her elbow, then spun around and kicked him in the chest with her slippered foot.

The slipper saved him. If she'd been wearing boots, he'd have fallen flat on his arse. As it was, he stumbled back and caught her ankle before losing his footing, so she fell too. They tumbled down together in a heap of arms and legs and the frilly things ladies wore under their dresses. What the hell was happening? Had she been training with Gentleman Jackson? Most—no, *all*—ladies he knew would have fainted rather than fight back. But she had not only fought. She had fought well.

She was not going to win.

When the world stopped spinning, he turned his head to the side and was rewarded by having it trapped thus. She crouched above him, looking little worse for the tumble they'd taken, and dug her forearm across his throat. "You are going to stay down for the count of ten, and I am going to walk away. Understand, Mr. Griffyn?"

"Where did you learn to fight like that?"

She grinned. "Want a lesson?"

"No, but I'd like to breathe again."

Her arm came up. "You can breathe while I walk away."

"I don't think so." She might have more skills, but he had more strength. He grasped her wrists and pulled her down on top of him. He expected her to kick, so he shifted to the side and rolled over, pinning her beneath him. He straddled her, his knees on either side of her ribs and her hands pinned beside her head. This was much better.

"Move off me before I scream," she seethed.

"Go ahead. That would make your aunt and my mother very happy indeed. We'd be forced to marry." Her breath puffed in and out in quick bursts, and from this vantage point, he had a nice view of the curve of her breasts as they rose and fell at the low neck of her bodice. They were both wearing gloves, which meant he couldn't feel her skin, but he could feel the pulse in her wrist racing. Or perhaps that was his own pulse?

In the moonlight and shadows, her skin was almost iridescent, and her eyes a shade of unearthly blue. She looked like some sort of mythological sprite brought to life from the pages of a storybook.

"You'd run if I screamed," she said confidently.

"Would I?"

Their gazes met and held, and he saw the flicker of doubt in her eyes.

"Have I done anything you expected?"

"I could throw you off."

"Maybe you could, but I'm willing to bet the effect on your hair and dress would be about the same as if you screamed." He should release her. He'd made his point, and he'd more than paid her back for the insult in the supper room. He didn't really intend to ravish her. Despite the rumors, he was no barbarian.

"Off!" she yelled.

He almost released her. His fingers flexed, but he simply could not do it. "I don't think so."

"Irritating man! What do you want?"

"I believe I was promised a kiss."

"That is not at all how I remember the conversation. Now allow me to go, or I will be forced to—"

He liked the sound of her voice. It was low and seductive, but he could not bear to hear another word from her lips. He lowered his mouth to hers and cut off her protests. She tensed beneath him, her lips going rigid again, but he found that with gentle pressure he was able to coax them into softening. He brushed his mouth over hers, prepared for the velvet softness of her lips, but not for the taste of her. She was honey and cherries and the slightest hint of something darker. He'd intended to kiss her lightly, leave her wanting, but once he had a taste of her, he had to know more.

He teased her lips open, kissing her deeply, releasing her wrists and locking his fingers with hers. He was painfully aware that he was straddling her. That he was leaning over her, holding her down. He was in control, and he liked it that way. She moaned slightly, and he was instantly hard. He knew he should release her. They'd been missing far too long, but he could not seem to stop touching her. And then he did the unthinkable, something he had never done before.

He dipped his tongue between her lips and met her tongue with his. The effect was electric. She jumped beneath him, and the shot of arousal he felt was all but dizzying. He knew he must stop. This was a gentlewoman, the niece of Lord Melbourne. He could not kiss her this way.

But there was that dark, erotic taste of her, hovering just out of reach, pulling him deeper and deeper until he was on the verge of losing control.

That realization finally cooled his ardor. In one motion, he released her, stood, and backed away. She lay on the ground below him, her eyes closed, her hands on the ground where he'd pinned them, and her chest rising and falling rapidly. Her cheeks were flushed, her lips swollen. She was the picture of debauchery. Slowly her eyes opened, and she stared at him. Looking down at her, he should have thought she was the one who was completely vulnerable and completely at his mercy.

But that was not the case at all. In fact, it was very much the reverse.

Dominic walked away without looking back.

⁓

Jane lay on the ground, a half-dozen tiny pieces of gravel digging into her back. What had just happened? Why had she allowed that…brute to kiss her, hold her down, make her feel…how did she feel? Out of sorts?

"Well, that was interesting."

She sat and cut her eyes to the hedgerow above her. Blue was still there, smiling at her with that sort of knowing smile she hated. "Are you still here?" she barked, rising and brushing her skirts off. She could not return to the ballroom. She would raise every eyebrow in the house.

"I have yet to pass on the intelligence you seek."

"As I tried to indicate a few moments ago, this is not the time or the place. Could it not wait?" She'd all but jumped when she'd seen the other spy in the garden. He was following her from the top of the hedgerows, and she had to do everything she could think of to keep Mr. Griffyn from looking up and seeing Blue.

Griffyn continued to frustrate her all the while Blue

was trying to capture her attention. She was an expert at reading lips, but with the darkness around her and the distraction of Griffyn, she had not been able to make out a thing. And then Griffyn had almost spotted Blue, and she'd had no choice but to kiss the infernal man.

"I am sorry to interrupt your tête-à-tête with your lover." Blue hopped down, and she was annoyed to see how perfectly pressed and unrumpled he looked, although the orange waistcoat he wore clashed monstrously with his gray coat.

"He is not my lover. I met him only a few moments ago."

"Well, I had no idea you were so friendly."

"Stubble it, Blue. Why were you sent to give me intelligence? I thought you had retired." She glanced down at her gown and brushed at the dirt where her knees had hit the path.

"I am merely developing my other interests."

She frowned at the recalcitrant dirt. "What other interests?"

"I have a keen interest in opera. In fact"—he consulted his pocket watch—"I am due back at Covent Garden momentarily, so let me be brief."

"Please."

"One of Agent Wolf's contacts sold him information on Foncé's whereabouts."

Jane blinked. "Wolf? I thought he retired."

Blue shook his head. "No one sleeps easy while Foncé is still walking free. Your uncle will order a report from Wolf, but it would be more expedient if you actually talked to Wolf face-to-face." He handed her a slip of parchment. "You will find him here."

Jane frowned. "You know M frowns upon this."

"You cannot remain the Barbican's secret forever. He already has you training Butterfly."

"How do you know that?"

He gave her a bemused look. "We are running out of operatives. If anyone can apprehend Foncé, it's you."

She took a breath and nodded. Blue stepped forward. "It's an enormous responsibility, I know, but I have worked with you before. You can do it. Now, turn around and let me do something about your appearance before you embarrass yourself and Melbourne."

He tugged and he poked and he fussed with her hair until she wanted to scream, *Enough already!* Finally, he turned her in a circle and pronounced, "You'll do."

"Thank you." She headed back toward the ball.

"I had better not catch you in the garden again!"

"Don't you have an opera singer waiting for you?"

He grinned. "As a matter of fact..." And he was gone. Jane knew he'd merely cut around one of the shrubs, but he did it so skillfully he seemed to disappear.

With a sigh, she made her way back to the lights and music of the ball. She skillfully evaded the half-dozen or so of her acquaintances who attempted to detain her and made her way through the throngs until she found the card room. She stepped inside, spotted her uncle, and met his gaze. When she stepped back out again to wait, a footman with a tray of champagne passed, and she snatched a glass and downed it.

She pressed her hand to her belly and attempted to still the fluttering. It bothered her how much Griffyn's kiss had affected her. She'd been kissed before. True, she had never been kissed on the gravel path in a garden before, but she'd been kissed in far more romantic places—Venice, Paris, the Egyptian pyramids at dusk. And all of those kisses had been bestowed by men she liked, and none of those kisses had made her feel even one one-hundredth of what she'd felt when Griffyn but brushed his lips over hers. Her whole body had seemed to come alive. It was as though she'd never smelled flowers before, never felt the cool evening breeze, never noticed how bright the stars or how vast the heavens.

Another footman passed, and she grabbed another glass of champagne. She downed it as well. She didn't even like champagne, but her belly was still fluttering and her pulse was still racing and she needed to be calm and collected for what was to come. She closed her eyes and saw *his* eyes dance before her. They were dark and sensual and promised he could make her feel oh, so much more than she had experienced even tonight.

The air around her stirred, and she opened her eyes to find her uncle standing before her. "You should at least give him a chance," he said.

Jane would have staggered back had the wall not been at her back. "How can you say such a thing?" Her uncle had always been her protector, her confidant, her ally. How could he betray her like this?

He beckoned her toward the library and away from the rest of the ball-goers. "You have to marry at some point, Jane. You know it as well as I do," he said when they'd stepped inside the library and ascertained they were alone.

"I know no such thing. I am an agent, not a wife. Most agents never marry, at least not until they retire."

Her uncle shook his head. "You are not like other agents. You are a woman."

"That shouldn't matter."

"But it does. The freedoms you have now cannot be allowed to continue unless you marry."

Jane gripped the back of a chintz couch. "Why?" But she knew. She knew as well as he did.

Her uncle gave her a patient smile. "Must I detail the reasons?"

She knew them already. She was too old to claim to be studying abroad. And because she was not expected to be in the schoolroom, when she disappeared for any length of time, rampant speculation commenced that she had eloped or left to have an illegitimate child.

"I thought you were on my side," she said petulantly. She knew how it sounded, but she could not seem to stop the childishness from flaring up for a moment.

"It is because I am on your side that you must marry. I want you to keep working. I need you to keep working. Foncé came very close to assassinating the prince regent last fall. We cannot allow him to come that close again."

"And how am I to find him and destroy him if I have a husband to answer to?"

Her uncle gave her a long look. "You are Jane Bonde. You will find a way."

"And I'll find the husband as well," she told him.

"What is wrong with Dominic Griffyn?"

"It won't work with him."

"Why not? I'll admit he has a somewhat question-able past—"

"That's not it." But she immediately regretted interrupting. Griffyn had a questionable past? That might be the perfect reason to disavow him.

"Then what is it?"

Jane clasped her hands behind her back. She could not tell her uncle he'd kissed her, and she certainly could not admit that she enjoyed the kiss. "Trust me when I say it will not do," she said. That had always sufficed in the past.

But this time he shook his head. "I cannot."

Jane frowned. "What are you saying?"

"My hands are tied."

"No. What does that mean?"

"It means I have already given my consent, Jane. I had no other choice. You *will* marry Dominic Griffyn."

Four

DOMINIC TYPICALLY ARRIVED AT THE STABLES EARLY. He liked to be the first one to greet the horses. Although Edgeberry had a full complement of grooms, stableboys, and trainers, Dominic often brushed, walked, and trained the horses himself. There was only one way to truly know a horse, and that was to spend time with him or her. Dominic found that a half hour picking out a horse's hooves told him a lot about that animal.

When Dominic started for the stables that morning, the sky was black, and the rolling hills around the estate were shrouded in a low, eerie fog that swirled about his boots as he moved through it. He might have stayed at the marquess's town house in London last night, but then he would have missed walking through the fresh dew this morning and the clean smell of the pasture.

He anticipated the scents of the stable—hay and leather and horse. Dominic hoped the familiar smells would help him forget the lingering fragrance of laundered linen and fresh violets. It would take longer to forget the taste of Miss Bonde, but he was determined.

He did not know what accounted for his behavior the night before, and he did not want to know. He wanted to go for a long ride on one of his most spirited stallions and forget her altogether.

But he was still thinking of Miss Bonde when he reached the stable and was therefore surprised to be greeted by Old Connor. The man was so named because a decade or so ago, a Young Connor had been briefly employed.

"Sir, I am glad to see you."

"What's wrong?" Dominic wasted no time on pleasantries and did not expect Old Connor to do so either.

"It's Lily's Turn, sir. She's showing signs of the colic."

"What?" Dominic arrowed for the mare's stall. "That's the third horse in a month."

"Yes, sir."

Dominic opened the stall door and found Lily's Turn on the floor. She rose quickly, bared her teeth, then went back down. "Do you have the oil and molasses ready?"

"Yes, sir. Do you want me to wake the other lads?"

Dominic waved his hand. "Not yet. Bring me the supplies."

Old Connor rushed away, and Dominic bent to study Lily's Turn. There was pain in her deep brown eyes. Dominic put his hand on her muzzle to comfort her. He closed his eyes for a long moment and sat with the horse in silence.

Dominic was not obligated to work with Edgeberry's horses. As a part of the marquess's family, Dominic did not have to do anything. Dominic's mother had ensured he would receive a generous allowance yearly. Dominic had been free to act the wastrel, buy a commission in the army, join the clergy, or tour the Continent.

He'd chosen to stay here, at Edgeberry's country house just outside London, and breed Edgeberry's Cleveland Bays. In Dominic's mind, there was not a better breed than the Cleveland Bay. He'd even come to blows once when another breeder insisted Yorkshire Trotters were better carriage horses. Cleveland Bays had regal blood. Dominic's horses were especially prized because of their bright bay color and completely black points. He'd also had great success in breeding and training matched pairs, which were highly sought after by the *ton*. Members of the royal family owned Edgeberry horses, and when Tattersall's had a request for a particularly fine Cleveland Bay or an exquisite matched pair, the auctioneer knew where to come. The name of the Marquess of Edgeberry had become synonymous with fine horseflesh.

Bur Dominic hadn't taken this on for his adopted father. He hadn't even done it for the horses, though he cared about them. He'd done it for himself. There was a peace when he was with these animals. The turmoil inside him ceased for just a little while, and he could forget.

Unfortunately, he was still close enough to London to find trouble. He'd found it last night in the form of Jane Bonde.

Old Connor returned, and he and Dominic set to work, administering warm water and oil. Dominic offered Lily's Turn molasses in her feed bowl, and she ate it eagerly. "Do you want to walk her, sir, or shall I?"

"You take a turn. I'll see to the other horses."

The other grooms were arriving now, eyes heavy-lidded and hazed with sleep. Dominic greeted them as he checked the other horses. So far all appeared well. He returned to Lily's Turn's stall and studied it. Had she eaten something poisonous? He made certain his horses ate the best food to be had. He walked to her feed bucket and studied it. It was empty. He checked the manger and the water bucket. Nothing. Walking the stall, Dominic saw nothing else that pointed to a reason for the colic.

Old Connor returned, and they repeated the treatment, then Dominic walked Lily's Turn. By midmorning, the horse had moved its bowels and was doing better. Dominic had one of the younger grooms watching her for any signs of distress. Dominic sat in the small office and read correspondence from gentlemen seeking to buy horses or hoping to breed their stock with that of Edgeberry's. Dominic savored the time he spent in this stable, in this office. It felt more like home to him than his chambers in Kenham Hall. The sight of the rectangular red-brick building, with its row of windows and carefully tended paddocks, never failed to loosen any tightness in his chest. Even now, with a pile of tiresome correspondence before him, he felt at peace.

He heard a shuffle and glanced up, spotting his mother in the doorway. For a moment, he merely looked at her. She was still a beautiful woman. Even as her son, he could appreciate her beauty. As petite and dainty as she was, he could have lifted her with very little effort. But she did not need his protection. She was tough, tougher than any man he'd ever known. Men seemed to want to protect her, though, and when it was in her interest, she allowed it. She could pretend to be helpless. She was an excellent actress; she could pretend anything.

There were times, when she'd first married Edgeberry, he thought she pretended to love the man. But over the years, her behaviors had become less practiced and more natural. Dominic thought she probably had fallen in love with Edgeberry after all.

There was no question that Edgeberry had fallen in love with Titania upon first meeting her. He would not have defied convention by marrying her if he had not been desperate for her. Growing up, Dominic was used to seeing men desperate for his mother. She possessed a sensuality and voluptuousness that appealed to men, and she used it to her advantage. He could hardly blame her. She'd been born into poverty and squalor, and now she was the Marchioness of Edgeberry. But there had been casualties associated with her rise. His childhood was one of them.

"Do not frown," she said, sidling inside. "It makes me feel unwelcome."

"You are always welcome." He stood and pulled out a seat for her. It had been months since she'd last been here. She preferred London, even in the winter.

"I've interrupted you." She gestured toward his letters.

"It will wait." He sat. "I presume you are here about the ball last night."

She smiled. "I should have known you would cut straight to the point. There is an art to chitchat, Dominic."

"I am not interested in art."

"As I am well aware." She steepled her white-gloved fingers. "So tell me, what did you think of Miss Bonde?"

"She is attractive."

"Attractive? The chit turns heads every time she walks into a room." She leaned back. "You should have seen her mother, God rest her soul. She was a true diamond of the first water."

"How did her mother die?"

"A fire. It was tragic. Only the little girl and her nanny escaped." Dominic could picture a cherub-faced child being carried from a burning building by a nurse dressed in a long night shift. He could all but see her crying, reaching back for her lost mother and father.

"How old was she?"

His mother cocked her head. "Ask her, or is she incapable of conversation?"

"She seems intelligent and able to converse."

"Good, because you will need to converse with her tomorrow evening."

"Mother…"

"I was deadly serious when I told you to marry, Dominic. Your father—"

"He's not my father."

She held up a hand. "Very well. Lord Edgeberry has had enough. You either marry, or you will be disowned."

"That babe was not mine." He fisted his hands in his lap, still fuming about the woman who had appeared at the Edgeberry town house with a baby she claimed was his on her hip. She hadn't known he was the bastard son and not the heir to the title. Too late, she realized she'd been seduced by the wrong brother.

The marchioness plucked at her fashionable ruby gown. "So you never touched the chit?"

Dominic clenched his jaw.

"So you *did* bed her."

"Mother."

"What term would you prefer? Swive? Or perhaps the Old English word? Fu—"

He rose. "Mother!"

She grinned, and he knew she enjoyed this game of poking at him. "I have four children, Dominic."

He sank back in his chair and covered his eyes. Now he had images of his mother and Edgeberry in his mind. He shuddered.

"I have done the deed a time or several hundred." She paused, and Dominic allowed his forehead to thud on the desk. "Now that I think of it, it has been much more than that. Perhaps thousands of times."

"Save me," he muttered.

"So did you have relations with that woman or not?"

He sighed. "I did." It was easier to speak of…it if he did not look at her. "But I did nothing that would produce a child. She—er…" Could he not simply fall into a hole and disappear right now? "She pleasured me, if you understand my meaning." But of course she understood his meaning, and his fear was that she would illustrate how well she understood. The silence went on for several moments, and Dominic finally looked up.

"That doesn't seem very fair of you. You gave her nothing in return?"

"Of course, I—" Dominic stood. "I am not having this conversation, Mother. God knows I am no saint, but that child is not mine. The last thing I want is to bring a bastard into the world." He closed his mouth abruptly, aware he had said too much.

"Dominic." His mother stood and reached for him, but he avoided her. He did not want to be touched at the moment. She clasped her hands together in front of her. "It has not been easy for you. I know that. I am so proud of all you've accomplished. The Edgeberry name is revered among anyone who knows horseflesh."

But it wasn't his name, Dominic thought. None of this was his.

"Lord Edgeberry wants you to marry. *I* want you to marry. I'd like to see you with a family and children."

Dominic shook his head. The thought of children made him physically ill. He could not be responsible for a child.

"Dominic, there is no longer a choice. You must marry or you lose everything, including these horses." She swept her hand, indicating the stable.

"Change his mind," Dominic said. He hated to ask for anything, but the thought of leaving his horses was devastating.

"I cannot. I have tried, and really, there's no reason you should not marry—"

"I don't want to. That is reason enough."

She gave him a sympathetic look, the kind she had given him when he'd been a child and stomped his foot, declaring, "I don't want to go to bed!"

She did not say *too bad* now, but he saw it in her expression.

"You are a grown man and able to make your own

decisions." She collected her reticule and made her way toward the door. "If you choose to consider marriage, I expect you to be at Lord Melbourne's home tomorrow evening for dinner."

His mother was almost through the door when Dominic said, "Why her? Why Miss Bonde?"

She looked over her shoulder. "Because I always want the best for you."

∽

Jane had climbed out of many windows, but she had never climbed out of her own. She'd never had to, but Blue's information had intrigued her. She had to meet this Wolf and find out what he'd learned about Foncé. Her uncle had always tried to keep her away from the other agents. She understood and respected the decision, but the situation with Foncé required extreme measures. The man had to be caught. They were all his targets now.

The drop from her window was steep, with little to cling to. Part of the way down, a tree branch touched the wall, and she thought she might be light enough to catch hold and use it to aid her descent. But the straight drop from her window was another matter.

She went to her wardrobe and pulled down a wooden chest with an embellished gold Q on it. It was the right size for jewelry, but it held something infinitely more valuable. She took a key from her dressing table and unlocked the box, pushing the cover back on the hinges. Inside lay a pair of ordinary gloves, an inkwell, and a brush. She opened the inkwell and gagged at the smell. What had Miss Qwillen mixed in here?

She dipped the brush inside, and it came out covered in what looked like black honey. Was it tar? Tree sap?

Jane did not know, but she had learned to trust Miss Qwillen, or Q, over the years. She pulled on the gloves and painted the palms with the awful mixture, then waited a quarter of an hour for it to set. She thought she remembered Q saying to wait a quarter of an hour. Perhaps it had been three-quarters of an hour? Oh, bollocks! Jane did not have time to waste. She would go and hope for the best. Nine out of ten of Q's inventions worked.

Jane stood at her window and looked down at the drop. *Please let this be one of the nine.*

She climbed out of the window, resting her hands on the ledge. The gloves felt sticky, which was encouraging. She looked down at the drop between her window and the tree branch she hoped to catch. It was quite a fall. Taking a deep breath, she moved her feet so they rested on a narrow foothold. She'd tied her skirts up and out of her way, and she looked down to be certain of her footing before she moved. Jane closed her eyes and inched her hands off the window casement one by one. She gripped the wall and wobbled slightly, but when she pressed her hands flat, so that the glue made complete contact with the building, she had a more secure hold.

Inch by inch, she made her way down the side of the town house. It was slow going, and she had to steel her nerves so as not to panic the few times her hands slipped and she slid down the side of the house. Finally, her feet touched the branch, and she lowered herself onto it. But the moment she was sitting securely on the branch, she heard an awful crack and jolted downward. The branch did not snap, but it hung onto the tree by a few layers of thin and peeling wood. Jane held on to the end of the branch, swaying in the breeze.

She almost laughed. She had been in far worse situations. If she fell to her death outside her own window, it would be the ultimate irony. The branch still swayed, and she used her legs to further the momentum, moving them as she might if she were on a swing. The branch dipped perilously close to the tree trunk, and Jane almost wrapped her legs around it, but then she swung back.

And the branch made another ominous cracking sound. She was running out of chances. She swung her legs again, this time catching the trunk at the same time the branch snapped. She let go, but too late, and fell backward, her legs gripping the trunk and her arms hanging down. Fortunately, the ground was not so far below her now. She latched on to the trunk with her hands and flipped her legs over, scratching her neck as she turned. She landed on the ground with a soft thud that reverberated all the way to her forehead. It had been a longer fall than she would have liked. She sat down, took inventory, and decided her neck had borne the worst of it. She would have to wear her hair down for a few days to cover the scratch. She touched it gingerly, wincing when the raw skin flared and burned.

Rising, she pulled the gloves off, then untied her skirts and brushed them off. She scanned the ground and finally spotted the cape she'd dropped down earlier. With a twirl, she dropped it over her clothes and pulled the hood up. She did not want to attract attention, and her blond hair was a beacon in the dark. She'd memorized then burned Blue's note, which had directed her to Charles Street, not far from her own home in Mayfair. The streets were congested with carriages ferrying the *ton* to one engagement or another, and she quickly decided she had better take the side streets rather than the main thoroughfares. If the hood of her mantle fell back or a group of foxed gentlemen accosted her, she did not want to be where her aunt and uncle's acquaintances might recognize her. She cut through an alley behind a row of terraced houses and crept along a line of mews, listening as the horses stabled there pawed and stamped. Gradually, she became aware of another sound.

Footsteps. Quiet and stealthy, but she knew when she was being followed.

Her skin prickled and her senses heightened, but she did not slow or show any sign she had heard her pursuer. The path alongside the mews grew darker and narrower as she continued down it, a situation that was not in her favor. She needed open space to fight, and she did not have it. Her only other option was to run. She took off at full speed, glad she was wearing her half boots. She lifted her skirts and ran with her head down. Her heart began to pound when she heard the echo of heavy footsteps running behind her.

And gaining.

She cut across a busy thoroughfare, skirting carts and carriages and hoping to lose her pursuer. But when she looked back, he was still right behind her. It was a quick glimpse, but she could see he was a man in a greatcoat and hat. He jumped over a crate of coal, ignored the coalman's curses, and all but flew. She might have remained on the busy lane. Certainly someone would have stopped to help her, but she could not chance being recognized. She cut through another alley between town houses, knowing her pursuer was gaining on her. She felt it the moment he reached for her, and instead of futilely pushing ahead, ducked and rolled. He stumbled and ran by her, and she had enough time to pivot and run back the way they had come. She'd been looking for an escape, and she'd seen a promising ironwork gate. She could evade him in a garden. There were shadows and shrubs to conceal her. But when she reached the gate, it was locked. She swore and launched herself onto it, scrambling over just as he caught her foot. She kicked him somewhere near his neck and fell back. Backpedaling, she scurried into the garden, snagging her cape on a rose bush and diving into a scratchy line of shrubbery. She pushed her way through the tightly packed shrubs, crawled into another patch of shadows, and spotted a low wall at the far end of the garden.

Ducking and running, she angled for it, uncertain where her pursuer was. He was quiet and stealthy. She half-expected him to pop up in front of her. She reached the wall unmolested, jumped up, and rolled over, then flattened herself against it and listened.

Nothing.

Had he not followed her into the garden? She looked to her left and to her right. The wall marked the property line beside a small stone church. It looked Norman in design and perfect for her purposes. She pushed off the wall, and hugging the side of the building so she would remain in the shadows, she slithered around to the small cemetery in the back. Appropriately, it was shrouded in a low mist that looked rather unearthly. Jane did not believe in things she could not see or touch. Real danger did not come at one in the form of a specter. It came in the guise of a man in a caped greatcoat, an assailant firing a pistol, or the knife-wielding thug.

She scooted into the cemetery and leaned against one of the small, stubby trees growing there. She watched and waited for several minutes, looking for any sort of movement or sound.

There was nothing, and yet she felt a sense of unease. She felt as though she was not alone. She shivered. She was being ridiculous. The dead beneath her feet had moved on. She was alone here, and she had better make her way to Charles Street before it grew too much later.

She stepped away from the tree and started for the other end of the graveyard. Once she was away from the churchyard, she would determine how far off course she had traveled. Wolf had better have important information, but even if he did not, she had learned something very valuable tonight.

Someone was after her. She could not be certain it was Foncé or the Maîtriser group, but someone was looking for her. And someone knew where to look, which meant her aunt and uncle were no longer safe. And that made finding Foncé all the more pressing.

She reached for the latch on the cemetery gate, but instead of the cold metal, she touched something warm and soft.

"Allow me."

Five

JANE PIVOTED AND ASSUMED A FIGHTING STANCE BEFORE
the man's words were even spoken. He was fortunate
he had spoken. He was fortunate she knew his voice—
that her efforts to annihilate every remembrance of
him from her mind had failed. She did not strike.

At the last second, she pulled the round kick she'd
been about to deliver and merely stumbled ungrace-
fully backward. She would have died of embarrassment if another agent had witnessed such clumsiness,
but here it worked to her advantage. The move made
her appear startled and scared.

And Dominic Griffyn had no idea how close he'd
come to having his neck broken.

"What are you doing here?" she demanded.

He gave her a dark look, his eyes too deep in the
shadows for her to accurately gauge his expression.
Those thick, sooty eyelashes worked in his favor.

"Opening the gate for you." True to his word, he
swung it wide. Jane hesitated. This could be a trap.
Nothing about the situation screamed *trap*, but if he
was not here to trap her, why was he here? He had

either followed her or hunted her. She disliked both possibilities—the second more than the first.

"You followed me," she said, taking a guess.

"You have a high opinion of yourself." He casually held the gate open, his arm draped over the decorative pikes.

She narrowed her eyes. "Are you saying you did not follow me?"

"I can't get anything past you." He stepped out of her path, but she still hesitated to leave the relative security of the churchyard. She could hide in the cemetery and the nooks and outcroppings of the ancient church building.

"*You* interrupted my solitude," he said. "You tell me what you are doing here without"—he glanced around, feigning curiosity—"a chaperone or footman."

He implied their meeting was coincidence. She didn't believe it. This cemetery was not Drury Lane or Vauxhall Gardens. The odds of the two of them meeting here, randomly, were...well, larger than her mathematical skills allowed her to calculate. And she would not forget that she'd been pursued. It was far more likely that Griffyn was that pursuer than that they'd met randomly, and now he would lure her into trusting him.

"I don't have to answer to you," she said, turning back the way she'd come. She didn't go far before he caught up. She'd expected him to grab her elbow. She was prepared to knee him, and then shove his face into the mud beneath her boots. But he didn't touch her. He walked backwards, matching her stride for stride.

She was striding quickly, and though he had to peer over his shoulder time and again to be certain he didn't trip over any objects in their path, her pace did not seem to discourage him. "You don't have to answer to me, Miss Bonde," he said, "and by all that's holy, I wish we two had not crossed paths. Then you could go on your merry—albeit suicidal—way, and I could go on mine."

She stopped, and he mirrored her. "But?" she prodded.

"But we did cross paths, and I'd be the worst sort of gentleman to allow my intended bride to continue on unescorted."

Jane opened her lips to respond and found she didn't know where to begin. There was so very much in that statement to refute. She decided on the most obvious point. "I don't need an escort. You do not know me well, sir. If you did, you would know I am perfectly capable of looking after myself."

"While I do not doubt the veracity of that statement, Miss Bonde, the fact remains I am obligated now to escort you."

A clock tower chimed somewhere nearby, and Jane's pulse quickened. Time was slipping away. She could not afford this delay. She put her hands on her hips and glared at him. "You are not obligated to do anything, sir. And I use that term of respect lightly. You and I both know you are no gentleman. Stop this masquerade and allow me to pass." She swept past him, her skirts parting the fog swirling about their feet.

He followed her, of course. She could easily lose him once away from the churchyard, but as she neared the low wall she'd scaled to gain entry, she realized she would have preferred to exit through the gate. And now she would feel foolish retracing her steps. This—*this*—was why she worked alone! Now she would have to scale the dashed wall again.

Resisting the temptation to glance at her shadow, she took two steps back, broke into a run, and leaped onto the low wall. Her hands caught the top, and she was pulling her leg over, when she felt his hands on her bottom. With a jerk of shock—and perhaps something more—she released her hold on the wall. Too late the folly of that impulse registered, and she fell backward.

He caught her, of course. Dashed man. She would have preferred to land on the cold, hard ground. She would have preferred to smash her bones against a pile of unforgiving rocks. She would have preferred...she closed her eyes. She was not even convincing herself. His arms were solid and his chest warm. He smelled of soap and horse and leather. Her body heated and tingled, remembering their kiss the previous night. It was a purely animalistic instinct. She knew this, and yet it was forceful enough that she wanted to give into it. She wanted to turn toward him, press her breasts against his hard chest, wrap her arms around his neck, and press her lips to his sensual mouth.

But she was not so green as to be confused by the conflicting desires at war within her. Her mind wanted to escape him. Her body wanted to ravish him. Her mind would win.

She hoped.

She pushed out of his arms, knowing she'd lingered too long for her protests now to make sense. She would make them anyway. He did not expect her to be logical; men never expected as much from a woman. "Let me go."

He released her as though she were a hot poker. "I was merely attempting to assist you."

"I do not need your assistance," she said through clenched teeth. She'd made the mistake of looking at him, and all that inky hair and those black eyes made her stomach clench in such a way she almost pressed her hand to it to ward off the spirals of heat coursing through her body. "I came in that way, and I can leave that way as well."

He raised a brow. "And you claim I'm no gentleman."

Oh, now this was too much. She had no time for it, but she couldn't seem to stop herself. "Are you implying I am not a lady?" She took a menacing step toward him, and though he did not retreat, she thought she saw a flicker of concern in his eyes. "A piece of advice, Mr. Griffyn. A gentleman never even hints that a woman is not a lady, no matter what insult she has given you."

His brow arched. "I believe we've already established I am no gentleman."

Yes, yes they had. And why did that make her belly flutter? Ridiculous body! She would not be at the mercy of her desires. She stomped away from him and headed for the garden gate. She told herself her change of direction was due to the fact that her pursuer—if, indeed, it was not Griffyn himself—might be lying in wait by the garden wall. It was not because she could not risk Griffyn touching her again.

He followed, which she expected, but he did not

attempt to play the gentleman and open this gate for her. He let her struggle until she'd broken the lock and then watched as she jerked at its heavy weight until the rusty rails cleared the overgrown weeds that had grown up around it. She finally passed through and would have slammed it on him, but it caught on yet another creeping weed. Instead, she gave him a potent glare.

And he said she wasn't a lady.

She made her way through a dark uneven street. She moved gingerly through the mud and the muck, attempting to keep the hem of her skirts clean. She righted her cape, which had twisted about her shoulders, and pulled the hood over her hair and down to conceal her forehead. Griffyn was right behind her, but as soon as she was out in the open, she would leave him behind. No one followed her if she did not want to be followed.

But he must have anticipated her, because right before they stepped out onto the busy thoroughfare, clogged with carriages and the *ton*'s town coaches, he took her arm and tucked it into his. She tried to jerk away, subtly, so as not to draw attention, but he held tightly. "Which direction?" he asked.

"Release me."

"We have had this conversation already."

She stared at him. She could threaten to scream, but that was patently ridiculous, even as a threat. He knew she would not do it. She'd rather deal with him than a swarm of well-meaning rescuers who would gossip about Miss Bonde's scandalous appearance on—she glanced around—Chesterfield Hill late at night.

He met her gaze, and she knew he understood her dilemma. She saw the triumph in his eyes. It made her want to scream just to spite him. And that was the sort of unprofessional behavior she always loathed. "This way," she said sweetly, pointing toward Charles Street. This was not over. He might think he had won, but she would be the victor in the end. She never lost.

They strolled, arm in arm, as though they were a couple walking home after a night's entertainment. He skillfully steered her away from the less desirable men and women they passed, made certain she did not step in so much as a puddle—even when it meant he could not avoid soaking his boots—and kept her safely on the sidewalk, while he walked along the curb where carriages rolled by, splashing mud onto his trousers. She kept her head angled down so the hood concealed her features and ignored the way her cheeks heated at his closeness and how her heart wanted to melt at his chivalry.

Just because he could act the gentleman did not mean he was one.

Just because she had never particularly cared for gentlemen, at any rate, did not mean she had to push this one up against a wall and take his mouth with hers in a kiss she knew would leave them both breathless. Clearly, his thoughts were not along the same lines. A moment later he asked the perfectly logical and reasonable question, "Are we going to Charles Street?"

"As you see." She sounded petulant. She was far too old for petulance.

"Meeting your lover at The Running Footman?"

She let out a short laugh. "Hardly. I assure you I am going to a respectable home." At least she assumed it appeared so on the outside. "You may leave me there without qualm."

He made no reply, and she could only hope he did not intend to actually see her inside. She could not exactly discuss Foncé or the Maîtriser group with Wolf if Griffyn insisted on chaining himself to her side. It would be humiliating enough to make an appearance with Griffyn beside her. She was supposed to be a spy. She should be able to evade an unwanted tail. Of course, she'd never had to escape the man picked to be her husband. If she could not escape him now, it did not bode well for the marriage.

Not that there would be a marriage. She had not agreed yet. She would find a way out of this conundrum.

She glanced at Griffyn. Surely he did not want to wed her. Perhaps he had thought of an alternative. Perhaps there was some other woman he could marry instead. "You know they expect us to marry." She didn't think it necessary to mention whom *they* comprised. He knew.

"So I have been told." He steered her around a small group of men watching a bootblack shine a gentleman's shoes. It was probably prime entertainment for the night.

"And?"

He frowned at her. "I'm not going to bend down on one knee, if that's what you want."

She shuddered. "No! Please *do not* even entertain the idea."

"I assure you I am not. I cannot promise not to entertain *any* ideas, however."

She supposed he was trying to shock her, but she could hardly find his statements shocking when she herself had pondered the odd fantasy or three involving him. "What I meant was what will you do about it?"

He shrugged. "That is the benefit of being a man. I don't have to do anything. If I do not act, we do not wed."

She rolled her eyes. "Are you truly so naive?"

He stopped walking, forcing several people to circumvent him, and turned to face her. "I believe that is my line."

"I am not naive, and I know my aunt and uncle. They will have their way if steps are not taken to prevent it. I could act alone, but they know most of my stratagems."

His lips curved into a dubious smile. "You have stratagems?"

"It might be better if you acted."

"Better for whom?" His gaze was intent but bemused, and she could not discern whether he was angry or on the verge of laughing at her.

"For both of us, obviously."

He merely looked at her. She had to curb the urge to dig the toe of her boot into the sidewalk. "I thought..." But she hadn't thought this through very well. Perhaps she should wait to discuss it with him. Unfortunately, their next discussion might be at the altar.

"You thought?" he prompted.

"Perhaps you might marry someone else. Then you and I could not marry."

He didn't speak for the length of seven heartbeats. "You are serious?" he said finally.

"Of course. You simply need to choose a woman to marry. Unless there is a woman you have in mind already. Is there?"

"Are you asking if I have a mistress?"

"Shh!" She glanced around, forgetting for the moment she wore her cape. Still, if they continued talking of topics like one's *mistress*, curious passersby would surely look more closely. "Need you be so blunt?"

"*I* am being blunt?"

Vexing man. Why must he be so difficult? No wonder he did not have a mistress. "Fine. I will be blunt."

"This I have to hear," he muttered.

She ignored him. "There must be women who would have you."

"Because of my relationship with the marquess?"

"No, because…" She gestured to him.

"Pray, madam, do continue."

She waved her hand. "Because…look at you." She felt her face flame. He really could not be such a complete dolt. "Do not play games with me, Mr. Griffyn. Surely you realize you are an attractive male specimen."

"An attractive male specimen! Bloody hell. Next you'll want to dissect me."

Her face was red by now. She did not need a mirror to tell her she was blushing. This night was turning into a complete failure. Was she to be completely humiliated? "I am simply saying—"

"I know what you are saying, and the answer is no."

"No?"

"I will not marry to avoid marriage. In fact, were the situation to reach such dire straits, I find I would vastly prefer you."

❧

Her blue eyes widened, looking like enormous sapphires glittering against the velvet night of the cape. She intrigued him, this woman who was full of contradictions. One moment she was bold and audacious. The next moment she blushed like a schoolgirl. Who was the real Jane Bonde?

Whoever she was, she did not want anything to do with him. She'd made that, if nothing else, clear enough. Suddenly, he was eager to finish this duty and be done with her. He should have left her back in the cemetery. It wasn't chivalry that persuaded him to escort her; it was curiosity. What was she doing in that cemetery? Why had she been breathing heavily as though she'd been pursued? He'd heard her breathing before anything else. She was light on her feet, but she couldn't stop her breath from dragging in and out. Most likely her stays were laced tightly and constricted breathing.

And the image of her in only her stays was not one he ought to dwell on at the moment.

So what or whom was she running from? One moment all had been quiet and peaceful. He'd been alone with his thoughts and, if he'd been a praying man, his prayers. The next she had raced past him and dove into the shadows of the old Norman church. For a moment, he'd actually thought he'd fallen asleep and was dreaming. He did not know her final destination, but wherever it was, she did not want him to accompany her.

All the more reason to insist on accompanying her.

"Miss Bonde, the hour grows late. Shall we

continue?" He offered his arm and found he was actually somewhat offended when she did not take it. She muttered something about not needing his assistance and stomped away. Several men parted to allow her to pass, and he had to hurry to catch her. They did indeed pass The Running Footman, but she barely gave the tavern a glance. She finally stopped in front of an unassuming town house. Several lights still burned in the windows, but it did not appear the owner hosted any sort of social event. Did she intend to make a social call this late?

"This is it," she said. "You may go now."

He might have considered departing, but he certainly wasn't going to be ordered to do so. Not to mention, he was still curious. Whom was she meeting? What was so important that she needed to rush out, on her own, at night? A lover? A blackmailer? Exactly what was Miss Bonde trying to hide?

When he didn't take his leave, she scowled and climbed the steps to the front door. She peered over her shoulder before knocking, seeming resigned to the fact that he was not quite so easy to dismiss. She rapped on the knocker three times and waited. Dominic ascended the steps quietly and stood beside her. He heard faint footsteps, and then the black door opened. A distinguished-looking butler with black hair that had silvered at the temples looked down at her. His face was expressionless granite.

"Good evening." His voice betrayed nothing of what he must be thinking; namely, that it was too late for a social call. The butler did not appear to recognize Miss Bonde, and she hesitated, glancing back at

Dominic, then frowning in annoyance when she saw
he was beside her.

"Good evening. I am Miss Jane Bonde. I have
come to call on Mister…"

The butler's brows rose slightly.

"Lord…"

The butler's brows paused in their ascent.

"Yes, Lord…" She drew the title out, almost as
though she waited for the butler to prompt her with
the man's name. Did she not know the man she was
calling on? Oh, Dominic was most definitely not
leaving now.

"Lord…Wolf?" she finally asked.

"You are here to see Lord Wolf?" the butler asked,
his voice betraying nothing. "And who is your companion, Miss Bonde?"

"He's not my companion," she said, shooing him
with her hand as though he were a fly. "He is leaving."

Dominic stepped forward. "Dominic Griffyn."

"Also to see Lord…Wolf?" the butler asked.

"Why not?" Dominic retorted. To his surprise,
the butler opened the door and admitted them into
a small but well-appointed vestibule. The floor was
pale marble and continued up a rather wide staircase.
Two richly upholstered armchairs stood on either
side of the door, presumably for footmen forced to
sit up at night.

"I am Wallace. I will fetch his lordship."

"Thank you, Wallace," she told him, smiling
brightly. As soon as he started up the stairs, she whirled
on Dominic. "Go away."

He gave her a long look. "I much preferred you

when Wallace was present. Do you even know the man you are calling on?"

"The matter does not concern you!" She circled him and opened the house's door. "I am safe inside. Good night."

"A simple yes or no will suffice," he continued, ignoring the open door. "Do you know Lord Wolf?"

"Why must you be so difficult?"

"Why will you not answer the question?" He heard voices, and she quickly closed the door and rushed back to the spot she'd occupied before Wallace had gone to fetch his master. The butler descended the marble stairs alone.

"His lordship bids you come to the drawing room. Follow me, please."

She gave Dominic a triumphant grin. Dominic had a feeling her victory celebration might be somewhat premature when she realized he'd followed her up the stairs. Wallace opened the white-paneled door of the drawing room, a small but comfortable chamber, and Dominic spotted a heavily pregnant woman and a tall man with light brownish hair and what was obviously a hastily tied cravat, waiting for them.

Wallace cleared his throat. "Miss Bonde and Mr. Griffyn." The butler closed the doors, and Griffyn looked at Miss Bonde. She was looking at the woman. Clearly, she hadn't expected her to be present.

The pause stretched for a long moment, and the man finally stepped forward. "Miss Bonde, I do not believe we have met."

"No." She pushed the hood of her cape back, revealing her golden hair, which was still almost perfectly coiffed, despite her adventures that evening. "I am sorry to disturb your evening, Lord Wolf." She nodded. "Lady Wolf."

The couple in question did not glance at each other, but Dominic had the feeling, nonetheless, that some sort of communication passed between them.

"You are friends with Lord Melbourne?" the woman said, rising from a chair upholstered in some sort of rich ivory material. She did so slowly, using her hand on the arm of her chair to assist her. She was obviously in the last stages of her condition and well into her confinement. Dominic recalled his mother at this stage when carrying his younger half brothers. She was chronically tired and unable to find a comfortable position in which to sleep.

"I am his lordship's niece."

"I see." The woman nodded. "Won't you please sit down? I am Lady Smythe, and that is my husband, Viscount Smythe." It was a very smooth correction, but Dominic did not miss the fact that Miss Bonde had not known the correct names of the people she called on. Had she created a name randomly, or was there some reason behind it?

"Are you also friends with Lord Melbourne?" Lord Smythe asked.

"Yes," Dominic answered.

"No," Miss Bonde countered. This time the Smythes did exchange a look.

Dominic feigned injury. "This is news. I shall have his name struck from the engagement-party guest list."

She glared at him. "There is to be no engagement party."

"Another shock," Dominic said. "I don't think my nerves can take many more."

Miss Bonde looked on the verge of attack, but Lady Smythe, who had resumed her seat, began to rise again. "Do you need a moment alone?"

"No," Dominic said at the same time Miss Bonde answered, "Yes."

"Really!" she huffed then smiled apologetically at the Smythes. "Please do not stand on our account. We shall step outside for a moment."

"Very good," Lady Smythe said. "Shall I ring for tea?"

"Yes," Dominic said.

"No," Miss Bonde argued.

Lady Smythe sighed. "I had a feeling that might be your answer."

Dominic had to walk quickly in order to reach the door of the drawing room and open it for Miss Bonde. Whatever anyone else said, his mother had raised him to observe some conventions. He needn't have bothered, as the butler opened the door before Dominic could touch the handle. He then closed it and moved away. Miss Bonde waited until Wallace was out of sight before hissing, "As you can see, I am perfectly fine. You may return to"—she waved her arm vaguely—"whatever it was you were doing."

"That would be rude. The Smythes are serving tea."

She gave him an exasperated look. He rather liked her when she was angry. She looked less perfect and more human. "The tea is not for you. You do not even know them."

"Neither do you."

"They are friends of my uncle."

"As am I."

She clenched her hands into fists. "Mr. Griffyn, there is a private matter I wish to discuss with the viscount. If you would be so kind—"

He grabbed her wrist and unfolded her fingers. "No, I am not kind. No one has ever accused me of that vice, and I won't begin now."

"Let go of my hand."

"You'll only clench it again. You, Miss Bonde, are hiding something."

"So says the man who was lurking in a church cemetery."

He allowed that to pass without a reference to glass houses and stones, which he thought showed a rather formidable amount of forbearance. "You intrigue me, Miss Bonde. Much more so tonight than when we first met."

She gave a disbelieving snort. "And so you accost every woman who does not intrigue you?"

"Are you referring to the incident in the hedge-rows?" he asked.

"You know I am."

"In that case, need I remind you that *you* kissed *me*?"

"No, I did *not*."

"You quite lost yourself in my arms."

"I most certainly did not!" Her eyes, so darkly blue they were almost violet, flashed with anger.

"Must I show you again?" He tugged on the hand he still held, pulling her closer. Damn. He was going to kiss her again. All of this kissing would wreak havoc on his reputation as a heartless seducer.

"You wouldn't." She was flush against him now. "Do not dare!"

That sealed her fate. He pressed his mouth to hers, merely intending to give her a taste of what they'd shared the other night. And perhaps he intended to remind himself as well. He hadn't quite forgotten the first taste of her. He did not think he ever would. She'd pressed her lips firmly together, and he brushed his own against them until he felt hers soften. She exhaled, a tiny puff of air that feathered against his lips. He clenched her hand more tightly and wrapped his other arm around her back, holding her in place. Holding her against him. He could feel her body trembling now as he used his tongue to tease her lips open.

He could have explored her lips for hours, perhaps days. She had perfect lips—moist, plump, and warm. He licked her lower lip then took the ripe flesh gently between his teeth. One of her hands came up to grasp his coat. He thought she might push him away, but instead she moved the wool coat aside and spread her hands on his chest, only the thin, finely made linen separating their flesh. He moved quickly, clenching her hand and removing it from his body. He held it trapped at her side. If this were to continue, he would have to explain the rules to her.

He slanted his mouth over hers. He was in no hurry and took her slowly, completely. His hands sank into the softness of her flesh as their bodies came together. But he wanted more of her. Using gentle pressure, he opened her lips to his. He eased his tongue inside, tasting her, reveling in the heat of her. A frisson of white-hot arousal shot through him when his tongue rubbed against hers. She must have felt it as well, because she gasped, and her body went rigid in his arms.

And then she wasn't rigid. Then she was soft and pliable, her warm body melting into his. Her breathing matched his breathing, and he trembled when she did. For a long moment, he didn't think he could release her. Ever. For three beats of their hearts, he was afraid he would never be able to walk away from this woman again.

His head swam; his vision dimmed as blackness swirled. Dominic had to make a conscious effort to open his fingers from her wrist and release her. Even more difficult was the act of separating their lips. As soon as he'd pulled away, he had the overwhelming urge to pull her to him again.

"No!" He stumbled back, putting several feet between them, and still had to clutch the wall for support and to resist taking her in his arms again.

She blinked at him, looking like a woman who had just stepped from a dark room into the sunlight.

"What the devil just happened?" he asked, more to himself than to her. She looked as surprised as he did. He stared at her. Had she bewitched him? How else could he explain how he felt? How desperately he wanted her? How close he had come to wanting to break more of his own rules?

She put her hands to her pink cheeks. "I think you had better go," she said, her voice low and sultry. Hearing her speak, he wanted to do anything but walk away from her. And that was precisely why he had to walk away.

"I think you are correct." He glanced about, surprised to note they were standing outside a drawing room. He had not known where he was for a long moment there. He was with Miss Bonde—no, not Miss Bonde. He was with *Her*. "Where is my hat?" he asked, looking about.

The door to the drawing room opened, and the butler emerged, holding his beaver hat. "Here you are, sir. If you will follow me, I will show you out."

Dominic opened his mouth, then frowned. "How…" It did not matter. He took the hat, placed it on his head, nodded to Her, and started down the stairs without looking back.

Once outside the town house, once on the street, he did not think of her. Rather, he did not allow himself to think of her. When he was not in her presence, the effect she had on him diminished. He couldn't begin to imagine what had come over him when he'd kissed her. He did not want to spend another moment considering what was between them. She was dangerous. That much was clear to him. He would do well to avoid her.

Easier said than done, of course, considering they were to be engaged and then married.

He'd think about that tomorrow.

Without planning to, he'd made his way to Edgeberry's London residence. It sat behind a large wall and iron gates. A footman stood just inside and recognized Dominic as soon as he stepped into the light cast from the lamps on the columns flanking the gates.

"Mr. Griffyn, sir. Just one moment." He heard the clink of a key, and then the gates swung open.

Dominic tipped his hat at the footman and made his way up the short walk to the house. Edgeberry's butler opened the door, looking weary and frazzled.

Dominic paused. "Has his lordship returned from the country, Danbury?"

"No, sir," Danbury said. "But Lord Phineas is here."

Dominic almost groaned aloud. Phineas was his mother's third son, Edgeberry's second. Phineas was not the heir to the marquessate, but the spare. He had all of the privileges of his father's position and none of the responsibilities of his elder brother's future. If there was a vice, Phineas subscribed to it. His main vices were as cliché as his rakish ways—wine and women. As if on cue, Phineas—or one of his reprobate friends—guffawed loudly.

"Perhaps he will retire soon," Dominic said to the beleaguered butler. Danbury was a relatively new addition to the Edgeberry staff. He did not feel as though he had enough authority to impose much order on the young gentlemen of the household. When Edgeberry was present, it was not necessary. But tonight, Edgeberry and Dominic's mother were away.

"Yes, sir." Danbury nodded but did not look hopeful. Dominic was not hopeful either. The best the butler could hope for was that Phineas would be rendered unconscious from overimbibing, sooner rather than later.

For his part, Dominic intended to steer clear of the party and seek the solace of the room he occupied when in Town. He climbed the stairs, glad the drawing-room doors were only partly ajar. The men inside were so raucous they could not have heard him pass. He reached the landing of the second floor and frowned. It was dark, and Dominic had not thought to bring a candle or lamp. The lamps had either sputtered out, or the servants had forgotten to light them. Dominic took a deep breath. It was not so very dark. Light shone at the bottom of the stairs. He stepped forward, the floorboard creaking as he moved. His room was at the end of the corridor. The distance was not great when the lights blazed, but it seemed the other side of the world at the moment.

Idiot, he chided himself. He clenched his hands and walked confidently forward.

Behind him, a floorboard creaked.

Dominic paused. Had that been his imagination? Was someone else up here with him? He turned back, and that was when the attack came. Later Dominic would take comfort in the fact that he did not scream. He would take comfort in the fact that his brother would wake up in the morning with a sore jaw.

Phineas jumped out from a dark alcove and yelled, "Got you!"

Dominic hit him, sending him sprawling onto his skinny arse. He would have hit him again if he hadn't recognized him.

"What the devil was that for?" Phineas complained, his words slurred from too much drink. "Jus' having a bit o' fun."

Dominic grabbed his half brother by the shirt and slammed him against the wall. "Listen, and listen well, *Brother*. Do not ever—do you hear me? *ever*—come at me from behind again."

"Very well."

Dominic released him, and Phineas all but slumped to the floor before picking himself up. "What is wrong with you, anyway?"

Dominic shook his head and continued to his room. "Pray you never find out," he muttered before opening the door. The lamp in his room burned, and he welcomed the light. He slammed the door, leaning back against it and closing his eyes tightly. His entire body shook, and it was a long, long time before his legs were strong enough to carry him to his bed.

Six

JANE STOOD OUTSIDE THE DOORS TO THE DRAWING room for a long moment after Lord and Lady Smythe's butler escorted Mr. Griffyn away. Her cheeks were still burning, but it was not from embarrassment. She did not embarrass easily, and she could not remember ever having blushed so often. She was not the blushing sort—or at least she hadn't been.

She was the sort to feel annoyed when she allowed the personal to interfere with the professional. She was here on business for the Barbican group. That business had nothing whatsoever to do with Mr. Griffyn. In fact, he was in the way. And yet, she had allowed him to escort her to the residence of one of the Barbican group's best operatives—Agent Wolf.

And then she'd allowed him to kiss her senseless within feet of that operative and his wife. She was obviously in need of more sleep or a knock on the head or a long stint in the Barbican group's filing room, affectionately referred to by agents as the Dungeon. And she might opt for any or all of those possibilities after she destroyed the Maître group.

With that thought, she took a breath and glided into the drawing room. The Smythes, heads together as they sat beside each other on the settee, had obviously been in the middle of a discussion, because their whispered conversation ceased, and Lord Smythe stood.

"I am afraid Mr. Griffyn was called home," she said, making her way to a gilt armchair with lions carved on the front legs. "That might be for the best, as he is not...a friend of Lord Melbourne." She looked pointedly at Lady Smythe and then at Lord Smythe. It might not be proper for Lord Smythe to be alone with her, but she could hardly discuss classified Barbican cases in front of a civilian. Not to mention, the deeds of a monster like Foncé might cause the poor woman to give birth prematurely. Her belly was huge on her small frame, and Jane rather thought the lady looked ready to fall forward from the enormous size and weight of the babe she was carrying. The child looked as though it would be more horse than human.

Of course, Jane had no experience with women in Lady Smythe's condition, so perhaps all of them looked as though they were carrying a foal at this stage.

Lord Smythe correctly interpreted her glance at his wife and sat beside the woman, taking her hand. Jane was a bit uncomfortable at such displays of affection, especially considering holding the woman's hand was probably the beginning of what had caused the condition the woman was in now, but the woman was not hers to contend with. Surely Lord Smythe knew how to dismiss his own wife. Considering her difficulty in ridding herself of Mr. Griffyn earlier, she should probably take notes.

"Miss Bonde," Lord Smythe began, "you said Lord Melbourne sent you."

Actually, she hadn't said that, but she had let it be assumed. "I am his niece," she repeated.

"And did he mention who I was?"

Jane's gaze slid to Lady Smythe again. Really, the poor woman should probably go lie down. It could not be comfortable to sit in her position. Or stand. Or…exist.

"You can speak in front of Lady Smythe," he said. "If you know I am Agent Wolf, then you might as well know she is Agent Saint."

If he had pulled out a pistol and shot her, Jane would have been less surprised. She actually fell back against the seat of her chair, all the air whooshing out of her lungs. She shook her head. "I don't understand." She knew it was rude, but she could not stop staring at Lady Smythe's—Agent Saint's, *the* Agent Saint's— belly. How could this hugely pregnant woman be an agent for the Barbican group?

"I see you are somewhat surprised," Lady Smythe—Jane could not think of her as Agent Saint in her condition—said. "Believe me when I tell you Lord Smythe and I were equally surprised. We had been married five years when we discovered, quite by accident, that we were both agents for the Barbican group."

"And M knew?" Like many agents in the group, she often called her uncle M to protect his identity and save her the time and trouble of using his courtesy title.

"Of course. He managed to keep the secret from everyone."

That did not surprise her. What was truly extraordinary was that these two were such good spies that they kept their roles from each other. It underscored what she already knew: Wolf and Saint were the best—save herself, of course. She had studied their previous cases and the techniques they'd used to fulfill their missions. She had read and reread Saint's amazing feats, never once considering Saint was a woman.

Until very recently, women were not allowed in the Barbican group—or so her uncle had told her. That was one reason her identity was kept so secret. At least, that was what she had believed. But how could a woman so hugely pregnant be an operative? Did they have other children? How had she fought with that huge belly? She certainly couldn't run.

"We are retired," Agent Wolf told her.

"I had heard that," Jane said, snapping her gaze back to him. "But I also know no one can rest easy with Foncé free."

"That is true," Saint said. "It's only a matter of time until he uncovers our hidden identities and comes after us. He abducted Baron's wife, and he sent his assassin after Blue. Foncé has more reason to hate us. We've almost had him twice."

Jane nodded. In other words, these two had come face-to-face with Foncé and lived. Not many could say that, especially agents of the Barbican group.

"We'd rather not risk a third encounter," Wolf said. "And we have every reason to believe Foncé wants every member of the Barbican group dead. He will not stop until he achieves his purposes."

"But why has he targeted us? It's almost as though he has a personal vendetta against the Barbican group."

Wolf spread his hands. "If we knew that, it might give us some insight into how we might apprehend him."

"That is why I'm here," Jane said. "I was told you are in possession of information as to Foncé's whereabouts."

Wolf and Saint exchanged a look. There seemed to be an entire conversation in that brief meeting of their gazes.

Saint spoke. "We've been told you are the best."

"I am." It wasn't false pride or braggadocio behind her boast. She *was* the best. She'd never yet failed a mission. She was the operative sent in when other agents could not complete their missions.

"I believe it," Agent Saint conceded, "but M didn't send you."

Jane schooled her face. "How do you know that?" she asked, keeping her voice level.

"Because he doesn't know I have this information," Wolf said.

Bollocks. She had fallen for the trick—and it was not even a new trick. "Blue," she swore under her breath.

"Yes." Saint nodded. "We wanted to know whom M considered the best of the best. We wanted to assess whether we thought you could really capture Foncé."

They were assessing *her*? Jane's brow rose. "And?"

"We're undecided," Wolf said. "You seem young."

Jane stood. "Am I young or merely female?"

Wolf held his hands up as though to ward off an attack. "Do not put words in my mouth. We are as invested in capturing Foncé as you are. We have been trying to destroy the Maîtriser group for almost a year."

"I *will* destroy the Maîtriser group," she said. "I never lose."

The two spies exchanged another glance.

"Stop doing that!" Jane said, moving to stand before them. "Say what you're thinking. You don't believe I can do it."

"It's not that," Saint said. She rose, pushing herself up, belly first. Jane had to step back to make room for her distended form. "You are just so very young."

"And you are so very pregnant! A tortoise could move more quickly than you at the moment. You are not going to apprehend Foncé. If I were you, I would go into hiding."

"Don't think we haven't considered it," Wolf said. "As yet, we don't believe Foncé knows who we are or where we live. But we might be wrong, and time is running out." He gestured to his wife. "There is more than the two of us to consider."

"Then give me the information in your possession. Blue said one of your contacts sold you Foncé's whereabouts. Or was that a ploy to arrange this meeting?"

"No, it's true. I don't know how much to trust the information, however. It might be a trap."

"Whatever trap Foncé has laid, I assure you, I can elude it."

"You are very confident," Saint said. "But we don't want to send you to your death."

"I'm not afraid of death, and I'm not afraid of Foncé."

"You should be," Wolf said quietly. Jane started to ask what he meant, but he turned away. "Come with me. I have something to show you."

Jane followed the other agent out of the drawing room. Behind them, Saint said, "I'll come with you."

Wolf looked back, his eyes narrowed, and his lips parted as though he would contradict her. Jane waited for him to object, but the seconds ticked by, and he said nothing. Instead, he took his wife's arm and walked down the stairs with her, while the butler appeared seemingly from nowhere and led the way to what Jane assumed was Wolf's library, on the ground floor of the residence.

Wolf paused outside the closed door. "If you will give me one moment." He went inside, leaving the door slightly ajar. Jane could not help but peek inside, but before she saw much more than dark wood and a shelf of books, the butler moved to block her view.

"Have you ever been in the Dungeon?" Saint asked while they waited.

"Yes, have you?"

"Once." She shuddered. "That was quite enough." She inclined her head toward the butler and the library behind him. "Adrian has his own version of the Dungeon inside."

Jane's eyes widened. The Dungeon housed all of the Barbican's files—stacks of boxes filled with maps, agent notes, drawings, secrets, and information about some of the most dangerous and notorious men and women in the world. Jane found it fascinating. Just not as fascinating as working in the field. Still, she liked to spend an afternoon there when she had free time. She could lose herself in old maps and reports.

"I'd love to see it sometime," Jane told Saint.

"Catch Foncé, and I'll give you a key," Wolf said, appearing at the door. "Come inside."

She entered the library, disappointed it appeared much like any other library in London. Desk, couch, chairs, books. She shrugged to herself. No sign of any enormous file warehouse here. On the desk, a small sheaf of papers was stacked neatly, and Wolf gestured toward these. "Sophia, sit in my chair," he said.

Saint's brows rose. "You really are worried about me." She took the chair and glanced at Jane, who sat opposite her. "He doesn't like me to climb up and down the stairs."

"You should rest in your condition."

"Traitor!" Saint said playfully. "Just you wait. Ten to one when you are increasing, all the resting your husband tries to force on you will drive you mad."

For a moment Jane couldn't breathe. *When she was increasing?* She was *never* going to be increasing. She was not going to have children.

Except if she married Griffyn, she supposed she would be expected to have children. They would lie together, and children would be the inevitable result. She'd be forced to rest and be kept away from the action—just like Saint. It wasn't that she didn't like children. She did like them, but she also liked traveling the world, hunting double agents, and priming a pistol.

Men had always been secondary considerations compared to those central to the Barbican group. She'd known men. She was still a virgin—by most definitions—because she did not want to find herself with child. But in her travels, she had occasionally met a handsome man who intrigued her. She'd shared kisses and more. She'd known passion—or so she'd thought. Nothing she had experienced thus far could compare to what had passed between her and Griffyn tonight. She had all but lost herself in his arms. That had never happened to her. She always knew what she was doing. She was in control and quite capable of telling a man to stop what he was doing—and enforcing her command, if necessary—when she felt he or she was becoming carried away.

Tonight Jane was not so certain she would have stopped Griffyn. Her skin felt warm when she but considered the kiss they'd shared in the very public space just outside the Smythe's drawing room. What had she been thinking?

She *hadn't* been thinking. That was the problem, and that was why she could not possibly consent to marry Griffyn.

Wolf was saying something, and Jane tried to concentrate. She stared at the papers before her on the desk, but found her gaze drifting to study the two of them. They loved each other. It was so clear, so obvious. He had his hand on her shoulder, and she leaned toward him. Jane had seen men and women in love before. Her own aunt and uncle certainly had an affection for each other. But nothing she had ever seen had made her want what others had.

The Smythes were different. She wanted a man to worry about her, to want to protect her, to cherish her, as Wolf so obviously cherished his wife. And she wanted someone to lean on, someone who would make her feel safe and valued for more than the way she could flutter her eyelashes or toss her hair. She wanted a man who would see the real her—the woman and the agent—and love them both.

"Bonde?" Wolf asked.

"I'm sorry." She blinked. "I'm listening." She focused her gaze on the papers in front of her.

"As I was saying, this is the information I've"—he looked at Saint—"*we've* gathered. The top page is where my source believes Foncé is hiding."

Jane scanned the foolscap, lifted it, looked for another sheet, then frowned. "That is all?"

Wolf shrugged. "Now you see why I didn't rush to inform M."

"Westminster is a busy area—the river, Whitehall." She shook her head. "He could be anywhere. Not to mention, your source notes only having seen Foncé in that area on…" She consulted the parchment again. "On *numerous occasions*."

"It's a start," Saint said. "It's more than we had."

Jane tapped her fingernails on the desk and shifted through the other papers in the file. They were more informative. She knew quite a lot about the Maîtriser group, but Wolf's research filled in several gaps. "If the Maîtriser group is intent upon"—she read from the page—"*furthering anarchy by disrupting and destroying government*, it certainly makes sense for Foncé to frequent Westminster. That is the seat of power."

"He could be planning another attempt on the life of the prince regent."

"It's a possibility." But she didn't think so. "He has something big planned. A grand finale. It will take him years to kill every member of the Barbican group, even if he could uncover all of our identities. But he could cripple us in other ways. Make us look ineffective and useless."

"He's tried that," Wolf said, "when he went after the regent."

Jane rose. "Next time he will make certain he doesn't fail."

❧

Dominic felt edgy. It wasn't simply the close confines of Edgeberry's carriage, though it was quite cramped with two of his brothers and both his parents inside. Carlisle prattled on endlessly about an upcoming horse race, and his mother, always vivacious herself, asked dozens of questions. It wasn't just the incessant chatter and cramped squabs Dominic was forced to share. The entire day had been rainy and cold, and he'd been cooped up inside for the better part of the afternoon.

He missed his horses. He hated being away from them for this long. He'd spent the morning in Edgeberry's mews, tending to the marquess's town hacks. He knew these animals. He'd bred them, trained them, and they were some of the finest animals the stables at Kenham Hall had produced. But the mews were a far cry from the open air and land of Edgeberry's country estate, and London was as loud and damp and foggy as ever.

Dominic hated London, and he hated being away when one of his horses was ailing. Though he trusted Old Connor implicitly, he could not help but wonder how Lily's Turn was getting on and whether any other horses had been struck down with colic.

"You're quiet tonight, old boy," his brother Arthur said. He was Lord Trewe, the oldest of Dominic's three half siblings and the heir to the marquessate.

Like his brothers, he possessed fair hair and large brown eyes. He was more serious than Phineas, who was most likely carousing again tonight, and not quite as carefree as Carlisle. And at five and twenty, his hair was already thinning, making him look older than his years.

"He's saving his conversation for dinner. He's allowed only a thousand words a day and must portion them out," Carlisle said, chuckling at his own cleverness.

Edgeberry laughed, and Arthur covered a smile. Even Titania, his mother, allowed her lips to quirk slightly. The family was not unkind, but it was obvious to everyone Dominic was not one of them. The Houghton-Cleveborne family laughed easily, talked copiously, and loved generously. Dominic shared none of those characteristics.

"Leave your brother alone," his mother said, defending him as always.

"When there is a battle to be fought, Mother," Dominic said, "I will fight it on my own."

"Dominic knows we're only teasing him," Carlisle said. "He speaks at least fifteen hundred words a day, if one counts the conversations with his horses."

"Their conversation is a vast deal more interesting than that of some humans." Dominic looked pointedly at Carlisle. Carlisle laughed, and Arthur slapped him on the shoulder.

"He has you there, puppy."

"I am certain Mr. Griffyn is considering the importance of the evening," Lord Edgeberry said, pulling on the sleeves of his wool superfine so that the coat was perfectly fitted. As though mirrors of their father,

Arthur and Carlisle adjusted their own coats. Dominic hoped his own was wrinkled, though his valet would never have stood for it.

"I envy you, old boy," Arthur was saying. "If Miss Bonde was titled, I'd pursue her. She's tempting, even without the title."

Titania put a hand on Arthur's arm. "She's not for you."

Arthur shrugged genially. "Plenty of debutantes this year." But there was no hurry for him to marry. The heir had several more years before his father would demand he choose a bride. Arthur was no saint, but he was circumspect. Dominic was the one who caused the family scandal. And it was true he was the most tainted of all of them. But the marquess still had it all wrong.

"She's not for me either," Dominic said. "She is a perfectly acceptable girl—"

"Perfectly acceptable?" Carlisle sounded as though he were choking. "She's a diamond of the first water."

"She certainly has many facets," Dominic agreed. Most young women of the *ton* were not found climbing cemetery walls and sneaking about on midnight errands on Charles Street. She had secrets, as did he, and the last thing Dominic needed was more secrets. No, the last thing he needed was an attraction to a woman like Jane Bonde. If he allowed himself to be swept up in this farce of a courtship, he would soon find himself in the parson's mousetrap.

"Give her a chance," his mother said, reaching over to pat Dominic's knee. He suddenly felt five again. His mother had said the same thing about Edgeberry.

Dominic glanced at the marquess, who was seated beside his mother. Her plum gown sparkled in the coach's low lights. One of the marquess's hands rested possessively on his wife's arm. He had been good for her, and the marriage had saved Dominic and his mother from the squalor they'd been living in. The marriage had saved Dominic's life, though in other ways, it had also taken it away from him. As Titania Griffyn, his mother had been free to choose her own destiny. As the Marchioness of Edgeberry, she had innumerable responsibilities, and Dominic often felt he was the least of these. He'd been sent to Eton and Oxford and the Continent, while she assumed her new position and raised three more sons.

Had she thought the dorms of Eton or a summer in Italy would make him forget? Had sending him away lessened her own feelings of guilt? Dominic could forgive her, because he saw her in a different light now. She was only human, and she had done the best she could. But the boy he'd been would never forgive her for abandoning him when he'd needed her most.

"We are here," Edgeberry said, sitting forward with something akin to excitement. Dominic was more subdued. His mother and the marquess descended first, followed by Arthur. Dominic couldn't remember whether protocol dictated he or Carlisle descend next, and he did not care. He motioned the boy to go ahead. When he climbed out, Lord Melbourne greeted him warmly. "Welcome, Mr. Griffyn. My niece is inside." He gestured to an unassuming terraced house of white limestone. Window boxes blooming with pink flowers adorned the facade, and lights burned in all but the uppermost windows.

Dominic caught his mother's eye. She looked nervous, and he gave her a nod to reassure her. He would see this evening through, but he would not be compelled to marry.

Hats and walking sticks were handed over at the entrance, and Lady Melbourne greeted everyone enthusiastically. Her bright, cheery tone all but grated on Dominic's nerves. The house seemed too bright, and he longed for the shadows. When she reached him, Lady Melbourne said, "I see where you inherited your exotic looks. You and your mother are similarly favored."

"Gypsy blood," Dominic said, because he knew it annoyed Edgeberry.

"Rubbish," the marquess said as if on cue. Titania gave Dominic a quelling look.

"Where is your lovely niece?" Lady Edgeberry asked.

"In the drawing room," Melbourne said. "Will you come up?"

As one, the family clomped up the stairs. Dominic took his time, studying the paintings and artifacts in the vestibule before following. Melbourne was reputed to be a senior official in the Foreign Office, part of the Secret Service. He had certainly traveled widely. The house had a warm, distinctly Continental feel. The drawing room was no different. The walls were dark, the furnishings covered in sumptuous fabrics and jeweled tones. Interesting objects and artistic pieces had been placed here and there, not demanding attention but adding to the flavor of the room.

And in the center of it, wearing a silk gown that rippled like the deepest lake, stood Miss Bonde. She was pale, a porcelain object surrounded by the dark wood furnishings and luxurious velvet coverings of the room. The drawing room was darker than the vestibule, and Dominic had the urge to step into a shadow and observe. He had forgotten how difficult it was to drag his gaze from Miss Bonde once he had fixed it. The blue of her eyes matched her gown. The pink of her lips perfectly matched the delicate roses in a vase on the side table. The slope of her exposed shoulders seemed made for his hands. She was an alabaster statue he dared not touch again.

But he would not be allowed to set himself apart. Not tonight. He was propelled forward, and before he knew what was what, he stood before her and had her gloved hand in his. "Miss Bonde," he said, bowing to her.

"That's two," Carlisle whispered to Arthur. "Five pounds he doesn't say twenty-five in the next quarter hour."

"Make it a half hour, and I'm in."

Miss Bonde curtsied but did not speak. Her eyes were unreadable tonight. She could not possibly have forgotten about the kiss they'd shared the night before, but nothing in her face betrayed any emotion. Dominic stepped away, and his brothers moved forward. They reminded him of a pack of lions, with their golden manes, moving in for the kill. His fingers itched to claw at them, grab them by the scruff of the neck and toss them back. But he was little more than a jackal. The choicest cuts should go to the kings of the jungle.

And indeed, her reaction to his brothers was much as any other woman's. She smiled, and her face seemed to flood with life and color. Within a matter of moments, she was smiling and laughing at something Carlisle said, while Arthur was less amusing but obviously vastly interesting, if one gauged by the rapt expression on her face when he spoke.

Dominic took the claret he'd been offered and sipped it, standing off to the side while his parents conversed with the Melbournes. He'd learned his natural expression was somewhat dark and foreboding, and he did not expect anyone to attempt to draw him into their circle. He preferred it that way. But he could not stop his gaze from straying to Miss Bonde. And once or twice he caught her blue eyes on him. Something seemed to leap between them when their gazes met, and she quickly looked away, smiling at Carlisle and saying something that had both his brothers laughing.

She might be standing in the middle of the room, but she was as distant from all of this as he. She played the part of the proper young lady, but he'd met the real woman in the cemetery the night before. And there had been none of the tittering laughter or fluttering of eyelashes he saw now.

Oh, yes, she had secrets. How he would enjoy uncovering them—if such an act wouldn't put his own secrets at risk. Better to stay away from her.

He glanced at the bracket clock on the table. A quarter hour had passed. Did he want Arthur or Carlisle to win the wager? He'd allow Carlisle to win this time, and he lifted a book from one of the tables and began to peruse it, not speaking again until they went down to dinner.

Despite his brothers' determined flirting, Dominic

was the one asked to escort Miss Bonde to dinner. He waited for the hosts, and then his parents, and then offered his arm. Her body was warm beside his, though her gloved hand rested very lightly on his sleeve. He knew she could walk quickly and efficiently, even run with admirable agility, but she took slow, dainty steps, and he was forced to match her stride.

"Your brothers are quite gregarious," she said as they started down the stairs.

"Economy is not in their natures." He felt her gaze on his face.

"Is that what you are, a word economist?"

"I dislike idle chitchat."

"I believe that. I cannot imagine you doing anything idly."

He cut his gaze to her. Had he imagined her inflection on the word *idly*?

"Tell me, Mr. Griffyn, what do you like, if not idle chitchat?"

He hadn't intended to answer. The question had all the trappings of chitchat, despite her introduction. But then she looked at him, and that indefinable something passed between them again. And he found himself speaking to her, because otherwise he would have bent her over the banister and kissed her.

"Horses," he said, his voice husky.

"Racing or breeding?" Her voice hesitated slightly on the last word.

"Breeding. His lordship's stables are renowned for the quality of their stock."

"You will have to show them to me sometime. I enjoy a breathless ride now and again."

Dominic met her gaze, and she raised an innocent brow. Still, he doubted they were speaking entirely of horses. He also knew she would never come to Edgeberry's stables. "When you visit, you must allow me to mount you."

"You have a stallion in mind?" she asked.

"Griffyn, don't bore the lady with talk of horses," Carlisle interrupted as they were directed toward the dining room. "My brother talks of little but horseflesh. I thought we might talk of the theater."

Carlisle was on her left and Dominic her right as they took their seats. She sat before him, and as he moved to take his place, she happened to lean forward, causing her bodice to gape slightly. Dominic was no gentleman, but even had he been, he could not have looked away quickly enough to avoid the sight of her rounded breasts swelling at the edges of her stays. But it was not the flesh that held his attention. Nestled between her breasts glinted a long, deadly dagger.

Seven

DINNER WAS STRAINED. PERHAPS NOT FOR HER AUNT and uncle, or for Lord Trewe or Lord Carlisle, who really could talk without ceasing, but Jane simply wanted the evening to end. Her face hurt from smiling so much—tight smiles she knew her aunt recognized as false. But every time she looked at her aunt, pleading for her to intervene, her aunt simply notched her chin higher and straightened her shoulders. Jane understood the message: chin up and bear it.

And what could her aunt have done anyway? It wasn't the chattering boys that unnerved her. It was the dark silent man beside her. Dominic Griffyn was a presence, no matter how little he vied to capture her attention. In fact, he could not have appeared less interested in her. He made no attempt to speak with her, no attempt to look at her, no attempt to extend even basic common courtesy to her aunt and uncle. He was not rude, but he lived up to his reputation—a man who cared little for others' opinions or for the customs of Society.

It was obvious he wanted to be anywhere but here.

She might squirm in her seat at being seated so close to him. She might catch her breath watching his fingers curve around his spoon. His fingers had curved about her waist as well, had pulled her to him, so close she had felt his heart slamming in his chest.

Or had that been her heart?

Surely he had not been as affected as she. If he had been, he could not have ignored her so thoroughly. But there again, he met expectations. In the two days since the ball in Grosvenor Square, she had researched more than the Maîtriser group. She'd researched Dominic Griffyn. He had a reputation as a seducer of women. He didn't dally with debutantes or the demimonde, but there seemed to be a number of widows, actresses, and barmaids who had been the recipients of his attentions. And from what Jane had heard, those attentions were rather remarkable. In fact, if the accounts she'd heard were to be believed, he cared much more for the woman's pleasure than his own, though considering he was a man, she hardly believed that. What she could believe were suggestions that he was different than other men—he did not like to be touched, and he was very, very careful not to do anything that might produce a child. And yet recently, one woman had accused him of fathering her bastard child.

Jane was not certain what to think, but as a good spy, she knew she would eventually root out the answers. One thing was certain—he seemed to chafe at being forced to spend time in her presence. Well, she was hardly thrilled to be in his. It had been torture to touch him, walk with him down the stairs. They exchanged banter, innuendo, what he called meaning-less chitchat. She wasn't capable of anything more. She'd deliberately not thought of him again after putting her research on him aside and reading through Wolf's notes on the Maîtriser group. But it was easy not to think of a kiss or an embrace when she had a mission on her mind. It seemed a completely different person had been kissed in the Smythes' town house. She'd gone to sleep and dreamed of Foncé slitting her open like a fish. She'd woken sweaty with fear, not lust, and until her aunt had reminded her of this dinner, had not thought of Griffyn.

Now she could not stop thinking of him.

Irritating man!

Her uncle began to recount a story she had heard a half-dozen times—he was an interesting man, but only five of his best stories could be told to anyone outside the Barbican group—and she slipped a hand into her reticule and withdrew her small watch, its gold chain glinting in the light from the chandelier overhead.

It was after ten, and she had to leave soon or risk missing her appointment. Wolf's contact had agreed to meet her and show her where he'd seen Foncé. This morning a note from Wolf had arrived, stating that his contact had new information as to Foncé's whereabouts. He wanted to meet her at a warehouse in Westminster, on the Thames. He had heard Foncé was expecting a shipment delivered there. Wolf advised her against going. He wanted time to verify the source and see the warehouse himself. But Jane didn't have time to wait. She kept thinking that someone had been following her the night before. If it wasn't Griffyn—and more and more she doubted he cared enough even to open a door for her—then who was it? Foncé or one of his men?

If he knew where she lived and who she was, then Melbourne and the entire existence of the Barbican group was at risk.

But she had to depart soon if she were to arrive at the rendezvous on time. The rest of the company was in no hurry. They seemed happy to chat endlessly, until Jane was afraid she would have to feign sickness in order to escape. Perhaps her aunt saw something of the desperation Jane felt, because Lady Melbourne finally rose and left the men to their port. Jane, Lady Edgeberry, and Lady Melbourne retired to the drawing room. They had barely taken a seat before Lady Edgeberry excused herself.

The door closed behind her, and Lady Melbourne said, "You might have tried a little harder, Jane."

"I do not even think the doors to the drawing room are closed yet," Jane said.

Her aunt huffed. "I am sure the marchioness would agree with me, at any rate."

"Ha! Well then let her look to her son. He did not even notice me."

Lady Melbourne rolled her eyes. "Jane, you might be a very good spy, but you are hopeless at gauging men."

"Tell that to the agent in Verona, whom I—"

Lady Melbourne held up a hand. "Dominic Griffyn wants you."

Jane's eyes widened. "Are you certain you should say such things?"

"Don't pretend to be innocent, Jane."

"It's not that. I had supposed *you* were more innocent."

"I have been married longer than you have been alive. I know something about human nature, and something about men. You are a smart girl, but you don't see how men look at you."

"Yes, I do, and Dominic Griffyn was *not* looking at me. He paid no attention to me whatsoever."

"He kept his gaze on you the entire evening. You think if a man doesn't openly ogle you, like Lord Carlisle, he doesn't want you. Mr. Griffyn isn't the sort of man to compete with another. Not outright. He'll allow his brothers to flirt and play the role of lovers all night, but in the end, if they attempt anything more, he'll swat them away like flies."

Jane narrowed her eyes. "How many glasses of wine did you drink?"

Her aunt was silent. Jane rose, feeling the need to pace, to move after the long dinner. "That's a powerful image, my lady, but I see no evidence for it. It's just as likely that Mr. Griffyn is happy his brothers court me, because then he does not have to bother. Tomorrow he will go home to his horses, and this will all be over."

"You had better hope not."

She turned. "Why?"

"Because if you don't marry Griffyn, you will have to marry someone. We've been through this."

A clock chimed the hour, and Jane knew she was out of time. "I have a megrim. Would you make my excuses?"

Her aunt sighed. "Of course."

Jane did not start for the stairs to the second floor when she left the drawing room. She made her way along the corridor, opened a door at the end, and slipped down the servants' stairs. She waved at the kitchen maid and stepped outside. There was a well here and a small herb garden. The garden proper was on the other side of the house. Jane could easily slip out through the back gate and into the alley where the mews were housed. She started across the lawn but froze when she heard murmured voices.

She almost ignored them and continued on, but something about the way they rose and fell drew her back. She pushed herself against the wall of the house, dropped down to pass under windows, and finally stopped beside the French doors of the morning room, which were open to the garden. In the light cast from a lamp, she could clearly see her uncle and Lady Edgeberry standing close together.

She slid soundlessly behind a large potted tree and pushed back against the wall of the house, listening.

"I don't like to make threats," Lady Edgeberry was saying. Her voice was not quite so cultured as it had been at dinner. Her dark dress melted into the shadows, and she was but a petite figure beside that of Jane's uncle.

"But you make them anyway," Melbourne said.

"Most women fall over themselves to attract Dominic's attention. Your niece appears quite immune."

"I cannot force her to marry your son any more than you can force him."

"Do not worry about Dominic. He has reason to marry, as does Miss Bonde. Do not fail me, Melbourne, or I will make good on my promises." She moved to return inside, but her uncle spoke before she could cross the threshold.

"If women fall over themselves to attract Griffyn's attention, why not choose one of them? Why do you want Jane to marry him?"

She turned back. "Precisely because she does not fall over herself." And she strode back into the house.

Jane waited a moment to ensure the marchioness was gone, then stepped into view. Melbourne's shoulders dropped. "I should have known you would be lurking somewhere."

"It's what I do. Lurk. Creep. Scuttle." She shrugged. "Care to explain that conversation?"

"Not particularly." A single lamp lit the room, and her uncle looked out of place among the frilly upholstery patterns and dainty chairs her aunt had chosen.

"What does Lady Edgeberry have to hold over you?"

"You can add *interrogate* to your list of vices."

"Skills. You taught me each and every one."

"Too well." He ran a hand through his hair, and Jane watched in some amazement. Her uncle was distraught. She had never seen him so unless one of his agents was in danger. "I don't like to tell you this, Jane."

Her spine prickled with unease. "I think you'd better."

"Lady Edgeberry and I were once lovers."

Jane stepped back, wishing she had stayed hidden in the garden. Oh, she did not want to hear this. She did not want to think about what her uncle did in the dark of the night. Her aunt and uncle had no children, and Jane preferred to believe that was because they had never consummated their union. She knew it was ridiculous, but it was easier than imagining them pawing each other the night before, when she caught them smiling secretively over breakfast.

She cleared her throat. "Before or after…"

"After." He turned away from her, clasping his hands behind his back. "I'm ashamed of what I did, Jane. Your aunt and I have had our difficulties, but I should not have strayed." He turned back. "Titania was beautiful, seductive, a promising actress. Every man wanted her."

"Eh—" Bollocks! Why did she continually stumble into conversations like this tonight?

"It was over within a few weeks. She met Edgeberry, and I realized I really did love your aunt."

"And you never told Lady Melbourne?" That was not like him. He did not avoid difficult situations. He faced them.

"No, and I don't want her to find out. She would never forgive me."

That was true to a point. Her aunt loved long and loyally, but if someone betrayed her, she could also punish the offender for years. She would not be persuaded this was a youthful mistake, but she would eventually forgive.

Poor Melbourne. Poor *her*! Jane was going to have to marry Griffyn to keep the marchioness quiet.

"Perhaps if *I* speak with Lady Edgeberry—"

"It won't do any good, Jane." Melbourne moved closer to her, and she saw the weariness in his eyes. He looked as though he'd aged ten years. "She has made up her mind. She can be very persistent when she wants something. If you can't marry Griffyn, tell me now. I want to speak to your aunt before she hears of this from Titania."

Jane stared at him. How could she marry Dominic Griffyn? And how could she not?

"You will have to marry someone, Jane. Remember that. You cannot continue with the Barbican group if you do not. But I won't force you to marry someone you cannot live with. It was my mistake, not yours, and you shouldn't have to pay for it."

She took a breath. "Marrying him wouldn't be so awful a price," she finally admitted. "He is attractive."

Melbourne's brows rose. "Is he?"

"And he kisses well."

He crossed his arms over his chest. "Does he now?"

She could have said more, could have tortured him with tidbits of knowledge, but she did not want to discuss intimate matters with her uncle. She could talk to him about anything but that. Finally, she said, "I will think about it. Tell Lady Edgeberry I am considering."

"Very well. Thank you."

She laughed and gave him a hug. "I love you, Uncle. No need to thank me."

"Shall we go inside? Griffyn has already left. He said he wanted to rise early and travel to Edgeberry's stables. You're quite safe from him." He offered his arm.

She stepped back. "I have an appointment."

"Oh? Anything I should know about?"

"Not yet. I'll brief you in the morning." She started for the back gate, waving at him over her shoulder.

"Jane!" he called.

She looked back.

"Be careful. This one…he's not like any other foe you've faced."

"Yes, my lord."

She reached the gate, opened the latch, and stepped into the alley. The mews were just across the short lane, and she opened the door soundlessly, reached inside, and retrieved the sack she'd secreted there hours before. Standing in the shadows, she tied her skirts up and out of her way, discarded her slippers for a pair of sturdy half boots, and retrieved the dagger from her bodice. She'd had a sheath sewn along the wooden busk that ran the length of the center of her stays. The busk ensured she maintained good posture, not that she was likely to forget with a sharp dagger to prick her if she forgot to sit straight. Now she slipped the dagger into one of her boots and donned a black cape, pulling the hood over her bright hair. Jane stuffed the items she'd removed back into the sack and shoved it into the mews. She closed the door again, hearing the horses shuffle curiously, but otherwise disturbing nothing.

She turned, and Dominic Griffyn stood before her.

❦

"This is interesting," he said, scrutinizing her attire. "Is there a reason you don capes and sneak away from your cozy home each night?"

"What are you doing here?" she demanded, her eyes flashing even under the shadow of the cape.

"What are *you* doing here?" he answered in kind.

"I live here."

"This"—he pointed at the dirt lane—"is a street, not a residence."

She blew out a breath. "You are the most exasperating man. Go home. This does not concern you."

"That may be, but I'm curious."

"I assure you there is nothing of interest. You are supposed to be at home." She actually gestured down the lane. It wasn't even the direction of the Edgeberry town house, but he didn't point that out.

He crossed his arms. "I'll go home."

"Good."

"If you tell me where you are going and why."

She pressed her hands together, threading her fingers. "I cannot. I would if I could, but I am sworn to secrecy."

"Then I'll have to follow you."

"No!" She stepped close to him and took his hands in hers. She still wore her gloves, as did he, but somehow the contact between them was just as heated as it would have been had their skin been bare. He jerked his hands back.

"Do not touch me."

"Do not follow me." Then her eyes softened. "Please, Mr. Griffyn. Go home."

He actually wanted to give in to her. She was beautiful with her large blue-violet eyes pleading with him. He wanted to please her.

But he wanted to follow her more.

"Tell me what I want to know."

Her eyes turned stormy. "I can evade you, you know. I know how to lose a tail."

"Even a tail who yells out your name when he loses sight of you? Even a tail not afraid to wake the whole city to find you?"

She tapped her foot. Clearly, she had not considered this tactic. Equally clearly, she was torn between giving up on her errand for the night or allowing him to accompany her. "It's late," she said. "I don't have time to argue." She began to walk, and he was so surprised it took him a moment to catch up to her.

"If you come with me, you take your life in your hands." She walked quickly and efficiently, making her way past the dark mews with a confidence that told him she had done this many times before.

"That doesn't sound promising."

"And I won't answer your questions. No matter what happens." She glanced over her shoulder. "You'll be left with more questions than answers."

"Very well."

She scowled at him. "Do not say I didn't warn you. When you end up dead, do not blame me."

"I shall come back as a spirit and haunt you."

"That's amusing now. It won't be if something goes wrong."

"What could go wrong?"

"Nice try. End of discussion." And it was. She began to run at an easy pace, and he was forced to run to keep up with her. She ran with sureness and speed, hesitating only when she reached a busy street. Then she slowed to a walk so as not to rouse suspicion. Once away from the bustle of carriages and young bucks making their way back to bachelor quarters, she began to run again. Gradually, he realized they were headed for the river.

He smelled it before he saw it, and when they paused under a tree, he tried not to breathe too deeply. "Why...did...we...not...take...a...hack?" he finally managed.

"I don't want anyone...to know where...I am." She was hardly out of breath, and he found himself impressed almost against his will. Growing up with brothers and among the boys at Eton, he had thought women frail creatures who needed to sit for long hours and be escorted when walking. But Miss Bonde was in far better physical condition than he. She was barely winded, while his lungs burned.

"We're going to the river?" The question might as well have been thrown into the wind. She ignored him and looked into the distance. He followed her gaze, attempting to see what, if anything, she searched for. Suddenly, for no reason he could discern, her stance changed, and he saw the glint of the dagger in her hand.

"You the one they call Bonde?" a voice called out from the darkness of another tree.

"Yes. Are you Applewhite?"

"I thought you were coming alone."

She glanced at Dominic over her shoulder and scowled. "Change of plan."

"You're late."

She let out a frustrated sigh. "And you talk too much. Will you take me to the warehouse, or must I find it myself?"

"Oh, I'll take you," the man said, emerging from the dark. Dominic couldn't manage a good look at him. His hat had been pulled low on his brow, and he wore his coat collar high to protect him from the chill in the air. "You agents are all the same," he grumbled. "In a hurry to die."

Agents? Dominic thought as he followed the man closer to the river and along its edge. What sort of agent was she? Customs agent? Was she inspecting illegal cargo? It made no sense. Women did not work as customs agents.

A row of warehouses came into view. At this time of night, they appeared deserted. Tugs designed to transport goods from the large vessels in the crowded river to the riverside wharves stood as dark sentries on the Thames's murky waters. In the distance the newly constructed Millbank Prison loomed over them all.

"I thought there was a shipment arriving tonight."

Applewhite shrugged and spit. "I only know what I heard. The wind or tide might have been against them. Made it slow going."

"Is Foncé here?"

"Shh!" Applewhite grabbed her hand, and Dominic stepped in immediately and shoved the man back.

"Do not touch her."

Miss Bonde gave him an amused look and turned her attention back to Applewhite.

"I'm trying to save her life. Those that speak that name aloud don't live long."

"Fair enough," she said. "Has the man in question arrived yet?"

"No." He pointed to a warehouse painted putrid yellow. "That's the one. When you step inside—"

"You're not coming with us?" she asked.

"That wasn't the deal. The deal was I show you the warehouse. Wolf isn't paying enough for me to stay."

Something that looked like concern flickered in her eyes and was gone. "When I step inside…" she prodded.

"Stay to the right. There's a stairwell. Take it to the second floor. There's an office no one uses up there. It has a view of the floor on one side and the river on the other. Good luck to you." With a tip of his hat, he was gone.

For a long moment, she didn't move. Dominic waited for her to say this was all some sort of hoax, but she seemed to be studying the warehouse.

"You're not actually going inside," he said.

She glanced at him as though she'd forgotten he was present. "You'd better wait here. Stay hidden. I don't trust this."

"Then we should return home. I'll escort you." He reached for her arm, but she shook him off.

"I'm not going home, and I don't need an escort." She flashed the dagger. "I'm going in, and it would be immensely helpful to me if I did not have to worry about you."

"I suppose I'm not going to be very helpful then. I'm coming with you."

She shook her head at him, and he felt her annoyance. Hell, he was annoyed with himself. Why the devil was he doing this? He was no knight in shining armor. What did he care if she wanted to traipse about London in the middle of the night or hide in old warehouses? It was nothing new to her—that much was obvious. He should have gone home tonight instead of waiting to see what she'd do. But now that he had, he couldn't leave her. He felt responsible for her somehow. After all, she was his betrothed—or she would be if he ever asked for her hand.

And he certainly wasn't doing that until he knew something of her secrets.

"I thought you were a rogue who cared nothing for Society or its rules."

He nodded. "Apt description."

"Then act like one! Abandon me. Leave me to fend for myself. Say something truly despicable and stomp off to some brothel or other."

"All good choices, but I'm staying right here."

"I hate you," she seethed. "You are no better than the rest of the *gentlemen*." She said the word as though it was a curse.

"It occurs to me, Miss Bonde, that if you want me to leave and I accommodate, that is actually the more gentlemanly act. If I stay where I am not wanted, I act much more the disreputable rogue."

She gave him a disgusted look and shook her head.

"Are we going inside?" he asked.

"*I* am going inside. You can go to the devil." She started for the warehouse, but when he made to follow, she turned and put a hand on his chest, which he allowed. This time. "Follow me. Step where I step. Do what I do."

He looked down at her, so stern and serious. She was actually giving him orders.

"If you ruin this mission for me, I will personally see you flogged."

"How wonderfully fifteenth century."

She held up a finger and jabbed it at his nose. "Don't tempt me."

He had the strangest impulse to kiss her right then. Why he should be attracted to her, he couldn't say. Why he wanted to kiss her, when he never kissed, he could not fathom. Miss Bonde was annoying the hell out of him. The one thing he could not tolerate was being ordered about—by a man or woman. But there was something about the way she did so that made his blood thrum. He might have kissed her then, too, if something she'd said didn't niggle at his mind. *Mission.*

She moved forward again, keeping to the shadows as a cat might. She really was rather good at this, and he followed her as best he could. He was neither as sleek or small as she, but he thought he did a tolerable job of slinking. They reached the warehouse, and she stopped to stand on tiptoes and peer into one of the grimy windows. Her eyes barely cleared the casement, and he leaned close to whisper, "Would you like me to lift you?"

She jumped as though startled. "No. Step back," she hissed.

He shrugged, but he didn't step back. Compared to the stink of the river, she smelled sweet and fresh. He liked the way one tendril of hair curled about her jawline. Since he was at a level with the window, he peered in as well. "No one inside," he said.

"I can see that." Again, staying in the shadows, she made her way to the door. It faced the river and was not in shadow, and she paused for several moments before moving into the open. When she did, it was lightning quick. She stepped out, tried the door, found it locked, and slid back into the darkness before he had even thought about moving.

"Locked." Her breathing was more rapid now. "Padlock. I could break it, but I don't have time, nor do I relish being exposed as I do so."

"Now we go home?"

"Now we go in through a window."

"I bloody knew you were going to say that." The windows were small and square. She could fit inside, but he would have a more difficult time.

"Feel free to return home at any time." She moved back to the window they'd stood beside. He could see the marks from their hands on the dirty windowpane. She stood on tiptoe again and pushed at the glass. "It's latched, but the latch isn't very secure." She pushed on it, but she didn't have the angle to do any damage.

"Want me to try?"

"Can you break the latch without breaking the glass?"

"I don't know."

She pursed her lips and considered. In the distance, he heard the sound of men's voices. He couldn't tell if it was coming from the river or the road, but he had the feeling they were headed this way.

"Lift me," she said.

He raised his brows. "Pick you up?"

"Yes. Hoist me up, and I'll break the latch. Then I'll push the window in, and you can push me through."

He considered refusing her, but she would only find another way. And then there was something appealing about being given permission to touch her. "Come here."

She stood in front of him, facing the window, and he hesitated only a moment before putting his hands on her waist. He had to adjust his hold once he was through the folds of the cape, but when he had her securely, he lifted her. She was more solid than she looked—not heavy, but not light. He braced a knee against the building, while she gave the window a firm tap from the palm of the hand. She tapped it again, and it swung free, closing again. "I have it. Can you raise me a bit higher? I think I can make it through."

But as he lifted her higher, her cape caught on a splinter or nail, and she had to tug it free. "Just a moment." He set her down and watched as she unfastened the cape and tossed it into a shadow. She'd tied up her skirts, and a long stretch of white leg was visible before the skirts covered her thighs. She wore silk stockings with silk garters. She'd ruin them when she climbed through the window, and for some reason, he thought that a pity.

"Done ogling me?"

"I wasn't—" Oh, why deny it? "For the moment. Turn."

She did so, obediently, and he lifted her to the window. She rested her chest against it and shook her head. "A bit higher."

He adjusted his grip, lowering it to her rounded hips and the edge of her buttocks. With a push, she scrambled over. But not before he had a flash of her white bottom. He swallowed, willing himself not to return to the image now. This was not the place for it. The top of her head appeared on the other side of the window.

"Coming?"

With a grunt, he hoisted himself up. Without anyone to give him a push, he had to exert a great deal more strength, but he managed it and slid through soundlessly.

"Shh!"

Apparently, she didn't agree. He had the urge

to take the flat of his palm and lay it against those firm white cheeks of her bottom. Of course, if he touched that skin, he would forget about spanking her. He could think of more pleasant ways to spend an evening.

"Griffyn?"

He gave her a dark look and willed the image away again. "The stairs, correct?"

"This way." She led, as usual, though he could see where the stairwell was as easily as she. The voices from the men grew louder now. They were definitely headed this way. She moved quickly, despite the darkness in the warehouse, stumbling only once over a tumbled crate. He avoided it because he'd seen her trip, but he seemed to knock his knee on everything else imaginable. She must have had cat eyes to see her way around the debris.

She climbed the stairs silently, with him right on her heels, as they heard the padlock being opened. A sliver of light danced through the door's crack, and they dove into the upper room, closing the door behind them. For a moment, they both rested against the door, catching their breath. The voices of the men were inside now, and Dominic watched the light of the lamps make long shadows on the ceiling. He counted two, no three or possibly four men's voices.

On hands and knees, she began to crawl toward the center of the room, nearest the open area, where she could look down on the floor. Why the hell did he have to see that flash of flesh? He could think of little else as he watched her crawl along the floor. Dominic supposed he should worry about the men below. They would be none too pleased to find the two of them in their warehouse. Perhaps he should have tried harder to make her return home.

She paused and rose on her knees, looking over the ledge to the floor below. Whatever she saw caused her to gasp and jerk back down. She swore—oaths a lady should not even know, let alone utter.

"Problem?" he asked.

"No. Everything is fine." She fumbled in her skirts, giving him more than a flash of her upper thigh, and pulled out a small pistol. Dominic's brow rose. It rose farther when she also produced a shooting bag with balls, powder, and a priming horn.

"Do you have a cannon under there too?"

She didn't even smile. This was new. He'd seen women shoot hunting rifles before, but he'd never seen one with a pistol. And this one seemed to have been made for her. It was small and feminine. Why did she need a pistol, and why did she carry one on her person?

He had that uneasy feeling again. It was becoming familiar. *Mission.* The word echoed in his mind.

Dominic made his way across the floor in much the same manner as she. When he was beside her, he peered over the ledge. It took a moment for him to make sense of the scene below. Two men were moving about, while one man tied a fourth to a chair. That man did not look as though he needed restraints. He slumped over, head on his chest, face bloody and swollen. A fifth man stood, arms crossed casually, and watched. He glanced toward the spot where Dominic and Miss Bonde hid, and Dominic ducked down again.

"What's going on?" he whispered.

"There's no shipment," she said, finishing priming the pistol. It made him nervous to note how comfortable she was with such a task—as though she had done it many times before.

"Perhaps it's merely late."

"The idiot contact didn't understand the code. The cargo isn't from a ship," she whispered. "The cargo is that agent."

"You know that man?"

She nodded. "He works for my uncle."

"So he's a spy."

"More or less."

"And the man below?"

"The tall, thin one with the dark hair in the blue velvet coat?"

"That one."

"Foncé, leader of the Maîtriser group. And all you need know is that he and the Maîtriser group are very, very dangerous."

"I have a bad feeling."

She peered over the ledge again. "It's mutual."

"And voilà!" the man said from below. "It is complete."

Dominic noted he had a French accent.

"I have a bad feeling this—"

"Now, where is my *amie*? *Bon soir*, Mademoiselle Bonde. Where are you?" Foncé's tone might have been playful, but the malice in his voice was not.

Dominic cut his gaze to Miss Bonde.

"—is a trap," she finished.

Eight

THIS WAS BAD. VERY, VERY BAD. SHE HAD BEEN IN worse situations. She had escaped them, but she had never been in this sort of situation with a civilian beside her and a wounded agent below. Did she save Griffyn or Viking?

Or did she simply say to hell with all of them and kill Foncé here and now? Yes, his men would storm the room. Yes, she would end up dead herself, but the world would be free from the leader of the Maîtriser group. He wouldn't be able to carve people up for his amusement any longer. Killing him and sacrificing herself would probably be the least selfish thing to do. But she was, unfortunately, rather selfish. She did not want to die, nor did she want Griffyn dead. Viking might already be dead. She hadn't seen him move since he'd been brought in, though his body didn't appear as stiff and inflexible as dead bodies grew after even a short period of time.

Griffyn was looking at her. She supposed he expected her to devise some sort of plan.

She didn't have one.

"Oh, mademoiselle! I know you are here! Where are you?" Foncé sang.

"Go to hell," she hissed, still crouching beneath the ledge. *Think. Think!* There was another window in the office, but even if she managed to pry it open and slide through before Foncé's men reached her, the drop was substantial. She could break a leg. Then she'd be Foncé's prisoner and suffer a broken leg. And if she did manage to escape, it would mean leaving Viking behind.

She'd never left a fallen agent.

"Are you behind those crates?" Foncé asked. She imagined him gesturing to the stack of crates, and a moment later she heard them tumble to the ground as his men toppled them. "Hmm. No. What about under that table?"

"There aren't many more hiding places," Griffyn pointed out.

"Good. I'm ready for the conclusion."

"How foolish of me. I was actually hoping we might live another day." He leaned his head back on the wall where she overlooked the ledge. "Is there any chance of survival?"

"Oh, there's always a chance. I could take a cue from Baron and set the place on fire, but I don't have a tinderbox. Do you?"

"No," he said, voice ominous.

"Scratch fire, then. I have enough pistol balls to shoot all of them, but they will probably take cover while I reload. Then we'd be at a stalemate."

"Behind the door?" Foncé called from below. "I will find you!"

"If you actually know how to fire that thing, I am in favor of shooting them."

Jane rolled her eyes. Of course he doubted her. Men always did. She usually used that to her advantage, but Griffyn's skepticism made her a little sad. "I know how to fire it, but I think the better course is to let them find us."

He glowered at her. "I have to disagree."

"You don't merit an opinion. Roll those two barrels near the door."

He didn't jump to do her bidding, which annoyed her, but what had she expected? Finally, he moved in a crouch to the two wine barrels and pushed them quietly toward the doorway. He had an easy enough time that she deduced they were empty. That was unfortunate. Still, she rose on her knees and peeked over the ledge. "Oh, Foncé!" She waved her handkerchief. "Up here!" She dropped back down as the sound of a shot being fired reverberated off the walls of the warehouse. She wasn't certain where the ball struck, but it wasn't terribly close. Foncé might have light below, but it couldn't penetrate the shadows up here.

"That missed me," Griffyn said low. "Perhaps you are not trying hard enough to see me killed."

"Ye of little faith," she muttered. The barrels were in place, and that had been all she asked. She heard the men's footsteps on the stairs, and she moved to the door, keeping low. "Step back," she said, motioning Griffyn out of the way.

"I'll help," he said, refusing to budge from her side.

She huffed out a breath. "This is no time for chivalry."

"It's not chivalry. It's survival."

She had no time left to argue. The sound of the footsteps grew closer and closer. Beside her, Griffyn leaned forward with anticipation. She put a steadying hand on his arm. Timing was crucial. She could hear him breathe faster as the footsteps crashed down on them, and still she waited. Finally, at the last moment, she threw the door open, knocking one of Foncé's men backward. "Now!" she yelled, and Griffyn heaved a barrel down the steps. They rolled mercilessly, striking first the man, who reeled from being hurt by the door. He tumbled down, taking the other man with him. When they tried to rise, Griffyn launched another barrel at them, sending them tumbling down the stairs.

"Follow me!" Jane yelled, running down the steps. She didn't look to see if Griffyn followed. She could protect him better by killing Foncé. She leaped over the two men, who were lying unconscious at the base of the steps, and spotted Foncé making for the exit door. "Oh, no you don't," she murmured pulling her pistol from her pocket. She aimed, cocked the hammer, and fired, but she missed—barely—and Foncé scooted out the door.

She uttered a scream of frustration and followed, only to be pulled back by strong arms. "Griffyn!" she yelled.

But it wasn't Griffyn.

The men at the base of the steps weren't quite as lifeless as she'd hoped. One of them had her by the arm, and when she turned, he punched her in the stomach. Her breath whooshed out of her, and she doubled over, but she recovered before he could hit her again and kicked his shin.

He didn't release her arm, though she yanked hard enough to tear her sleeve. Foncé was escaping! "Let. Go!" She tried to kick him, but he danced backward and struck at her again. This time she saw the glint of steel.

He laughed at the surprise on her face as Griffyn grabbed his shoulder from behind and spun him around. The man released Jane, but she watched long enough to see Griffyn's strong right smash into Foncé's man's nose. "Thank you," she called.

"Go!"

She was already gone. She raced out of the warehouse, hearing the thud as the door slammed behind her. Immediately, she pressed her back against the outside wall. Foncé could be waiting out here. This might be a ploy to lure her outside. She scanned the area for him and saw nothing and no one. She edged along the wall, stopping to listen.

Plop. Plop.

Was that the Thames lapping against the dock?

Plop.

Was it Foncé? Had he been wounded?

She felt something plink onto her boot and looked down. Hellfire and damnation. She was the one wounded.

Blood stained the front of her gown, and she pressed a hand to her belly. Foncé's man had stabbed her with his dagger. She'd thought it only his fist, but this wasn't the first time the excitement of the moment cushioned the pain. She felt it now. Keenly.

She drew her hand away, staring at her crimson-stained palm. Head dizzy, she lurched back inside the warehouse. It took her a moment to catch her bearings. Griffyn was being useful. He'd tied up the man with the knife and was working on the other man, utilizing a long piece of rope of the sort found on sailing vessels. He glanced at her then looked again. Whatever he saw caused him to drop the rope and abandon the man he was binding. "What the hell happened?"

She waved her hand as though the wound was nothing. And no organs were spilling out, so she considered it a mere flesh wound. "I'm fine," she said. "Secure him."

"You're bleeding," Griffyn pointed out.

"It's a stomach wound. Those take a long time to kill a person."

"That's reassuring."

She ignored him, focusing on Viking instead. He still hadn't moved. It might already be too late for the other agent. "Viking," she said, walking toward him. She wobbled unsteadily, her legs swerving off to one side without her permission. Jane fell to her knees beside the other agent. He had a shock of blond hair, pale blue eyes, and wide shoulders, an appearance that had earned him his sobriquet. She lifted his square face from his chest, and his eyes fluttered and rolled back. "Oh, Viking."

Griffyn came up behind her. "He's still alive," she said without waiting for him to ask. "Help me untie him."

She had intended to assist in the untying, but she couldn't seem to force her legs to hold her. She stayed kneeling beside him, which might have been for the best. As soon as the agent's hands were free, he tumbled to the floor. She caught him, breaking his fall and noting the blood on his chest.

"What happened?" she asked, listening to his ragged breathing. Tears she refused to shed stung her eyes. She knew the sound of the death rattle.

"Listen," Viking said, blood gurgling in his throat. "Not much time."

"Nonsense. I'll take you to Farrar. He'll patch you up in no time."

"Bloody butcher," Viking croaked, but he was smiling. "Keep him away."

"Just hold on." She began to rise, intending to pull him up beside her, but he grabbed her gown.

"Listen, Bonde." His voice was low now, almost inaudible. She bent close.

"I'm listening."

"He knows. Watch your back. Tell…"

He coughed, blood spilling out of his mouth and onto his chest. A good deal of it splattered on her, but she didn't flinch. Griffyn—she'd all but forgotten him—handed her a handkerchief, and she used it to wipe Viking's chin.

She wanted to tell Viking to save his strength. She wanted to be kind, but she needed to know what he knew. Swallowing her disgust at herself, she prompted, "Tell…"

Viking nodded. His eyes closed, and his breathing stuttered. She was losing him. "Viking. Tell what? Tell someone?"

He nodded. "M," he rasped.

"Tell M. I will. What should I tell him?"

The silence was loud, punctuated by the slow, labored breathing of Viking. She could hear the struggle his lungs made to pull in one last breath. She was killing him. Making him talk was killing him faster. No matter that he would die despite any action she took. She would never forgive herself for this. She would add it to the list of all the things she'd done for which she could never forgive herself.

"Foncé," Viking whispered.

"Yes." Jane nodded. "What about Foncé? What should I tell M?"

He pulled in a ragged breath. "Knows him."

Jane waited. She waited for Viking to exhale. Waited for him to speak again. After a long moment, she realized he never would. She was shaking when Griffyn put his hand on her shoulder. "He's gone."

"Do you think I don't know that?" she spat at him. Then she closed her eyes. "I'm sorry."

"No apology required. You're wounded. You need a doctor."

"I know." She allowed him to help her rise. Her head was spinning too much for her to manage it on her own. Her stomach churned at the smell of blood and death clinging to her. She would not allow herself to cast up her accounts. To do so would serve no purpose but to split her wound further. Straight spine, Bonde, she told herself. Her uncle had said it enough times that the words were almost her own.

"No argument?" he asked when she'd gained her feet.

"I know when I need help."

"Good." And the next thing she knew he'd swept her into his arms.

"No!" Now her head reeled. "I can still walk. I want to walk."

"You don't always have your way. I'm taking you home."

"No." She *would* have her way on this. "Take me to Piccadilly."

"Piccadilly?"

"There's a doctor there," she said.

"This Farrar you mentioned?"

She nodded, struggling to keep her head up. Finally, she gave in and rested it on his shoulder. She didn't want to be close to him. She simply needed the support. But she couldn't stop herself noticing how clean and wonderful he smelled. She had no choice but to smell him.

"Where on Piccadilly?"

She opened her eyes and started. She was sitting on his lap, and they were inside a carriage. "Where are we?"

"Hack. Where on Piccadilly?"

She gave him the address and fought to keep her eyes open. She had never lost consciousness before, and she refused to believe she'd done it tonight. Knife wound or no.

Griffyn gave the jarvey the direction, and the carriage jerked into motion. She hissed in a breath as her wound was jostled.

"Besides a doctor, what is on Piccadilly?"

She might as well tell him. It was a bit late for secrets, and he'd soon see, at any rate. "The offices for the Barbican group."

He took her chin in his hand. "Stay with me, Miss Bonde."

She realized she'd closed her eyes again, and she nodded and fought to keep them open.

"What is the Barbican group? And do not tell me you cannot say."

She swallowed. "I *can't* say, but I might as well. Remember you did not hear this from me."

He gave her a look bordering on amusement. "I am the soul of discretion."

Fine. Let him jest now. "The Barbican group is a subset of the Foreign Office. It's the most elite group of spies England has to offer."

When he didn't respond, she glanced at him. It was a short glance as, slowly, she realized she was still sitting on his lap. Why did he not put her down?

His face was turned away from her, his jaw clenched.

"Griffyn?"

He stared at her. "I bloody well knew it."

❧

He didn't know why he expected to see a sign on Piccadilly directing the hackney to the headquarters of the Barbican group. It wasn't as though the Foreign Office wanted to advertise the location of the offices of its most elite spies.

Spies! Bloody spies! He glanced at Miss Bonde, who had moved out of his lap and was now sitting beside him, looking out the window. "We're almost there," she said. She said it as though going to spy headquarters was the most normal thing in the world for her. And it probably was. He didn't want to believe she was a spy. *His* betrothed, a spy!

Well, she wasn't actually his betrothed yet, as he hadn't asked for her hand in marriage. But she was as good as betrothed to him. Women were not supposed to work as spies. He'd thought his mother's career as an actress about the most outlandish career a woman could have.

Apparently, he'd been wrong.

He didn't want a wife who was unconventional. He didn't want a wife at all—not from the beau monde at any rate—another prim and proper miss who would look down on him because he was the bastard son of an actress. He'd lived all his life with the taunts and jibes of others because of his mother's career. If he ever were to marry, he wanted a wife who stayed home and…did whatever it was women did. They did not carry pistols and suffer knife wounds.

Women wrote letters and…embroidered. That's what they did.

Whatever the hell embroidery was.

He would raise horses. She would raise children. And that would be that.

Except it would not be the end of it. Bonde was not going to give this…occupation of hers up lightly. And the last thing he wanted was to be saddled with a spy. Bloody hell! He didn't even think women could be spies.

No, he would cross Jane Bonde off his mother's short list of marriageable ladies. She would have to find another bride for him. Not that ladies were exactly lining up. Yes, certain sorts of women were eager to trade favors, but they weren't the sort one brought to dinner at Kenham Hall. Miss Bonde was that sort, but the others of her ilk were not so keen to marry a bastard—even the bastard of a marchioness.

Miss Bonde hadn't seemed to mind his illegitimacy. Initially, he'd thought her disdain for him was the reason she tried to avoid him. Clearly, she had another reason. She was the one with secrets, the one who was not what she seemed. Did her uncle know what she was involved in?

Of course he did. Lord Melbourne worked for the Foreign Office, which meant he'd probably brought up his niece to continue in his footsteps.

"Why does your uncle want you to marry?" he asked suddenly.

She dragged her gaze from the window, where she was monitoring their slow progress along Piccadilly. "The usual reasons," she said smoothly.

"You lie quite easily," he remarked. "But then that's your profession."

"My profession is to stop madmen like Foncé and groups like the Maîtriser group, who are intent on destroying the sovereignty of the British nation. At times I cannot reveal certain aspects of my life. That doesn't make me a liar." She was in pain. Her voice was strained and higher pitched than normal. But otherwise she didn't show it. He couldn't help but admire her for that. She was no simpering miss.

But admire her or not, he wasn't going to marry her.

"And you haven't answered my question," he said. "That was quite the patriotic speech, however."

She opened her mouth, and he held up a hand. "Do not say *the usual reasons*. They do not apply in this case. A husband and the children accompanying marriage would be more hindrance than help to your *profession*."

The hack slowed, and she turned her attention back to the window. "We've arrived. Do you have any blunt? If not, I'll ask the jarvey to wait and have Moneypence pay."

He gave her a scornful look. "I have coin enough for a hack. Who is Moneypence?"

"My uncle's clerk." With a nod, she moved to open the door, but he grasped her arm. "Our conversation is not over."

She looked down at his hand on her arm, and he pulled it back. "Good." She met his gaze with her clear blue eyes. "Because I have more to add."

"Do not open the door," Dominic ordered her. "That's for me to do."

"I don't need assistance opening a door."

"I don't imagine the majority of ladies need assistance opening doors. That isn't why it's offered." He opened the door, jumped down, and lowered the steps, then held out a hand to assist her. She rose unsteadily, and Dominic realized she was too weak to make it down the steps on her own. Not that she would ever admit as much. He leaned forward, putting an arm around her so she might lean on him. He would have carried her, but that would be too much of a spectacle in the middle of Piccadilly, even at this late hour. The street still teemed with life.

He tossed the jarvey a few coins and followed the nod of her head to a small, unmarked brown door beside a men's haberdashery. "That's it? The door to the chamber of espionage?"

"Yes. Did you think it would be gilded and ornamented with diamonds?"

"That's what they have you for, I suppose."

The fact that she made no retort spoke for how

exhausted she must be. Keeping his arm about her, he helped her to the door. She moved slowly, and he more or less carried her, dragging her feet. When they stopped before the door, he reached for the handle, but she shook her head and indicated a bellpull. Dominic pulled it. Nothing happened.

"Wait," she said. "He's slow."

Dominic waited. And waited.

Finally, a rectangular slit in the wood opened, and two ancient rheumy blue eyes appeared. "Are you here to see Miss Leighton?"

Dominic shook his head. "No, we're—"

Miss Bonde held up a hand. "Yes. I hear she cobbles shoes."

The blue eyes narrowed and focused on Dominic. "She also makes blackberry pies."

"Which I hear she sells in twos."

The rectangular slit closed, and Dominic heard a clang inside. Secret codes? Hidden chambers? Dead spies? How had he become involved in this?

"Let me speak," Miss Bonde told him.

"Gladly. I know nothing of pies or shoes."

"It was the code to gain entrance. I had to give two lines of it, because you made Felix suspicious."

"Doesn't he know you by now?"

"This isn't Almack's, Griffyn. If someone is trying to find a way in, he or she will be much smarter than a debutante and far craftier too. We take no chances."

The door opened slightly, and the two of them squeezed through. It was immediately closed again, shrouding them in semidarkness. Before them stretched a long, surprisingly wide hallway. It seemed carved into the building and cavelike, with walls of stone on either side and an arched stone ceiling above. Dominic began to move forward, but he realized Miss Bonde hadn't moved. She leaned against the wall near the entrance, eyes closed and hand pressed to her belly. The crimson stain had grown larger, and even in the dim light, she looked pale. "Where is this doctor?" he demanded, but Felix was already gone.

"Moneypence can summon him," Miss Bonde said.

"Fine. Where's Moneypence?"

"End of the hallway." She gasped in a breath. "There's a door on the right."

The hallway seemed to stretch endlessly. She was never going to make it.

"Miss Bonde." The man she'd called Felix appeared again. Damn these spies and their appearing and disappearing. He was beginning to feel as skittish as a new colt.

"Are you injured?" Felix asked.

"A scratch," she answered.

Dominic refrained from rolling his eyes. He had a feeling that even if she'd lost a limb, she'd call it a *scratch*. "Go find Moneypence," he ordered Felix before he disappeared again. "Tell him to fetch the doctor."

"Farrar," Miss Bonde supplied.

"Yes, Bonde." Felix shuffled down the long hallway, moving rather more quickly than Dominic had assumed was possible for a man his age. He turned to Miss Bonde, who had pushed away from the wall. His gaze caught the smear of blood she'd left behind. He moved to catch her as she stumbled forward and swept her into his arms.

"Put me down."

"When you can stand on your own, I will." He followed the hallway in the direction Felix had gone. He was about halfway to the door Bonde had pointed out when it burst open, and a slim, dark-haired man in tailored black shot out.

He skidded to a stop when he saw her being carried and put a hand to his mouth, which had formed an O. "Bonde!"

"I'm fine, Moneypence," she said. "Griffyn is overreacting."

The clerk's gaze shot to Dominic for a moment, lingered with not a little distaste, and returned to Bonde. "What happened? Shall I send for your uncle?"

"Send for the doctor," Griffyn said. "She's lost a lot of blood."

Moneypence's gaze didn't leave Bonde's face. Finally, she nodded. "It would be helpful to see Farrar."

"I'll fetch him. He's downstairs."

"I'll wait in my uncle's office."

But Moneypence was already gone. He'd opened a door in the wall and disappeared. Damn spies. Griffyn moved forward, but wherever the door had been, he couldn't see any sign of it now. "Where's Melbourne's office?"

"Through that door." She gestured to the one she'd indicated earlier. "You have to forgive Moneypence. He has a *tendré* for me."

"Is there a man who doesn't?" Dominic asked, sounding surlier than he'd intended.

"Plenty. I have my share of enemies."

They reached the door, but before Dominic could grasp the latch, Felix opened it.

"Haven't you disappeared yet?" Griffyn asked before turning to survey the room. It was brightly lit by both a chandelier and several lamps, and Dominic stepped inside, wondering if he'd somehow stumbled into White's. It wasn't as luxurious as the gentleman's club—or what he knew of it, since he was not a member—but it was certainly not what he expected to step into after traversing the austere hallway.

Dark wood tables with lion's-paw feet had been placed throughout the room, which was about half the size of a ballroom. Couches with plush pillows and sumptuous fabrics served as seats alongside padded armchairs. Desks, with clerks dressed in black, were located near shelves full of books and files. Stacks of paper piled like towers on every desk. About half-a-dozen men were at work this night, and every single one of them looked up at his entrance. All conversation ceased as they took in the situation. He was carrying a woman—one probably familiar to them—and she was obviously injured. He looked down at her, dismayed to see she had her head on his chest and her eyes closed. "You had better not die on me," he grumbled.

"You won't be so lucky," she answered, but her voice was thin and weak. Where the hell was that doctor?

"Terribly sorry to interrupt," Dominic began. The doctor wasn't present yet, and light as Miss Bonde was, his arms were tired. "I'm looking for Lord Melbourne's office."

A clerk—judging by his dress and youth—stepped forward. "That area is restricted."

Dominic raised a brow. If he hadn't been holding

a woman, he would have punched the man. "Shall I set her on a couch here to bleed to death, or is there somewhere more private?"

"I'll show you." A man not much older than Dominic stepped around from behind one of the tables and gestured to the far end of the room. He was short and unassuming, with dark brown hair and a confident gait. No one challenged him as he led Dominic out of the room and into a smaller antechamber. There sat an empty desk before a closed door. "You must be the reason Moneypence went scurrying into the unknown a few moments ago," he said.

"He went to fetch the doctor."

The man nodded as he opened the door to the office and gestured for them to proceed inside. He followed, going to the lamp and lighting it. "Farrar. Good man."

"And you are?" Dominic asked.

The man smiled, though it didn't reach his eyes. "Never ask a spy his identity. Put her down on the couch there," he said. Dominic followed his gesture toward a leather couch in the far corner. The room was dark and masculine, and Dominic imagined the couch had cost a pretty penny. He didn't think the blood would easily wash out of the furnishing.

Dominic set her down gently, placing her head on the arm. She'd kept her hands over her abdomen, and they were covered with blood now.

"Stomach wound," the spy said. "Those are rarely fatal, if treated." He shrugged. "And if they don't succumb to infection."

"That's reassuring," Miss Bonde said, surprising

Dominic. He hadn't realized she was still conscious. "Any other words of comfort?"

"No. But you don't look as though you need any, Miss…"

"I'll tell if you do."

Dominic watched the two spies volley verbal balls back and forth. He had no doubt she would win, but he didn't intend to sit here and wait for the inevitable outcome. "Is a doctor actually coming, or shall I fetch one myself?"

"Allow me to inquire about the good doctor's progress," the spy said and took his leave, closing the door behind him. On a table behind the large desk set against a wall, Dominic spied a decanter of what looked suspiciously like brandy. He had neither time nor inclination to study the room, but he did note the large painting. It seemed to depict a group of men in a tavern, heads close together in earnest conversation, while all around them the patrons of the tavern engaged in one folly after another.

"It's good brandy," she said.

He gave her a curious look.

"I saw you glance at it."

"I didn't think ladies drank spirits," he said, going to the table.

"Ladies, no. Spies, yes." She swallowed and paused, as though gathering her strength. "Farrar is good, but he is not exactly delicate. I'll need a drink for what's coming. Unfortunately you should never, never give liquids to a person with a stomach wound."

He poured himself two fingers and drank it down. Kneeling beside the couch, he helped her position her head more comfortably. "Thank you." She closed her eyes and laid back. "I'm sorry you must play nurse-maid. If you want to go—"

"Do not insult me."

"I don't mean to, but you must know you don't owe me anything. We are not engaged, or, I think, likely to be."

Silently, he agreed. But he did enjoy playing the devil's advocate. "Oh, I don't know. I may still ask for your hand. If you live."

She gave him an annoyed look. "Is that an incentive to die? It won't work. I'll live, but I won't say yes."

"Why not? Your uncle seems quite keen to marry you off."

"As does your mother," she shot back with more venom than he thought she had strength for. "I overheard her threatening my uncle in the garden."

"When?" he demanded.

"Tonight. When the ladies retired and the men drank port, the two of them had a tête-à-tête. Apparently, you are to marry me…or else."

Dominic shook his head. "Or else what?"

"You don't know?" She'd slipped down off the couch cushion again, and he helped her lift her head. She felt warm. Was it simply his imagination, or did she feel too warm? Where the hell was that doctor? He looked in her eyes, which were still steady, not overly bright, but the color in her cheeks was high. She swallowed and lay back again. "Your mother threatened to reveal her liaison with my uncle to my aunt."

Dominic cursed and rose.

"So you did know."

"I knew of no such…liaison. But I do know my mother. I do not doubt the veracity of her claim, or that she will follow through with her threat."

"So you see." She closed her eyes. "It is not me who *must* marry, but you." Her eyes opened again. "Why?"

He paced the room, stopped before the decanter, and poured himself another brandy. He was not a man given to drink, but tonight he felt the need of it. He didn't know how much to tell her. He preferred to say nothing, but that would not do. She had been thrust into something that had nothing to do with her, and she deserved an answer. Not that he pitied her; she'd thrust him into something far worse.

"There was a woman," he began, sipping his brandy.

She gave a bitter laugh. "There always is."

"She—that is to say, I…" He sighed. How the hell was he supposed to say this? "She made an accusation. I am not guilty, but she—well, I—"

"Oh, dear, Mr. Griffyn," Miss Bonde said, her lips curving in an expression that appeared suspiciously like a smile. "This is not a promising beginning, I fear."

At that moment, he was saved from continuing by the sound of footsteps. The door opened, and a man of medium height and advanced years entered, followed closely by the clerk Moneypence. Moneypence went straight to Miss Bonde, all but shoving Dominic out of the way.

"Miss Bonde, are you badly injured?" He knelt beside her, grasping her hand.

Dominic studied the doctor, who seemed to take stock of the situation as he entered. His hair was white, as was his beard, and his eyes were a piercing green.

He'd stopped midstride upon seeing her laid out on the couch, and now he moved cautiously forward. "Knife wound, Miss Bonde?"

"I'm afraid so. Just a scratch, but it might require a stitch or two."

Moneypence drew in a deep breath. "Your uncle is on the way. May I fetch you anything?"

"No." She squeezed his hand. "Could you meet my uncle at the door? Assure him I am fine. He will be worried."

Moneypence jumped to do her bidding. When he was gone, and the door closed behind him, Farrar said, "That was nicely done."

"You know he feels weak at the sight of blood," she said.

"What about you, sir?" the doctor said to Dominic. "Can you stomach the sight of blood?"

"If I must."

"I may need assistance. I can call one of the men outside—"

"No!" Miss Bonde all but rose off the couch.

The doctor raised his brows.

"If this is going to hurt, I prefer to have Mr. Griffyn present. He won't mock me if I scream."

"Don't be so certain," he said.

She gave him a look indicating she was less than amused, and the doctor gestured for him to stand near her head. Farrar knelt beside her abdomen. "I'll have to lift your dress."

"The blood is dried to the fabric," she answered. "You'll have to cut the material."

"Very well." He took a sharp blade from his bag

and pressed it just under her breasts in the center of her abdomen. With quick strokes, he slit an opening down the material, baring a swath of white flesh.

And baring a great deal of blood. The material was indeed stuck to the wound, and Farrar studied it, then gestured to a corner behind the door. "Would you be so kind as to fetch me a basin of water, Mr. Griffyn, is it?"

Dominic dragged his gaze from the wound. "Yes." He made his way to the pitcher and poured the water into the basin with shaking hands. She'd said the wound was a scratch, but that was no scratch. She was cut, perhaps not so deeply as to injure any organs, but deep enough. He couldn't imagine how she'd had the strength to stand, not to mention remain upright for as long as she had.

Steadier now, he returned with the water and held it for the doctor. The doctor motioned to the edge of the couch. "Set it there," he said, taking a length of clean linen from his bag. "I'll need you to hold her."

"Hold her?" Dominic glanced at Bonde. Her eyes were closed, and she was so still that if not for the faint bloom in her cheeks, he would have thought her sleeping…or dead.

"This will hurt, and she will not be able to stop herself from flinching. Hold her down, if you will."

He looked at her again, trying to decide the best place to hold her. Arms? Wrists? Shoulders?

"Lay your hand across her chest," the doctor suggested.

Her dark blue eyes opened, and when Dominic met her gaze, they were filled with amusement. With a sigh, he knelt beside her and laid an arm across her chest. Since the wound was rather low, he had to hold her across her breasts. He tried not to notice how full they were under his arm. How warm and firm. He swallowed and kept his gaze on the wall just above the couch.

"Ready?" Farrar asked.

"Ready," Dominic said through clenched teeth.

"I think he was asking me," Miss Bonde said. "I'm ready."

Dominic heard the sound of the cloth being dipped in water, and the drip as it was wrung out. And then the doctor moved, and Bonde's entire body convulsed. "Bollocks!" she yelled.

"Hold her, Griffyn," the doctor ordered, and he realized he'd released her. He was not used to touching anyone, least of all holding a woman down.

He placed his hand over her again. A sweat had broken out on his forehead, and he was unaccountably warm. Desire and revulsion warred within him. He wanted her, and he hated that he must touch her under these circumstances. He heard the sound of the water, and she jerked, but not as violently as before. "Is this making you…uncomfortable, Griffyn?" she asked between clenched teeth.

"No," he said. "I do this sort of thing every day."

She almost smiled, and then she screwed up her face, and he assumed Farrar had acted again.

"I suppose we will have to marry now." She looked down at his arm, which was clearly draped across her breasts. "This is highly improper."

"Correct me if I am wrong, but I do not think propriety is of much concern to you."

"Not at the moment." Her gaze focused on the doctor beside him. "God's nightgown, man, what are you doing? I'm already wounded. Are you trying to kill me?"

"I'm cleaning the wound. You will need a stitch or two." Farrar sounded unmoved by her obvious pain.

Dominic glanced over his shoulder. The knife slash did look cleaner. Much of the blood was gone. "Only two stitches?" he asked.

The doctor reached into his bag. "Do you know anything about wounds, Mr. Griffyn?"

"Only when it comes to horses."

"Like a horse, she's going to buck when I insert the needle and sew her closed."

Dominic imagined she would indeed. He'd never received stitches, but he'd watched an animal or two sewn up. If the animal was conscious, it often acted as though the remedy was worse than the injury.

"I'll hold her down."

"I am right here, you know." Bonde sounded surly. "And I've received stitches before. I won't move."

"Hold her," Farrar said. He had the cat gut ready and the needle in his hand. Dominic held her tighter and pressed down. Their faces were inches apart.

"I apologize in advance," he said.

"Kiss me."

Dominic blinked. "I don't think—"

"Good. Just kiss me." Her body stiffened. "Now!" She gave him a pleading look. "Please."

He lowered his lips to hers, kissing her tenderly, but she'd have none of that. Her mouth closed desperately over his, taking him with a fierceness he hadn't expected. For a moment, he rebelled at the violence of the kiss, and then warmth flooded his body and desire flared. He tried to resist it, tried to tamp it down, but it was impossible. His hands moved from holding her down to cupping her face. He angled her face, kissing her deeply and gently, willing all the pain away, replaced by pleasure. He drew back when he felt the wetness on his thumbs. He looked into her eyes and saw the tears running down her cheeks. "Jane." He swiped them away. "Bloody hell. I'm sorry. I don't know—"

"It's not you," she said, her lips trembling. "This hurts like the devil."

As much as her strength and courage shocked him, he wasn't prepared for her vulnerability. He felt almost panicked at the sight of her shaking lips.

"And don't call me Jane," she added, clenching her teeth. "I haven't given you leave."

He would have laughed if he hadn't needed all his strength to keep her down. Strange. He hadn't exerted any pressure at all when he'd been kissing her.

"That should do it," the doctor said, standing.

"Off me," Bonde demanded. Dominic released her as though she were on fire, almost tripping over Farrar in the process.

"I don't suppose you want a pain tonic? I have morphine."

"I'm fine."

"I knew you would say that," the doctor said, collecting his supplies.

Dominic shook his head and stepped over the doctor. "You cannot stitch her up and leave her without anything for the pain."

The doctor glanced up at him, the older man's eyes weary and fatigued. "She's like the rest of the men. She won't take them. If I leave it, it will only go to waste."

"I don't need pain medication," she added. "It dulls the senses." She tried to sit, to see the wound, but she couldn't quite manage it. Her face was as white as a sheet, though, and she could not hide the pain from the wound.

Dominic could see it. The doctor had done good work. The wound looked like little more than an angry red slash on her pale belly. It was then Dominic realized he was looking at her bare abdomen. Her skirts were pulled up so he had a view of her long legs as well. Hastily, he looked away, and not a moment too soon.

He turned as the door opened.

Nine

Pierce Moneypence stood outside the door. He'd spent half his life outside M's door, and he knew the exact spot to stand so he could hear the goings-on inside. He might be more clerk than spy, but he had learned a thing or two during his tenure with the Barbican group. Moneypence could hear Bonde's muffled curses and protests, and he clenched his hands in sympathy for her. He hated that she was in pain.

Even more, he hated to see her with the dark man who'd been all but carrying her. She'd called him Griffyn—appropriate, as the man was guarding what Moneypence considered a priceless treasure. Not that the treasure knew he was alive. Jane Bonde thought of Moneypence as her uncle's clerk, nothing more.

He'd often thought if he could do something brave and daring, she'd see him differently, but Moneypence was not the brave and daring sort. Oh, he'd done his share of espionage, but it was not the sort that earned any glory. He ciphered letters, researched, filed, collected information spies like Wolf and Bonde used to track England's most dangerous foes.

He liked his job, and he loved the Barbican. But after ten years here—ten years of being half in love with Jane Bonde—Moneypence was beginning to think she was never going to love him back.

And he'd seen in her face, in the way she looked at Griffyn, that Pierce Moneypence would never be anything more than a friend to her. With a sigh, he moved away from M's office door. She'd asked him to look for her uncle, and he could do that much. He moved through the adjacent offices without really seeing them. He'd seen all of the men and the rooms a thousand times. He moved so blindly, he almost didn't see Q.

"Moneypence!" she cried when he'd all but bowled her over.

"I'm terribly sorry, Miss Qwillen," he said, catching her elbow to steady her. They were in the great stone corridor now, and the stone would hurt her if she were to fall.

"That's quite all right," she said, shaking her skirts and stepping back. He released her elbow, blushing a little at the contact. If he'd touched Bonde's elbow, he would have fainted. "Are you thinking of an important mission?" she asked. "Is that why you didn't see me?"

"Mission?" he blinked. "Oh, no—why, actually, yes. I am to meet M when he arrives. Bonde asked me to wait for him."

She gave him a sad shake of her head. "Bonde? That explains it then." She began to walk away, and on any other day, Pierce would have shrugged at the cryptic comment and let her go. But today was not a normal day. Today he felt peevish. He turned and grasped her elbow again. She wore a long-sleeved gown, and her elbow felt rather pointy beneath the fabric. But his hand slid to her upper arm, and he noted the flesh there was pleasantly full and round.

"What do you mean, *that explains it*?" he asked.

"I mean, that explains why you are woolgathering," she said, frowning down at his hand on her sleeve. "You have a dreamy look in your eye whenever Bonde is mentioned."

He did? "I do?" He cleared his throat. "I can't think why. Certainly, you must be mistaken."

She arched a brow. She was a small woman with a mass of curly brown hair and large spectacles. Moneypence actually thought she was rather pretty, in a bookish sort of way. Of course, when one considered his model of beauty was Jane Bonde, it was difficult to think of any other woman as anything more than *pretty*.

"Right. I am certain you have no idea what I am referring to," Q said, freeing her arm.

"You would be correct in that assumption." He moved aside slightly, so another clerk might pass.

"And I am certain you are not madly in love with Jane Bonde."

"I—" He glanced around, suddenly terrified the clerk might have heard. The man didn't look back.

"You needn't worry he might overhear," Q said. "Everyone knows."

Pierce felt rather dizzy at that revelation. "Everyone knows what?"

"Deny it if you will," she said, "but it's obvious to everyone that you're in love with her." And after throwing that blade at his chest, she began to walk away again. Pierce stood still for a long, long moment, and then he chased after her, skidding around her, and coming to halt in front of her.

"What are you doing? Are you mad?" she asked.

"Yes—no! I have to ask."

She was staring at him as though he'd lost his mind, and perhaps he had. She put her hands on her hips. "Well, ask then."

"Does she know?" He did not need to say who *she* was.

Q looked at him for a long time. "Of course she does, Moneypence."

He had no idea what his face looked like, but it must have fallen, because she put her hand on his arm. "I'm sorry. But everyone knows."

And she walked away. Pierce's legs felt weak, and he wobbled on them for a long moment before sinking into a crouch, his face burning with shame and embarrassment.

❧

The door to M's office flew open, and a voice boomed, "What the hell happened?" Melbourne stormed into the room. Moneypence followed closely on Melbourne's heels. Jane tried to arrange her skirts into some semblance of order that would afford her privacy, but Moneypence did not look at her.

"I want an explanation," M demanded. "Moneypence told me you were fine, but if you are fine, why is Farrar here, and whose blood is that?"

Jane saw Moneypence's gaze dart toward the couch.

He must have seen the blood on Farrar's linen, because his face went white, and his eyes rolled up.

"Catch him!" she ordered Griffyn.

The man moved quickly for a civilian. He reached Moneypence before the man hit the floor and set him gently on the rug.

"You!" her uncle hissed. "What are you doing here?"

"That's my fault," she said immediately. She had her own quarrel with Griffyn, but she was not going to allow him to take the fall for her.

"That goes without saying," Melbourne said, shaking a finger at her. She'd rarely seen him so angry. His face was turning an alarming shade of purple. "And I am not speaking to you. You're in no condition to talk."

"If you no longer need my services," Farrar said, gathering his bag and instruments, "I shall take my leave."

"Doctor," she warned.

"She is perfectly capable of speaking." Farrar moved toward the door, stepping over Moneypence in the process. "It's a minor wound. I would tell you to have her rest for a few days, but I know she won't." The doctor exchanged a look with Griffyn, who looked as though he'd like to escape with Farrar. "That was one of the more interesting procedures I've performed, Mr. Griffyn. I hope that is not how you perform treatment on your horses."

Griffyn didn't bother to respond, but Jane smiled. It might not have been conventional treatment, but when she'd kissed Griffyn, she hadn't noticed the rest of the world. He'd made the stitches bearable.

"What is the dashed man going on about now?" Melbourne asked.

"Nothing," she answered. Moneypence moaned and rubbed his head. The poor man still refused to look at her, and his face was red with humiliation.

"Here." Her uncle removed his cape and draped it over her. "That ought to save me from having to unearth the smelling salts. Moneypence, send for Baron. I have a feeling we will need him before this night is through." He nodded to Griffyn, who assisted the clerk to his feet. "Go with him."

"He might as well stay," Jane said. "He already knows everything I'm going to tell you. If you send him out, he might find out something else we don't want him to know."

Her uncle glared at her. "We don't want him to know about Foncé and the Maîtriser group." He made his way to his desk, while Moneypence dashed out the door with his head down. Poor Moneypence.

"There are other sensitive cases," Jane said. "And I'm afraid we have a bigger problem."

Melbourne gave her a look that almost made her change her mind about telling him. She ran her gaze over him, realizing he looked older than she remembered, and haggard. His expression was one of resignation and...dare she think it? Defeat. But she was an agent before she was his niece, and she knew what she had to do.

"Foncé knows about you."

Melbourne's face went blank, almost as though he had wiped it clean of expression. "How do you know?"

"Viking told me. I'm sorry. He's dead."

Her uncle sat back in his chair and ran a hand through his hair. "I figured as much. He didn't check in. You spoke to him before he died?"

"Wait a moment," Griffyn interrupted. "A man is dead, and you two dismiss it in a matter of seconds?"

Melbourne's gaze locked on his. "We don't have time to mourn him. He wouldn't have wanted our grief, in any case. He knew the risks."

"And what if it had been your niece killed tonight? Would you have been as cold, as callous?"

"Griffyn," she began, but she didn't press. A part of her wanted to know, had always wondered if she was any different to Melbourne than the other agents.

"I'd mourn her privately, and do my job publicly. As I will with Viking."

"I can't be a part of this," Griffyn said.

"It's too late for that," Jane said.

Griffyn looked at her, and she felt her breath catch. It was such a dark look, so full of danger and mystery. She was not afraid of danger, but there was something in the mystery that made her uneasy. She should have kept her distance from him. She should have built up her defenses, plugged the chinks in her armor, called in the archers and the cauldrons of boiling tar. All she had was a dry moat and a weak drawbridge—scant protection against such a dangerous foe, especially one she rather wanted to conquer her.

She turned back to her uncle. "As I said, Foncé knows about you. Viking wasn't able to elaborate. I don't know if the Maîtriser group knows where you live or where the offices are or if I'm your niece. But he has come for you this time."

Melbourne said nothing. He rested his chin on his closed fist and considered. His eyes were cold, and his silence a bit unnerving, but she didn't interrupt.

She had her own ideas as to how to proceed, but she would wait until consulted. If she were consulted.

"London isn't safe. We must close the town house for the remainder of the Season."

Jane nodded. She'd come to the same conclusion.

Melbourne continued. "Viking did not say Foncé knew the location of headquarters, only that he knew me. I can stay here. I should be safe enough underground."

"I'll stay with you."

"No." Melbourne shook his head and glanced at Griffyn. Jane frowned, not liking that glance. "Your identity is compromised—"

"And Foncé hasn't seen Baron and Wolf and Saint? We have no reason to suspect he knows I'm your niece."

"I give the orders here, Bonde," Melbourne said, and she closed her mouth. She wasn't going to like what came next, but she knew who was the leader of the Barbican group. "You'll go with your aunt, protect her, watch to see if Foncé follows, and take a few days to heal."

She didn't speak. It was worse than she'd thought.

"You cannot go somewhere Foncé could trace you. That means we must send you somewhere he won't suspect." Melbourne looked at Griffyn again. "I will pen a note to Lady Edgeberry, begging the use of Edgeberry's estate in Richmond."

Griffyn started visibly. Before he could object, Jane did. "Uncle, no! We should not involve Mr. Griffyn or Lord and Lady Edgeberry any further."

"That will be difficult once your betrothal is announced. However, we may be able to put that off until after we've taken Foncé into custody."

She felt beads of perspiration form on her back and had to stop herself from breathing too shallowly. The rapid motion would hurt her already throbbing wound. How had this happened? How had she been all but pushed into an engagement with Griffyn? Given time, she might have found a way to avoid marriage—convince her uncle it was unnecessary, or persuade Lady Edgeberry she was not a suitable match for her son. But the more time she spent with Griffyn, the more likely an engagement and subsequent marriage. "Surely I should stay in Town. Perhaps my aunt could go alone."

"You are injured. I want you safely away from here so you will fully recover." Her uncle gave her a long, determined look. Jane sighed. She was out of options. That did not mean she had given in, but she would have to formulate exit rather than avoidance strategies.

"You are forgetting one key point, Lord Melbourne," Griffyn said quietly. She'd almost forgotten he was in the room. When he spoke now, she turned at the hint of anger in his voice.

"What is that, Mr. Griffyn?" Melbourne asked. Jane felt a chill race down her spine. She knew that look. She'd seen it in the card room at one too many balls. Her uncle had not yet played his winning hand.

"You speak of betrothals, but I have not asked Miss Bonde to marry me."

Jane was tempted to look at Griffyn as he said this. After all, it was not every day a man discussed marriage with her. She did not dare move her gaze from her uncle. She wanted to see his expression if and when he betrayed his secret—whatever it was he was holding in reserve.

"You have my permission to ask her, if that is what you wait upon."

Jane couldn't stop herself from cutting her gaze to Griffyn. He certainly was not waiting for permission to ask her. His face revealed nothing, though she would wager a fortune he was furious. He would have made a good spy. Even some of the best agents could not hide anger.

"I don't know what game you are playing, my lord, but I will not be a pawn. I am not asking Miss Bonde to be my wife, nor will I support a visit by her and Lady Melbourne at Kenham Hall. I'll take my leave."

"I wouldn't do that if I were you," Melbourne said. "I was left with the impression that Lord Edgeberry has had enough of your wild ways. And now matters have progressed to the point where I insist you ask my niece to marry you, or we meet on a field at dawn."

Jane laughed. "Ha! And when have *you* ever cared about my virtue, Uncle? Or, for that matter, my minor injuries?"

Melbourne didn't deny or contradict. He merely gave her that same steely glare. "I mean what I say, Jane."

"You would issue a challenge?" Griffyn asked. To his credit, he still sounded confident. The silence in the room lengthened. Her uncle was a master at the use of silence. Right now, Griffyn was going over every encounter they'd had and wondering if Melbourne knew of it. If Jane actually thought her uncle cared about her more intimate relationships, she would have been doing the same. But she knew he turned a blind eye. And he'd sent her in the field with more serious wounds than she possessed now. Why the sudden protectiveness?

She was beginning to think this banishment and this marriage was not for her sake at all, but her uncle's attempt to hide something. His liaison with Lady Edgeberry? Was he that desperate to keep a love affair from the past hidden? Surely he must know he could trust his niece, his best operative, not to betray his confidence. So perhaps it was something more, something he feared Jane would discover if she remained in Town. But what?

"I have been nothing but a gentleman to your niece. If there was any impropriety in my being alone with her tonight, I assure you it was only out of concern for her safety. As you see, she is wounded. I would not use her injured state to my advantage."

"That is true," Jane added. "He insisted on accompanying me because he feared for my welfare. Although I told him I did not need his assistance."

Griffyn scowled. "And that is why you lie on a couch in a blood-soaked gown. You might be lying in a pool of blood by the river if I had not been there."

She opened her mouth to argue.

"And was Miss Bonde injured at Lord and Lady Smythe's residence?"

Jane clamped her mouth closed. How did Melbourne know about that? She had not told him about the visit, and the Smythes had no reason to reveal it. But again, why should he care if she'd kissed Griffyn at Lord and Lady Smythe's?

"I'm not certain to what you refer, my lord."

Oh, he was good, she thought. Griffyn was very good. Unfortunately, Melbourne was better. Griffyn didn't realize it, but he was already doomed. They both were.

"I refer, Mr. Griffyn, to the kiss—a rather extended, quite passionate kiss, from the account I heard—you shared with my niece outside Lord and Lady Smythe's drawing room."

Silence.

Jane did not dare glance at Griffyn.

"Do you deny it?" Melbourne asked.

"No."

"Do you not think I have the right to ask your intentions toward my niece after such an embrace?"

"Yes."

"And what are your intentions, sir?" Melbourne rose to his full height and placed his hands palms-down on his desk. This position always intimidated his subordinates. It intimidated her. Interesting that he should use it now.

Griffyn did not speak. Jane glanced at him, surprised by his silence. He appeared to be weighing his options.

"And do not tell me it was an innocent kiss, or that it was the only one. I happen to know there were others far less innocent."

"Blue," she muttered. The next time she saw him, she would smash his perfect nose flat. Griffyn was watching her. He probably hadn't heard her, but he could certainly see in her reaction they were bested. "It's no use," she said. And at the moment, she did not care. She was weary of fighting it. She'd been fighting the parson's mousetrap for years. And really, would marriage to Griffyn be so awful? He already knew her secret, and she wouldn't mind kissing him again. And again. But if she had to marry Griffyn, she damn well wanted to know why—none of this defending her honor rubbish. What was Melbourne really up to? Could she even still trust her uncle?

Jane looked at Griffyn and then at her uncle, who for all her doubts looked very serious about his threats. She would see her way to the bottom of this mystery. "Uncle, may Mr. Griffyn and I speak alone for a moment?"

Melbourne crossed his arms. "Not until there's a betrothal."

"My lord, I am attempting to assist you on that point."

"Oh, really?" His eyes reflected merriment. "I rather doubt that, but I will give you five minutes. No more." He crossed the room, opened the door, and stepped outside.

"I say we call his bluff," Griffyn said as soon as the door closed. "He will not ruin his own niece by challenging me to a duel."

"Yes, he will. What you fail to understand, Mr. Griffyn, is this visit to Kenham Hall is not about securing our betrothal—although it does solve that problem for him. This is about protecting his wife and the Barbican group from Foncé. Lord Melbourne will do anything to ensure the safety of Lady Melbourne and the group." And whatever else he was hiding.

"What about you?"

"I am part of the Barbican group."

"You are his niece, and he threatens you while you lie here covered in blood."

The dear man actually looked offended on her account. "This is but a mere scratch," she said. "But thank you for your concern." She was not used to such solicitousness.

Griffyn did not speak for a long moment. She was half-afraid he would not speak again before her uncle returned. Finally he crossed to her. His gait was a bit cocky, but not quite a swagger. And he moved like a man who was confident of himself but wary and careful. He knelt beside her. "You are nothing more than a pawn in your uncle's game of spies."

"Pawn or not, I know this chess game very, very well."

He put a finger on her lips, and she instantly felt the room was too warm. "Do you not believe you are more worthy than a pawn in someone's game of chess? Do you not think you are worthy of your uncle's love?"

"Yes, but..." She trailed off, not certain what she would say next. *Did* she believe she was worthy? She had known she had worth as a spy, but what about as a niece, as a person? She swallowed. Griffyn still hadn't spoken, and she didn't know what to say.

"But?" he prodded. "What of your husband's love? I don't love you."

"Of course not." He barely knew her. Why would he love her? And yet the words pierced her very close to her heart. She couldn't tolerate such softness. "If you propose, we needn't actually marry. I will find a way out. We may have to cede this battle, but we won't lose the war. I never lose."

"Never?"

"No."

"What is *losing* in this case?"

She caught herself before she could make her reply—something to the effect that marrying him would be losing.

He shook his head. "That's what I thought."

She sat forward and winced at the pain. "But you just admitted you do not love me." She was at a level with his dark eyes now, and those chiseled cheeks that begged for her to caress them with a finger.

He shrugged. "There are other reasons to marry."

"Such as? Appeasing my uncle and your mother?"

"To begin. The marquess also wants me to marry. I have an interest in keeping him happy."

"So you are not even going to fight?"

"To what end? If I don't marry you, I'll have to marry some other chit."

"Chit? Chit!"

"Believe me," he went on, ignoring her protest, "I understand the sacrifice you make in aligning yourself with me—the bastard child of an actress."

Jane gasped. She didn't know whether to hit him or hug him. The circumstances of his birth had nothing to do with her objections, and while she wanted to reassure him as much, she also wanted to smack him. He'd called her a chit! As though she was interchangeable with any other girl in London!

"Before you act on that murderous look, I'd better call your uncle."

"No—"

Griffyn stood and faced the door. "Lord Melbourne, you may come in."

The door opened immediately. "Well?"

"Serve as witness, my lord." Griffyn faced her, crossed his arms, and glared. "Miss Bonde, will you do me the honor of becoming my..." He swallowed and scowled at her. "Wife?"

She blinked at him. It was the worst proposal she had ever witnessed. Not that she had witnessed many proposals, but she was certain had she witnessed a thousand, this would be the worst of the lot. Not that she could blame him if he really thought she cared on which side of the blanket he'd been born. Well, perhaps she could blame him a little. If she was forced to marry him, this was likely to be her only marriage proposal.

"Jane." Her uncle's voice had a warning in it.

She blew out an angry breath. "Fine. Yes." Then she glared at her uncle. "I am consenting to a betrothal, not a marriage."

"One leads to the other, Jane."

Not with that proposal. "We'll see." She looked at Griffyn, but he shook his head and turned away.

⤜❧⤛

Dominic did not know how it had all happened so quickly. It seemed one moment he was on his way home in the early morning light after a night rife with one too many revelations, and the next he was in a carriage seated across from Lady Melbourne and her niece.

It had been a day and a night, but already Miss Bonde—he supposed he had the right to call her Jane now—looked much improved. Her color had not fully returned, but she could walk on her own, though slowly, and seemed to be tolerating the ride to Richmond without complaint. Not that he thought she would complain. He could shove a hot poker in her eye and she would rather hit him than admit she was hurt.

She sat facing forward and staring out the window.

Beside her, her aunt was reading a book. It seemed no one wanted idle chitchat today. No one wanted to pretend this was a journey they all looked forward to. The sun peeked out from a cloud, shining its light on Jane's golden hair. Dominic would have sworn her hair sparkled. And even in the bright sun, he could not detect a freckle or blemish on her skin. She was a little pale, but her lips were a tantalizing shade of pink. It was an innocent shade. A sweet shade. He wanted to kiss her until her lips were wanton red.

He closed his eyes. He was on dangerous ground with her. She was the sort of woman who might make him forget all his rules. He could not allow that. Not with her or anyone. She was right to fight a union with him. He could offer her nothing a true husband should.

But he and his betrothed were the only ones not rejoicing. The marquess had been ecstatic at the news of the engagement, as had his mother. They had agreed to keep it secret for the time being—Dominic was not certain what excuse Melbourne had given for that—but he really couldn't remember the last time he'd seen them so happy. His mother, in particular. She'd actually started to cry.

Bonde had better hurry and figure out some sort of escape plan, if she really did not intend to go through with it. He looked at her across the coach. His betrothed. *His betrothed.* It didn't seem possible. No woman like the beauty that sat across from him would consent to marry him, and if she did, she would certainly scorn him until the end of her days.

But Jane Bonde had consented, albeit reluctantly,

but not because she objected to him. He'd seen the shock in her face when he'd accused her of not wanting a bastard as a husband. That was not why she did not want him. No. She objected to being taken away from her precious case—her mission. She objected to marriage and the freedoms it would curtail. Perhaps he had objections as well. For one, he didn't want the intimacy of marriage. There were some men—and perhaps women as well—who should never marry. They had secrets or pasts too vile, too shocking, too revolting. Such a one did not deserve a wife or children.

But this was not the sort of thing one mentioned to one's betrothed—even if she was only biding her time as his betrothed. This was not the sort of secret one mentioned to anyone. It was the sort one tucked away in the dark, forgotten folds of the cloak of one's mind and hoped it stayed hidden. It was the sort of secret that invariably reared its monstrous head after a long day, waking him with sweat pouring over his body and a scream on his lips.

How would he explain waking up screaming to his wife?

Not that a scream would scare Jane Bonde. She would probably roll over and go back to sleep. Little as he liked to admit it, that was actually a point in her favor. If he had to marry, better to marry a strong woman. A woman who would not flinch at what he was and what he'd done.

But she had points against her as well. Jane Bonde, spy—or whatever she wanted to call herself—for the Barbican group, was unconventional. His mother had been unconventional, and God help them all if the family added another like her. He closed his eyes, weary at the very idea. Memories and images assaulted him, and he opened his eyes to shut them away again. He could not abide the dreams today. He hadn't quite convinced himself that the night of his betrothal wasn't a bad dream. Had she really fired a pistol? Had she actually suffered stitches with barely a cry of pain, not to mention nothing to dull that pain?

And had he really kissed her while the doctor sewed her up? He didn't know why he'd agreed to that idea. And he couldn't have said why he'd kissed her the other times he'd done so. It seemed difficult *not* to kiss her. And when he kissed her, it was even more difficult to cease.

The only way to keep from kissing her, it seemed, was to avoid her, which would be difficult when they were living under the same roof at Kenham Hall. The only solution was for him to return to London. He always had a room there. It would mean neglecting his horses, but the animals had grooms to see to them. They didn't need him.

If only he could say the same. Already he was tense and edgy from having been away too long. The darkness lurked just on the edge of his vision. The hem of that cloak billowed in the breeze, and he needed to find a way to calm the breeze, restore the peace. His horses had always done that for him. Now, his only sanctuary had been ripped away from him, in addition to everything else he'd lost.

"I believe that is Kenham Hall," Lady Melbourne said, breaking the silence and gesturing to the view of the house from the rise they had just topped. It was an impressive view. The architect of the great country house had combined the best of the Palladian and neoclassical styles to create a pleasant red-brick edifice with white-stone dressings. The stable had been built with that same red brick and was just visible in the distance. Dominic looked from the vista to the lady and started, surprised to find her not looking at the view, but at him. "Lost in your thoughts, Mr. Griffyn?"

He glanced at Jane, who was studying him curiously too, and then back at Lady Melbourne. "I was, my lady. I should have pointed the house out for you. But then, no one has ever accused me of doing as I should."

She raised a brow. "You proposed to my niece. Should you have done that?"

"My lady," Jane interrupted. "Do you see the lake there? I imagine it is a lovely prospect in the morning. Perhaps we might walk there after we break our fast tomorrow."

"Splendid idea, Jane, but tomorrow is too soon, in your condition. A few days yet."

Lady Melbourne continued in that vein until they reached the drive. She was actually quite good at chatting about trivialities. He always struggled with inconsequential topics. She seemed able to go on at length about anything and everything. Finally, the carriage stopped, and the footman opened the door. Dominic stepped down first, followed by the ladies holding their skirts with one hand. Dominic handed each lady down then nodded to the housekeeper and butler, who'd assembled to greet the new guests.

Strangely enough, Old Connor stood before the house as well, wringing his hat.

Dominic didn't think; he simply acted. He bypassed the other servants and went straight to Old Connor. "What is it?"

"It's Nessa," Old Connor said. "She has the colic."

"No."

Nessa was one of his favorites. At sixteen hands and with a bright bay color and perfectly black points, she was one of the most graceful and certainly the grandest mare the marquess owned. If there was royalty among horses, she was it. She had birthed many equally regal foals, and she was older and perhaps more fragile than the other horses to suffer thus far. "Let's go." Dominic started walking, everything but Nessa forgotten.

Old Connor jogged beside him. "But, sir, your guests!"

Dominic glanced over his shoulder without slowing. "Millstone," he said to the butler, "see to the guests." And he continued walking. Lady Melbourne might stare at him in shock, and Jane Bonde might regard him with that puzzled look, but he did not have time for pleasantries and social dictates at the moment. He would save Nessa.

In the end, he could not save her. The grooms and Dominic worked all night, side by side, to no avail. The first morning light broke, and the beautiful mare lay still. Dominic dismissed the grooms, ostensibly sending the men to their beds, but in truth, he wanted to be alone with her. In the quiet dawn, he sat, hand on her neck, and grieved. He would not cry. He'd shed enough tears as a boy to know they served no purpose. But he mourned her nonetheless. It was the least he could do.

Finally, he rose and pulled the blanket over her. He stepped into the aisle and closed her stall door with a finality that tugged at something in his chest. He detected a movement and glanced down the aisle, then blinked.

"Am I disturbing you?" she asked.

He was relieved she'd spoken. He'd been afraid the lack of sleep had muddled his brain and he was imagining her. "You should be back at the house in bed." Not only was she injured, it was too early to be out for a morning walk. His voice came out raw and tattered, and he thought he must look like he sounded. Dominic was rather surprised his appearance hadn't scared her away.

But this was Jane Bonde. She feared little except failing at one of her precious missions.

She waved her hand, dismissing the notion that she should be in bed after suffering a knife wound. "I could not sleep and wanted fresh air."

He supposed he should make some response to that, but damned if he knew what it was. He was too tired to think of niceties. He closed his eyes, feeling them burn with dryness and fatigue, and ran a hand though his hair. It felt wild and unkempt, and he could feel the itch of the shadow of his beard, demanding he shave. He wore shirtsleeves and trousers, having long ago discarded his coat, cravat, and waistcoat. His shirt was open at the throat, and he supposed he was dressed inappropriately for a visit by a lady, especially one wearing not only gloves but a bonnet. She carried a parasol as well—as though the weak morning light would be any threat to her pale complexion.

He opened his eyes, and she'd come closer. Too close. He could detect the scent of her perfume. He moved away, grabbing one of the shovels set nearby. "You should return to the house. I have work to do." That much was true. He had horses to feed, stables to muck out, a new foal to evaluate, mail to address. The days he'd spent in London meant he was woefully behind.

He'd dismissed her, or so he thought, and he walked to the end of the aisle and opened Lily's Turn's stall. She was looking well. He would never have known she'd so recently been ill. He laid a hand on her nose, and she nudged it expectantly. He smiled. "No apples with me this morning."

"Where are your grooms?"

Dominic turned, feeling suddenly exposed, as though interrupted in a private moment. "I thought you had returned to the house."

She raised her brows. "I am not that easy to be rid of. You cannot really think to muck out stables."

Dominic put the shovel he held to use. "As you see."

"I do." She watched him, her eyes dark. He wondered what she saw, or thought she saw. "What should I do to help?"

He shook his head. "Nothing. Go back to the house."

But she was already peeling off her gloves. "Do not be ridiculous. You look exhausted, and you are doing the work of two men on your own and, from all appearances, without the benefit of any sleep."

"If my appearance offends you—"

"I have seen far worse than a man with stubble on his chin and shadows under his eyes." She removed her bonnet and set it, with her gloves inside, on a stool. She leaned her frilly white parasol beside it. Her dress was white as well, he noted. Not ideal for working in a dirty stable. He glanced down at her feet, pleased with himself for not lingering too long on the swell of her hip. At least she wore walking boots and not slippers.

"This is not the sort of work a lady does."

"It's not the sort of work a gentleman occupies himself with either," she countered. "But here you are."

"I am no gentleman, and I do this every day."

"And today you need assistance." She looked behind her. "Is there another shovel? Or perhaps I should climb into the hayloft and pitch hay for you?"

Lily's Turn moved forward now, and when Jane glanced back, the horse nuzzled her. Jane laughed, and Dominic had a moment of jealousy, though for the attention the horse gave to Bonde or the attention Bonde gave to the animal, he couldn't have said. He was better off not thinking too deeply about it.

"Do you want a treat?"

Lily's Turn's ears perked up.

"Of course you do. I have nothing with me this morning, but I promise to bring you something later."

"The horses are on a strict diet," Dominic said. "They eat at prescribed times, and only the best feed."

Jane raised a brow. "And yet this animal expects some sort of treat. How can that be?"

Dominic lifted the shovel again and went to work. She was too observant by far. Lily's Turn had been spoiled on occasion with apples and carrots, but since the colic...he did not want to call it an epidemic, as it was not contagious...instances might be a better term.

Since the frequent colic instances, he had outlawed any treats to the horses.

"Perhaps I could assist by feeding the animals. If I come after you, you could ensure I give each horse the proper amount in the correct proportions."

"Jane, this is not necessary. Go back to the house."

She did not move. "You realize I still have not given you leave to use my Christian name."

"We are betrothed. I believe the permission is implied in the contract I signed."

"Then shall I call you Dominic?"

"Call me whatever the hell you want, but leave me alone." Every woman of his acquaintance, and most men, would have run away at the tone in his voice. Jane did not even blink.

"In your time of need? I think not." She stepped out of the stall, and when she didn't immediately return, he was forced to follow her. "Is that the feed room there?" She gestured to the end of the aisle. There was a small room where he kept feed. She'd spotted it right away, most likely because of the various buckets stacked outside.

"Yes."

"And how much does…what is her name?" She gestured to the horse.

"Lily's Turn."

"How much does Lily's Turn receive?"

He told her, as much because he was tired of arguing as because he wanted her and that tantalizing scent of violets away from him for a few moments. Perhaps then he could think how to rid himself of her for the rest of the morning, if not the entire day.

He watched her go to the feed room then stepped back into the stall to continue the mucking it out. A moment later, she called, "Which grain should I use?"

He frowned. All of the horses grazed on the grass in the pasture and received the same hay in the stables. Each also received a measure of grain—the amount depending on the horse's age, health, and lactation status—at set times throughout the day. The grain was of the highest quality, and he always ordered it from one supplier.

"They are all the same," he called.

Silence. "No, they are not."

A shiver of dread made him drop the shovel and race to meet her.

Ten

JANE HEARD THE SHOVEL CLANG AND PEERED OUT OF the small room, only to jump back when she saw Griffyn racing toward her. Her stitches gave a small twinge of pain, and she remembered she was not supposed to make sudden movements. Obviously, she'd caused some sort of trouble. She did not mean to cause trouble, but she'd been doing it since she was a young child. Her aunt said she was too inquisitive by far. She saw things she was not supposed to.

Her uncle, of course, said this made her the perfect spy. But right now she had wanted only to be useful, and she could see that, instead, she had made Griffyn worry about something else. That had not been her intention. Surely, she had simply made a mistake, and he would explain her misstep to her.

Except, of course, she rarely made mistakes. Something here was not right.

She flattened herself against the wall of the tiny room as Griffyn's large frame filled it. He smelled of horses and hay and leather—all scents familiar to her. She had seen how exhausted he was before, but now that he was so close to her and the light of the lantern on the peg in the room shone on him, she realized the man was fortunate to still be standing. She had thought him a strong man, as well as an exceptionally handsome one, and she had not misjudged. And this morning, with the dark stubble bruising his jaw and the purple smudges under his already coal-black eyes, he looked not only exotic but almost feral.

A shiver of heat swirled through her, landing in her lower belly. Her gaze fell to his hands, large and strong and covered with dirt. She wondered what those dark hands would look like on her pale skin, on the pink of her aureole as he cupped her breast.

She took a sharp breath, and he gave her a curious look. But then he was all seriousness. "What did you do?" he demanded.

"Nothing." But she could see he wanted a full account. "I walked back here, took a pail, then set it down and lit the lantern. I saw the two sacks of feed and asked which I should use."

"You did nothing else?"

"No." She narrowed her eyes at him, watched as he lifted the grain to inspect the contents of first one sack then the other. "There should not be two types of feed," she surmised.

"No." His answer was short and to the point.

"One appears unadulterated," she said, pointing to the fuller bag, the new bag. "The other has been mixed with something else."

"And that's what I've been feeding my horses. This inferior grade." He pointed to the bag with the mixed grain. "I pay for the best, and unwittingly I kill my horses with this...this..." Words seemed to fail him, and a vein throbbed in his forehead.

"I suppose your supplier could be cheating you."

He gave her a sharp look. "But you don't think so."

She gestured to the new bag. "This is perfectly acceptable. I assume." She shrugged. "I know nothing of horse feed." She looked at the other bag, which was almost empty. "This is a mixture of that and something else. If I had to guess, I would say someone mixed the premium feed with something less desirable."

"That is my deduction as well."

"Are the stables in financial crisis?" she asked, then recollected herself. She was not on a mission and could not interrogate the Marchioness of Edgeberry's son about the marquessate's financial situation. "Of course, that is none of my concern. I withdraw the question."

"The stables are in excellent financial condition," Griffyn said, and she could see from the subtle way his chest swelled when he said it that situation was entirely due to his efforts. But if that was the case, why would they mix inferior grain with the superior?

"Oh." She gave him a cautious look. Perhaps she should not reveal any more. She had caused enough trouble.

"Out with it," he said, grasping her arm before she could back away, make her excuses, and return to the house. She should have listened to him the first time he ordered her to return. But she had never been very good at following orders.

"I do believe my aunt may worry if I am not at breakfast soon."

"It is far too early for breakfast or for your aunt to

rise. I already know what is happening. I want you to confirm my suspicions."

Well, if that was the case, she would not be the bearer of bad news, so much as the confirmer. "One of your grooms is stealing the superior feed, selling it for profit, and replacing it with an inferior grade."

He glared at her, and she considered shrinking back. But she did not shrink. She was Jane Bonde. Suddenly, he whirled and slammed his fists against the wall of the small room. It shook. It felt as though the entire stable shook, and she heard several horses emit concerned whinnies. She thought he would take out his rage in some dramatic way now—throw pails about, rip hooks off the wall. Instead, he leaned his head against his fists and did not move.

Jane could have dealt with an outward manifestation of rage. But this…what to call it? Internalization? This internalization was foreign to her. She stood still, feeling helpless. Finally, he turned and looked at her. Only his eyes burned with anger and the intensity of his emotions. His face showed nothing at all. "I am going to find this man," he said, voice low and quiet. "And kill him."

She swallowed at the razor edge to his tone. He sounded as though he really could kill the man responsible. "That might be a bit extreme," she ventured.

"Do you think so?"

No, not at all. I will keep my opinions to myself in future. I will keep my opinions to myself! But she said nothing, waiting for him to speak again.

"Nessa is dead."

She had not met anyone called Nessa, family member or servant. "Nessa is a horse?"

"She died of colic in the wee hours of the morning."

That explained why he had been up all night, and why he looked like he'd battled Satan and lost.

"Colic caused by inferior feed."

"Colic caused by rapid changes in her diet, or whatever the devil is mixed with her feed in this bag. It could be ground wood for all I know. She suffered horribly at the end. I have never heard a horse make the noises of pain that she made. And there was no reason for it"—he looked at the grain—"other than greed."

"I'm sorry." She wanted to touch him. She wanted desperately to reach out and take his hand or pull him into an embrace. But she had the distinct impression that if she did so, he would pull away. He did not like to be touched except on his terms. She could not say how she knew such a thing. It was something she sensed, not anything he'd said or done. She knew it the way she knew when an informant was lying or a man was a double agent or that an ambush waited ahead. These instincts kept her alive. Griffyn wasn't a threat to her life, but he was a threat nonetheless. He wouldn't take her life, but he might just take her heart. His grief over his horse, his obvious love of them, pulled at something inside her. He suddenly seemed human, seemed so much more than a dark mystery. She wanted to know more of that tender side. She must guard against him the same way she guarded against any enemy—by keeping him close.

Perhaps that was why she had sought him out this morning. Perhaps it was not merely that she was weak and longed for his company. Perhaps it was only a protective measure. It was better to know where he was and what he was doing. That way, she could avoid him in the future.

He was looking at her, his expression unreadable. Was that scorn or curiosity? "I'm sorry," she repeated. "Can I help in any way?"

"No." The statement was final, and she heard the tone of dismissal. Now was her chance to escape. She could hurry back to the house and avoid the stable in the future. She need not involve herself with this matter. Her time could and would be better spent strategizing how to defeat Foncé. Why was he in London? What was his plan? Was it to kill Lord Melbourne? Attack the Barbican group at the source? Or was there more to it?

She sensed there was more to it.

She needed time to think, time to plan how to return to London. Her uncle had sent her to the country, but he had not said she could not return briefly. Richmond was an easy distance from London. Perhaps she might make a quick trip to meet with Saint and Wolf. Or perhaps Blue might help. Lord Melbourne had sent for Baron. Did Baron know something she did not?

"Well, then, Mr. Griffyn," she began, glancing at him again. He'd been looking away, and he glanced back at her in surprise. For a brief moment, so very brief, she saw his face without its mask. It was back before she could even realize what she had seen. There was that look of scorn and coldness that made him resemble the devil himself. But she had seen something else.

Pain.

"Well…" she said again, her words failing her. "You clearly do not know me very well. I can and I will assist you. Tonight." The words seemed to hang between them, palpable and capricious things. She almost stretched out her hand to snatch them back. What had she been thinking? She wanted to spend less time with the man, not more! She had a madman to defeat, her uncle's life to save. Perhaps the sovereignty of England depended on her.

Oh, very well. That might be exaggerating her own importance a little, but the fact was that she did not have the time to keep watch in hopes of catching a grain thief.

"Thank you, but no," Griffyn said.

"Pardon me?" Oh, but how she wished she would shut her mouth. The man was politely refusing her. He'd said *thank you* and everything. She should take the opportunity to go now. Instead, she felt a bit insulted. Who was *he* to refuse *her*? She was the best spy in England. Did he not think her capable of catching a grain thief? She could have done it in her sleep.

"I do not need your assistance." He squeezed out of the small feed room, and she had to follow him. She would not call what she was doing *chasing* him. She did not chase men she did not intend to capture. She had no intention of capturing Griffyn.

"Mr. Griffyn," she said, catching up to him before a stall. He lifted a pitchfork and began to pitch hay. "Investigating, capturing criminals, lying in wait— these are the sorts of things I *do*. I could show you a dresser full of medals and honors for the hundreds of times I have done such things and been rewarded by the king. I can catch your grain thief."

He turned to her, still clutching the pitchfork. "I do not need your assistance." He scooped the hay again.

"Why?" She crossed her arms over her chest. "Is it because I am a woman?"

"No." Another scoop of hay.

"Because I am injured? Because if that is the case, I assure you I am perfectly—"

"No." Another fork of hay.

"Is it because you know I have more pressing matters to attend to? Matters that could affect the sovereignty of our country and the balance of power in the realm?"

He gave her a long look from under his dark lashes. "No."

"Then why?"

With a sigh, he dug the pitchfork into the hay. "Because it would require the two of us to be alone for hours on end throughout the night. That is a great deal of temptation."

"*I* will not be tempted." And that was a lie. She was tempted now. "I have conducted hundreds of surveillance operations, quite often with male agents. I have never been even remotely tempted." That was true enough, but he was not an agent. He was…Griffyn.

"Perhaps I was speaking of myself."

"You? But—" Suddenly her throat felt quite dry. She licked her lips and wished she had tea or water or a stiff brandy. "Oh," she finally said, because she could not think of anything else to say.

"So you see, Miss Bonde, it would be better, for me, if you are not involved."

"I do, Mr. Griffyn." She would have said more, though she knew not what, since her mouth seemed to have a mind of its own this morning, but she heard the sound of male voices.

"The grooms," Griffyn said. "We were all up late, and I told them to sleep a few hours. Doubtless Old Connor decided they had slept long enough."

"I should return to the house." But she did not move. She was reluctant to leave him. He seemed so tired. She was weary too, but there was something exhilarating about being in his presence, something that made her heart race and her blood pound through her veins. She felt alive, the same way she did when she was close to ciphering a code. Was that it? Was Griffyn a puzzle she wanted to solve, or was she no better than every other young lady? Enticed by his dark good looks and the mystery and danger surrounding him?

"You should go in," Griffyn said, looking as though he would not miss her in the least. Perhaps she was not quite so tempting after all.

"Good day then." This time she forced her legs to move and was able to nod to the grooms as she passed them on her way out of the stables. They hastily removed their caps and bid her good day. She started back for the house at a quick clip. By the time she'd arrived, she realized she was in pain. Her stitches throbbed. She should not have walked so quickly. She took a moment in the saloon to lean against the back of a chair and catch her breath. The pain would pass if she gritted her teeth and bore it for a few moments.

"Are you unwell, Miss Bonde?"

Jane spun about, wincing when her wound flared hot in agony. "Lady Edgeberry," she managed to gasp out. "I did not know you were in residence." But judging by the marchioness's dress, she had not been in residence. She was dressed for travel in a sturdy day dress and spencer. She wore a straw bonnet trimmed with green ribbon, rather than the sort of mob cap a lady would wear if she had been indoors.

"I fear I roused my coachman at an unholy hour this morning so I might arrive in time to break my fast with you and your dear aunt. Where is she? Allow me to fetch her for you. You do not look at all well."

Jane held out a hand. "No, please. I am perfectly well. I have been out walking and simply need to catch my breath. I...overexerted myself."

Lady Edgeberry looked doubtful but did not gainsay her. Jane knew her excuse flimsy. She was a young, healthy woman. There was no reason she should find a walk taxing. But Lady Edgeberry did not know her, and Jane supposed the marchioness might very well assume her son's young betrothed had a weak constitution.

The marchioness indicated the chair Jane had been clutching, and Jane could have cursed herself for unthinkingly giving Lady Edgeberry the opportunity to have a tête-à-tête. The lady was unaware Jane had overheard her threats to Lord Melbourne, and Jane did not particularly like the role the marchioness had played in this betrothal. But though Jane was an unrivaled spy, she was not as socially adept. Seeing no other alternative, she took the chair across from Lady Edgeberry. Sitting actually caused the pain to subside slightly, and Jane felt as though she could think clearly again.

"I understand felicitations are in order," the lady said. "I cannot tell you how very pleased I am that you and my eldest son are betrothed."

"Thank you," Jane answered. The marchioness really did seem pleased. Her smile appeared genuine, but Jane knew she had been a renowned actress. One look at her and it was not difficult to guess why she had been so successful in her chosen field. She was lovely in exactly the ways Jane wasn't lovely. Lady Edgeberry was petite, dark, and exotic-looking. Her thick, shiny blue-black hair was swept into a sleek chignon at the back of her long, slender neck. Her skin was warm olive, and her eyes a dark brown. The outer corners tilted up slightly, accented by her long lashes. She had a plump, expressive mouth that could probably pout as easily as it could smile.

The marchioness had four sons, which meant she was one of Lady Melbourne's contemporaries, but Jane could not detect any wrinkles on her face or neck. Her figure would certainly make her a favorite on the stage. She had voluptuous curves and a trim waist. Even dressed in a modest golden day dress, her figure was impressive. Griffyn was a bastard, and it was not uncommon for actresses to give birth without the benefit of wedlock. What was uncommon was for an actress with a by-blow to marry a marquess. The marriage had been quite the mésalliance at the time, or so Jane had read in her research of Griffyn.

"I knew you were perfect for Dominic the first time I saw you," the marchioness said.

Jane's brows rose. "Why is that, my lady?"

"Because you don't care a whit what Society says or does."

"That's not entirely true. I care very much what Society says about my aunt and uncle. I would never allow anyone to hurt them with actions or words."

The lady was quiet for a moment, and Jane did not know if she understood the veiled threat or not.

"And yet you turned down six marriage proposals— all from quite eligible men."

"*I* did not think them eligible."

"I venture to guess your aunt and uncle did." She pulled absently at the fingers of her fine kidskin gloves. "And what makes Dominic different? What makes him, in your opinion, eligible?"

Jane did not like the turn this conversation had taken. She did not like to feel as though she were being manipulated. She might accept this betrothal for the time being, but that did not have to mean she acted like a foolish, lovelorn nitwit. "Let us be frank, Lady Edgeberry."

The marchioness leaned forward. "Oh, yes, let's do. I must confess that most members of the *ton* have quite a different definition of *frank* than I do. In which case, I shall allow you to set the tone."

"I think you know very well that my aunt and uncle have all but insisted I marry your son. I have my own reasons for agreeing. These reasons have nothing to do with your son's *eligibility*, and everything to do with my need to marry."

"Are you with child?" the marchioness asked.

Jane blinked. "No!"

Lady Edgeberry shrugged apologetically. "You did ask for frankness."

"I did, and it is my understanding that your son's, shall we say trouble, with ladies precipitated your dictate that he marry."

Lady Edgeberry sat back. "Young unmarried ladies do not generally speak of such things."

"I hardly think I have shocked you."

"Not at all. In fact, this is exactly why I considered you the perfect wife for my son. You do not care that he was born on the wrong side of the blanket. You will not fear his black moods. A bit of youthful indiscretion will not shock you or deter you from marrying him."

This was all true, but Jane thought, considering Griffyn's connections, most young ladies could overlook all three of those concerns. She said as much, but Lady Edgeberry shook her head. "But would Dominic have such a young lady? Doubtful. He has an enormous amount of pride. He would never consent to marry a woman who looked down on him because of the circumstances of his birth. Do you understand why?"

"He does not wish to be pitied."

"He has too often been pitied and condescended to by young, beautiful ladies. From my perspective, he had quite given up on the notion of marrying any young lady I considered eligible. Perhaps given up on marriage altogether."

"And yet you say I am perfect."

"Because you are beautiful. You do not pity him. You are everything he did not think he could have.

And now I will see he has it." The marchioness's dark eyes met Jane's. "And has you."

"So I am a trophy." The thought was truly appalling. She was anything but a trophy. She collected trophies of enemies of the state. She was no man's trophy.

"A hard-won trophy. I do not know what you have heard about my son and his dalliances with ladies, but I assure you they are, for the most part, exaggerated."

From Jane's experiences with Griffyn thus far, she was not inclined to agree with the marchioness. Griffyn seemed quite experienced and lived up to his reputation as a man who knew how to please ladies.

"Are we still being frank, Miss Bonde?"

Jane was not quite certain what she should answer. She was not at all certain she wanted the marchioness to go on.

"Miss Bonde?"

"Y—" Jane cleared her throat. "Yes."

"My son had a difficult childhood. I blame myself. I was away too much. I consorted with men of questionable character. Dominic was hurt by my unintentional neglect. I do hope, if and when my son elects to tell you about those years, you will keep an open mind. Do not judge too harshly—neither him nor me."

Jane sat very still for a long, long moment. She was not innocent of the evils of the world. Her position in the Barbican had exposed her to more than many men saw in a lifetime. And still she could not imagine what the marchioness had done or allowed to be done. She found she had begun to shake slightly, not enough for the marchioness to notice. In fact, that lady had, by all appearances, decided the conversation was concluded.

She had risen and was pulling her gloves from her fingers, one by one. "Will you join me in the breakfast room, Miss Bonde?"

"I will," Jane said, surprised her voice sounded so calm and flat when she was shaking inside like a leaf in the wind. "After my exertions this morning, I would like a moment to change my petticoat and mud-caked boots." She gestured to her dirty clothing. She had not noticed them before, and she had never cared about a little dirt, but she needed an escape. She rose, and her wound gave a tinge of pain. She'd forgotten it as well. "Excuse me," she said and walked quite regally to the stairs that led to the west wing, where she and her aunt had been situated.

She held her head high, showing no sign of distress, until she reached her room. Miraculously, it was empty of servants or her aunt, who surely would have taken one look at Jane's expression and known something was amiss. Jane closed the door behind her, locked it, and sank into the dainty chair set before the dressing table. She caught a glimpse of herself in the mirror and closed her eyes. She was as pale as the first winter snow. Her wound throbbed, and she desperately wanted something much stronger than coffee or tea to ease the pain. She might be allowed ratafia later, but it would do little to dull the ache. Why hadn't she taken the pain medications from Farrar?

And why had she allowed herself to fall into Lady Edgeberry's trap? Jane was not going to see Dominic Griffyn as anything other than one of many of the men she knew. He was no different. She did not want to know anything about his childhood. She did not want to feel sympathy for him. She did not want to think that perhaps, in some way, her friendship might help Griffyn. She could not help him. She had to capture Foncé. She had to help her country.

And this was precisely why she should never marry. Her loyalties would forever be divided. Years ago, she'd had to make a choice, and she'd chosen the Barbican group. Why, then, did she have the urge to go to Griffyn? Why did she lie awake thinking about the feel of his lips on hers? Imagining what his hands on her bare skin would feel like? Why did she long to know more about him, yearn to know what secrets he hid behind those dark eyes? Why did she seek him out? For she had certainly sought him out this morning. She'd known he loved horses. She'd known he would be at the stables.

And why shouldn't she want to see him? She was a woman as well as an agent. She had desires and needs, as much as she tried to suppress them. Could she have possibly known, all those years ago when she'd begun training as an agent for the Barbican group, what she was giving up? Had she ever even had a choice? Had her destiny been set when her parents died and she was sent to live with her aunt and uncle?

Suddenly, Jane was angry—angry that her uncle had chosen a path for her without considering it might not be the path she wanted; angry that she could not seem to put Griffyn out of her mind, the way she had other men; angry at his mother for whatever she had allowed, even unintentionally, to happen to him when he was a young boy.

Another glance in the mirror revealed spots of

bright red in her cheeks. Jane took a deep breath. Foncé was in London. She could not afford to waste time fretting over what might have been. Her life, for better or worse, was the Barbican group. She had to find a way back into Town. A sharp knock sounded on the door adjoining her room to her aunt's. Jane turned as her aunt opened it. She took a quick look at Jane and frowned. "Goodness. Have you already been out?"

"I went for a walk."

"Is that wise, in your condition?"

"I'm fine."

"You would say that even if you were being drawn and quartered."

"Women aren't drawn and quartered."

Her aunt gave her a dark look.

Jane sighed. There was nothing wrong with being fussed over once in a while. "I may have overexerted myself. I came to rest and change into clean boots before breakfast. Lady Edgeberry has arrived."

"Has she?" Lady Melbourne smiled. "Oh, good! We can spend the day planning the wedding."

Jane inhaled sharply. She had walked directly into that trap. It was such an amateur mistake that she deserved her punishment.

"What is this nonsense about boots?" her aunt asked.

And here it comes, Jane thought.

"You do not need boots to embroider and discuss wedding plans." She looked about. "Where is your maid? I will tell her to fetch your slippers." She rang the bellpull, putting her plan into action. Jane could see no way to counter this plan, except to feign illness and stay in bed. She was not certain which was worse—staying in bed all day or being forced to discuss wedding lace and whether scones or crumpets should be served at the breakfast.

The maid entered, exclaiming over the state of Jane's petticoats. Soon day dresses were dragged out for inspection, and her hair was taken out of its simple style and repinned. Maids hurried to and fro, jumping to carry out her aunt's orders. Jane closed her eyes and focused on a piece of advice Agent Blue had once given her: When you've jumped into a strong current, sometimes the best strategy is to allow it to take you where it will.

Of course, they had been standing at the precipice of a particularly tumultuous stretch of the Seine, with three of Napoleon's agents closing in, and she had not been certain she would survive the jump, much less the journey down the river. Jane winced now as another pin was thrust into her already too-tightly coiled hair. The situation now was not so very different, except at present she had jumped into a much stronger current.

Eleven

DOMINIC HAD NOT SEEN JANE THE REST OF THE DAY. He had worked in the stables, or at least pretended to work, while keeping his ears open for any conversations that might hint at who the grain thief might be. But none of the grooms expressed anything but regret at Nessa's death. None of them seemed displeased with his lot or complained of his wages. By late afternoon, Dominic was no closer to finding the guilty party than he had been at dawn.

Finally, when Old Connor found him dozing in front of his correspondence, Dominic returned to the house, intent upon sleeping for a few hours. Jane's idea to keep watch in the stables all night seemed better and better the more Dominic considered it. A new shipment of grain had just arrived, so the thief would want to strike soon.

As he paused outside the drawing room, intending to greet his guests before retiring to his bedchamber, he heard his mother's voice. He eased the door open silently and glimpsed the three ladies sitting properly with teacups balanced on their knees. His mother was saying something about adorning the wedding carriage with silk streamers and white flowers. "What is your favorite flower, Miss Bonde? That is to say, which is your favorite white flower?"

"Uhh…" She looked and sounded weary, much as he would have had he been forced to endure the conversation. "Daisies?" Her eyes met his. He should have realized that she, a spy, would catch him lurking. Her eyes pleaded with him, and she mouthed, *help*.

"Daisies are a rather common flower," his mother said, dismissing his betrothed's suggestion. "I was thinking roses. Much more elegant." His mother spoke rapidly, as though discussing the wedding was a mere formality. She had obviously already planned the entire affair. Jane must have known this as well. If he were a hero, he would have swooped in and rescued her. She would have made a fine prize. She wore a frothy white gown that seemed to float around her body like storm-tossed waves. Her hair made a golden crown about her head, and not a single strand had escaped to mar the perfection of her high cheekbones, her straight nose, or her full lips. He'd seen her hair down, most recently when she'd been injured and lying on her uncle's couch in the Barbican group's offices. He did not know if she'd taken it down or it had fallen from the exertion of her efforts, but it had looked like a shiny silk skein against the dark leather of the couch. Looking at her now, Dominic had the urge to take it down again and let it tumble over her white shoulders and shapely arms.

"Roses would be lovely," Lady Melbourne responded. "Do not you agree, Jane?"

Jane blinked. She'd been staring at him, just as he had been staring at her. "I am in perfect agreement," she said, and he knew, without a doubt, she had no idea whatsoever her aunt was discussing. "If you would excuse me for just a moment—"

"What? No!" his mother objected, and Jane was trapped once again. Dominic could not suppress a chuckle.

"We must discuss the footmen's livery. I was thinking gold…"

Dominic moved stealthily away, praying he was not heard. No, he was certainly no hero to allow a lady to suffer through such tortures. But she was a good agent. She would find a means of escape on her own.

He took a long nap and felt refreshed and clear-headed when the bell rang for dinner. He would have avoided the meal if he could, but it was too early to return to the stables without arousing curiosity among the stable hands. He was expected to dine with his betrothed and her aunt.

Once again the company had convened in the drawing room. Dominic joined them, planning to greet his mother and then find his betrothed and make a show of kissing her hand. But the first person he'd seen upon entering was Miss Bonde herself, and he found it impossible to advance any farther. She slew him. Her beauty, quite simply, slew him. No matter how often he reminded himself he did not care for the classic English beauty, he found himself enthralled with her. Perhaps he had been wrong. He *did* care for the classic English beauty. It was her eyes, he decided, that drew him in. They were large and dark-fringed and the color of the ocean before a storm.

She wore a pink gown, probably more suitable for a debutante than for an elite spy with the Barbican group, but the color matched that in her cheeks. The neckline was modest for an evening gown, but his gaze lingered on the swell of her breasts pushing against the silk of the fabric. He could imagine the feel of them in his hands, their weight and firmness.

"Mr. Griffyn," she said. His gaze returned quickly to her face, and he felt rather like a naughty boy caught peeping through the slit of a half-open door.

"Miss Bonde." He made an effort to cross the small space between them, took her hand, and kissed her gloved knuckles.

"You look much better than you did this morning. I hope you were able to rest."

"I was. You look well. How is your injury?"

She waved a hand. "I hardly notice it. Have you decided what you shall do about the grain thief?"

He frowned. His horses and stables were his concern and no one else's. "I will deal with it."

She arched a brow. "You are not exactly one for conversation." She cocked her head. "Or is it that you do not think I, a woman, can understand the complexities of the situation?"

Dominic glanced over his shoulder to ensure no one else was listening. Everyone had moved away from them, giving them as much space as they could want in which to speak. He supposed that was one benefit of an engagement.

"That is not it at all. I am quite aware of your capabilities, Miss Bonde."

"Then I would think an intelligent man such as

yourself, a man who cares about his animals, would want the help of someone with my capabilities, in spite of the temptations. I will keep them at a minimum, I assure you. I will wear black and style my hair in an ugly fashion so I am quite hideous to look upon."

She must know she could never look hideous. He could not decide if she was teasing him or actually thought the color she wore or the style of her dress really would play some part in how much he desired her. He said nothing. He'd merely intended to greet her and exchange pleasantries, but it seemed every conversation they had turned into a debate.

"I will meet you in the stables tonight at midnight," she said. "Or would eleven be better? I forget that country hours are so much earlier than those kept in Town."

"I do not wish to argue with you, Miss Bonde."

"Then do not argue with me, Mr. Griffyn." And before he could speak again, she walked away, joining her aunt and accepting a glass of ratafia. He wondered if it had been shaken as opposed to stirred. He wondered how he remembered such a minute and unimportant detail about her.

All through dinner, he listened to his mother and Lady Melbourne discuss wedding preparations. Miss Bonde sat to his right, and she appeared to listen attentively, though surely she had heard it all before. She was probably plotting other ways to make his life difficult. He did not want to meet her in the stables, but he could see no means to keep her away. She would not be afraid to venture out in the dark, and she could probably elude any of the servants still awake. If he did not go to the stables, she would apprehend the grain thief on her own. If he did go and tried to persuade her to return home, she would only make a scene and probably alert the thief to their presence. He had little choice but to tolerate her involvement tonight.

"Dominic, are you listening?" his mother asked.

He realized everyone at the table was watching him and probably had been for several minutes. "I confess my mind was otherwise occupied." He should not have glanced at Miss Bonde in that moment, but he could not seem to stop himself. She had a knowing smile on her lips. Curse the woman. She probably knew very well that he was plotting how to avoid her tonight. Unfortunately, his mother mistook the glance.

"Oh, I see," she said, her voice low and teasing. "You are thinking about *after* the wedding. I can hardly blame you."

Lady Melbourne colored, and Miss Bonde lowered her eyes. Dominic refused to allow his face to flush. There were times he wished he did not have quite so earthy a mother. "Actually, I was thinking about an offer Lord Charing made for one of the foals born last year. It's a generous offer, but I am not certain I approve of his stables or the way he treats his hunters."

"They are horses, not children," his mother said.

"I think Mr. Griffyn's concern speaks well of him," Lady Melbourne said.

"So do I," Miss Bonde added, and this time when he looked at her, her eyes were dark with something that caused his groin to tighten.

❧

He never even heard her coming. He'd been listening for her as he crouched in Nessa's empty stall, keeping watch on the room where the new shipment of grain was stored. It was after eleven, and he'd been expecting her. He'd watched and he'd listened, and then without warning, something touched his shoulder.

He almost let out a howl when he saw her standing beside him. "Where the hell did you come from?" he hissed.

"The house," she said, crouching beside him. She wore a dark dress, black gloves, and a black shawl about her head to hide her bright hair. "My aunt wanted to chat more about the wedding—or, rather, what happens after the wedding."

His breath caught in his throat, though she did not appear chagrined to be having this conversation with him. She settled beside him, her eyes alert and scanning the stable, her voice a low murmur he could barely detect over the noises of the horses, owls, and other night creatures.

"I did not have the heart to tell her the discussion was unnecessary."

"Because you are not an innocent."

She looked at him, turning her head slowly until her eagle eyes met his. "Because we are not actually going to marry."

"Oh." He'd insulted her. He had not intended to, but he'd never been good at social graces, and he was not practiced enough not to misstep on occasion. She turned her gaze back to the stables and continued her surveillance.

"This is a good location," she said after a long silence

between them. "If he comes tonight, he must pass us to reach what he wants."

"Did you see anything on your approach?" There was no reason to ask if she'd been seen. He knew she had not.

"No. Everything looked to be as it should. But I do not live here. Perhaps if you'd made the walk, you would have seen something I missed." She spoke without looking at him, her attention on the stables. He wondered how many times she had done this sort of thing. It seemed to come to her naturally, and she appeared quite at ease. He, on the other hand, could not seem to stop looking at her. He could smell the scent of violets on her and feel the warmth of her body beside his. They did not touch, but she sat companionably close.

How many men had she sat with all night long on one mission or another? How many weeks or months had she roamed the Continent unchaperoned, free to do as she might? He did not begrudge her that freedom; she was no young miss of twenty. If she had taken a lover, who was he to judge? He was far from pure himself.

And yet, he found himself annoyed by the thought that another man might have touched her. She was his, if only in word, and only for the time being.

"What is it?" she asked.

"I didn't speak."

"Something is troubling you. You clench your fists when you are troubled."

"I do not."

She glanced at him, and he clenched his fists before

he could stop himself. He gave her a dark look. She shrugged.

"Should we be speaking? I would rather not alert the thief to our presence."

"We'll hear him before he hears us. Listen for a change in the sound of the chirping of the insects or the stamp of the horses' hooves. They will hear him before we do and alert us." She was looking at him now, not studying the stalls. He wished she would go back to her surveillance. "Very well. Don't ask me."

She knew the question in his mind. Of course she did. That did not mean he had to say it. He could keep silent. He should keep silent. If he asked her a question, she would ask him one. He did not want to answer her questions.

He looked away, and she murmured, "Coward" under her breath. He turned back to her so quickly that he nudged her and knocked her onto her bottom.

"I am not a coward."

"Then ask."

"Perhaps I do not want the answer."

"Don't you?"

He did. He really did. But he was not a man who gave into impulses and desires. He offered his hand and pulled her back to her feet so she was once again crouched beside him. He was thankful for her gloves. If he had touched her bare skin, he did not know if he could have resisted dragging her into his arms. As it was, he kept his attention resolutely on the stable and not on her. She said nothing, and for a very long time, all was silent. But there was no peace. He could not relax with her beside him. He was still fatigued from the long vigil last night, but with her beside him, there was no chance he would fall asleep.

"You are really not going to ask," she said when perhaps a silent hour had passed.

"It is not my concern."

"I am your betrothed. I would think my past lovers something of your concern."

He took in a slow breath. Was that confirmation, or had she been speaking generally? "This discussion can do little good," he finally said.

"Even if I tell you there has been no one?" She spoke the words earnestly, her gaze directly on him. If she was lying, she was very good at it—a fact that should not surprise him.

"I would not believe you."

"How utterly disheartening. You think me such a loose woman?"

"I think you have had freedom and opportunity. Women, given those options, act much as men."

"Much as your mother did," she said.

"Yes." He looked away. "I do not judge her or you. I am no saint."

"Neither am I, but nor am I an abject sinner. I have had lovers, but not in the sense you mean. I am still a maiden."

He turned to look at her, trying to gauge whether she was telling the truth. It was a foolish hope. He would never be able to tell, and yet, when he looked at her, her face looked different. Whatever mask she wore had slipped away. He knew it because he had seen it slip away in Melbourne's office when she was in pain. She looked very young and very beautiful.

He saw the truth of her words in her eyes, and he saw something else as well. She wanted him. Dominic took a ragged breath. She was not the first woman to look at him with desire in her eyes, but she was the first one he'd wanted in return—the first one he'd thought of as more than simply an object for physical release.

"I will admit," she said, "that I have kissed men. Perhaps too many men, a half dozen, I suppose." She looked down. "I have touched and been touched, but I have never lain with a man, never given my maidenhead."

"Why not?" His voice sounded ragged in his ears. "Are you not married to your work?"

"Yes, but perhaps I have always hoped there might be something else—*someone*—worth saving myself for." She looked down, and he realized at some point she had removed her gloves. In her hand she held a piece of hay. She'd broken it into tiny pieces. "And, of course, there was God."

"God?" He frowned.

She looked up at him. "He might smite me for fornication."

He felt a smile tugging at the corners of his lips. "Yes, that's a definite cause for concern. Of course, it's not very likely. If God were to go about smiting all those who engaged in fornication and adultery, most of the *ton* would be little more than black marks on an Aubusson rug."

"Is that what those marks are? I thought they were burn marks caused by sparks from unguarded hearths." She laughed, and he could not stop himself from laughing too. How long had it been since he'd laughed? And then, her broad smile on her face, she looked up at him, and he could not resist. He leaned forward, cupped her cheek, and kissed her. It was a light, friendly kiss, and it must have surprised her, because she did not kiss him back. It was brief and chaste.

And it was not enough.

For either of them.

She met him halfway, her mouth as hot and hungry as his. He felt as though she were a lodestone, and he could not escape his attraction even if he'd wanted to. He did want to, though at the moment he could not remember why. He cupped her face, plowing his hands into her hair and knocking the shawl to the ground. Her hair was fine and soft, and he stroked it even as his tongue stroked hers.

She had been kissed before. She undoubtedly had more experience at kissing than he, and she did not hide it. She was not shy or hesitant about kissing him back. Her tongue met his, stroking him, and then sucking him lightly until he fisted his hands in her hair, because otherwise he would be tempted to place them elsewhere. He'd pushed her up against the wall of the stall, and now she slid down it; he slid with her until he was kneeling before her, her body trapped between his thighs.

He pulled back and looked down at her. He could not breathe. His chest was tight, and his heart pumped furiously. She was so beautiful. Too beautiful for him. His hand reached out and touched the collar at her chin, and he saw his fingers tremble as they unfastened the tiny buttons and opened the material to reveal her collarbone and the hint of the swell of her breasts. His lips were foul. He would defile her by touching them to that alabaster skin, but he could not stop himself. He bent and pressed his soiled lips to her warm flesh, inhaling the scent of violets.

Her heart beat as quickly as his, and when he moved his lips to graze the soft flesh swelling above her stays, she took a shuddering breath. He laid his forehead on her chest, trying to regain control, listening as her heart thundered out of control for him.

She wanted *him*.

"You see the effect you have on me," she murmured. Her voice was low and velvet with his ear pressed against her. "Will you think me horribly wanton if I ask you to finish with those buttons and touch me?"

"Yes," he said, even as he reached for the next button. A tiny, round black button that his large hands had to fumble with to unfasten. And then there was another and another. He would be undressing her for days. "But I am as wanton as you, and I did warn you not to tempt me."

"I am very bad at heeding warnings," she said, drawing in a sharp breath when one of his hands grazed her breast. He almost had the bodice open. Then there were the stays, of course. Finally, he pushed the fabric back over her shoulders and watched as her breasts rose and fell from her rapid breathing. There was a small satin bow at the valley between them, and he loosened it, tugging the lacings apart. He slid the stays down until only the thin, fine material of her shift covered her. He imagined if he'd had more light, if he'd been outside in the light of the moon or in a bedroom with a lamp burning, that he would have seen the dark of her areola through that thin fabric. He could only imagine it now and see the outline of her hard nipple. He bent his head and took it in his mouth, material and all.

She bucked under him, her hands coming up to wrap around his neck and invite him to continue. He slowly withdrew, took her hands in his and removed them from his neck, setting them firmly at her sides. Then he looked down at the wet material. Her nipple was apparent. It was a hard, swollen peak straining against the fabric. Slowly, he moved to her opposite breast, swirling his tongue around her nipple until the fabric of her shift clung to the point of flesh.

"Touch me," she whispered. "Really touch me."

He longed to do so. His hands gripped her waist as a drowning man grips a shard of floating debris. He would not sully her with his hands; those hands had done unspeakable things. His mouth too was vile. He had already soiled her by touching his lips to hers.

"Then allow me to touch you."

"No."

But in typical fashion, she acted without listening. He could not have said exactly what happened, but one moment he was above her, and the next he was on his back and she straddled him. He felt his breathing hitch, an edge of panic creep in, but he held it in check. He could do this. He wanted to enjoy this. Her bodice gaped open, and he endeavored to keep his gaze on the precarious edge of her shift. Her breasts were about to spill out, and if she bent a little more, he could take one in his mouth. He closed his eyes and felt her hands on his neck. She'd loosened his neckcloth, pushed the standing collar aside, and begun to unbutton his shirt. Fire raged through him as she touched her sweet lips to his skin. He'd never been touched like this. Never allowed this.

"I know you want me," she said, her lips against his neck. "I feel your pulse beating here in a rapid staccato." She looked up at him, and his gaze shifted down. Her breasts had fallen loose of their confines, and they were as full and perfect as he had known they would be. He gritted his teeth and looked back at her face. "I cannot help but think," she said quietly, "that perhaps I have been waiting for you. You make me feel…" She touched his rapidly beating pulse. "Like this. I cannot stop imagining your hands on me." She took them from her waist, and he watched as she placed them on her bare breasts. He should have pulled them away. His skin was dark against her pale flesh, but she was so soft and so warm. Instead, he kneaded her, then plucked at one nipple until she gasped. He rose, taking it into his mouth and sucking hard. She arched back, and he sat, sliding his hands to her back and holding her pressed against his mouth.

Her hips moved against him, and he knew she must feel his hard cock straining against his trousers. He could release the fall so very easily. He could thrust into her, take her, give into this temptation.

Her mouth met his again, and his hands were on her generous breasts. Her hips continued to move, and he lowered a hand to still them, but found it sliding against the silk of her thigh. She moaned, and he slid higher, slid deeper until he could feel her heat. She slowed her movements then, as though waiting in tortured anticipation of what he would do next. He should not touch her. He'd already gone too far. He should not reach for her, but his fingers extended, and he felt the warm wetness of her center. He groaned at the fierce wave of need that crashed over him. He wanted to be inside her. He wanted to plunge into her heat, feel her tighten around him. He wanted...

His head swirled, and he shook his head to clear it. Suddenly everything was pitch black. *No,* he said in his mind. *You are in the stable.*

The stable was not completely dark. This was not real. It wasn't. But he heard his own breath wheezing in and out, and he felt himself curl into a ball on his hard pallet. If he could just make himself small enough, no one would find him. The room was dark. He'd begged his mother to leave a candle burning, but she said it was a frivolous expense, and they couldn't afford it. Now he was in the dark. He was not alone in the dark.

"Mama?" he asked. Please let it be her. Please. He'd heard her come in from the theater. He'd heard her talking to The Man. Please do not let it be him.

His mother did not answer, and Dominic curled tighter, trying to make himself smaller. It wasn't his mother. She was asleep, sleeping soundly from exhaustion and wine. She never woke. Never came to save him. The Man wasn't the first one to find him cowering in the dark. And his mother never knew. She couldn't protect him. She couldn't even protect herself from vicious men who slapped and hit and flew into drunken rages.

Dominic tried to still his breathing and listen. He heard nothing. Perhaps he had been mistaken. Perhaps he was alone. He didn't move, didn't breathe.

And then a hand clamped on his shoulder, and a deep voice said, "Hello, lovely."

Twelve

WITH THE CRY OF A WOUNDED ANIMAL, GRIFFYN threw himself off her. Jane blinked, the haze of arousal making her mind sluggish and slow to respond. Part of her wanted to protest his abrupt cessation. She wanted more. She wanted everything.

No! She didn't want that. What had she been thinking? She hadn't been thinking, obviously. For a few minutes of pleasure, she might have lost everything. What would she do if she became with child?

Saint was with child...

But she wasn't Saint. And she—Jane glanced with some alarm at Griffyn. Only a few seconds had passed, but she finally noticed his breathing was fast, and his face was white.

"Mr. Griffyn?" That sounded ridiculous. He'd been kissing her, touching her intimately only a moment ago. "Dominic." She rose on her knees and moved toward him. "Are you unwell?" He looked very poorly, indeed. His eyes were black and dead. He didn't seem to see her. He was staring at something else. Something beyond her. She looked over her shoulder, but there was nothing.

"Dominic?" She reached out and touched his hand. His skin was freezing cold. He jerked his hand away and hissed at her.

"Don't touch me. Don't *ever* touch me."

The voice was his, but it didn't sound like him. It was animalistic and low, almost a growl. Even his hand had curled into a claw, as though he were a wolf, prepared to strike at her. "I won't touch you. What is wrong? What's happened?" But she didn't expect an answer. She'd seen this before. He was in shock. He probably wasn't even aware she was beside him. Something had triggered this change in him. She couldn't think of anything she'd done. They'd been kissing; he'd been touching her, that was all.

"Stay back," he warned.

"I will." She took the moment to right her clothes, pull her hair up. His breathing was slowing, but he still did not look like himself. He still had not focused on the stall or on her. Something was horribly wrong, and she had better take him back to the house. The thief be damned at this point. And then she heard a sound. Good. If it was the thief, she'd make him help her move his master from the stables to the house. She thought about calling out and decided to wait until he entered the stable. If he thought he could escape, he might run in order to avoid being identified. She heard what sounded like a footstep, and then Griffyn began to rise.

She shook her head at him and hissed, "No. Stay still."

He didn't seem to hear her, and she heard another sound—something like a scrape. For some reason, her heart was thumping wildly now. Something was wrong, and it was more than simply Griffyn's current condition. The groom was too quiet, too stealthy. A common thief would never go to that much trouble to steal grain. Dominic tried to stand again, and she grabbed his hand to tug him down. His hand tightened on hers, and she was hauled against him then pushed against the wall of the stall. The prickly wood cut through the thin fabric of her gown and into her back.

"Three rules," he said through a jaw clenched with what she could see was enormous restraint. What was he restraining himself from? Hurting her? Taking her?

"I heard a sound—"

"Do not touch me is the first," he said, voice thankfully low and muffled. "I can touch you, but you never touch me. If I want you to touch me, I tell you where and how. Secondly, no kissing."

She was beginning to comprehend what he was saying. Had he not heard her? Did he not realize the thief was about? "Griffyn," she said. "You have to listen to me. There's someone coming."

"And last," he went on as though she had not even spoken, "never, ever surprise me. You won't like me if I'm surprised."

"Griffyn," she said again.

"Do you understand?" he asked.

"I understand," she said, though she didn't at all at the moment. "Do you understand someone is coming this way?"

He blinked at her, and she shoved him back, away from her. Now that she had space, she could listen again. She went absolutely still, concentrating as hard as she could...

Her body went on alert, and she cut her gaze to Griffyn again. He crouched a few feet away, raking his hands through his hair. It was not Griffyn who had alerted her.

Someone was entering the stable.

Jane flattened her back against the wall of the stall and forced her heart to slow its pounding rhythm. She needed all her senses. Griffyn was quiet, but she didn't know how long that would last. Should she try to intercept the intruder before Griffyn made their presence known or trust that he would remain quiet long enough for her to see who it was and what he wanted?

The stable door creaked, and several horses shifted and stamped their hooves. Jane had to strain to hear again, but the sound of the horses had captured Dominic's attention. He looked up, his eyes clear and focused. Thank God. He was back. She met his gaze in the semidarkness and put a finger to her lips. He nodded, rose, and joined her against the wall, keeping to the shadows. They were at the end of the row of stalls, but she could hear the horses near the entrance moving about uneasily.

"Who is it?" Griffyn asked, his mouth close to her ear.

She flicked her gaze at him. Interesting that he should not assume it was one of the grooms. "You don't think it's your thief?"

He shook his head. "The horses don't know him."

That was it. The horses' restlessness had made her suspicious as well. She did not know who would be lurking about, but she intended to discover the man's identity. She held up a hand, directing Griffyn to stay where he was. He gave her an incredulous look before she sidled toward the stall door.

She hadn't gone far before he pulled her back. "This is my stable. Stay here," he hissed in her ear.

This was not the time for arguments or the time to point out that she did not take orders from him. He peered out of the stall doorway. They had left it open enough to squeeze out of, and she considered allowing him to go and get himself killed. But that would have violated all sorts of oaths pertaining to protecting King and Country with her life. After all, a country's innocent people comprised it. With a sigh, she joined him, but not before she could stop him from slipping out of the stall. Any protest she might have made caught in her throat when the sound of a pistol boomed through the building.

Instinct told her to drop to her belly and lie flat. Training told her to run after the intruder. Something else—something she did not want to think too deeply about—told her to save Griffyn. She burst into the stable aisle, not taking any care to conceal herself. They were discovered now, and in a moment the stable would swarm with grooms, if not the entire estate staff. The sound of a pistol on a silent night carried a long, long way.

As she scrambled out of the stall, she noticed two things. First of all, Griffyn was on his knees. Secondly, the horses were calling and screaming with fear. She ran to Griffyn, but he pointed toward the exit. "There!"

She saw the retreating figure and gave chase. Griffyn followed her, and the sick feeling in her stomach subsided. This was why she could not fall in love with him. One day there might come a time when she had to choose again between love and duty. What would she choose?

She skidded onto the drive and then darted left, colliding with Griffyn and knocking him down. It saved them both from another bullet. "Bastard had another gun," she said to herself, reaching into her boot and unclasping the small pistol she had holstered there. Griffyn gave chase to the attacker, but she paused a moment to prime the pistol. She cocked the hammer, aimed—and bollocks! Griffyn was in her line of sight! And now the distance was too great to ensure her aim. Still holding the pistol, she broke into a run and quickly closed the distance, passing Griffyn, pausing and aiming the pistol. She stopped breathing, stopped her hands shaking, stopped every thought racing through her mind. With deadly accuracy, she fired, flinching back from the recoil.

She shook her head, clearing it, then allowed her knees to give way when she saw the attacker was down.

❧

It seemed an eternity before Dominic reached Jane. She was down, and he grabbed her, checking her for blood. "Where are you wounded?" He felt wetness on his hand and pulled it away from her belly. His gaze met hers.

"My stitches came out," she said, her breathing ragged. "The devil, but it hurts! Help me up."

He gave her a long look. "Maybe you should sit here a moment." He heard the sounds of people coming. He'd have more servants than he knew what to do with in a matter of moments. One could carry her into the house and fetch the local doctor. But the look in her eye wiped that thought away. She was not going to be reasonable.

"Either help me up or move out of my way," she said, struggling to rise. He grabbed her elbow and assisted her. She pulled away and marched to the body. The man lay motionless on the grass. She stared at him a long moment, then bent and pushed his coat aside. A red stain in the center marked where a small pistol ball had entered. Dominic had imagined there would be more blood, more gore. But the pistol she'd used was small, and so was the ball. But small or not, she was deadly accurate. She'd hit him straight through the heart. He was probably dead before he hit the ground.

"So my thief isn't one of the grooms."

She turned to look at the stable hands running toward them. "This isn't your thief," she said before they were both surrounded and swept into the maelstrom of shock and confusion.

Several hours later, near dawn, Dominic was finally able to go to his bed. He'd answered every question, told his side of the story countless times. The sheriff had been summoned. The local magistrate had been summoned. The doctor had come. He hadn't been able to save the dead man, but he'd stitched Jane again—or so Dominic assumed. Because of her injury, she'd escaped most of the questioning. Her aunt had put her to bed, but as Dominic climbed the stairs to his bedchamber, he doubted she would stay there for long. In about an hour, the house would settle down. In about an hour, he could wash, shave, and change his clothing.

And so it was, when she stepped into the stable—presumably intent upon stealing one of his horses—he was waiting for her. She gave a small jump of fright, and he was sorry for that. He could see by her wince the jump had pained her, though surely her pride injured her more than her knife wound. "Going somewhere, Miss Bonde?"

"For a ride, Mr. Griffyn. Surely you would not begrudge me that small indulgence after the night's excitement." She was dressed in a tight-fitting light blue riding habit, her golden hair tucked neatly under an ostrich-plumed shako hat. She looked quite fashionable and quite desirable with her impressive figure displayed to advantage. It was difficult to believe he had kissed her last night, touched her. Matters had gone too far. He'd been forced to explain his rules to her—rules meant more for temporary encounters with willing barmaids than a lady, than this women he was beginning to care for.

From now on, he would not allow himself to touch her, and he would protect her at any cost. Most especially, he would protect her from himself.

"I would not, no," he said, "but I cannot allow you to return to London."

"I'm not—"

He raised a brow.

"Very well. I have to go. It's urgent."

He took a deep breath. "I know you cannot trust me after…what I did last night. But I give you my word, it will not happen again. You are in no danger here, with me. You are quite safe as long as you do not touch me again."

She blinked at him, her blue eyes strangely clear despite the fact that she had probably not slept. "Shall we walk, Mr. Griffyn?" she asked. "I fear we might be overheard here, and I have something to tell you."

"You are injured."

But she was already walking toward the door. He followed, and they stepped out into a day that seemed intent on being neither sunny nor rainy. Clouds threatened to open up with rain, but the sun broke through in patches. He walked beside her, keeping a small distance between them. She turned to look back at the stables, and then obviously liking what she saw, said, "I am not leaving because of what happened between us last night." She looked at him, her gaze direct. "I liked it. Not the part where you berated me, but the other. I liked it far more than I ought."

"Miss Bonde—"

"Jane. You don't scare me, Dominic. Nothing you could do will ever scare me. Even my own response to you doesn't scare me." She looked down as though struggling to be honest. "Well, it doesn't scare me much."

"You must allow me to apologize for speaking to you that way."

"I wish you had told me sooner. One needs to know one's parameters. You understand why I am confused. You have a policy that forbids kissing, yet you have kissed me on more than one occasion."

"It will not happen again."

"Yes, it will, and I won't follow your rules either. You can't have me on those terms, Dominic. We decide on mutual terms or none at all."

Fury rose in him at her tone. What the hell did she know about terms? Who was she to tell him what he would and would not allow?

"I can see you do not want to discuss it. Your look is as black as those thunderclouds." She pointed to the distant clouds. "But I have been through a few traumas myself. One thing I know is that talking about what happened does help. Keeping it inside only makes it seem that much bigger, and makes one feel that much more alone."

He rounded on her, and she stepped back. She was scared now, and she should be. He had rarely been this angry. "I am alone, Miss Bonde. You cannot possibly imagine the things I have endured."

"Can't I? I'm not so innocent or gently bred, Dominic. I have traveled the world. I have seen all manner of atrocities, and it does not take much imagination for me to surmise what happened to you."

They were standing closer than he thought, and she reached out a hand and placed it on his newly shaved jaw. He flinched back immediately, shocked at her touch, and even more shocked that she would willingly consent to touch him. If she really had any idea how sullied he was, she would never touch him.

Then why did he look at her and think she had some inkling? And if that was so, how could she bear to stand beside him?

"I am here," she went on, "if you ever want someone to talk to. I know our betrothal is not in earnest, but I would like to be your friend." She leaned forward, and again he was shocked, because he could see she intended to kiss him. He made to move away, but she put her hand, feather light, on his cheek again. "It is not that sort of kiss," she said, and brushed her lips across his cheek. Indeed, he did not think a woman other than his mother had ever kissed him so sweetly, so innocently. He did not know how to feel. Part of him wanted her to kiss him again. Part of him wanted to flee.

He stood his ground.

"As I said, I am not leaving because of you."

Ridiculous woman. "You cannot leave at all. You shot the thief. The magistrate is undoubtedly on his way. He will have questions."

"I cannot afford to wait to answer them. He will not believe I shot the man anyway. He will think you did so, and I am claiming to have done it to save you from a charge of murder, though we have the man's pistol and the evidence that he shot first. Not to mention he was no thief."

Dominic shook his head. He was not certain he was following. He had assumed the thief would be one of his own men, but he was not shocked it was an outsider. "If he was not the thief, who was he?"

"One of the Maîtriser group. His name is Tueur."

Dominic stared at her. "You knew that man?"

"He and I are—were—old rivals. He's an assassin. We were both extremely fortunate to escape. He is very good at what he does, or rather, did."

"You are not sorry at all that you shot him?" The thought struck Dominic with all the weight of a wheelbarrow of bricks. He had thought she would feel guilt and repentance. He had thought she would leave not only because she feared him, but because she could not stay where she had killed a man. But, of course, she'd killed men before. Exactly how many? Ten? A dozen? Two dozen?

She'd spoken of traumas…

"Sorry? I am glad. If he had lived, we would all be in grave danger right now. As it is, we do not have much time."

"Foncé knows you are here."

She nodded. "He is not certain. He sent his assassin to kill me if he found me. If he knew without a doubt, he would have sent enough men to make certain I died. He might have killed everyone here, just because he could."

"But you killed his man. He doesn't know now."

"But when Tueur doesn't return, Foncé will suspect. I have to find him before that. You must stay behind to protect your mother and my aunt. Better yet, move them to another of Edgeberry's estates."

"The devil I will. I'm going with you. I can better protect them by destroying the threat."

"You are staying here." She began to march back to the stables. Apparently she considered their conversation at an end. He was of a different opinion.

"I am going with you."

"You will only be in my way. I do not need an impediment."

"Harsh words, if I really believed them. But I can help you. If nothing else, I can protect you." Of course, he hadn't protected her last night. But he would not think of that now. Perhaps, if he could save her from these assassins intent on killing her, he could make amends for his own behavior.

She'd reached the stable and gestured toward the
stalls. "Do you want to choose, or shall I?"

He ignored the question. "It will take me a few
moments to speak with Edgeberry's butler. I will
ensure footmen keep watch on the house all night and
escort the ladies wherever they wish to go. And we
cannot go without giving your aunt and my mother
some sort of explanation."

"You give them an explanation, then," she said,
turning to him, her pistol in her gloved hand. Bloody
hell! She was pointing it at him. "I said you are staying, and if I must ensure you stay, I will."

❦

Jane hated to make threats. She always made promises,
but pointing the pistol at Dominic was definitely a
threat. She would not shoot him, not even in the foot.
Still, she had to find some way to keep him here. She
could not allow him to risk his life in London with
her. As soon as she'd seen him in the stable, she'd
known he would be difficult. She'd thought that telling him about Tueur would help him to understand.
Apparently he had some misplaced sense of chivalry.
She didn't need his chivalry. She much preferred he
choke her than kill her with his kindness.

He looked at the pistol and then looked at her. His
dark eyes told her nothing, except there was no fear in
him. "Go ahead and shoot me then," he said. "That's
the only way you will keep me here or stop me from
following you."

She wanted to curse him aloud. She'd known
he would not be easily deterred. The man was

extraordinarily vexing. She should shoot him for that reason alone.

"I wouldn't even blame you for shooting me. I deserve it after last night."

Jane rolled her eyes. "You deserve it? Because you kissed me senseless? Because your touch made me want to do things I have never considered doing with another man? Risking what I have never been willing to risk before?" She lowered the pistol and stepped closer, trying to force her point through his thick skull. "We were both experiencing intense emotions, and yours triggered a memory. I have seen it before. Do you think what happened to you as a child makes me want you, the man, any less?"

She had said too much. She could see in his eyes the complete shock and disbelief. He really did think it mattered. He really did think his past defined him. If she'd believed that about herself, she couldn't have rolled out of bed in the morning.

She would have to change the way he thought about himself. But not today, not when she had to stop the Maîtriser group from overthrowing the government. Her love affair would have to wait until King and Country were safe again. Unfortunately, she had forgotten that she was dealing with an extremely obstinate and clever man. She'd lowered her pistol in the heat of her speech, and he took advantage of that now. He leaned forward and swiped it from her hand.

"No!" Damn this man who was neither friend nor enemy. She forgot to keep her guard up with him.

"I ask you to give me half an hour. That is all," he said.

"I am not negotiating with you!"

"I have your pistol."

She all but rolled her eyes. "As though you would shoot me. I can fetch another in London. You go to the house and arrange your footmen. I will be gone by the time you return." And they would see if he could catch her.

"In that case, you leave me no choice." He pocketed the pistol and reached for her. She was ready this time, and she kicked him soundly in the shin. But he was still stronger than she and quicker than she anticipated. Added to that, he was her betrothed. She couldn't exactly stick her dagger in his belly or break his nose, as she would have done with an actual attacker.

"Release me, or I promise you will regret it."

He'd all but carried her into one of the stalls. A brown horse blinked at her then continued to graze on feed. A line of rope hung just outside the stall, and he quickly went to work. She did not make it easy for him. She wiggled and darted, but he had too much experience in dealing with recalcitrant animals. He tied her quite easily, her arms locked at the wrist and held above her head. He allowed her some give, probably because he did not want her to stretch her wound, but she was secure. For the moment. She was cursing at him, and she saw him reach for his handkerchief, obviously considering gagging her, but deciding against it. Good. She would scream, and the grooms would untie her.

"I'm going to tell the grooms to stay out of the stable."

"I am going to make you extremely sorry," she said.

"I know you will." And then he leaned forward and kissed her forehead. She tried to smash his nose with a violent jerk of her head, but he moved back too quickly. "I will return in a half hour." He walked away.

"Griffyn!" she yelled. "Griffyn! Come back here!" No answer. Torture would be too good for the man. But he'd underestimated her. She could escape any situation. She needed only to locate the knots and… she looked up. The knot securing her arms was far out of her reach. She would have to manage the ones around her wrists. That would be difficult with her wrists pressed together. But Griffyn was not cruel. He had not tied her as tightly as he might. She worked her wrists, pulling and stretching, until she found a knot and began to work on it. If only she could reach her knife. But this would have to do. It would be time consuming, but standing here, waiting for him, would drive her mad. She should be on the way to London by now.

When the Maîtriser group was defeated, she would delight in overturning their betrothal. She did not care that such a thing would harm her reputation. If this was what men were like, then she could do without them. She didn't want to marry anyway. She didn't want children either.

At least, she never had before… But seeing Saint with child, seeing that children were a possibility for another agent, had made an impression. Now she found when she thought of babies, she did not feel quite so panicked. She actually felt a little pull of longing.

The horse she was sharing quarters with finished eating then and looked at her curiously. "Hello, horse," she said. "Stay over there." It was a large horse. She could barely see over its shoulder.

She started on the knots again. She worked the knot as best she could, then realized her gloves were making such a manipulation impossible. She struggled to remove them just as the horse grew braver. It took several steps closer. "I do not have carrots or apples or sugar or whatever it is you want from me," she told the horse.

It breathed warm air on her, sniffing at her gown. Its teeth closed on the fabric of her gown and tugged.

"Step back, horse!"

It raised its head, looked at her, and when she could not back her command with any action, it took her riding habit in its mouth again. Oh, this was humiliating. She could not even fend off a horse.

"That is not food," she told it, twisting away. "Stop. Boo! Boo!"

The horse looked up at her curiously.

"She's not scared of you."

Jane looked up at the thin, white-haired man standing in the stall doorway. He did not appear surprised to see a woman tied inside it. He did remove his hat out of—she assumed—respect. In her current position and with her riding habit now dirtied with horse saliva, she was hardly worthy of it. "I realize that," she said. "But as you can see, I have no other means of dissuading her."

"I do see that." He held out an apple, and the horse took it, munching happily. "I'm Old Connor."

"Jane Bonde. Would you mind untying me, Mr. Connor?"

"I would not, Miss Bonde, but I'm afraid Mr. Griffyn would have my head. I will stand here and make sure Little Molly doesn't accost you any further."

Little Molly? Good God. She could not imagine what Big Molly would look like. "I assure you no harm will come to you if you release me, Mr. Connor."

"It's Old Connor, miss. No *mister.*"

"Fine. But you can hardly leave a lady tied in a stall."

"I don't ask questions, Miss Bonde. I've learned to trust Mr. Griffyn over the years. He and I didn't always see eye to eye. But he's a smart man, and he has his reasons for what he does."

"He can have no reason for tying me. It is unpardonable!"

"Oh, I don't know about that." He scratched his head. It was still bare as he continued to press his hat to his chest. "I've known him since he was a boy. He doesn't generally act rashly. Taught him everything he knows about horses. He learned everything he could, taking it all in slow and deliberate like. He knew he wanted a free hand in this stable, and he made it so Lord Edgeberry couldn't refuse. The stable and these horses have prospered because of him. But for all that, I think he needs the horses more than they need him."

So she wasn't the only one who knew of Dominic's trauma. She wondered if he'd spoken of it to this man, or if Old Connor, like she, was merely deducing. Old Connor looked back. "Here's the man now. I've been keeping Little Molly away from her, sir."

"Thank you." Griffyn moved into sight. He'd changed and was now dressed in riding boots and coat.

"I see you rushed back to untie me," she said. "You look quite fashionable. Now, release me."

"One moment." He moved out of sight, and she heard him speaking quietly to Old Connor. The nerve of the man. Really! The nerve. How dare he leave her tied here while he had a leisurely conversation?

Finally, he returned, leaned up, and began to unravel the knots. She looked up, but when she looked down, she saw his gaze was on her. She also realized his body was pressed against hers. She took a shaky breath as heat flooded through her. Desire so strong she felt dizzy ripped through her. She wanted him to press her up against the wall of the stall and kiss her until she forgot everything but the feel of his mouth. "You're touching me," she murmured, wishing her voice did not sound quite so seductive.

"I don't mind it so much at the moment."

Her arms sagged, and he took her wrists in his hands and began on those knots.

"Would you like me to stop touching you?"

She knew what he meant. His body was still pressed against hers, though such intimacy was not necessary to release her hands. She wanted to say yes, but she could hardly catch her breath. She closed her eyes, trying to calm her mind, control her desire.

Then her wrists were free, and she opened her eyes again. He'd stepped back, and she resisted the urge to grab his coat and haul him up against her again. Instead, she swept from the stall without looking back. She would not allow desire to sway her from her purpose. She would not allow Dominic Griffyn to sway her. He might follow her now, but she would lose him at the first opportunity.

Thirteen

IT WAS NOT CHANGING HIS CLOTHING THAT HAD TAKEN Dominic the additional few moments Jane seemed to object to. He'd written to Edgeberry to come to Kenham Hall immediately and to bring additional footmen. Dominic hadn't liked leaving his mother and Lady Melbourne alone at Kenham Hall, but he saw the logic in going straight to the threat, rather than waiting for this Foncé to come to them. Jane was no fool, nor was she a coward. He might have wished she had less bravery. Time and again he'd watched her dive into danger without a second thought, and he wondered how she'd survived as long as she had. He wondered if she would survive until the wedding.

And then, as he rode beside her on the road to London, he wondered when he had started to think of marrying her as inevitable.

It should not have been inevitable, despite the efforts of his mother and Jane's uncle. They had done nothing indiscreet, not in public at least, and engagements could be called off. Such a thing was not done without consequences. He did not mind consequences, except for the embarrassment they would cause his family. He felt as though he was embarrassment enough at times without contributing more. He knew his mother did not see him that way, and he did not think his half brothers did, but Edgeberry was altogether different. The marquess would have preferred the bastard son of his wife respectably married and out of the public eye.

If Dominic called off the engagement, he would not only ruin Jane's reputation, he'd be quite prominently in the public eye. Everyone would assume there was some mark against Jane's character, and she would be virtually unmarriageable. Dominic did not want to marry, but he'd known when he accepted the betrothal that such an outcome was likely. He would not be the source of dishonor for any lady. He knew only too well the pain that came with Society's derision.

Jane would have to call it off, and while he did not think she had any such qualms about doing so, he also thought if she truly considered her options, she might decide marrying him was the best choice from a long list of undesirable choices. She had to marry someone. Why not him?

Because your touch made me want to do things I have never considered doing with another man? Risking what I have never been willing to risk before?

She wanted him. It still shocked and confused him. She seemed to suspect the truth about him, and she wanted him anyway. There was no doubt he wanted her, but he could not even allow himself to consider lying with her. Look what had happened the night before. The nightmares were bad enough when he was sleeping. He had never experienced one when awake, and he did not want to risk it again.

He could not go back to that time, to the little boy he'd been. He could not risk it, not even for the chance to bed Jane Bonde, not even for the chance at a normal life—a wife and children. His life would never be normal. He could never hope to have what other men had. It was better that he confine his needs to the occasional willing woman who would not question his rules—a woman he could touch but who would not touch him except when his cock finally demanded release and either his own hand or that of his lover's was necessary.

Dominic had never paid for a woman. In London, he'd seen firsthand how respectable women were reduced to selling their bodies. A woman's body was not something to be bartered, in his opinion. People were not commodities.

But what would he do with a wife? If he married Jane, he would not be able to keep himself from her bed. What then? Would he strangle her unwillingly? Pound her to a bloody pulp while in the throes of some memory? Force her to kill him to protect herself?

In the fading light, he caught the glint of Jane's blue eyes as she peered back at him, and his chest tightened. Despite the risks, he still wanted her.

She'd insisted they pause this afternoon in order to ensure they would reach London as night fell. He suspected she also needed a brief respite from riding, since she moved stiffly, favoring her injury. But she would not allow them to tarry long. They were nearing London proper now, and the travelers on the road were still plenty. Farmers and country laborers left the city for the night, while those in the *ton* who had been spending the day in the country returned. She had been right to wait until now. No one watching the roads would have been able to spot her. There were simply too many people traveling to and from the capital.

They rode straight to Piccadilly and the offices of the Barbican group. Jane swept inside, removing her hat and gloves as she walked, and he followed in her wake. He observed that men made way for her, their eyes watching her, not with desire but respect. Their gazes fell on him with curiosity.

She led him down the hallway and to the central area where they had been before. Tonight it was all but empty of men. However, there was a woman.

"Butterfly," Jane said, stopping her march toward Melbourne's office. Dominic glanced at the woman rising from a table covered in documents. She must have been a spy if she was here, but she looked like any woman he might have passed on Bond Street. She was attractive enough, with her dark hair and large brown eyes. She wore a gown that accentuated the lushness of her figure and yet was still perfectly respectable. She was several years older than Jane, but she had an air of youth and excitement about her.

"Bonde!" The two women embraced, and Dominic saw the other woman's gaze flick to him.

"This is Mr. Griffyn," Jane said without looking at him. "He insisted on accompanying me." Jane gestured to him carelessly. "Lady Keating, Mr. Griffyn."

Lady Keating moved forward and held out her

gloved hand. Dominic took it and bowed slightly. He was never one for these formalities. "A pleasure, Mr. Griffyn. Thank you for returning her safely to us." She moved toward Jane again. "But why have you returned?"

"Foncé sent Tueur to kill me."

"Tueur?" Lady Keating asked, her brow furrowing.

"Foncé's assassin," a male voice said as a wall of a man stepped into the room from the direction of Melbourne's office. He glanced at Griffyn, assessing him, then slid his gaze to Jane. "Bonde. I didn't think you had clearance to return."

"And when did you become my superior, Baron?"

"Your uncle is in the field. I have command until he returns." He stepped toward Dominic. "I don't think we've had the pleasure, sir."

"Dominic Griffyn."

"Ah." The man's sharp green eyes returned to Jane. "Your betrothed. Should he be here?"

"No, but he refused to stay behind."

"You should have stayed behind."

"I was only endangering everyone by remaining. I can do more good here."

The man seemed about to argue, but Lady Keating spoke. "We do need help. Every available agent is searching London for Foncé. We are no closer to finding him, but I thought if we uncovered his plan, we might be able to intercept him before he could carry it out."

"And what are these?" Jane gestured to the papers littering the table.

"Every piece of correspondence we have

intercepted in the last year. I thought perhaps if I went through it…"

"Yes." Jane was nodding and moving toward the papers. Dominic watched her, saw the way she continued to favor her injured side, and the stiffness in her movements. He caught Baron watching her too.

"Bonde, you were sent to the country to recover from your injury," Baron said, his gaze meeting Dominic's. "I do not think sufficient time has passed for you to recover."

"I'm fine."

Dominic shook his head. He'd be damned if he was going to allow her to come all this way and then fall ill because she refused to listen to her body when it was in pain. "You need to rest. You did not sleep last night and just rode all the way from Richmond."

"He's right," Baron said. "As your superior—"

"You are not my superior," she said, eyes blazing.

"As your temporary superior, I insist you rest for at minimum three hours before working."

"I can read papers. That is not taxing."

But Dominic could see Baron would not allow her to naysay him. He stood firm, arms crossed over his wide chest. "You are ordered to the dormitory at least until nine. I'll have provisions sent to you. Griffyn, I am afraid I cannot allow you to leave. You know too much at the moment. If you were to fall into Foncé's hands, it could be disastrous."

"I have no intention of leaving. I'm here to protect Miss Bonde."

Jane rolled her eyes and shook her head, but Baron nodded. "Good. Jane knows the way to the dormitory."

❧

Jane stared at Baron for a long moment. She narrowed her eyes, willing him to back down. Ridiculous man. Did he really think she did not know her own limits? And did it really matter at the moment? So what if she was in pain? It was the least she could endure to do away with Foncé once and for all.

Baron leveled his gaze at her, and she let out a sigh and started for the door. She didn't really care if Griffyn accompanied her or not—which was a complete fabrication. She wanted him to leave, go far away from her. He was a constant distraction. She should never have allowed matters to progress as they had the night before.

The country was in jeopardy, and this was no time to think about bedding a man. And yet her thoughts kept returning to the way it had felt when his lips pressed against hers, when his hands caressed her, when his body molded to hers. He was strong and hard, not an ounce of fat on him. And those shadowed eyes turned impossibly large and dark when he was aroused. She could lose herself in those eyes.

She led him down a flight of stairs into the dormitory area. Kitchens and workrooms were also on this level, and she was pleasantly surprised when she turned from the stone steps and spotted Q in the corridor. Her workshop was on this level, and she was about to turn into it. She wore a plain brown gown with an apron over it, her curly hair pulled into a messy bun at the back of her head. She was petite and thin, with a pointy chin and large eyes that peered at the world from behind large spectacles. Q paused when she spotted Jane, smiling at her friend and then allowing her smile to fade when she spotted Griffyn. Jane almost rolled her eyes. She knew that look. Probably every woman who saw Griffyn gave him that look, knowingly or not.

Q pushed her spectacles onto her nose and darted her attention quickly back to Jane. "Bonde! It is good to see you."

"Miss Qwillen. I did not realize you were still here." Jane gestured to Dominic. "This is Mr. Griffyn."

He gave a short bow. "I am Miss Bonde's betrothed."

Jane felt like punching him. Was it necessary to tell *everyone* about the betrothal?

"Congratulations!" Q said. She looked at Jane, a question in her eyes. "I had no idea. Does Moneypence know?"

Jane frowned in confusion. Why should Q care about Moneypence? "I suppose. Why?"

Q fluttered her hands. "No reason. Come. I have something you simply *must* see." She started for her workroom then glanced over her shoulder. "You too, Mr. Griffyn."

"Miss Qwillen is in charge of weaponry design," Jane told him before they followed.

"Interesting," he said, his voice low and close to her ear.

She felt a rush of desire and immediately countered it with indignation. "Why? Because she is a woman?"

"No." He tucked a strand of hair behind her ear. "Because I had never before considered that weapons needed to be designed." He held out a hand, as though *he* was inviting *her* into Q's workshop. Vexing man.

"Weaponry design is an old and fascinating pursuit," Q said as she bustled behind a long table covered with wheels and cogs and spring of all shapes. Jane took a moment simply to gaze about the room, noting any changes. She'd always loved Q's workshop. She remembered when Miss Qwillen had joined the Barbican group. She was Jane's age or a year or two older, and the two had immediately become friends. Jane had sat for many hours in the workshop, watching Q work.

It was a rather small room, about the size of a parlor or a small sitting room, but far less comfortable. The stone walls and floors were bare of any and all decoration. No rugs or paintings in here. The surfaces of the plain wooden tables, two against one wall and one very large table in the center, were covered with pieces of metal, string, various tools, and jars with cryptic labels like *innards*.

Shelves lined the back wall of the room, housing books and more jars, as well as the area Q had warned Jane she should never touch. That shelf held powder and explosives. A fire burned in a hearth on the other side of the room, and jars and vials were suspended above it by a metal contraption. The contents of the containers bubbled and hissed.

"What do you have in those?" Jane asked, indicating the hearth.

Q glanced at them as though only just seeing them. "A witch's brew. But I have something I want to show you." She beckoned the two of them toward the shelves in the back, toward the area usually restricted. She reached onto the shelf and removed a quill. The large swan feather was quite lovely, and Jane noted it had a metal nib, which meant it was a rather expensive pen.

"Do you know what this is?" she asked.

"A pen," Dominic answered. Jane knew better than to assume anything Q possessed was as simple as what it appeared to be.

"Very good," Q said with a smile. Jane was suspicious of that smile. "Would you like to write something with it?" Q looked at Jane. Jane shook her head. She was not risking it, no matter how much Q smiled. "Mr. Griffyn?"

He took the quill, and Q produced parchment and ink. He dipped the metal nib in the ink and pressed the point to paper. Jane cringed and scooted back slightly. But Dominic scrawled his name on the parchment without incident.

"Anything strike you as odd about the pen or ink?" Q asked innocently. Jane took another step back.

"No. It appears ordinary enough."

"Good. Watch this." Q produced a large ring with several keys hanging from it. She walked to a book lying at a forty-five-degree angle on one of the shelves and slowly shifted it to the opposite angle. A panel in the wall at the back of the room sprang open. Jane jumped and ducked. Dominic gave her a curious look, but Jane took her time climbing back to her feet. Q went to the panel, inserted one of the keys into the lock hidden within, and the rest of the panel opened. A door had been hidden behind the panel. It was a thick stone door with a large peephole at eye level.

"What is that?" Jane asked.

"My secret chamber," Q said. "Haven't you seen it before?"

"No." And Jane was not so certain she wanted to see it now.

"Why do you need a secret chamber?" Dominic asked. "The entire building is secret."

Q gave him a look that spoke volumes of her opinion of civilians. "Because some secrets cannot be shared even with spies." She inserted another key, pushed the heavy door open, and stepped inside. She lit several wall sconces and then placed the pen on a small wooden table in the center of the room. Other than the table, the room was bare. The plain stone walls and the square shape reminded Jane of a gaol cell. She did take note of one aspect of the room. The walls were blackened in irregular patches. If she had moved closer, she might have inspected the black and determined its origin, but Jane was not stepping into that room.

"Watch carefully," Q said. She lifted the pen from the table and broke the metal nib. "One."

"Oh!" Jane cried. What a waste.

"Two, three." Q reached the door to the room and closed it. "Four, five, six—watch through the peephole. Eight."

"What happens at ten?" Jane asked.

"You will see. And ten!"

A small spark leapt to life at the point where the quill's tip had broken. Jane winced as the spark became a black plume of smoke, and then a burst of light caused her to raise her arms to shield her eyes. The building shook, and she stumbled into Dominic, who caught her and pulled her down, covering her with his body. Despite the fact that she was shaking, she smiled at his chivalry. She spent far too much time among spies, and they were too focused on their missions to worry about antiquated notions such as chivalry.

When the floor stopped shaking and all was quiet, Dominic moved aside and pulled Jane to her feet. Q was smiling at them indulgently. Dominic did not look quite so amused. "What the hell was that?"

"Exploding quill. Impressive, isn't it?"

"Yes," Jane agreed.

"No. I was writing with that pen a moment ago. What if I'd pressed too hard and broken the tip?" He peered through the peephole, and Jane followed suit. Oh, dear. Not only the pen but the table had splintered into a thousand pieces, and more black marks marred the stone walls.

"I suppose we would have had to make a run for it," Q said calmly. "That is why I used a delay feature."

Dominic blinked at her. "You are mad."

"I want one," Jane said.

Dominic rounded on her. "You are both mad!"

"I thought you might," Q said, ignoring Dominic and moving toward her shelves again.

"You cannot think to traipse about London with a pen that might explode at any moment."

Jane smiled at him. "I promise to be careful."

"And I have just the thing," Q said, holding out a slim, rectangular wooden box. "This is a case to protect the pen." She opened it, and another ordinary quill, this one made with a peacock feather, lay inside, cushioned by velvet one might see in a jeweler's box.

"Perfect!" Jane said, taking the box and slipping it into her reticule.

"Yes," Dominic drawled. "I feel safer already."

"Now," said Q, "off to the dormitories with you. I have more work to do." She led Jane and Griffyn to the door, but when Griffyn stepped out, Q pulled Jane back inside. "Oh, I almost forgot! I made the repairs to your fan!" she said loudly—far louder than Jane's proximity to her required.

"I will be just a moment," Jane told Griffyn.

He shrugged. "I am more than happy to wait outside the workshop."

Jane frowned at him, and when she turned back to the room, Q pushed the fan, which had a handle equipped with a magnifying glass, into her hand. "Thank you."

"Do endeavor to be more careful with it," Q said.

"Yes, the next time I'm forced to jump from a window onto an awning, I will be certain to protect the fan."

Q nodded, looking thoughtful. "You've led a dangerous life, Jane."

Jane opened her mouth then closed it again. She didn't quite know how to respond to that statement. It was certainly true, but it was so true, that stating the fact seemed almost ridiculous.

"Do you ever wish there was something"—Q wiggled her fingers—"more in your life?"

Jane narrowed her eyes. "Like morning calls and evenings at the theater?"

Q smiled at her. "No, not that sort of thing, but perhaps your betrothal is a good thing. There is more to life than the Barbican, Jane."

Jane laughed. "So says the woman still here long past dark."

But Q didn't give her a rueful smile as Jane expected. "You are right, and I plan to make a change. I don't want to end up alone. I don't want to crawl into a cold bed the rest of my life with no one to hold me."

Jane gaped at her. In all the time she'd known Q, the woman had never so much as mentioned a man. Now she wanted one in her bed?

"Do not look so shocked," Q said with a laugh. "I am a woman." She pointed at Jane. "And so are you. Don't always subordinate the woman to the agent." And with those words, Q retreated to her bomb room. Jane didn't know if that was the term Q used, but it was certainly how she'd think of that small chamber henceforth.

Jane turned to step out into the hallway, but her feet didn't move. She thought about Baron and his wife, and then Wolf and Saint. Did she have to choose between being an agent and being a woman? Being Bonde and being a wife? What would her life be in ten years or twenty, if she lived that long? Would she go home to an empty chamber, an empty bed? Would she never know the feel of a man's body sleeping beside her, the sound of her child's laughter?

There is more to life than the Barbican.

But there hadn't been more to her life up until this point. Her uncle had trained her as an agent from the very first. She'd never had any choice but to spy for the Barbican. No one had ever asked her if she wanted a normal life, if she wanted a husband and children. She hadn't ever considered the option. She loved being an agent, but wouldn't she love being a wife and mother too?

Jane moved into the doorway and peered into the corridor. A little way down the hall, Griffyn leaned negligently against the wall, arms crossed over his chest, eyes closed. Just looking at him made her heart beat faster, made her belly flutter. She wanted him. She'd not denied that, but up until this moment she had been unwilling to accept the truth of the situation they were in.

She was going to marry Dominic Griffyn. She could fight it. She could argue. But her uncle and his mother would have their way. Even Griffyn seemed resigned to their union. The longer she looked at him, the more she wondered why she fought it. Why not marry him? Why not take him to her bed, make lovely dark-eyed children with him? Was she going to risk her life for M forever? Didn't she deserve love and affection?

Of course, the question remained as to whether Griffyn was willing or able to give her either, but she had faced worse odds before and come out ahead.

He opened his eyes then, and his gaze met hers. The look sent a slow spiral of heat through her, centering in her lower belly and pulsing. Oh, yes. She wanted him. And rules or not, she would have him.

She took a shaky breath and moved into the corridor. Griffyn said nothing, merely followed her. She could feel his presence at her back, feel his warmth in the cold stone passage. Finally, they reached the end of the hallway. She opened a door on the left, and lifting one of the candles burning in a sconce outside, brought it into the room. She made a quick study of the dormitory, noting the rows and rows of simple bed frames. Only one had any sort of mattress upon it. The others were bare, the lattice work of ropes that comprised their innards exposed.

She settled the candle into a sconce and eyed the one acceptable bed. It had been laid with white sheets and a plain white blanket. One flat pillow leaned against the open iron headboard. "It must be cleaning day," Jane said, feeling him step into the room behind her. Her entire body seemed to vibrate with awareness of him. "The maids have taken all of the bedding out to beat and wash."

"I'm not sleeping with you," he said.

"I believe that is my line," she said. She turned and found him so close to her that she almost bumped into him. Despite his words a moment before, he didn't move back. She wanted desperately to reach out and touch him, stroke his cheek, allow her fingers to wander from his jaw to the open collar of his lawn shirt. But she knew she could not touch him. It seemed so unfair, so impossibly cruel. In that moment, she wanted him more than she'd ever wanted anything— more than she even wanted to capture Foncé.

He shook his head, reading the look she hadn't bothered to disguise. "Do not look at me that way."

"What way?"

"Like you want to devour me."

"You're an attractive man, Mr. Griffyn. One could hardly blame me for wanting to devour you."

"And you're a beautiful woman, Miss Bonde—"

She raised her brows. "Do you really think so?"

He frowned at her. "You know you are."

"It's nice to be told," she said, moving a little closer. "It's arousing to know that the man I want, wants me."

He shook his head, but he still didn't back away. "This is not going to happen."

"What if I agree to your rules?" Her gaze darted to the tail of his neckcloth dangling from his coat pocket. She reached for it. "What if I promise not to touch you?" She wound the cloth around her hands, binding them loosely. She saw his chest rise, saw him take a slow, shuddering breath.

"Those rules..." He had to pause and swallow. "They aren't for you. You're—" He gestured to her vaguely.

"Your betrothed?" she supplied. She moved closer, so if either of them breathed deeply they would brush against each other.

"Yes."

She nodded. "When we marry, you will have to bed me at some point, Dominic."

"*When* we marry?"

She shrugged. "I know when I'm defeated. Maybe I want to be defeated." She rose on tiptoes until her lips brushed against his. "Kiss me, Dominic. Break your rules for me. Again."

Fourteen

BLOODY HELL. HOW COULD HE RESIST HER WHEN SHE was looking at him with those large blue eyes, when her lush body was all but pressed against him, when that enticing violet scent teased his nose and made him want to bury his face in her hair, her shoulder, the valley between her breasts? His gaze flicked to his cravat wound around her wrists. She could free herself from the bindings if she but maneuvered her wrists, and yet there was something impossibly erotic about having her bound and offering herself to him. Oh, yes, he wanted her. He wanted her like he'd never wanted any woman…and she *had* agreed to his rules.

But could he make her follow them? She was his future wife, not some barmaid. And if he did not ask her to follow his rules, would he be able to continue, no matter how much he desired her?

"Kiss me, Dominic," she purred, and he gave in, pressing his lips so lightly to hers that neither of them was fully satisfied. He should stop this now. He needed more time to think, to plan how this marriage would work. But while his mind wanted time, his body wanted hers. He found his hands coming up to cup her face, slide in her hair as he lowered his lips to hers to take her completely. Their mouths met in a hot, passionate fusion of lips and tongues. She allowed him to ravish her mouth, and when he would withdraw, she caught his tongue and sucked it gently. His whole body exploded with fiery desire, and he had to break the kiss, step back, take a breath.

"I'm sorry," she said. "You didn't like that?"

"I like it." His voice was husky and low. He was staring at her, his gaze dipping to her bodice, his hands aching to take her breasts in his palms.

"And yet you pulled away."

He nodded. "I want you. But on my terms."

He thought she would walk away, would give him one of her perfect scowls, but she merely raised a brow. "Then take me. On your terms."

He moved toward her, and she put her hands between them. "Be gentle with me, Dominic. I've never done this before."

"Nor have I." He put his hands on her waist, drawing her close, and felt her body go rigid.

"What do you mean?"

He looked at her face, saw her look of disbelief.

"I know you've been with women. I know your reputation."

He nodded. "To hell with my reputation," he said. "You're the only woman I've kissed or allowed to kiss me. You're the only woman I've considered…" He paused, not certain how to say this delicately.

But she understood him. "You're a virgin?"

He wasn't a virgin. No one who had done the

things he'd done could be a virgin. But he'd never actually penetrated a woman, thrust himself inside her, made her his, and so he supposed what she said was true, to a point.

"Yes."

"Then we will figure this out together."

He refrained from telling her there was not much he needed to figure out. He knew what he wanted. He knew even without ever having had it. But when he would have reached for her again, she turned and presented him with her back. "Help me remove this gown."

He tried to step back, but the wall was behind him. "Why?" Ridiculous question. He knew why. He wanted her out of the gown, wanted her bare before him.

She looked at him over her shoulder, her lashes lowered over eyes that were almost violet. "It's terribly uncomfortable. The pins are sticking me," she lied.

"We cannot have that." He motioned for her to turn around again, and she complied without saying anything further. He had no idea how women's garments worked. He reached for the back of her gown and immediately hesitated. He saw no buttons or ties. How was the thing fastened together?

"You have to remove the pins," she said.

"I know." Pins, right. But where were the dashed pins? He narrowed his eyes at the thin line of gold. Ah. Not stitches. Those were the pins. He reached for one and plucked it out. The gown remained stubbornly closed. He plucked another out and another, revealing the swath of pale skin at the base of her neck. Dominic took a deep breath and tried not to notice how soft it looked, tried not to imagine how she would shiver if he pressed his lips to it. He needed time to think. It seemed everything happened too quickly. He wanted to bed her, but what then? Could he take her without the nightmares grasping him in their clutches and taking hold with a vengeance?

He pulled another pin and noted his hands shook slightly. How many damned pins held this gown together? At this rate, it would take him hours to remove it. He pulled another pin, and the gown widened to reveal the space between her shoulder blades. She had a small freckle there, and he wanted to touch it, kiss it. Instead, he attempted to pull another pin, and all of the pins he held tumbled to the ground.

They made no sound, but Jane looked down, then over her shoulder at him. "Are you feeling well?"

"Perfectly well. Turn around."

She turned, and he thought about retrieving the pins. No, he would fetch them later. He wanted this task completed. He pulled two more pins, and then wondered why the devil he wanted to finish this. He'd revealed some pretty underthing that clearly held her breasts in place. A light pink ribbon circled it, and he could imagine how it would look, the small pink bow nestled at the valley of her breasts. Her bodice gaped now. Thank God he was standing behind her. Or perhaps he should curse God. He had never noticed how lovely the rounded slope of a woman's shoulder could be, or how alluring was the slim tapering of her waist. He pulled the last pin, and the bodice of the gown fell open.

She unwound the cravat from her wrists and allowed the garment to fall to the floor. Her hands were free now, but she still held the neckcloth, still refrained from reaching for him. She stood before him, wearing only her skirt now and the underthings, which seemed rather ineffectual, as they were so sheer he could see her pale skin through the linen.

She turned, and he forgot to take a step back. His gaze dropped immediately to the pale pink bow, which was indeed nestled at the perfect curve of her breasts. The underthing pushed them up slightly, so half moons peeked out from the lace and ribbon. It would take more than a tug on that ribbon to reveal her to his gaze, but he wanted to tug it nonetheless. When his gaze finally met hers, she was watching him. Her eyes were dark and hungry. She wanted him as much as he did her.

He closed his eyes. He would resist. He had to resist because...bloody hell. Why did he have to resist?

"Could you help me?" she asked, voice low and husky.

He opened his eyes. She was looking down at her skirt and tugging at a string. "I cannot work out this knot." She continued tugging it.

"Let me see."

Ignoring him—why had she even asked for his help anyway?—she yanked on the skirt. She was probably tightening the knot and making it worse. "Ah! So frustrating."

"Move aside." He pushed her hands away and stepped close, leaning down to take a look at the knot. It was only knotted twice, and he quickly undid it then looked up. His gaze was at a level with her breasts. He blinked as her skirt fell in a puddle at her feet, leaving her clad only in flimsy underthings. He forced himself to look at her face. "Is this a ploy to seduce me?"

"Did it work?"

He was as hard as a rock. His gaze drifted to her hands, still gripping the neckcloth. She followed his look and wound the material around her wrists again. "Better?"

Dominic stared at her. Did she have any idea how beautiful she was? How much he wanted to touch her? Dominic clenched his hands together to stop himself from dragging her into his arms, to stop his hands from sinking into her thick hair, caressing her soft skin.

"You could tie this more tightly," she said. "Make me powerless." She lifted her hands. "You could tie me to the bed, then you'd know I wouldn't break the rules. I couldn't touch you."

Dominic blinked. "I am not going to tie you." She was a virgin, for God's sake. He wasn't going to take her maidenhead with her tied to the bed.

"I trust you."

The words speared straight through him. No one had ever said that to him. No one had ever looked at him the way she did, like he was absolutely delicious. No one had ever trusted him enough to give up all power.

"This is daft." But he was imagining her tied to the bed, and his breathing had already quickened. Her hands would be secured above her head, forcing her breasts up. He could kiss them, kiss her. Anywhere.

"Loosen this knot." She turned to him, presenting

her back. Without thinking, he loosened the knot, and the heavy garment over her midsection sagged. She pulled and tugged and then slid it over her hips, taking the garment she called a petticoat with it. When she rose again, she wore only what looked like a nightgown, except it ended above her ankles. She had small ankles, slim and delicate.

"Do you want me to remove my chemise?" she asked.

Yes. "No. Do you…" He swallowed. "Do you have anything underneath?"

"No. I've never stood naked before a man Dominic. But I trust you." There it was again. That word. *Trust.* She freed one of her hands and reached for a white ribbon he hadn't noticed just above her breasts. "It scares me to stand naked and vulnerable before you. And that is how I know I must do it." With a tug, she pulled the ribbon, and the chemise opened then slid down her body.

Dominic realized too late what she intended. Too late, he decided he would not look. He would turn away and tell her to dress. He was not going to tie her naked to a bed. He swallowed. No matter how much the idea appealed.

But his eyes and his brain were not in agreement. His body had sided with his eyes, and he could not look away. She was the most beautiful creature he had ever seen—all porcelain and pink and gold. She was round and soft and everything a woman should be. He had seen the female form before, but always in paintings or statues or in tantalizing glimpses during a stolen rendezvous. He had never gazed at a woman like this, a woman who looked at him with a mixture of desire and uncertainty. A woman who wanted him, despite what she must have deduced had happened to him.

He had never wanted any of those women the way he wanted this one. Need burned in him. It terrified him too. But, as she'd said, perhaps the fear was something to confront rather than turn away from.

She backed toward the bed, settling herself so her back was against the pillow. She held out the cravat and wound her hands into the iron headboard. "I'm ready."

He shook his head. Everything in him wanted to go to her, but he resisted. "I can't tie you. I can't make you powerless."

"Will you stop if I ask?"

"Yes."

"Then I am not powerless. I cannot do it myself. Tie me."

As though he were walking in his sleep, he went to her, took the cravat and wound it around the iron frame and then her wrist. He tied it, but she looked up at him and shook her head. "Tightly."

"I don't want to hurt you."

She smiled. "I'm not so fragile."

Dominic tightened the fastening until he knew she could not free herself. Then he repeated it with the other wrist. And then he stepped back and gazed at her. He could have looked at her forever. She was that beautiful. She sat as demurely as could be expected, naked and tied to the headboard. She watched him watch her, and finally, she said, "You can touch me. I can't touch you back, not with my hands."

He moved forward, knelt on the bed. Raising his hand, he pressed it to her cheek. He leaned forward and kissed her gently. She moved her lips against his and sighed softly. His hand slipped down to her jaw, her neck, her shoulder, and then slid down her long, silky arm.

He repeated the gesture with her other arm, still kissing her. "Is that all you want to touch?" she asked. "Only my arms?"

"No."

"Where else do you want to touch me? Show me."

She was giving him permission, but he did not have to comply. He could move away. He could stop. His hand shook slightly as he moved it over her breast. He hovered several inches above her flesh, and she drew in a breath of anticipation. Her nipple hardened and peaked, and she whispered, "Please." He couldn't resist her. He filled his hand with her breast, her warm, ripe flesh pushing eagerly against his palm.

He bent to kiss her again, kneading her flesh and listening to the soft mewling sounds of pleasure she could not contain. His mouth dipped to take her nipple and rub it along his tongue. And then he took the other one, suckling until her hips rose and pressed against his hard flesh. His hands skated down her body, worshipping the curves and the indentions, careful of the wound on her belly, until he slid to the juncture of her thighs. He had never taken his pleasure in this moist place. He knew what to do. He knew the mechanics of the act that caused bastards to be born. But Jane was his betrothed. A child of theirs would not be a bastard.

He cupped her sex then slipped a finger so it lay against that warm wetness. She moaned and arched her hips, and he slipped inside her. His cock ached, but his entire being rebelled against taking her when she was bound. He did not have to complete the act, though. He could give her pleasure. He stroked her, in and out, and she moved against him. He knew she liked this. He knew what to do to please a woman in this way.

"The way you touch me," she gasped. "I didn't think…didn't know."

He felt his control waning at the sound of arousal in her husky voice. He used a knee to nudge her thighs apart and gazed down. She was pink and gold, and his hand was dark against her flesh. He touched a small nub at the apex of her folds, and she cried out. He glanced up at her, amazed at her responsiveness.

"Oh, yes. Touch me there," she said, pushing against him.

He slid a finger over her, and she cried out again. Her face was flushed now, her eyes closed, her wrists straining against her bindings. Could he have done this without binding her? He was in control. She could not touch him, and yet she had so much more control than she could ever realize. He was having difficulty restraining himself. He flicked a finger over her again, and she stilled. Her whole body stiffened, and she gasped out his name.

He had never heard his name said in such a way. There was desire and pleasure and…love in every syllable. He watched her climax slide through her, and could not help but fall in love with her. Had any woman ever been as beautiful as this one? In the throes of ecstasy she took his breath away. He forgot, for the moment, his own needs and desires, and knew only that he wanted to give her more pleasure. He wanted to feel her stiffen, see her face when she found pleasure.

She opened her eyes, and they were impossibly dark and blue. She gave him a lazy smile. "You have done that before," she said.

"Have I? I don't remember anyone but you."

She smiled, and he watched her. The color in her cheeks was high, and her lips were red and slightly swollen from his kisses.

"Oh, yes. I feel extremely wanton now. You are far too handsome. One look at you and I begin to imagine your hands on me."

This was intriguing. He did not think he was particularly attractive. Not when one considered his blond, fair-skinned half brothers. Not when one considered her perfect blue-eyed beauty. He was dark and Gypsy in appearance. He looked at his dark hand against her thigh and felt as though his touch sullied her. But she wanted his hands on her. "Where have you imagined me touching you?" he asked.

"All over. But it's not just your hands I imagine. Your mouth and your body feature quite prominently in my daydreams. I want to feel your body pressed against mine."

Her invitation was tempting. She was ready for him. He could loosen the fall on his trousers and plunge into her. He thought if he could last and he could move the right way, he might be able to please her again.

And perhaps if he concentrated on the feel of her

body beneath him, the scent of violets, he would not think of the past. The nightmares would keep at bay. He took a deep breath. "Are you certain you want this? It is not something either of us can undo once it is done."

"I want you, Dominic," she said, her voice caressing him because her hands could not. "Make me yours."

He reached for his trousers and then paused. He could not do this with her restrained. He wanted her to be a willing participant. He wanted to trust her, wanted to give himself to her as she'd given herself to him. He reached for her bindings and tugged at first one and then the other. She watched him, brows arched. "You don't have to do that."

"I want to."

She lowered her hands. "May I touch you?"

He nodded, wanting her touch and fearing the nightmares lurking in the shadows. She wrapped her arms around him, bringing his mouth to hers. She kissed him slowly but with building urgency as her hands tangled in his hair and cupped his jaw. He'd never been touched like this, with gentleness and love and passion all combined. He felt his emotions churning and tamped them down. He would not allow himself to think too much. He would only feel.

Her hands slid down his body, which was still fully clothed, and cupped his erection. She slid her hand up and down it, then loosened the fall on his trousers so he sprang into the warmth of her palm. He'd never allowed himself to be touched like this, but he gave her freedom. Jane kissed him, stroked him, loved him. He had not known one could be touched this way.

And then she raised her hips, and he felt her warmth, knew he was poised to enter her. He hesitated just a moment and slid partly inside. She stiffened, and he looked into her eyes. "They say there is pain the first time." He did not know how to bed a virgin. He did not know how to bed any woman. He pulled away, but she clutched at his shoulders.

"It has passed. Don't stop. If you go slowly, I think I shall be well."

How the devil was he supposed to proceed slowly, when every single one of his instincts told him to drive into her with hard, fast thrusts? He clenched his jaw and moved inside her again. She was so tight and so small. He could not catch his breath for the fierce desire he felt. He paused again until he felt her body relax, and then slid farther into her until he was embedded to the hilt. She stiffened, and he waited. He was in agony of waiting. Finally, after a bloody eternity, she murmured in his ear. "Yes. Now."

He needed no further prodding, no instruction. He allowed his body to move as it would, to follow instinct and desire. She stiffened again, and he waited until she relaxed and sighed. He moved again, and this time when she stiffened, he could not stop.

"I can't..." He clenched his jaw, but his body had taken over. He thrust one last time and felt his seed spill into her. He had not intended to allow that. He had thought to spill his seed on her belly or the blanket. But now it was done. Now he lay panting, his head on her shoulder, her arms around him.

She held him tenderly, stroked his back, whispered his name. He wanted to tell her he did not deserve this sweetness, this gentleness, but he was afraid if he spoke, his voice would break. And so he held on and concentrated on the steady, rapid pounding of his heart.

❧

The act had not hurt as much as Jane had anticipated. It had been uncomfortable, but there had also been moments when she sensed she might have felt pleasure if it had not all been so new. If she had not been so concerned for him. His breathing had slowed now, and he pulled back to look at her. His dark eyes were even darker. The candle lighting the room had burned down, and the dormitory was darker than it had been.

She wanted to say something. She was afraid she wanted to tell him that she loved him. She did not even know when she had fallen. Perhaps in the stable, when she'd realized how vulnerable he was. Perhaps when he'd kissed her as Farrar stitched her. Perhaps the first time she saw him. She could not tell him, even if she wanted to. What would he say to that revelation? He would probably leap off her and run screaming for Piccadilly and the first coach he could take out of London. She was going to marry this man. She would have the rest of her life to tell him how she felt.

If she could keep him safe until Foncé was captured. If she could avoid becoming Foncé's next victim.

"I apologize for any pain—"

She put a finger over his lips, half-expecting him to protest that she was touching him. But he allowed it. "I am not so fragile. And I did not feel pain. I felt a little discomfort. I am certain, given time and practice, that will fade."

"I…did not take precautions."

She furrowed her brow, uncertain what he meant. At times she thought the most difficult aspect of being a lady was having to talk around every taboo subject.

"We may have to marry now." He pulled away, and she felt the loss of him keenly. But he did not leave her side. He lay beside her, facing her, his head propped on an elbow.

"I told you, I already intended to marry you. Even before…" She gestured to the bed, noticing she was still nude and still uncovered. She had never been overly modest, but she still found it strange that she should not be uncomfortable to be so exposed before him. Especially when he was still dressed and she had seen almost nothing of his body.

He closed his eyes. "You do not want to marry me, Jane. If you only knew…"

When he did not go on, she said, "If I only knew what? Tell me, and then I shall know. We can put your fears to rest." She met his dark gaze, and for a long moment she thought he might actually tell her. She saw the conflict, saw the war within him. And then he closed his eyes.

"I cannot. It is not a fit subject for a lady."

"I assure you," she said, "I have discussed many subjects not suitable for ladies. We have just done something many might consider not acceptable for ladies. I am no saint. Just a woman. You can tell me. Anything." She yawned, her sudden fatigue surprising her.

He touched her stitches, and she realized he had been careful of them earlier. How could she not fall in love with him when he was so careful with her? "You must be exhausted," he said, moving to sit.

But she cupped his neck and brought him back down beside her. "I am. Stay with me. Sleep with me."

He gave her an indulgent look, and she knew he was humoring her. Well, so be it. If she but fell asleep with him beside her, it was enough. She wrapped her arms around him and burrowed into his chest, resting her head against his heart. She could hear the steady thump of it, smell the scent of leather on his clothing and skin. She knew his scent now. She knew his taste, and yet she did not know him at all at times.

But they would have a lifetime to learn everything there was to know about each other. Her eyes drifted closed, and she was vaguely aware that he pulled the blanket over her and moved away. He was not ready to hold her, to allow that much intimacy. Jane fell into a light sleep and was almost as instantly awake and reaching for her dagger.

"What is going on here?"

Bollocks! She was naked, and her dagger was God knew where. But then she remembered she was in the Barbican headquarters. She was safe.

She knew that voice. It was familiar to her. She had heard it—

Her eyes adjusted to the semidarkness, and she spotted her uncle hulking in the doorway. She snatched the blanket over her breasts.

His face was red, his eyes bulging. "I told you to go to Kenham House." He glanced across the room, and her gaze followed. There was Dominic, standing stiffly against the wall.

"I did go to Kenham House," she said, "but when the assassin found us, I thought I should come back and notify you."

His gaze went to her again, and his eyes widened with interest. He took in her state of dishabille. "I see," he said.

Jane did not like the way he was looking at her, as though his scheme had gone exactly as planned. "What do you see?" she asked.

"Griffyn took advantage of you. He has ruined you."

"He is my betrothed."

"Exactly," her uncle said with a smile.

Rage burned through her. How dare he act as though what had happened between her and Dominic was some sort of stratagem? How could he reduce it to that? "This has nothing to do with you."

"I should congratulate you, Mr. Griffyn," M said. "You have done exactly what I hoped."

"If you want to congratulate someone, then it should probably be me." She wrapped the blanket around her, jumped off the bed, and stood in the line of fire. "I seduced him. I wanted him to ravage me."

"Jane," Dominic said, his voice low. He stepped beside her, unwilling to allow her to shield him. "Enough."

"Oh, no." She shook her head. "I will not allow you to play the martyr." She looked back at her uncle. "The truth is I stripped nude and begged him to—"

"For the love of all that is holy, do not say another word!" her uncle yelled. He closed his eyes tightly and shook his head. "I do not want these images in my head."

"I do intend to marry her, my lord. I know initially neither of us intended to honor the betrothal agreement, but we have reconsidered."

"Oh, you will marry her," M said. "And you'll go back to Kenham Hall this moment and continue the wedding preparations."

"No." Jane shook her head. "Foncé knows we were there. He sent Tueur to kill me. There's nowhere left to hide, my lord. We act now, or..." She didn't continue. She didn't know what else to say. The alternative was too awful to consider. Her aunt dead or one of Griffyn's brothers carved open by Foncé. It was past time the man was stopped.

Her uncle seemed to consider her words for a long moment. Jane didn't understand why he was hesitating. What was there to think about? Why did he want her away from London so badly?

"Very well," he said. He turned his gaze and his pointing finger on Jane. "I expect you in my office in one hour."

"Yes, my lord." Perhaps she was wrong. Perhaps she was imagining his eagerness to be rid of her.

He started for the door to the dormitory then looked back one last time. "I've summoned all the agents in London, and most should have arrived by now, so do endeavor to look considerably less debauched."

Fifteen

DOMINIC WATCHED THE DOOR CLOSE AND SWALLOWED. The lump in his throat did not budge, nor did the weight pressing on his chest, making every breath he took labored and difficult. He was going to marry. He looked at Jane, his gaze lowering to her belly. He might have a child. Panic clawed at the edge of his thoughts. What kind of father would he be? Who was he to deserve a child?

"Do I look debauched?" Jane asked, blinking at him.

She looked adorable, wearing only a blanket, with her hair mussed and her lips red and slightly swollen. "Thoroughly."

She arched a brow. "I have the feeling you rather like it."

"I will not answer that."

He did not know if it was deliberate, but her blanket slipped then, revealing the swell of one breast. He swallowed again. God help him, but he wanted her again. He hadn't realized that the act could be like that, that there was more than the simple release. So much more. For the first time in years, he thought he might be able to forget about the past. He might be able to begin again. Perhaps if he concentrated on how lovely his betrothed looked in only a thin blanket.

Perhaps if he concentrated on removing that blanket... Then he might keep the past at bay. He might even forget it one day and begin again.

"I suppose if I am not to look debauched, I must dress,," Jane said, looking about at her discarded clothing. "I do not have much time. I could use your assistance."

He shook his head. "I will fetch Miss Qwillen. I know nothing about women's clothing."

"This could be your opportunity to learn."

Not if she actually needed to put clothing on. He backed toward the door and started for Q's lab.

Closer to a half hour later, Jane emerged, looking fresh and pretty and perfectly innocent. No one would guess she had been tied to the bed for his pleasure just under their feet. And thank God her uncle had not seen her thus.

"Are you ready?" she asked Dominic as Q stepped out behind her.

"I was not summoned."

"Rubbish," she told him. "You need to know the latest intelligence as much as I do. Q? Are you coming?"

Q yawned. "No. I have worked all night to make the specifications Baron requested to his pistol. He should be able to prime it even faster than before. You still have the quill?"

Jane patted her reticule, and Dominic sighed. He'd forgotten the exploding quill. It would be a miracle if they all survived.

"Good. I have done all I can then. Be careful, Bonde."

"I always am."

"And kill that bastard Foncé."

Jane smiled. "You know I will."

Dominic shook his head. That was the strangest conversation between two ladies he had ever heard, but nothing since the night he'd met Jane had been ordinary. He did not think anything in his life would ever be ordinary again.

He escorted Jane to the upper floor and to the threshold of Melbourne's office. He could overhear voices inside, both male and female. He still thought it wisest to wait outside, but she pulled him in with her. The room quieted when they entered, but Jane ignored the stares and silence and led him to the only available seat. It was an armchair. She took it, leaving him to stand beside it.

"I apologize for my tardiness," she said.

Melbourne made some sort of growl, and the man standing beside his desk raised a brow in amusement. The man had remarkable blue eyes, and Dominic almost wondered if they could possibly be real.

"I would introduce everyone," Jane said, "but we are spies, and that is sort of against the rules."

But Dominic already knew Wolf and Saint, Lord and Lady Smythe, and of course he knew Lord and Lady Keating from the night before. He did not know the man with the blue eyes or any of the other men standing in the shadows, but Dominic did not wish to know them. At times, the less one knew, the better.

"When you interrupted," Melbourne said, eyeing Jane, who looked absorbed in examining her nails, "Blue was telling us the latest intelligence."

It was not difficult to ascertain who Blue might be. He was the man with the vivid blue eyes. "I thought Blue had retired," Lady Smythe said.

Blue cocked his head. "And we all thought you would have had that baby by now, but you are still here."

"Touché," Lord Keating remarked.

"In any case," Blue said, "I *am* retired, which makes it even more remarkable that it was *I* who overheard the latest intelligence and not one of you."

"You are a lodestone for intelligence," Lady Keating said. "It falls into your lap as though it were a wounded bird."

"It rather does, doesn't it? In any case, I overheard a conversation—I won't bore you with details—M knows them—that seemed to indicate Foncé has plans to assassinate a large group of important personages."

"I assumed his target was still the prince regent," Lord Smythe remarked.

"As did I, but it appears he has expanded his diabolical plans," Blue said. "He has a scheme in place. I do not know when it will be executed, but my impression was that we—you, rather—have no time to waste."

A rumbling of voices moved through the room, and Blue sauntered to the couch and sat beside Lady Smythe. Dominic had to admit she did look close to bursting. Finally, Melbourne lifted his hand, and the room quieted. "Thoughts?"

"He could be planning anything," one man said. "I do not know where to begin."

"I think it might be a ploy to distract us from the

real target," another man interrupted. "I do not think we should take our focus from the prince regent."

"We need more information," Lord Smythe said, "if we are to formulate any organized plan of attack."

"And we can discuss it all day," Jane said quietly. Dominic noted everyone looked at her, and silence descended. "But what we really need is action."

"A spy after my own heart," Lady Smythe murmured.

"If Blue is correct—and when has Blue ever been incorrect?—Foncé plans to kill a large group of important people. Well, where is it large groups of important people gather?"

"The theater," Blue said.

"Vauxhall Gardens," a man suggested.

"Hyde Park."

"At one of the balls."

"At Almack's."

"Or one of the gentleman's clubs," Lord Smythe added.

"Good work, Bonde," Melbourne said. "I suggest we divide and conquer." He began to assign the agents to various locations.

"Mr. Griffyn and I will take Hyde Park," Jane said, standing.

"No. You two will stay here," her uncle instructed her. "Go to the Dungeon and review the files on the Maîtriser group."

"My lord—" Jane protested, but at his stern look, Jane clamped her lips closed. Her murderous expression said what she did not. She whirled and started for the door with the other agents. Dominic followed, but Melbourne stepped in front of him.

Jane turned "My lord, now what are you——"

Melbourne closed the door on his niece's protests and turned to look Dominic in the eye. "Do not think because I'm allowing you to stay here that I have forgotten your obligation to my niece."

"The thought never crossed my mind."

"If you even think of crying off, I will see you charged with a crime of high treason. When you are drawn and quartered, I'll stand close enough so that your blood spatters on my coat."

Dominic winced at the image of his intestines outside his body and Melbourne's red-splattered face. "I understand your concern, my lord."

"Good."

"I have every intention of making Jane my wife." The words caused his heart to slide into his belly, but he could ignore the feeling of nausea for the moment.

"See that you do." Melbourne turned back to his desk, and Dominic realized he'd been dismissed. And still, he stood rooted in place.

"Jane tells me you knew my mother."

Melbourne looked up from the stack of papers before him. With a sigh, he poured a glass of whatever amber liquid the decanter behind him held. "Sometimes, Griffyn, having a spy for a niece is a curse. Yes. I knew your mother." He lifted the decanter as though offering it, but Dominic shook his head. He rarely drank anything stronger than wine with dinner anymore. He'd tried to drown the past with spirits for years and found it only dragged him deeper into the nightmares.

"I don't remember you."

Melbourne shook his head. "We never met. Your mother had recently become involved with the Marquess of Edgeberry, and she needed help with a difficult situation."

Dominic could only imagine the sorts of situations in which his mother had found herself embroiled.

"She wanted a favor from you."

"She did. I don't know how she found me, but I could hardly refuse her."

"She asked you to make an investigation go away."

Melbourne narrowed his eyes. "What do you know about it?"

He knew everything about it. He would never forget that night, and he had always wondered why his mother had not been hanged. There could be little question she had murdered… Dominic could not even think his name without revulsion. And so Melbourne had saved his mother and saved him as well. "I know I owe you a debt," Dominic said.

"Do you? Time and again I have wondered if I should not have allowed her to face the consequences for her act, no matter what provoked it. I wondered it again recently when she threatened to reveal our relationship to Lady Melbourne if Jane did not marry you."

"I don't think she would have done it."

Melbourne raised his brows. "If you think that, you do not know your mother very well. She will do anything to achieve her aims. Even murder."

"You're wrong," Dominic said. "About her and about me. I will do my best to make Jane happy."

"You will make her excessively happy." Melbourne

lowered himself into his chair and looked Dominic straight in the eye. "You have no other choice."

~

Finally M's door opened, and Jane pounced on Dominic. "What happened?"

"We came to an agreement about your future happiness."

Oh, cryptic, cryptic answer. What did it mean? Was he pleased? Displeased? She could not read his expression.

"He cannot force you to marry me."

"It is not force if I agree to it."

Her throat seemed to close, and slowly she forced air back into her lungs. But was his agreement freely given, or would he marry her and grow to resent her?

And with Foncé free and threatening England, she hardly had time to worry about such personal, seemingly inconsequential matters. Jane looked around at her fellow agents talking quietly in small groups or reviewing documents. "We had better begin our research. There are quite a few documents pertaining to the Maîtriser group."

"And those are in the Dungeon?"

She nodded. "I promise it is not as awful as it sounds."

Unlike most other agents of the Barbican group, Jane did not hate the Dungeon. The official name for the Dungeon was the Records Room. She actually rather enjoyed the Records Room and its rows and rows of files and documents. She'd often found illuminating information here, and considered the agent who served as the records keeper one of the most valuable members of the Barbican group.

Every agent feared being taken off assignment for some muddle or other and being sent to the Records Room as punishment. Rumor was some agents had been consigned to the Records Room indefinitely and had never been seen again. Thus, the name Dungeon had come into use.

Jane led Dominic into the Dungeon now. She had chosen a lamp from the selection outside the door, lit it, and held it aloft while she shoved the heavy stone door to the Dungeon open. Or at least she intended to shove it open. Dominic pushed her aside and completed the task for her.

The Dungeon was as black as coal. Nothing flammable was allowed to remain burning without supervision. The stone room was seemingly endless, so it was possible someone was inside and the light from his lamp was not visible, but Jane did not think so. Everyone was looking for Foncé or preparing their strategy. She stepped inside, her boots echoing on the stone floor.

"What is this place?" Dominic asked.

"We keep records here." She shoved the door closed. "I think at one time it was a crypt, but as long as I have been here, it has been used for records storage. The entire room is stone, which makes it relatively immune to fire, and therefore the files are safer."

"You have a file to show me?"

She looked at him, increasingly aware that they were alone together. She had so often been alone with men, but she never thought anything of it. Now the air seemed charged with heat. Dominic's eyes were dark and exotic, and when he focused his attention on her with those Gypsy eyes, she found it difficult to think or breathe or…do anything but look back at him.

He raised a brow, and she realized she had not responded. "A file on the Maîtriser group. I hope it doesn't scare you away."

His mouth curved slightly, and he leaned forward to whisper in her ear. "You are not the only one not easily frightened."

She shivered at the feel of his warm breath on her skin. Heat flooded through her, and her legs felt inordinately heavy. "The files we want are this way." She waved at him to follow her and led him down one of the center aisles, marked with the letter *K*. Shelves towered above them on both sides, bowing with the weight of containers filled with documents. Each shelf had a string of numbers, and one had to consult the key book to find the appropriately numbered shelf for the topic of interest. She glanced idly at one of the numbers, reading K7865398. If she remembered correctly, this aisle contained information on poisons and the royal family of Russia.

The system made little sense, but no one was brave enough to challenge the ancient records keeper. He might suggest the agent reorganize.

After several minutes passed, Dominic cleared his throat. "Exactly where are you taking me? The Americas?"

She glanced over her shoulder. "Large, isn't it?"

"Massive. We could become lost. Hell, we are probably already lost."

"I'm not lost." She held her lamp aloft and hoped

she wasn't lost. No. There was the end of the row just
ahead. "I have requested these files so often I know
their location by heart. We need the row labeled *T*."

"*T*? For…?"

Jane shook her head, leading him through the
towering shelves. "Do not question it. The last thing
we want is to be assigned some organizational task."

"I see."

Finally, they reached an intersection, and she
led him along the row until she found the section
she wanted. A small stepladder had been propped
against the shelf, and she handed him the lamp and
climbed the ladder. Using the fan Q had repaired,
she positioned the magnifying glass on the handle
and studied the small numbers. Finding the file she
wanted, which was about as thick as her arm, she
extracted it and handed it down. Careful not to trip
on her skirts, she descended.

"Is this all?" he asked, looking dubiously at the file.

"Not much, is it?" she said, nodding for him to
continue the way they'd come. "We would have
more information, but every spy we send to investi-
gate Foncé ends up dead."

"That's reassuring."

She grinned. "Isn't it?" They'd reached the end
of the row, and she gestured to a room hewn out of
the stone. It was an alcove really, but large enough to
hold a stone table and one uncomfortable stone chair.
She stepped inside, set the lamp on the table, and took
the chair. She opened the file and began to peruse its
contents. Everything inside the file was familiar to
her, as familiar as one of the books she'd read over

and over in her childhood. She studied several of the pages with her magnifying glass, wanting to be certain she had not missed anything, but she found no hidden text. There was nothing new here. No hint of where Foncé intended to strike. She searched through the file for the last document that had been added and did not find it. Another search proved it was not there, and she remembered taking it home to read it. It must still be there. It probably would be as useless as the rest of the file, but she would have liked to see it again nonetheless.

Melbourne wouldn't allow her to leave, though. She was all but a prisoner here. She and Dominic. She peered at him now. He leaned against the wall, arms crossed. His stance said everything she needed to know. He was closed to her, closed to the world. She did not know what went on behind those Gypsy eyes, and she might never know.

But she had to try.

"It was never my intention to force you into marriage," she said finally. "The last thing I want is to trap you."

"I don't feel trapped," he said. She waited for him to elaborate, and when he did not, she struggled to think of what to say next.

"I only mean to say, you do not have to marry me simply because we—you—" How to say this?

"Ruined you?"

"I was going to say *took my virtue*."

"Ah, that is much better then." Once again, he said no more. He stood across from her, his dark, hooded eyes telling her nothing. Finally, she could stand it no longer. She'd seen glimpses of the real man beneath this hardened exterior. She could find him again. She rose and crossed to him, stood so close they were almost touching. He seemed almost amused by her actions. His eyes crinkled slightly. She wished she could be amused. Her head swam when she was this close to him. She could feel his warmth in the cold stone chamber, and she wanted to burrow into it.

"You are forcing me to be blunt," she said.

"Yes, as shy and demure as you are, it must be a trial."

She poked him with a finger, but he caught it and brought it to his lips, running it across them. She inhaled slowly and tried to slow her heart. Was he trying to seduce her, or was she still not allowed to touch him? "I am trying to tell you that you are free to walk away from me. I do not pretend to know what you and my uncle discussed, but whatever promise you made him, I will not hold you to it."

"Do you want an escape?" His face remained stoic, but she heard the undercurrent of anger in his tone.

"No. Not at all. I—" She should simply say it. If he laughed at her, he laughed. But she was not a coward. She hated cowards. "I want to marry you. I think—" She looked down. Why was this so difficult? She would rather have shot a man or hung by her fingernails from a roof. Her finger was still poised against his lips, or she would have clenched her hands. Instead, she straightened her back and looked up at him. "I love you."

She saw something flash in his eyes, but before she could interpret it, it was gone. He released her hand. "No, you don't. You only think you love me because…" He made a meaningless gesture. But she understood nonetheless.

"Because you bedded me? I am not so naive as that. It's true I was a virgin, but I have some experience, and I have never felt this way about a man before. I love you."

"No. You. Don't."

Did she have to argue with the man? "Yes, I do." She waved her hands in frustration, and he caught her wrists and spun her around so her back thudded against the wall. She might have countered him, but she wanted to see what he would do. He placed both hands on either side of her head and leaned down so his mouth was inches from hers. Jane forgot all about any argument. Now she wanted only to kiss him.

"You cannot love me."

"Why?" she whispered, entranced by the lock of hair falling over his forehead and the dark stubble on his jaw. She remembered the feel of it on her bare skin. It had been rough and erotic, all at the same time.

"Because I am not worth it."

Jane blinked and shook her head. "I…what?"

He pushed away from her. "If you only knew what I really am, you could never love me."

"I do know what you are. You're the man who practically carried me back here when I'd been cut open with a knife. You're the man who didn't flinch or leave my side when I was stitched up. You're the man who thought more of my pleasure than his own. The man who all but weeps when a horse dies. The man who insists on protecting me, even when I tell you a thousand times I don't need protection. If that is not you, then who are you?"

He stared at her, his expression one of shock and amazement.

"Tell me who you are. Tell me what happened, and see if it changes how I feel."

He stepped back, shaking his head, but she wouldn't allow him to go. She grabbed his arms and felt him stiffen. Before he could pull away or remind her of his rules, she slid her hands down to twine their fingers. "Let me love you, Dominic. Let me show you that your past doesn't matter."

"It does matter. Do you think I can forget?"

"No. But I think you can replace the pain with happiness, if you let me make you happy. Was there pain in what we shared earlier today?"

He stared at her for a long moment. She tugged his hands and pulled him closer. Rising on tiptoes, she brushed her lips across his. "Kiss me. Touch me. Let me love you until everything that happened before cannot possibly compare with what you have now. What we have."

He lowered his mouth to hers, and her head swam. Her skin burned, and her heart thumped so loudly in her ears she could not think. She wanted so badly for him to kiss her, she nearly shook with desire and want. Finally, he brushed his lips against hers. She moaned from the sheer pleasure of the light kiss. She wanted more, needed more, but she knew better than to push him. She allowed him to kiss her gingerly, and when he slipped his tongue inside her mouth, she could not stifle a moan. His demeanor changed then. He growled, and lifting her hands, he pinned her against the wall and devoured her mouth, his lips taking until she could barely gasp a breath. His tongue mated with hers, showing her what he could do with his body, how he could please her. She moaned, her legs weak and wobbly. She began to shake, and her skin burned with longing.

But this was not enough. She couldn't allow it to be enough. "If you want me," she said, pulling away, though it pained her to separate from him, "you have to give too. I won't let you marry me out of obligation."

He pressed against her, and she felt the hard length of him. "Does this feel like obligation?"

"No, it feels like desire. I desire you too. I'm wet for you, Dominic. I'm hot…everywhere. I think if you touched me now I would burst into flames."

She heard him draw in a long, slow breath. "You are killing me."

"Good. I want you to take me. Here. Against this wall or on that table. Take me, but you must give me something too."

He looked at her long and hard, his chest rising and falling rapidly, and then he released her and stepped back. She felt the coldness now that he no longer touched her. He was going to walk away. She wanted to pull him back, but she could not live in a loveless marriage. She could not love only part of him. She was willing to give him all of her, though she knew the sacrifice it would entail. Was it even a sacrifice? She had not chosen the path of her life. For once she would choose what she wanted, and Dominic was worth every sacrifice. If he could love her too. If he could trust her with all of himself, she would make the sacrifice.

She leaned her head against the wall and shut her eyes against the sting of tears. She would not cry. She never cried.

"Damn it!"

She opened her eyes in time to see his fist thump hard on the table. She winced, knowing the stone must have hurt his flesh. He rounded on her, and if she had not been against the wall, she would have stepped back.

He stalked forward, his eyes black. "Do you want to know what happened to me? Do you want to know all the sordid details of what I did? What I allowed?"

She swallowed, afraid now that perhaps she didn't want to know. Perhaps there was too much pain in him. But the pain had made him who he was. The pain had made the man she loved. She took a breath. "Tell me. Everything."

Sixteen

"I WAS BORN A BASTARD. I NEVER KNEW MY FATHER."

"I know. I'm sorry," she said quietly.

He rounded on her. "Did you know your father well?"

"I remember him. He and my mother died when I was six. I remember he kissed me good night and carried me to bed when I fell asleep in the carriage. But I didn't know him. Not really."

"I know where mine is buried. I suppose that should be some small comfort. It should be a comfort that she even knew who he was."

"That explains why you were in the cemetery that night."

He'd forgotten that meeting between them. He nodded. "I had gone to see his grave. He died of consumption. My mother said he was a great actor until he grew too ill to perform."

"I thought…oh, it does not matter what I thought. Do you often go to his grave?"

He could see if he answered affirmatively her eyes would turn misty, and she would probably sigh. He did not want her pity. He could not make it through the rest of this confession if she pitied him. "I do not go to honor him. I go because he left my mother with nothing. Perhaps my life would have turned out the same, regardless of whether or not my mother had blunt or security. As it was, she found it necessary to supplement her meager income. Her male admirers were only too happy to support her in return for her favors."

"I am sure she wanted only to take care of you."

He shook his head. "That might have been true in the beginning, but she longed for jewels and fine clothing, and selling her body was the only way to finance her greed."

"You're angry with her." She stepped forward and touched his arm, but he drew it away. He did not want her to touch him. Not now.

"She brought men to our flat. Some of the men were kind. Some were violent. Many were drunk. My mother was often drunk too. There were loud quarrels in the middle of the night, violent altercations, and even more violent couplings. I went to sleep each night, tucked in by my nurse, never certain whether I would wake to the sounds of screams or if my mother would even be home or conscious in the morning. And then one night—" He had to clench his fists in order to continue speaking. He forced the memory away and spoke as though he had not been there, as though the terror were not a burning sensation in his throat.

"One night my mother was drunk and asleep, and my door opened. I thought it was my nurse, but it was one of my mother's men. I recognized him. He came to the bed where I slept. I had no idea what he wanted, but he made it clear soon enough. He... touched me." Nausea made his belly roil and churn, and a light sheen of perspiration sprang to his forehead.

"Dominic, no."

He gave her a quelling look. "Yes." He fought the memory down and spoke in a detached voice. "He pushed my face into the mattress, lifted my nightshirt, and took what he wanted. I cannot describe the pain or the fear. I thought I was dying. I was only four." He looked at her again, expecting to see tears in her eyes, but she stood strong and nodded at him to go on. If she'd been crying, it would have broken him.

"I didn't tell. He said he would kill my mother if I did. And so it happened again. I was relieved when my mother found a new lover. She knew something was wrong by then, but she would never have guessed what it was. A year went by. Almost a year, and then another of her lovers found me desirable. This one did not rape me, not in the way the other did, but he forced me to touch him." He met her gaze then, and to his surprise, she did not seem shocked or even disgusted. She was a very good actress.

"One night my mother walked in and found me on my knees in front of him. She ordered me out of the room, and I heard a terrible row. One of the neighbors called a constable, who called Bow Street. She'd killed him. She claimed it was self-defense, but the wounds were not consistent with that account. She might have gone to the gallows if your uncle had not intervened and saved her."

"My uncle?"

"You said you overheard my mother discussing their past. She killed for me."

"But he said—" She shook her head. "The liar." She looked at him. "He lied to protect you—even all these years later." Jane stepped forward, so close he could smell the scent of violets. "You know none of that is your fault. You were a child."

He shook his head. "I could have done…something. Screamed or told someone."

"No, Dominic. You did nothing wrong. Those men were wrong to use you thus."

He felt a sharp sting behind his eyelids and realized it was tears. But he would not cry. He'd cried rivers when he was a boy, and it had not changed anything. It would change nothing now. He closed his eyes and willed the tears away. "You see why I defile you when I touch you. What happened to me was unnatural."

"Dominic, you did nothing wrong, and it changes nothing for me. I still love you. I love you more now because I understand you better."

He opened his eyes, wondering if he could be imagining what she was saying.

"I understand why you reacted as you did in the stable. But I'll never hurt you, and I want you to touch me. I love when you touch me. And when you want me to touch you, I want that too."

He stared at her. He did not understand why she did not find him repulsive. There were times he could not even look his mother in the eye because of what she had seen. Because of what he had caused her to do.

But something was changing. Something inside of him let go. The hurt was still there, but some part of it, some heavy, lonely part had lessened. He felt lighter. He felt as he did on the rare day he woke in the morning having forgotten what had happened to him. Perhaps given time, he would heal.

"Touch me now," he said, watching her face for any sign of hesitation. She reached out and took his hand. Her own was soft, though far from perfect. He'd seen her without gloves, seen the scars she bore. But she wore hers on the outside. His own were far more hidden. She brought his hand to her mouth and kissed his palm.

He slid his palm along her jaw and up to cup her cheek. His dark hand looked like a shadow against her pale flesh in the dimly lit room. He ran a finger along her cheek, and she closed her eyes and leaned into his touch as though she craved it. And then she stepped closer and wrapped her arms around his neck and pulled him into an embrace. He had thought she might kiss him, but she pulled him tightly against her and held him. He stood stiffly, uncertain what he was supposed to do, what was expected of him. But as the minutes passed, he realized she wanted only to hold him. He relaxed into her, rested his head on her shoulder.

She was shorter than he, feminine and rounded, but also muscled and solid. She would not crumble under pressure. She would not balk because he was not perfect. But she was perfect—well, she was far too stubborn and reckless, and she didn't take orders very well.

And she loved him.

He chuckled at the thought. Jane Bonde—a

diamond of the first water, an elite spy for the Crown, the bravest woman he knew—loved him. *Him*. She pulled back. "Why are you laughing?"

"No reason."

Her look said she thought he had gone daft.

"Because you love me," he explained, not that his explanation changed the expression she wore.

"One day, when you tell me you love me, I shall be certain to laugh."

"You are so sure of yourself? So sure I am going to fall in love with you?"

She raised a brow. "You haven't already?"

How he envied her confidence. He probably was in love with her, but he did not want to speak about love or the past or the future. He wanted to think about the moment—about the way her body felt pressed against his, the way her hair smelled like flowers, the way his heart felt lighter now. *She* loved *him*.

He bent his head and captured her lips in a light, teasing kiss. His hands tightened on her back, pulling her closer until their bodies were flush and he could feel the way her breathing increased. She was warm, and every rise and fall of her breasts pushed them deliciously against him. He caressed her lips with his, not kissing her, just tasting her, sampling her, teasing her. She made a sound of frustration, and he darted his tongue out and ran it along her lower lip. She stilled and did not breathe at all. And then her hands came up and cupped his head, tangling in his hair.

His first impulse was to remove her hands. The old panic rose in him. He would not be trapped, would not be forced. He tamped the impulse down. This was Jane. She loved him.

"More," she whispered. It was a command he was eager to obey. He trailed his mouth to her jaw and traced the curve with his lips until he reached her ear. He kissed her just underneath and felt the way her body shuddered. She was trembling against him, not out of fear, but out of need and want. She wanted him that much. And he wanted her. There was nothing sordid in this need. Nothing ugly or violent. He wanted to give her pleasure.

He stroked his hands down over her breasts, feeling their heavy weight in his hands. Her nipples hardened and pushed against the thin material of her gown, and he caressed them until they strained and she was panting. Then he bent, putting his mouth over the fabric and tracing the hard nubs with his lips. Her hands fisted in his hair, and she made a moaning sound. Earlier she'd been completely naked, and that had been erotic as hell, but there was something equally erotic about taking her fully clothed.

His hands continued to knead and palm her, but he lifted his head and met her gaze. Her eyes were impossibly blue. He couldn't remember why he hadn't liked blue eyes before. They were beautiful, stunningly so. And hers were like the sky before night fell, so dark and lovely. Right now they were hazy with desire for him. Her pale cheeks were pink and flushed, and her tender lips moist and red. The hand wrapped in his hair urged him to close the distance between them, and he slanted his mouth over hers. She responded immediately, opening her lips for him and darting her pink tongue out to touch his lips tentatively.

She tested his control, his reserve, and he slid his hands to her waist and pulled her closer. He opened his mouth to hers, and their tongues met and tangled. He stroked her, explored her, teased her, imitating the movements of his mouth with his body. He was painfully hard for her, but she had been a virgin, and she was not ready for him again. He knew that much. He knew the last thing he wanted was to hurt her.

She was flush against him, clinging as though she might fall if he released her, and it was an easy matter to turn her and lift her so her bottom rested on the stone table. She broke the kiss and glanced at the table, then reached over and closed the open file and moved it and her fan/magnifying glass aside. He chuckled softly. "Always an agent."

She met his gaze. "Does that bother you?"

"Quite the opposite. I want to see the aloof, controlled agent lose that control."

"I lost control the first time I saw you," she said, pulling his head down and whispering in his ear as her hands stroked his chest and worked down to his waist. Again, he struggled not to push her away. His instinct was to resist being held by her, to rebel against her touch. But he liked it; he liked knowing she found him desirable.

Her lips grazed his ear. "I knew I was in trouble when I saw how beautiful you are."

He shook his head. "Men are not beautiful."

"You are." Her hands brushed over his erection,

and he sucked in a breath. "I want you, Dominic," she whispered. "I cannot seem to take my fill of you."

"A challenge," he said with a smile and pushed her gently back on the table.

❧

Jane watched him, her lids heavy, her breath quick. She wanted to see him again, hard and thick with his desire for her. Instead, he stepped back, lifted the hem of her gown, and kissed her ankle. No one had ever kissed her there, and she felt a jolt of heat all the way up her leg, straight to her core. He turned her ankle, bending her knee slightly so he could gaze at her with wicked intent as he brushed his lips up her calf until he reached her knee.

When his tongue darted out, tickling the sensitive skin behind her knee, she jumped. "What are you doing?"

"Always analyzing, aren't you?"

"I'm curious."

"So am I." He pushed her skirts higher, and she was aware that she was exposed to him. She could feel the cool air from the Dungeon in that most private place and see the way his eyelids lowered slightly until his gaze was heavy-lidded. He took her breath away in that moment. He was the perfect incarnation of a dark angel painted by Rubens or Maffei. He was all sensuality and sultry heat and wicked intention.

His mouth moved higher, just above her knee, and she felt her leg begin to tremble against the hand with which he held it. "So am I," he repeated. "I may regret asking this, as I want no account of your former lovers."

"You have been my only lover," she said. "You know that."

"In the strictest sense, yes. And in that same sense, I have been only with you." His eyes clouded for a moment, and she willed his gaze back to her face.

"Yes," she said when he looked at her and seemed to return to the present. "We both began again tonight. Nothing not done with the intent of pleasure matters anymore. It's forgotten. Wiped away."

He took a breath, nodded, and then he returned to her. His lips were on her thigh again, moving upward. She was trembling quite noticeably now, and the ache between her legs was hot and insistent.

"I have never kissed a woman here," he said. "I've never slid my mouth to the heat between her thighs and teased her to climax with my tongue."

Desire stabbed through her so strongly she had to close her eyes and dig her hands into the table to gain control again. She wondered if he could bring her to completion simply by speaking.

"But I have read of such things."

"Such naughty books," she said, surprised at how husky her voice sounded. "I've never read anything so scandalous."

"Has any man ever put his mouth on you?"

"No," she said firmly. She had known attentive men, but none had ever kissed her there. She did not think she would have allowed it if one had. It was too intimate. It made her too vulnerable, and yet with Dominic it seemed right. She would have agreed to anything he wanted.

"Then it is another first for both of us." His hands

rested on her thighs, and he slowly pushed them upward, taking her skirts with his fingers. And then her skirts were at her waist, and he stood between her legs, looking down at her. "You are beautiful. So pink and perfect." His hands slid higher, and one cupped her. "Hot and"—his gaze met hers—"wet."

She could not stop the moan as his hand pressed lightly against her, taking all the yearning in her body and centering it in that one place. Without even thinking, she raised her hips and pushed against his hand, wanting more pressure, wanting to feel his fingers toy with her, then press hot and hard inside her. But the pressure of his hand lessened rather than increased, and he bent to kiss the inside of her thigh.

"Oh!" Her fingers scratched at the table, desperately seeking purchase. The rough scratch of his days' growth of beard against that too-tender skin made her dizzy with pleasure. She was falling, her body languid and heavy with need. And yet she knew Dominic would never let her fall, not in truth. Of course, he could not stop her falling in love with him.

His mouth brushed lightly over her center, and she jumped then sighed in frustration when he kissed her other thigh. He had her legs spread now, and she was so hot, so desperate with arousal. "I want you inside me," she said, again not only shocked at the breathlessness of her voice but the wantonness of her words. He did this to her. He made her forget everything else—the Dungeon, the Maîtriser group, the all-important mission. She was not Bonde with him. She was just Jane—but that was not even true. She was more than Jane when they were together. They became something new.

She squirmed and quivered, and finally he raised his dark head and met her gaze. She thought she might climax from the image of him between her legs like this. She had never thought she could be so close to climax without going over the edge. His hands slid down until she felt his fingers part her folds. "May I?" he asked.

He slew her. In that simple request was everything about him she loved. She felt the sting of tears behind her eyes and willed them away. "Yes."

He lowered his mouth, brushing his lips against that sensitive flesh. Jane dug her nails into the stone of the table and could not stop her hips from lifting slightly. And then his tongue darted out and scraped over that small, sensitive nub, and she cried out, shaking violently with need. He tongued her again, using the tip to tease her and circle her. She had not known anything could feel this wonderful. The pleasure was almost pain, and she felt her body tightening and spiraling. He flicked his tongue over her again, and she heard someone cry out in ecstasy, and she knew it was herself, but she was no longer present. She existed only on a plane where pleasure burst inside her, filling her, then crashing over her again and again.

It went on and on, and she had never known anything could feel this good. She had not imagined she could experience pleasure like this. As the sensations ebbed, she was aware she was still crying out, aware her legs were spread and she was open to him. And then he slid a finger inside her, and the jolt of arousal cut through her again. There could not possibly be more. And yet there was. His finger stroked in and out, and he bent to lick her again. She was almost too sensitive, and the feel of his tongue almost painful. Except that the pain was exquisite pleasure, and she rode that sensation and the fast stroke of his finger, the hot flicks of his tongue, until she came undone again.

This time she could not even manage a scream. She whimpered and arched, taking every last drop of pleasure he could give her. And then she pooled on the table, lying in a boneless heap.

Finally, years and years later, she opened her eyes. His mouth had curved up at the corners, and he'd pulled her gown over her legs, covering her. "That was interesting."

She was not even certain she could speak, but finally she managed to move her lips. "Not the words I would use."

"What words would you use?"

"Looking for compliments?"

"Oh, I think your reaction was all the compliment I need."

She put a hand over her eyes. "I was a bit more expressive than I intended."

He took her hand, kissed it, then pulled her up so she was sitting. "Always give me an honest reaction. I think if this marriage is to succeed, we will both have to be excruciatingly honest with each other." Besides the fact that her heart soared at the realization he was now speaking of their marriage as a given, she knew what he said was truth. Neither of them was used to honesty. He had a past he was ashamed of, and she had a present she was honor bound to hide. Could they even find a way to reveal those dark, vulnerable parts of themselves?

He tugged at her hands, and she slid off the table. "Now I believe you have a file to read."

"But…" She gestured helplessly. "I haven't given you anything in return. Allow me—"

He put a finger on her lips. "You have given me your love, and that is more than I can ever deserve."

"Dominic." She shook her head. He deserved that and so much more. "Unfortunately, there's nothing in this file I haven't seen. But there is a file at my town house."

"Shall we go there?"

She shook her head. "Foncé surely has a man watching for me, especially now that Tueur has not returned. Foncé must know he was not successful in his mission to kill me. I will have to send another agent in my stead."

"I would go for you."

"Too dangerous, and you are not trained."

"I suppose that is for the best, because I intend to go to Edgeberry's town house."

She shook her head. "You cannot. Melbourne won't allow you to leave."

"Jane." He took her hand. It was ice cold. He had his greatcoat with him, and he slipped it over her shoulders to warm her. "My brothers and my mother's husband are there. Surely you understand my need to warn them of any danger."

She sighed. "Of course I do, but M won't allow you to leave."

He raised a brow. "And you expect me to believe that you know of no secret passages or hidden exits?"

She gave him a long look. "Follow me." She led him through the Dungeon to the darkest, blackest section. This was the *A* section, and she had never required a file from this row. But she had been here once before when her uncle showed her this door to the outside. He'd made her promise not to reveal it to anyone, but he wanted her to know where it was in case the Barbican was ever invaded and she needed to escape. "This opens into an alley not far from Piccadilly. You can find your way from there. How much time do you need? I will return and open the door for you."

"Two hours?" he said. "Three if they are not at home and I must go to White's."

"I will be here."

He nodded then cupped her face, kissing her gently. She removed his coat and helped him don it, buttoning it for him and smoothing the material down. "Be careful."

He opened the door and was gone. For a moment, she wanted to go after him. She had the urge to protect him, but then she shook her head. He was safer without her. Foncé did not know him.

And she had not left him completely defenseless.

She retreated through the winding maze of the Dungeon and back to the main floors. No other agents were about, and the place seemed strangely deserted. She had seen it thus only a few times before, during the war with Napoleon, when stakes were the highest. This was another of those times. She did not know what Foncé planned, but she had to stop him. King and Country were counting on her to keep them safe so they might continue their blissful rides in Hyde Park, continue to dance the night away at their balls, continue to live their lives without looking over their shoulders.

She was tired and thought she might lie down in the dormitory for an hour. When she turned into the passage, she all but collided with Moneypence.

"Miss Bonde!" He caught her arm to steady her unnecessarily and released her just as quickly. "I am sorry." He looked past her, probably expecting Griffyn to appear and take him to task.

"Mr. Griffyn is not with me at the moment."

"At the moment," he murmured, and she thought he looked rather sad.

"Are you well?" she asked.

"You love him," Moneypence said. It was not a question, though she supposed it should have been.

Jane opened her mouth to tell Moneypence they had more important issues to discuss, but it occurred to her that she should set him free from his long infatuation with her. She should have done so years ago. "I do. I love him and am going to marry him."

"I see. And there is no chance for me then?"

She was not so cruel as to suggest there never had been, but she had an idea. "Mr. Moneypence, is Miss Qwillen in yet?"

"I do not think she ever left, though what she could be crafting now, when all of the agents she might help are out on assignment, I cannot begin to imagine."

"I need her assistance. Will you take me to her?"

"Of course." He offered his arm, and Jane took it, walking slowly. She had plenty of time to detail all of Q's charming qualities before they reached her lab. As a rule, Jane did not play matchmaker, but she supposed when one was in love, one wanted everyone else to feel similarly.

Moneypence knocked on the door to Q's lab, and when she opened it and saw him, the annoyed scowl on her face melted away. A pink blush spread across her cheeks in its place. Jane felt a swell of satisfaction at having guessed correctly at Q's feelings. "Mr. Moneypence." Q's gaze darted to Jane and then back to Moneypence.

"Miss Qwillen." He bowed. Jane watched anxiously, wondering if, now that he had delivered her to her destination, he would walk away. "It is a pleasure."

"Is it? I mean, thank you."

"Bonde needs you." He glanced at Jane, and Q followed suit. Jane had intended to ask Q if she might borrow a clean gown to wear, but one look at Q's current attire, and Jane reconsidered. It was covered with green flecks of some sort, and small holes had burned through the muslin in several places so she could see clear through to Q's petticoats.

"I actually need both of you," she said, inspiration striking. Jane Bonde was never one to ignore inspiration. "I have a mission for you."

Q frowned, but Moneypence shook his head. "Only Lord Melbourne has the authority to assign missions."

"Yes, but he has forbidden me to leave, and I find I need a file from my town house."

Moneypence sighed. "I suppose Mr. Griffyn has gone for you."

From the corner of her vision, Jane saw Q roll her eyes. Moneypence was obviously still holding out hope for Jane. She had to turn his attentions elsewhere. "Not at all. He has not been trained as an agent, unlike"—she gestured to them—"you two."

"You want us to fetch a file from Melbourne's town house?" Q asked.

"Exactly."

"I should think Miss Qwillen might go alone," Moneypence said.

Jane shook her head. "Considering the dangerous situation with the Maîtriser group, and the fact that my town house is being watched, I should think you might offer to go along and protect her."

Q opened her mouth, probably to protest she did not need protection. Jane tended to agree. Q had more weapons than the army of Luxembourg, but Jane gave her a meaningful glare, and Q closed her mouth. The woman was no fool.

"Oh." Moneypence blinked. "Of course. Miss Qwillen, I would be happy to accompany you."

"Thank you." She looked at Jane, her expression knowing. "If you will pen a note, I will present it to your butler in order to gain entrance to your room and clothing."

Jane shook her head. "If my town house is being watched, that will not do at all. You will have to gain entrance unnoticed."

Moneypence's eyes widened. "Do you mean we should break in?"

"It is not really breaking in if you have my permission to be there." She looked at Q. "The file is in my bedroom, in the desk drawer. It is locked." She told them where to find the hidden key. "While you are there, can you fetch me a fresh gown as well as the necessary underthings?"

Moneypence cleared his throat, apparently reminding her that she should not speak of *underthings* in his presence. Jane suppressed a sigh. *Men*.

"Of course."

"There is a large tree in the back, whose limb juts quite close to my bedroom window," Jane said. "I have used it and your glove grips on numerous occasions." She looked at Moneypence. "Of course, I leave it to your discretion to determine the best means of access."

"We will not fail you."

"Is two hours enough time?"

"I will do my best," Q said. "Let me look through my tools and see what I should take."

Jane backed away. "I will leave you to it." With a smile, she strode away. Not only had she begun a lovely romance, she had given herself at least an hour's rest. She could have gone to her town house herself, sneaked in and out without being seen. Q undoubtedly knew this, but she had been waiting for her chance with Moneypence, and sometimes, when a chance was available, one had to grasp it and hold on.

Seventeen

Dominic was relieved to see the footman at the gate of Edgeberry's town house. He'd often thought it a bit strange that the marquess always employed additional footmen for security, but now he was glad. He didn't immediately recognize the man, but he was allowed to enter after he explained who he was. The footman apologized profusely, explaining he had been hired recently. Dominic waved him back to his post and went inside in search of his brothers. The house was quiet, which did not surprise him. He opened several doors off the dark vestibule and noted the rooms were empty. It had been a gloomy, cold summer thus far, and the cold and gray encouraged everyone to stay in their warm, cozy beds.

"Danbury!" Dominic called when he didn't find the man in the parlor or the dining room. Danbury stepped out from one of the servants' doors.

"Yes, sir. Good to have you home, sir." The servant's eyes widened as he took in Dominic's disheveled clothing and days' growth of beard. "Shall I send Lord Trewe's valet to your chambers?"

"No. I'd like to speak with Lord Edgeberry. Where is the marquess?"

"He's gone to his club, sir. Lord Trewe accompanied him."

Dominic had expected this, but it still frustrated him. One more step. Another hour within which his family might be in danger.

"Lord Phineas and Lord Carlisle have also gone."

"They're all at White's?" He turned back toward the door, and Danbury hastened to open it for him. "I'll go directly."

"Yes, sir, but if I might make a suggestion?"

The cold air blew in through the open door, chilling Dominic. He felt uneasy, and it wasn't simply the unseasonal cold. "What's that?"

"I do believe a bath and a fresh coat might be in order if you plan to stop at White's."

Damn. Danbury was correct. Dominic could hardly show his face at the exclusive club looking like this.

"And your mother would undoubtedly like to speak with you."

Dominic's head jerked up. "My mother? She's at Kenham Hall."

"She returned this morning, Mr. Griffyn."

"She has to go back," Dominic said. And he would make his case after a quick bath and change of clothing. "Very well. Send a valet to my room. I hardly care whose, but I'm in a hurry."

"Yes, sir."

Dominic took the stairs two at a time, cursing propriety and the etiquette that demanded he look presentable to warn his family of danger.

"Are you warm enough, Miss Qwillen?" Pierce Moneypence asked as he and the weaponry designer made their way on foot to M's town house. She had her cloak pulled tightly about her slender frame, and the chill breeze whipping it about her ankles had turned her cheeks a lovely shade of pink.

Moneypence had decided it was perfectly acceptable for him to note the pleasing color of her cheeks at the moment. Once they reached the town house, he would concentrate on the mission. This was his first mission in the field, and he was actually rather excited. That excitement likely accounted for why he did not feel the cold. He was to obtain top secret documents from M's own residence, from Bonde's bedchamber. The thought actually made him lightheaded. Bonde's bedchamber! The place where she slept, breakfasted, undressed…

"I'm quite comfortable," Q said, interrupting his thoughts. "I'm from north of York and used to the cold."

That explained her seeming immunity to the elements then. Moneypence was glad. One quality that always appealed to him was hardiness. He wished he had more of it himself.

"There it is," Q said, pointing to a white limestone town house. It was rather unremarkable in appearance, but Moneypence supposed that was the idea. The leader of the Barbican hardly wanted a sign proclaiming his residence.

"Miss Bonde mentioned a tree we might climb to access her room. In which case, we should probably approach from the rear."

Q looked at him. "Are you skilled at tree climbing, Mr. Moneypence?"

Pierce considered. He'd climbed one or two as a boy, usually to escape larger boys intent on beating him to a bloody pulp. "I have some experience," he admitted.

"Good." By tacit agreement, they circled around the house, entering the garden through a gate in the alley where the mews were housed. They were both keenly aware the house was probably being watched, but the ease with which they gained entry to the premises did not surprise them. That did not mean the house itself was unguarded.

Keeping low to take advantage of the shrubbery, Moneypence and Q made their way to the tree closest to the house. They hid behind the tree trunk for a few moments, studying the house and the area. "I do not think we have been spotted," Q said.

"No one and nothing has moved," he agreed. His heart was beating rapidly, his blood racing through his veins. No wonder the operatives enjoyed fieldwork. It was rather exciting.

"Shall I climb up first?" she asked.

"I—" He began to protest, but she had already stood and was reaching for the lowest branch, which hung just out of her reach.

"Would you give me a boost, Mr. Moneypence?"

"Of course." He bent and made a cup of his hands. She placed her boot in it and stepped up. Her thigh pressed against his shoulder, sending warmth and the scent of gunpowder and smoke into his nostrils. It was a surprisingly pleasant scent, rather comforting. She reached for the branch, wrapped her legs about the trunk of the tree, and began to pull herself up. Without meaning to, Pierce caught a glimpse of the white of her calf. He felt his breath catch slightly. Despite Q's slight stature, her leg had appeared rather shapely to his eye.

He forced his gaze down. He was a man of principle and strong moral fiber. He did not look up ladies' skirts. That vow made, he began to climb, keeping his gaze on his hands or the tree until he was beside Q on the limb across from one of the house's windows.

"This is Bonde's room," Q whispered. "I've been inside before and remember the location within the building."

"Perhaps I should go in first. She might have laid booby traps."

"She didn't use any I didn't teach her to lay," Q said with something that sounded like pride in her voice. Logically, she should be the one to go first, then, but he was feeling a bit dizzy from the height of the tree limb on which they balanced. Certainly, it was strong enough for both of them, but did the breeze have to blow so bloody often? He felt as though he were swaying as much as a sailor on a ship.

"What should I watch for?" he asked, scooting forward.

"Anything that would set off an alarm."

"Right." An alarm did not worry him. An alarm would not kill or maim. He reached for the window and shoved the pane up. It was locked. Keeping one hand on the tree trunk for balance, he wrapped the other in a handkerchief and used it to break the thick glass. He didn't cut his hand, but it rather ached by the time he'd smashed through. He reached inside, turned the latch, and pushed the window up. Quickly, he climbed inside, turning to give Q a cheeky smile. With a scream, she jumped on top of him, smashing to the floor just as the whoosh of a blade cut the air where he had been a moment before.

✑

Dominic knocked on his mother's door and waited for her to admit him entrance. At the sound of her voice, he strolled inside and found her seated in front of her hearth in an antique chair upholstered in yellow-and-blue chintz. She held out her hand. "You are safe. Oh, Dominic." With a sob, she pulled him into an embrace. Dominic was used to her theatrics, but these were more dramatic than usual.

"Mother." He gently extricated himself and sat across from her, glad for the warmth of the fire. "I told you I was coming to London. I wrote to Edgeberry, told him to leave for Kenham Hall. London is dangerous at the moment. You are much safer in the country."

She sighed as though she had had this argument many times before. "Yes, I mentioned all of this, and the dead man at Kenham Hall to the marquess, but he says he has an important vote in Parliament tonight and will not quit Town until it is over."

"So you came home?"

She gave him a sheepish look. "I was lonely. Lady Melbourne is pleasant enough, but I missed my husband. Besides"—she pointed an accusatory finger at him—"how was I supposed to sleep easy knowing a man had been killed just yards from my bed?"

"How will you sleep easy knowing the man who sent him is here in London and may do you more harm?"

She shook her head and leaned forward. In the light from the hearth, he could see her face looked older than usual. There were more lines than he remembered, and she had a bit of gray in her hair at the roots. "Why would anyone want to harm me? I've done nothing. Edgeberry has done nothing."

"It's not you they are after. It's Melbourne and Miss Bonde."

"Miss Bonde?" Lady Edgeberry sat back with surprise. "Why would anyone want to harm that sweet girl?"

"Because she followed in her uncle's footsteps."

He had to give his mother credit. She did not even blink. "What footsteps?"

"Mother, please. Do not pretend you have no idea what Melbourne does."

"Something for the Foreign Office. I assumed he was some sort of clerk. Have they taken to employing women now?"

She was an amazing actress, but he knew her too well. Her gestures were a bit too heavy-handed. "She's a spy, Mother. Just like her uncle. And right now…well, the less you know, the better. But I am ordering Danbury to put more men around the house. And I'll find Edgeberry at his club and make him leave the city until this is over."

"And will you be coming with us?" she asked.

"No." He stood and raked a hand through hair, still damp from the bath. Dominic had never even considered leaving. "I can't."

"You love her," his mother said.

Dominic didn't answer. Did he love her? Was he even capable of love? "I don't know. I do not need to love her to marry her. That's what you wanted, is it not?"

"I wanted you to fall in love," she said. "But I will take marriage as a beginning."

"You did not give either of us much choice."

She studied her nails intently. "Oh?"

"Jane says you threatened to reveal your affair with Melbourne if she did not agree to marry me."

"Affair with Melbourne? I have no idea what you are talking about!"

"And that is the first truth you've told me all night. Tell me, Mother, why would Melbourne lie to his niece? Why would he want her to believe you were blackmailing him with a secret relationship, when you and I know the truth?"

Her eyes narrowed. "Do we?"

"Melbourne and you did not have an affair, but you do have a secret together. You killed a man, and he hid the evidence."

She stood. "I do not know what you are talking about." She whirled so her back was to him. "That girl has filled your head with foolish ideas. You had better go now if you hope to catch Edgeberry before he starts for Westminster."

"There are still hours before the session begins. What are you afraid to talk about, Mother?" He turned her around. "Did you think I didn't remember?"

There were tears glimmering in her eyes, unshed tears, and for that he was thankful. "I hoped…" She swallowed. "I hoped you had forgotten some of it. All of it."

"I haven't forgotten. I never will."

"Oh, Dominic." She threw herself into his arms, and he allowed her to weep for a moment before gently setting her aside. "I'm so sorry, my darling boy. So sorry. It's all my fault. You must believe me when I say I didn't know what…that man was doing to you. He threatened to come back, to keep hurting you. I did not mean to kill him. I was so angry."

"You were drunk," he said, and saw her flinch.

"I was. I was a horrible mother. I would have gone to prison if the truth had been known. Melbourne saved me. He saved us."

"And you repay him by blackmailing him?"

She waved a hand dismissively. "He needed to marry off the girl anyway. I was merely helping him. I do not know why he lied to Miss Bonde. He must have had his reasons. I wanted only the best for you. That's all I've ever wanted. That's why I married Edgeberry, why I want you to marry Jane Bonde. I want you to have what I could not give you all those years before."

"Mother." Dominic moved close to her. "All I ever wanted was you."

The tears that had filled her eyes spilled down her cheeks. "I'm so sorry." She fell to her knees, burying her face in her hands. "Can you ever forgive me?"

He bent and pressed his lips to her hair. "Yes. I do forgive you." And then he turned and walked from the room, leaving her to sob and mourn the past. For his part, he was done with it. It might take years to remove the talons of the memories from his mind and his heart, but he would no longer dwell on what was and what had been. He had a new life ahead of him, and tonight he would turn toward it.

The meeting with his mother had also presented some interesting questions. Why *had* Melbourne lied to his niece? Why not tell her the truth? Surely adultery was as great a sin as covering up a murder. As the leader of the Barbican group, Melbourne had undoubtedly hidden many murders. Had Melbourne lost faith in his niece? He'd sent her away to the country in what appeared to Dominic to be the agency's greatest hour of need. And now he had restricted her to headquarters. True, she was injured, but even Dominic had to admit the injury did not seem to hamper her much. It was more than a scratch—as she claimed—but it warranted only two stitches, and therefore, not much more.

And so it stood to reason, what else was Melbourne lying about?

Danbury was waiting for Dominic in the vestibule with his greatcoat in hand. Dominic donned it and said, "I am going to White's. If I miss Edgeberry or my brothers, tell them I've asked that they stay here tonight. In addition, gather every available footman, groom, and valet. Set up a rotation of guards. I want the house secure for the night."

Danbury's face paled. "Is there cause for concern, sir?"

"Yes. I hope it is nothing we need worry about, but I want to take every precaution."

"Yes, sir. I will see to it."

Dominic felt a sense of relief when he left the house. For the moment, his mother was as safe as could be expected, and soon he would see his brothers and the marquess safely inside the town house as well. Perhaps that feeling of relief was the reason he did not see the man coming for him. By the time he sensed something was amiss, the hood had been pulled over his face, something crashed over his head, and all went black.

෴

Pierce Moneypence raised his head gingerly. His head had thudded on the floor when Q tackled him, and his ears still rang. "What the devil—" he began.

"Booby trap," Q said, raising her own head. Her face was alarmingly close to his own. Come to think of it, her body was pressed to his, and she was still lying on top of him. He followed her gaze and inhaled sharply when he saw the blade gleaming beside the window. It was attached to a string and had swung down, in the manner of a guillotine, when he'd climbed through the window.

"You must have tripped it when you went through," Q said.

"Yes." He glanced at her, and their gazes met for a long moment. Pierce became aware that Miss Qwillen's body was rather warm and soft. Her breasts were pushed against his chest, and the feel of them was a rather pleasant thing. His gaze dipped to her lips, and he wondered how it would feel to kiss her.

And then, quite suddenly, she scrambled to her feet. "I apologize for my conduct," she said primly.

"It appears Bonde forgot to warn us there might be death traps." She brushed at her skirts, diligently avoiding looking at him. Pierce rose to his feet, his heart thumping, but with quite a different sort of excitement now.

"We must be careful," Miss Qwillen said.

"Right." Back to the mission then. He could not forget the reason they were here, and it was not to think about kissing. Though he hadn't quite forgotten how lovely a shade of pink her lips were.

They found the key Bonde had told them about and unlocked her desk drawer. There was another booby trap there, but it consisted solely of ink, which spattered Moneypence's face and chest. Q offered her handkerchief, and he rubbed it off as best he could, but from the way her mouth quirked each time she looked at him, he had the feeling he had not quite succeeded.

He would not have minded the ink so much if they had found anything of use in the drawer. They did find a document pertaining to the Maîtriser group, but it was little more than a summary of the action Wolf and Saint had taken against Foncé last year. He perused it quickly, and then stood rooted firmly in place. Q was reading it over his shoulder. Her hair had come loose at some point, and a lock of it rested on the sleeve of his coat. He had the urge to touch it, to see how it felt between his fingers.

Slowly, he turned and met her gaze. "Sorry!" she said quickly and stepped away. Was it his imagination, or had her cheeks turned bright pink?

"Should we continue to search?" he asked.

"I can't think where else Bonde might keep

documents," Q said. "Or was that an excuse to paw through her chemises?"

Now he blushed. "The thought did not occur to me. I meant we might search Melbourne's library."

She cast her eyes down. "Oh."

"Jane Bonde is not the only thing I ever think of, you know," he said curtly.

"Ha." Now she looked up, her hazel eyes glittering. "You could have fooled me. You've been mooning over her for as long as I've known you."

"I'm not mooning over her now."

She crossed her arms over her chest. "Really? Only because Dominic Griffyn will flatten your nose if you look at her too long."

"I'm not afraid of him. And he has nothing to do with it."

"Then why aren't you pining for her?"

Daft woman. Couldn't she see? "Because I'm thinking about kissing you!" Pierce could not have said what came over him, but he didn't question it. He reached out, clamped his hands on her upper arms, and dragged her to him. Before she could slap him, he planted a swift kiss on her lips and released her. "There. See?"

She stared at him, her eyes wide, her mouth agape. "I-I—"

He felt a strange sort of pleasure knowing he'd flustered her with the kiss. "We don't have time to stand about all day. Follow me to the library."

Either they were extremely fortunate, or better spies than they'd been given credit for, because they managed to find the library without alerting any of the servants. In fact, Moneypence wondered if Melbourne had dismissed them for the day. The house was eerily quiet. Once in the library, he and Q rummaged through the desk. She seemed particularly intent upon her work, and he supposed that was because if she looked at the desk and the bookshelves, she did not have to look at him.

Had she disliked the kiss that much? She hadn't slapped him, which he thought was a positive development. But he'd never kissed a woman before. Perhaps he had not done it correctly. Perhaps he should ask if they might try it again. He looked at her, on the other side of Melbourne's leather desk chair, and found her looking at him. With a scowl, she went back to her work. So right now might not be the best time to suggest another kiss.

All of the drawers in Melbourne's desk were locked, but Moneypence had the keys to his desk at the Barbican, and the keys also fit this desk. Pierce had known this, because once, M lost his keys and had to borrow Moneypence's spare set until he located those he'd misplaced. However, the lock for one drawer at the bottom of the desk did not match any of the keys he possessed. He'd tried them all twice, when Q approached. "Would you like me to try?"

"I think I can bloody well open a desk drawer." He sat back. "None of the keys fit."

"Hmm." She studied the drawer, her head cocked to one side. On her face was an expression he knew well.

"I do not like that look," he said.

"Which one?" She didn't glance away from the desk.

"The one that says you will shortly use explosives."

She grinned at him, and fiend seize it if she did not look beautiful when she smiled. He almost kissed her again. "Stand back," she said and drew a letter opener from her reticule.

Pierce did not need to be told twice, and from across the room, he said, "Are you intending to force the drawer open?"

"In a manner of speaking." She inserted one end of the opener into the crevice where the drawer met the frame of the desk. She then bent, and he thought she might have tapped the edge of the letter opener, but he could not be certain, because the next thing he knew she was racing toward him. "Duck!" she screamed, and the room shook.

Dominic opened his eyes and immediately attempted to close them again. The world was too bright. He squinted and tried to thrust an arm up to block the light. But he couldn't manage to make his arm work. He might have wondered at that if his head did not feel like it had an axe sticking out of it.

"Mr. Griffyn," a voice said. The voice was away from the light, and Dominic turned his face to it. "Thank you, Tolbert. You may pocket the smelling salts and leave us."

Tolbert, whoever he was, made an unintelligible grunt and walked away. He must have been a large man, because the floor shook with every step. Dominic's eyes were beginning to adjust to the light, and he realized he was in a room—a drawing room from the look of it—and the room was bright because he'd been seated beside a window. The day was not particularly sunny, and so the fact that he could barely keep his eyes open spoke to the pain piercing his head at the moment.

"How are you feeling, Mr. Griffyn?"

It was the voice again. This time Dominic made a concerted effort to look at the man. He was seated in a chair a few feet away, one leg crossed elegantly over the other. His black hair flowed over his shoulders, long and thick. He was tall and broad-shouldered with light eyes and an air of ennui.

"Who the hell are you?" Dominic asked, his voice raspy. He still couldn't use his hands, and it occurred to him to look down. They were bound to the chair. Upon further inspection, he noted his ankles were bound as well. "What the hell is going on here?" Anger flared in him, but there was something else as well.

Fear.

"Oh, now, Mr. Griffyn, do I really need an introduction? I should think you know all about me by now. Your betrothed certainly has a keen interest in me."

"Foncé."

The man clapped his hands. "There, you see. You do know me. What a pleasure to finally meet in person. Your Miss Bonde has given me quite a time of it lately."

Dominic's blood chilled upon hearing the man speak of Jane. For all the man's charm and affability, Dominic could see in the man's eyes something was not right. "I'm not a spy," Dominic said. "I don't know anything about their plans."

Foncé waved a hand languidly. "No, no. I did not expect you to provide me with information. I can glean that very well on my own." He gestured to Dominic, proving by Dominic's very presence that he could gather information.

"What do you want?" Dominic asked. "I won't betray her or the Barbican."

"There is nothing for you to betray. I know it all already."

That was rather disheartening. Dominic twisted his hands, but the rope with which he'd been bound held. He needed to find a way out of here, to warn Jane and Melbourne.

Jane. If anything happened to her, if this man so much as touched her… Dominic clenched his jaw.

"I merely want to ask you one *petite* favor."

"I don't owe you any favors."

"No, no, monsieur, you do not, but I can be most persuasive." He reached into a large black leather bag resting at his feet. Dominic had not noted it before. He did now as Foncé withdrew a long, sharp blade. "Do you see this, Mr. Griffyn?"

Dominic swallowed. "Yes."

"It is called a scalpel. It will slice you open from neck to navel. Shall I demonstrate?"

"I have the general idea, thank you."

Foncé smiled. "I thought you might. And now, for that favor…"

Eighteen

JANE PACED THE EMPTY BARBICAN OFFICES, HER GAZE
on the bracket clock she'd taken from M's office
and set on the desk before her. Dominic should
have returned by now. She'd made three trips to the
Dungeon, all of them fruitless. He was not at the secret
entrance. Had something happened to him? She was
at war with herself, trying to decide whether or not to
look for him. But where would she start? And what
if he returned while she was out? And where was
everyone? She was the only agent in the offices at the
moment. Was everyone doing something productive
but her? She would have thought Q and Moneypence
might have returned by now.

This waiting and wondering was going to drive her
mad. With yet another glance at the bracket clock,
she decided to make one last trip to the Dungeon. If
Dominic was not at the secret entrance, she would
leave headquarters and search for him. She had just
stepped out of the offices when she heard voices in the
stone corridor leading to Piccadilly.

"Finally," she muttered, not knowing who had

returned and not caring. She stopped short when Moneypence and Q approached. Moneypence's face and chest were covered with smears of black. "You're back," she said, meeting them halfway. "Moneypence, what happened to you?"

"Your booby traps," he said, pointing a finger at her. "You might have warned us."

She blinked. "Oh, yes. I quite forgot about them." She waved a hand. "Did you find the document I told you about?"

"Yes," Q said, moving forward and handing it to her.

Jane read it over quickly, shaking her head when she'd finished. "This isn't anything new. It appears I sent you on a meaningless errand...although"—she tilted her head so she might see Q's face better. Was that ink on the woman's lips?—"it does not appear you lacked for amusements."

Q touched her lips absently. Moneypence reached into his coat and withdrew another document. "Actually," he said, "we were rather busy. We searched M's office."

Jane frowned. "You did what? Do you realize you might have gone to gaol for doing something like that?" She smiled. "I'm impressed. What did you find?"

"A very old document about our friend Foncé," Q said. "Apparently, at one time he used a code name."

"Really?" She took the paper and moved closer to one of the wall sconces to scan it. "Did he work for the French? The *Ancien Régime*?"

"Perhaps he worked much closer to home," Moneypence said. "His code name was Chameleon."

Jane rubbed the bridge between her eyes. The name was familiar. "I've heard it. You do not mean to say he worked for the Crown?"

"What we mean to say"—Q stepped into the light—"is he was a member of the Barbican."

⁓

Dominic's hands were untied. He considered that progress. A pistol was aimed at his head, and he was relatively certain that was a step back. The bearlike man pointed the pistol at him, while Foncé smiled slickly across the desk. He pushed vellum, an inkpot, and a quill toward Dominic. "You will write."

"Can't you write your own love letters?" Dominic asked. He was buying time. What would Jane do? If she were in his place, how would she escape?

"You are being humorous," Foncé said, "but in a sense, you are not incorrect. I want you to write my love letter to the Barbican group."

"I hate to be the bearer of bad news, but the Barbican group does not return your affections," Dominic said with an apologetic shrug. Foncé watched him like a hawk. Somehow he had to work his hands down and untie the bindings on his legs. He had managed to loosen them by straining his legs against the rope, but he needed to slice the knots if he was to free himself. If he could just grab hold of one of Foncé's shiny blades…

"Write, or I will kill you now rather than later."

He wasn't ready to die. Not before he'd seen Jane one last time, held her one last time. "Death now or later, what is the difference?"

Foncé leaned close. "Later, I will have Tolbert shoot you. Now, I will carve you like a succulent roast."

Dominic lifted the quill. "I'm ready."

Foncé nodded. "Begin with *My dear Lord Melbourne*." He waited until Dominic scratched the words on the vellum and dipped the quill again. *"I have returned your friend, Mr. Griffyn. Before he died, he penned this note. You wish to meet with me? Come to the Palace of Westminster in one hour. I will be waiting."*

At the words, Dominic jerked, and the pen fell from his palm and to the floor. Edgeberry would be in Parliament tonight.

"Did I surprise you?" Foncé asked.

"Yes." His palms were damp, and he rubbed them on the wool of his greatcoat. He paused when he felt something long and rectangular inside the pocket of the greatcoat. What was that?

"Hands where I can see them," Tolbert grunted.

Dominic put his hands on the desk. "I wondered why you would want Melbourne to come to Parliament." What rectangular object could be in his pocket? It felt like a box. Who would have put a box in his pocket?

"How else will they see the fireworks?"

"There are no fireworks tonight."

"There will be when I am through."

Who else had possession of the coat? No one but Jane. Jane...Q's pen! "Who do you think you are, Guy Fawkes?"

"Oh, much better, Mr. Griffyn. Much better. Only by the time your friends with the Barbican reach me, it will be too late. They will explode with the rest." Foncé looked to his assistant. "You know what to do?"

"Yes."

Foncé started for the door. "Good-bye, Mr. Griffyn. I'll see you in hell." And he strode from the room.

"The devil you will," Griffyn muttered. He had to lay hold of that pen.

"Finish the letter," Tolbert ordered. Right. And as soon as he finished, the minion would shoot him.

"I dropped the pen," Dominic said and nodded to the carpet.

"Fetch it."

Dominic glanced at his legs. "I'm bound."

Tolbert looked at the pen, lying beside Dominic's chair. He was obviously reluctant to bend and retrieve it himself. "I suppose you're not going anywhere." He lifted one of the sharp knives Foncé had left on the desk and slit the rope binding Dominic's legs.

"Thank you."

"The pen."

Dominic bent, and while his body shielded his hands, he slid the box from his pocket, opened it, and deftly removed Q's pen. It shook slightly in his fingers, and he caught it before he could drop it. For a long moment, his heart thudded painfully.

"Write."

Gingerly, Dominic dipped the metal nib into the ink pot and placed the quill's tip on the page. He hoped his keeper would not notice the fine peacock feather had replaced the goose feather of the original pen. Carefully, he wrote the letter of the word where he'd left off.

"Faster!"

Dominic jumped and caught himself before he pressed too hard on the pen. "In a hurry?" he asked casually, writing another word.

"I have to kill you and deliver the body."

"Surely Monsieur Foncé does not want my remains to arrive too early."

"No, I have to have you there at half six, but killing a man is hard work. I'll want my supper after I do it."

"I can imagine." He wrote the last word with a flourish. Now was the moment. He could easily kill this Tolbert and himself, but then who would warn Jane? Who would save her from Foncé? And he was lying to himself if he pretended this was only about saving her. He wanted to save himself too, because, like it or not, he'd bloody well gone and fallen in love with her. Damned inconvenient to fall in love with her when his death was so imminent. He flicked his gaze around the room, searching for an escape. How would Jane escape? It was now or never. Dominic's fingers shook as he pressed the tip hard on the paper and broke it. One…

Dominic rose. Two…

"Sit down." Three…

"I would ask you to kill me standing up." Four… He backed away from the desk. "Perhaps by this wall." Five…

"Stop moving." Tolbert moved in front of the desk. Six…

Tolbert looked to the priming of the pistol, and Dominic backed up farther. Seven…

Tolbert cocked the pistol. Eight…

Dominic knew he was almost to the window. A few more steps. Nine...

He lifted a vase, threw it, and ran. Ten... God, he hoped he'd counted correctly. Tolbert fired, and Dominic couldn't tell if the ball had hit him or not. He stumbled and looked over his shoulder. Tolbert was coming for him. Dominic cursed.

Where was the explosion? Damn, Q!

And then the world burst into flame.

~❦~

Jane stared at the document in her hands, barely lifting her head when the door to her uncle's office opened. M took one moment to note Q, Moneypence, and Jane inside, and thrust his hands on his hips. "What is the meaning of this? I did not give you leave to enter this room."

Ignoring her uncle's protest, Jane lifted the paper. "What is this, Melbourne?"

He sighed. "Good God, now what?" He crossed to her and snatched the paper from her hands. With a glance, he took it in. "Lists of code names for past Barbican agents. Did you take this from my files?" He gave Moneypence an accusatory glance. Moneypence did not shrink back. The expression on his ink-stained face remained cool and stern.

"Yes," Jane said. "I sent Q and Moneypence to our town house to look for a document in my room."

Melbourne looked at the two of them. "Looks like they found more than they bargained for. Q, is that ink on your lips?"

She blushed then cleared her throat. "When we

didn't find anything in Jane's room, we searched your library."

"What?" He slammed his fist on the desk, but behind the anger, Jane saw a flicker of apprehension.

"They found this." Jane nodded at the paper he still held, not waiting for him to peruse it again. "Why did you never tell me Foncé worked for the Barbican group? Why didn't you mention that he was one of ours?"

It all made sense now. Why had Foncé been so successful at picking off and killing the members of the Barbican? Because he knew their methods. He'd trained with them.

She watched Melbourne's expression crumble. He passed a hand over his eyes, and when she saw his face again, it was the face of an old man. "Yes, Foncé was one of ours. He was our best and our worst."

"What happened?" Jane asked. "Why did he turn?"

Her uncle held up a hand and arrowed for the glass decanters on the walnut side table behind his desk. But he ignored all of them and opened a cabinet underneath, pulling a bottle from it and pouring the contents in a small cup. "Whiskey, anyone? It's Irish."

"No," Jane said. Moneypence shook his head.

"I'll take a tot," Q said. Jane blinked at her. Q shrugged and took the tot from Melbourne.

"It's been an interesting day." Her gaze slid to Moneypence, and her cheeks turned pink again.

M sat at his desk and put his head in his hands. His voice was muffled but audible. "Marcel Foncé was one of our best. He was the first agent I trained when I took this post. He amazed me with his skill and his cunning. He was like a son to me." He glanced up at Jane almost apologetically.

"You never saw his dark side?" Jane asked.

"Oh, I saw it," M said, "but I preferred to justify his actions. It soon became clear he was not stable. His mental state was…precarious. I had to terminate his position with the Barbican."

"And he never forgave you," Moneypence whispered.

"But it's more than that," Jane added. "He wants revenge now. He wants you and the Barbican annihilated."

"Yes, he hates me. He wants to hurt me, watch me fail on an enormous scale, kill everyone I care for. That's why I sent you away, Jane."

"No, it's not."

Melbourne's gaze narrowed.

"You sent me away because you didn't want me to learn the truth. That you'd failed with Foncé. That you are responsible for the danger all of us—all of England—is facing right now."

"Now wait here, young lady." M rose.

But she faced him, ignoring his protests. "You said he was like a son. Am I not like a daughter? And as such, I understand what Foncé felt. You know that all I ever wanted from you was love. Affection. Acceptance. Instead, you turned me into an agent. All I care about is all you ever cared about—the mission. You don't care if I live or die. Except if I die before I carry out the mission."

"That's not true, Bonde. Why do you think I wanted you to marry? I want more for you."

"Is that so? Or was it just a convenient method of

sending me away? I know you never had a love affair with Lady Edgeberry. You helped her cover up a murder and allowed her to blackmail you because it served your purposes to send me to Kenham Hall."

"I wanted you safe."

"You wanted me to remain ignorant!"

His face was purple with anger. "What do you want from me, Bonde? My resignation? My admission of failure?" he roared.

"I want you to call me by my name. I'm Jane." The two stared at each other for a long moment. No one in the room dared breathe. And then someone cleared his throat.

"Jane?"

She whirled and saw Blue standing in the door. Behind him a few other agents peered in curiously.

"Blue, this is not the time," M said, voice weary now.

"Actually, I didn't come to speak to you." His vivid blue eyes never left Jane's face, and she felt a frisson of fear race up her spine. "The other agents are waiting to give you reports, but I have news for you, Jane."

"What is it?"

He hesitated, and she saw something like compassion in his eyes. Oh, no. She did not want compassion. She did not want pity. "Spit it out, Blue. Say it."

"Griffyn is dead."

Nineteen

JANE COULD NOT BREATHE. SHE FELT HER KNEES BUCKLE and thought: This is what it must feel like to faint. She grasped the back of a chair before she could go down, and thus saved herself the humiliation of crumpling before most of the Barbican. Blue rushed to her side, catching her elbow, but she shook him off.

"I'm fine," she snapped. She met his gaze and saw pity in his eyes. She did not want pity.

"How the hell can he be dead?" M asked. "He was instructed to stay here."

Jane closed her eyes. This was her fault. She should not have allowed him to go. She should have insisted he stay safely inside headquarters. Dominic was no trained spy. He never had a chance.

"My sources tell me that about two hours ago, he was brought to the house we've been watching," Blue said.

The house they'd been watching. Blue's words echoed in her mind. The only reason the Barbican would be watching a house was because they suspected Foncé was inside. Slowly, she lowered herself into the chair. She could not bear to think what Foncé might have done to Dominic. Her beautiful Dominic.

"Foncé left about an hour ago."

"Did you follow him?" Baron asked, coming into the room.

"Yes, but I lost him. When I realized he was gone, I doubled back. I returned to the house in time to witness the explosion."

"Explosion?" Q asked.

"A rather large one," Blue said. "The house burned to the ground—what was left of it. I did not see anyone escape." He looked at Jane. "I'm sorry."

But Jane was looking at Q. "Your pen," she said to Q. "I dropped it in the pocket of his greatcoat. Could it do that much damage?"

Miss Qwillen shook her head. "Not by itself."

A rumble of murmurs passed through the room as more and more agents filed inside. Jane spotted Lord Smythe, but he was without Saint this evening.

"Then how do you account for it?" M asked.

"There must have been other explosives present," Q said. And then her eyes widened. "You do not think Foncé had been planning to use them to target the royal family?"

"Oh, he'd been planning to use them," Blue said. "I'll wager those were not the extent of his armory. He has more somewhere."

"We will stop him before he has a chance to use them." M came around his desk. "Reports! I want to know what you saw, what you heard, what you learned."

Jane tried to concentrate on the reports of the other agents. She knew their information might be crucial, and now, more than ever before, she wanted to kill Foncé for what he'd done. But her mind kept drifting. She couldn't stop thinking about Dominic— little things, like the way he tucked her arm in the crook of his elbow, the way he held a fork as though it was more of a weapon than an eating utensil, the way his dark eyes turned even darker when he looked at her. Her breath hitched, and she felt a warm hand on her shoulder. She looked up and into the eyes of Butterfly, Elinor Keating. "Stay strong, Bonde. Think about now. Think only of this moment. Later you can grieve."

Jane nodded. The other agent was right. Later, Jane could fall apart, rail and weep and beat her breast. Right now she had a mission.

She took a deep breath and focused on Wolf's report. When all of the agents had given an account, M sighed deeply. "We're no closer than we were, but I'll be damned if I sit around and wait for Foncé to blow something up before we act. We—"

"I'm terribly sorry to interrupt."

Everyone, M included, turned toward the door. "Mr. Felix," M said impatiently. "Can it not wait?"

"I don't think so, my lord. There's a man here to see you with urgent news. He has an old password, so I haven't let him in."

M's brow furrowed. "One of Foncé's men?"

"I don't think so," Felix said. "I saw him with Miss Bonde before."

Jane rose and cried out, "Dominic?"

Felix shook his head. "He said his name was Griffyn…"

Jane grabbed Felix's arm. "Take me to him. Where is he?" But she didn't wait for Felix to tell her. She ran for the Piccadilly entrance without another word. Behind her, she could hear the footsteps of the other agents echo in the stone corridor. They continued on when she reached the door, which she threw open.

Dominic Griffyn stepped into the opening. He was covered in black soot, a cut on his forehead bled, and his coat was in shreds, but he was alive. She fell into his embrace, meeting his ash-stained lips with her own. She did not care that he smelled of smoke and charred wood. She cared only that he was alive, that his arms wrapped around her, that he lifted her and pressed her tightly against him.

"No, don't cry," he whispered when he pulled back for a moment. Jane wasn't even aware that she was crying. "I'm here."

"But Blue…" She was sobbing too much to speak. Jane was also aware of others crowding around them, pulling Dominic inside, closing and bolting the door, but she wouldn't leave his side. She wouldn't be separated.

"We thought you were dead," Baron said.

"Indeed, you look like a cat who's just lost one of its nine lives. Perhaps two, at that," Blue remarked.

"I'm not dead yet," Dominic said, squeezing her waist with the arm he had wrapped around her. "But we haven't any time to waste. I know where Foncé is going, and I know what he plans."

❧

Once he mentioned Foncé, Dominic was spared recounting the details as to how he'd survived the blast. He wasn't entirely certain himself. One moment he had been backing up, the next he'd been hurtling through the air, shattered glass flying around him. When he opened his eyes and came to, he deduced that he must have been close enough to a window that he was thrown through when the glass shattered. He wasn't entirely certain whether Tolbert had been thrown out as well, so he wasted no time putting distance between himself and the house. That proved to be a wise decision, as moments later, another explosion rocked the very ground under his feet.

Every single bone in his body ached, and his tongue was swollen and thick with the taste of soot. But he ignored the discomforts and made his way to Piccadilly. He received quite a few curious looks. It was but half past three, and he hoped most would take him for a chimney sweep, though he was a bit broad for that profession. No one stopped him, and now in Melbourne's office with a glass of whiskey in his hand, he glanced at the bracket clock. It was almost four. He was running out of time.

"And that is all you know?" Melbourne asked. "Foncé said he planned to blow up Parliament."

"Yes. He asked me to pen a note, which he wanted delivered to you, so that you might arrive in time to be caught in the explosion. If we go now, we might still be able to stop him."

"We need a plan," Lord Smythe argued. "Is he targeting the House of Commons or Lords? He cannot possibly have enough explosives to do away with the entire palace."

"Considering he was targeting the Prince of Wales

before, my guess is he will aim for the Court of Requests, where the House of Lords meets," Blue said.

"I concur," Melbourne said, "but we divide into groups. We want to cover all entrances and exits and every possibility." Melbourne went on, but Dominic didn't listen. Instead, he looked at Jane. She was looking at him. Her cheeks were streaked with soot where his hands had touched her. He should be ashamed to tarnish her beauty so, but he was curiously glad he'd marked her. She was his. She was the only thing he could think about when he'd realized Foncé intended to kill him—and would likely succeed. He wanted more time with Jane.

"I thought you were dead," she whispered.

"*I* thought I was dead," he murmured back. They were seated on a couch, crushed together, as four people were seated on the furnishing, which was meant for three. "But I'm alive, and I owe that to you."

"I think you owe it to Q."

"Yes, she deserves my thanks, but I don't think I would have been desperate enough to use the quill if I hadn't wanted to come back to you so badly. I kept thinking, *what would Bonde do?*"

She laughed, which earned her a frown from the agents nearby. "And what was your answer?" she asked quietly.

"Bonde would do the most outrageous thing possible—blow herself up."

"Well, yes, but I *am* a professional."

"Of course." He leaned forward and kissed her. There was a time when a kiss was foreign to him, when touching someone so freely was abhorrent. Now he could not get enough of kissing Jane, touching her.

"You're safe here," she said.

"No." He shook his head. "Edgeberry and Lord Trewe are at Westminster tonight. I'll not stay behind."

The agents were rising, each with his mission. Dominic rose too. No one would argue if he went along. They had no more time for talk. Jane was the only one he expected to protest, but she merely nodded and said, "Stay close to me."

He followed the other agents to a courtyard he hadn't known existed. A dozen horses had been saddled and were waiting for riders. Jane waved away his help in mounting, and he chose a thoroughbred that looked fast and eager. As one, they rode out of the courtyard gates and into the city.

❧

The sun was low in the sky, giving the horizon an eerie glow. Jane didn't like it. She was not superstitious, but even she had to admit the look of fire in the sky was a bad omen. She understood the need for strategy. She understood the need for a master plan, but she worried they had talked too long. Were they already too late? Or were they riding straight into Foncé's trap?

No one had suggested that possibility, though it had been on all of their minds. Perhaps Foncé was merely waiting for their arrival to light the fuse and send them all to the hereafter. The biting wind whipped through her hair as they drew closer to Whitehall. Jane was not afraid to die, but she desperately wanted to live. She'd never been afraid to die, but she'd also never before had a reason to live. She had to stop Foncé, or she would never know what her life with Dominic might have been.

Darkness was falling when she spotted the Palace of Westminster. The building was a mix of the old and the new, the architect James Wyatt's stone additions clashing with the original medieval structure. Jane had been inside only a handful of times. Women were not allowed inside Parliament, and she had never seen the chambers. But she knew the building was a winding maze of staircases, old rooms, new chambers, and passageways leading nowhere.

Dominic arrived just ahead of her, and while Melbourne and several other agents explained the situation to the guards at the palace, Jane followed Wolf, Baron, Blue, and Butterfly into Westminster. Dominic was right behind her, but she could not worry about him at the moment. She had a single focus: destroying Foncé.

Still, she did not want to drag Dominic into something he could not handle. She paused in the entrance they'd chosen and looked back at him. "Are you certain you wish to go along? You could wait outside."

"I'm going with you," he said, his jaw set. "I know the dangers."

"Don't get in my way," she said, realizing belatedly how the injunction sounded. But she did not have time to worry about offending him.

He grinned at her. "Don't get in *my* way." He gestured ahead of them where the other agents had started down the old stone steps and into the damp bowels of the building. It had been used in the sixteenth century as a royal residence. King Henry VIII had once lived here, but Jane doubted he'd ever ventured into this dank section. He and Anne Boleyn had probably confined their amorous embraces to the upper floors and courtyards. Only the most unfortunate or disfavored courtiers had ever been forced into this section of the palace.

The six of them moved silently. The palace had dozens of entrances and exits. Foncé might have used any of them. A quick consultation with Constantine, the master of the Dungeon, had produced an ancient drawing of the palace. The drawing was not detailed, but it appeared these steps led below the Court of Requests. Another group of agents was undoubtedly venturing beneath St. Stephen's Chapel, where the House of Commons met. Melbourne, Moneypence, and Q were alerting the parliamentary members of the danger and urging them to vacate the building. Still, Jane could not suppress a shiver. If Foncé acted now, he would destroy not only all of Parliament, but the entirety of the Barbican as well.

At the bottom of the stairs, Wolf, who had been leading the group, paused. "The passageway splits here," he whispered. "Baron, you and Lady Keating take that corridor. Blue and I will take this. Bonde, you and Griffyn take the third."

Jane nodded and pulled her pistol from her boot. "Shoot to kill," she told the other agents, who, likewise, had armed themselves. "Take no prisoners."

"Agreed," Baron said. "And God go with you."

Jane motioned for Dominic to follow her, and

they started down a dark, narrow passage. When the sounds of the other agents' footfalls faded, she thought she could hear the scurrying of rats and other small creatures. She longed for a light, one simple candle, but she could not afford to do anything that might alert Foncé to their approach.

"The ground seems to slope downward," Dominic murmured behind her. He was staying close, the heat of his body warming her back.

"Another set of steps," she answered, slowing so she would not be taken off guard. When she felt the ground give away at her toe, she paused and pressed her back against the wall. "Are you still with me?" If he was half as terrified as she, his heart must be in his throat. She had learned long ago that she thrived on the fear, fed on it. To venture down this black stair-well was utterly terrifying. And exhilarating.

"I'm with you," he said, his voice sounding steady. "I must be mad to follow you."

"I'm quite mad to go," she answered, taking his hand. It was cold and dry. "Ready?"

"Answer me this: Will we survive?"

"Doubtful."

"In that case, I'd better tell you." He yanked her around so she was crushed against him. He was so warm and solid, and his mouth was close to her ear when he whispered, "I love you."

Her heart pounded for quite another reason now. "You must. After all, you're following me into the depths of hell."

"Jane…"

She smiled. "You know I love you too." She rose

on tiptoe and kissed him gently. "If we survive, I'll show you how much."

"Incentive to live," he murmured against her lips and then gently released her. If possible, it was harder to begin the descent down that blind staircase now than before. But she did so. She clenched her hands on the pistol and stepped into the void.

The steps were steep and narrow, and her heart thumped as much from excitement as from the fear of falling. She seemed to descend forever, and when the staircase finally ended, she felt along the wall for some clue as to which direction to choose. She could feel Dominic behind her, staying close as they edged along the old stone. They moved silently and as one. Jane took long, slow breaths to keep the panic at bay. She was beginning to wonder if they might have become lost in the maze of the old palace when she heard something scrape along the stone. She paused, reached back, and squeezed Dominic's hand in question.

"Not me," he whispered so low she almost couldn't hear him. Her chest was tight with fear, and her legs felt as heavy as cannon balls, but she forced herself to move forward. The wall curved, and as she slid around, she saw the first sliver of light. It was coming from a door at the end of the passageway. That small shaft of light illuminated all for her. She glanced back at Dominic, craving the sight of his face. And when she saw him, she took comfort in the cool, determined expression he wore. She didn't need to tell him this was it. He knew Foncé lay ahead of them. She took another step forward, her gaze on the door. It was slightly ajar, and she watched for any sign of movement.

She did not see the bend in the corridor, the alcove just large enough for a man to fit his body if he made an effort. She did not spot it until it was too late, and Foncé's arm snaked around her, the blade of his knife at her throat.

Twenty

Q WATCHED AS MONEYPENCE USHERED A GROUP OF arguing members of the House of Commons out of St. Stephen's Chapel. They were not moving as quickly as she would have had she been alerted to the fact that a madman planned to blow up the building, but she supposed Moneypence and she were probably having an easier time of it than Melbourne, who had taken the House of Lords. She followed the last of the MPs out, and Moneypence fell into step behind her. Her spine tingled at his closeness. Considering their situation, her feelings seemed entirely inappropriate, but she could hardly fail to notice when he was near. After all, she'd been in love with him for years.

And now—today—he'd noticed her. He'd kissed her! How could she not tingle in his presence? And how could she not question his motives? Had he simply kissed her because he was upset about Bonde's betrothal? Q was not anyone's second choice. She was not anyone's first choice, either, but that seemed beside the point.

The point, or what should have been the point, was

that the madman Foncé was attempting to blow up the Palace of Westminster. That should have been her focus. But when the MPs slow shuffle caused her to pause, and Moneypence paused beside her, she gave him a sidelong look. He wasn't as broad or tall as the agents working for the Barbican, but men like Baron and Wolf intimidated her. Nor was Moneypence as handsome as Blue, but she was no diamond of the first water. Moneypence had a pleasant look and a regal bearing. He always stood straight and seemed sure of himself. He had lovely brown eyes, good teeth, and a keen mind. Not to mention, much like her, he was far too intelligent to rush headlong into danger. In her opinion, that made agents rather more foolish than brave. The Barbican could use his—and her—talents elsewhere.

He was quite obviously an intelligent man, and that was why, as they stood there with nothing to do, she had to know. "Why did you do it?" she asked suddenly.

He blinked at her in the adorable way he had when he was confused. "Pardon?"

She looked over her shoulder at the MPs, who were still shuffling, slow as snails. She stepped closer to him. "I asked why you did it. Why did you kiss me at Bonde's town house?"

"I…ah—did I offend you?"

"No."

"Good…then…must we speak of this now?"

"Why not now?"

He waved a hand quickly. "No reason. I suppose I kissed you because I wanted to. I think I've wanted to kiss you for quite some time, Miss Qwillen. I just did not know I did."

How was she supposed to react to that kind of sentiment? She wasn't the type to swoon, and smacking him because he had been such a dolt for all this time hardly seemed an appropriate reaction. "Are you going to kiss me again?" she asked.

"I might," he said cautiously.

"You had better," she told him. He nodded then extended his arm, indicating she should precede him to the exit of the palace. She did so, following the last of the MPs into the streets where the guards had stopped passing carriages and were ushering the parliamentarians onto the Old Palace Yard, a safe distance away. She did not spot Melbourne or any of the lords, but they were in another building and might have exited another way. She moved toward the guards, eager to be out of the shadow of Westminster, but someone caught her arm. She turned, and Moneypence was looking at her. He was only slightly taller than she was and not much more substantive, but in the moment, he seemed large and safe and secure.

"Miss Qwillen, before I kiss you again, I have one question. What is your given name? Mine is Pierce."

She'd known that. How many times had she whispered *Pierce Moneypence* to herself before falling asleep?

"It's Eliza," she said. "Eliza Qwillen."

"Eliza."

She liked the sound of her name on his lips.

"May I court you, Eliza?"

Foolish man! He'd already kissed her. Did he not know he could court her? "Yes, Pierce," she said. "You may."

"May I kiss you, Miss Qwillen? Dear Eliza?"

"Yes, Pierce." She smiled. "You'd better."

He bent and brushed his warm lips over hers, warming her through and through. She closed her eyes and leaned into him, and that was when they heard the sound of an explosion.

❦

The cold steel of the blade slid over the vulnerable skin of her throat, and Jane dared not do so much as swallow. She could feel Foncé behind her. He was taller than she'd thought he'd be, more solid and more muscled. This was no puny weakling. This was a man of power. He smelled clean, as though he'd bathed recently. She was dismayed not to detect the scent of fear on him. She was certain he could smell her fear. But this time she was not afraid for herself. She was afraid for Dominic. She tried to catch his eye, to tell him all was well. She would be well. It was a lie, of course. She was going to die.

Dominic saw her look, their gazes met, but he did not step back. His expression could only be described as murderous. That was not good. He would end up dead himself, at this rate.

"Agent Bonde," Foncé said silkily, his breath caressing her ear. "Finally, we meet."

"Foncé," she said, moving her mouth as little as possible. "I cannot claim this is a pleasure."

"Too bad. Call off your attack dog. Mr. Griffyn and I have met before. If we had more time, you would have to tell me how you managed to escape."

"I have a few surprises in me," Dominic murmured.

Jane glared at him, willing him to take himself and

his surprises to safety. She had to think now. She had to think and plot, and she did not want to consider anyone's safety. She might have to sacrifice herself to stop Foncé—she certainly would—but she did not think she could sacrifice Dominic. This was why she never worked with a partner.

This was why she'd never allowed herself to fall in love.

She stared at Dominic now, knowing that she could never allow any harm to come to him. More than that, she herself did not want to die. She wanted to live because he loved her.

"Would you like me to show you my surprise?" Foncé asked.

Jane took a breath. "Yes. I want to see it, but you have to let him go."

"What do I care?" Foncé asked. "It is too late for him to save you." The hand around her midsection tightened, and he dragged her toward the open door.

"Go, Dominic," she said, keeping her voice hard and emotionless. "Get out."

"I won't leave you," he said. Vexing man.

"How terribly touching," Foncé said, mocking them. "Shall I kill him and solve the dilemma?"

"Go, Dominic," she said. "I don't want you."

He knew she was lying, but she would have said anything to make him leave her. He couldn't save her. Foncé would kill her for half an excuse. He was already digging the knife into her flesh, and she felt the trickle of blood oozing down her neck where he'd pricked her with the point of the blade. This was a man who liked to cut, who liked to carve.

Dominic did not move, but Foncé continued to drag her. She blinked into the bright light of the room and stared at Dominic's face before Foncé kicked the door closed. Then he swung her around, and she blinked in shock at the monstrosity in the center of the room. It was a simple room, rectangular in shape, one entrance and one exit. There were no windows, as it was underground, and she noted the faint outline of furnishings on the floor where pieces had once inhabited the space. A storage room for clothing? No, too damp. Perhaps for plate or serving utensils?

But now it had become something else entirely. Crates and crates labeled *Gunpowder* had been stacked in the center, rising almost to the ceiling. Snaking out from the stack in all directions were long fuses. It would take but a single spark to ignite one and blow them all into oblivion.

"What do you think, *chérie*?" he asked. "Do you love it? My little creation?"

She didn't know what to say. She didn't know if it would help to say anything. Had enough time passed for the MPs and the lords to have escaped? And did it even matter? Dominic had said he would not leave her. Could she allow Foncé to kill him without even a fight?

"You do not have to do this," she said, feeling the knife point cut into her skin at each word. "I know you want revenge, but if you want to kill Melbourne, why not go after him? He is far away from the palace at this moment. You won't hurt him by your actions."

"Oh yes, I will. I will hurt him more than a simple death ever could. You know it as well as I. The shame of his failure will eat him alive."

It was true. God help her, but it was entirely true. This would ruin what had been a long and stellar career for Melbourne. This would tarnish his sterling reputation forever.

"Why do you hate him so?"

Foncé laughed softly. She felt him laughing more than she heard it. She hated being so close to him, having his hands on her. She itched to dig her elbow into his belly, kick his shin, smash his nose with the back of her head, but any such action on her part would leave her lying in a pool of blood from the gash in her throat. And Foncé would be free to strike a match to a flint and light the fuses. "*Chérie*, you know better than anyone else why I hate him. I hate him for the same reason you do."

"I don't hate him."

He laughed again; this time she could hear the mirthless sound. "Yes, you do. You despise him. Admit it, and I may allow you to live another minute."

Jane could play along. Another minute, and she might find a way to stop him. "Fine. I despise Melbourne." She was surprised at the vehemence in her voice, surprised that she meant what she said, even though she had been humoring Foncé.

"Of course you do. He used you. Just as he used me."

She shook her head, feeling the flat of the blade hot on her skin now. "We're nothing alike."

"There you are wrong." He moved her closer to the altar in the center of the room, pushed her away, and the sudden freedom startled her. She stumbled and fell onto one of the gunpowder crates. The acrid smell of it burned her throat and nostrils.

"We could be brother and sister," Foncé said, kneeling before her like a nervous suitor asking for the hand of his lady. "He took you in when you were lost and afraid. Your parents were dead, and you had nowhere else to go. He gave you security in a world turned confusing and frightening."

Jane stared at him, this handsome man who seemed to know all of her thoughts and feelings. It was true. When she'd lost her parents at the age of six, her entire life had changed. But Lord and Lady Melbourne had welcomed her. They had given her a home with no conditions.

Or so she had thought.

"You were grateful," Foncé said. "So grateful you would risk your life for him. You would kill for him."

"No." She shook her head. That was not why she had joined the Barbican.

"*Oui*," Foncé said, nodding his head. "You wanted love and the security of a family, and he turned your innocent desires into clay he could mold to his liking."

Jane felt her face burn. It was as though Foncé looked deep into her heart, into her mind, and read the story written there. But she was no naive child. She knew Foncé's tactics. Nothing he said was meant to soothe her. Here she sat, on his altar like a pagan sacrifice. He would kill her when he was finished tearing down her defenses. "You have done your research, Monsieur Foncé, but my story is not yours."

"Is it not? I too was an orphan. I fled the brutality of the revolution in France. I arrived in London home-less, penniless, friendless. Your uncle—he was no lord then—took me in, showed me kindness, and gave me a vocation. I was part of your precious Barbican. I made it what it is. The prestige of the Barbican group was founded on the blood of the traitors I murdered."

She stared at him, hating him and wanting desperately to discount everything he said. But she could not. There was too much truth, despite the madness she saw in his eyes.

"You think me a cold-hearted killer," he said. "It's true. I like to kill. I like to cut." Spittle flew from his lips as he spoke. "But who showed me how to kill? Who showed me how to make an efficient, clean cut with my knife? A flick of my wrist across a man's throat, and he is dead quickly and painlessly. It is not murder if it is done in the service of King and Country."

Jane closed her eyes. She knew her uncle's methods and his words. He'd taught her the same technique. Given her the same trite justifications.

"But in time I came to loathe myself, loathe what I was doing, and I began to hate. Do you understand that, Bonde?"

"Yes." She lowered her head, eyes still closed. Why did Foncé not light the fuse? Why did he not kill them all? She wanted to die. She knew the loathing Foncé spoke of. She'd felt it too. She'd taken lives. She'd played God. She was no assassin, as Foncé had been trained, but she had done her share of murder in the name of the Crown. And though she had her reasons, her *justifications*, she hated herself every time she took a man's life. She despised herself and the Barbican for what she did. "I understand the resentment," she said, opening her eyes and looking at him. She saw him differently now. He was one of them. He was part of the Barbican. Her brother in so many ways. "He never gave me a choice. He took any chance I had for a normal life from me and gave me"— she waved a hand at the madness of the altar Foncé had built in the hollows of the Palace of Westminster—"this in its place. For that I do resent him."

Slowly she stood. "But I am not a child any longer, and I have not been for years. I cannot blame my uncle for all of my choices. I made some on my own. You, too, made your own choices. You chose to become a traitor. You chose to kill the innocent. M did not force your hand."

"You still do not understand," Foncé said, shaking his head. "When will you ever understand?"

"When will you?" And she kicked out, landing a boot squarely under his jaw, jerking his head back so he lost his balance. The dagger he held clattered to the floor, and Jane jumped.

∾

He was lost. Dominic was lost. It had killed him to watch Jane disappear behind that door with Foncé. It had pierced his heart to walk away from her, but it had been the only way. Alone he could not save her. He knew horses, not combat. But he knew who could save her, and he'd retraced their steps, running and calling out until Wolf and Blue had met him, their gazes hard with anger and concern.

Now he led the two agents back, praying he remembered the way. If he made a wrong turn…if he did not remember correctly, he would lose her. He would lose the only person he had ever come to love. He could not lose her.

He lost his footing, and Blue caught his arm, hauling him back from the abyss. "I remember this," Dominic said when he caught his breath. "The steps lead to the chamber where Foncé has her."

"You're certain?" Wolf asked.

Dominic looked at the two men. They would follow him now, though they surely must know there was a distinct possibility that he was mistaken. There were hundreds of such stairwells. And if he was not mistaken, they would still follow him. They'd follow him to what might be their death.

"I'm certain." And he led the way.

&

Jane landed on Foncé and struck him before he could retaliate. But he was a trained agent, one trained by the same master who had trained her, and it took him only a second to recover and strike back. He kicked her in the belly, and she skidded across the floor on her back. Instead of advancing, of taking advantage of her weakness, he turned toward the lost weapon. He was no fool, this Foncé. With a cry, Jane bounced to her feet and went for the dagger too. She knocked Foncé out of the way and reached for it.

Her fingers grasped the cold metal before Foncé kicked her hand away. She elbowed him, and they both went down. She caught his leg as he crawled for the weapon, and he dragged her across the floor.

Belatedly, she realized he was no longer reaching for the dagger. He was moving toward a table where a lamp burned.

"No!" She released him, rolled, swiped the dagger,

and blocked his path. Calmly, he set the lamp down and inclined his head. She was breathing hard, but she managed, "This is...over."

"Not until I light it, *ma chérie*."

She gasped in a breath. "Never."

And the door slammed open.

※

From over Wolf's shoulder Dominic could see Jane. She had managed to wrest the knife away from Foncé, and now she faced him with the blade in her hand. But their entrance had taken her off guard, and Foncé moved quickly. Too quickly. He grabbed Jane about the waist and took hold of her wrist, raising her hand and the blade to her throat. She wore a simple day dress in dark blue with white lace at the rounded neck. It was a modest cut made gruesome by the crimson stain of her blood on the white lace. The man had already cut her, and he would make the deep, deadly one now.

"Agent Wolf. Agent Blue," Foncé said. He sounded completely at ease, while Dominic could see Jane struggled to catch her breath. "So kind of you to join us. I have a fireworks display to show you."

"Release her," Wolf said, training his pistol on Foncé. Blue cocked his own weapon and pointed it at the madman. Dominic fused his gaze on Jane's. She was watching him. There was no fear in her eyes, only resignation, only regret. He shook his head. It was not over yet. He would not lose her.

Foncé angled her body toward the table they stood beside. "Miss Bonde, if you would be so kind as to take hold of that lamp."

"No," she said. Foncé dug the knife deep into her skin, forcing her head up.

"Do it."

Her gaze flicked to Wolf. "Shoot him," she said. "It's the only way."

"Shut up and take the lamp."

She did not move, her gaze still locked on Wolf's. "Kill him. Kill me. I'm dead anyway."

"Take the shot," Blue said.

"No!" Dominic heard himself scream. He hadn't even known he would speak.

"If you won't take the lamp, I will." Still holding Jane as a shield, Foncé reached for the lamp. Jane managed to slide out of the line of sight, and the room exploded with the sound of a pistol shot.

❧

Jane pushed the dead weight off her and stumbled forward. She didn't see who caught her, but she knew by his scent and the feel of his body it was Dominic. She buried her face in his chest, feeling unaccountably exhausted.

It was over. She was still alive. But there was no triumph in the victory. She felt hollow and empty. For the first time she walked away from a mission without the thrill of success coursing through her veins. There was no glory in this.

"He's dead," Blue said. "Good shot, Wolf."

Jane opened her eyes and turned her head. Blue knelt beside Foncé's lifeless body. He withdrew a handkerchief, pristine white, from his ghastly puce coat and wiped the blood from his fingers. And then he allowed the cloth to fall over Foncé's face. Wolf turned away, the look in his eyes as dead as she felt inside.

"It's over," he said to no one and all of them. "It's finally over."

The four of them limped toward the surface, seeking fresh air and what remained of the light, like worms after a heavy rain. They met Baron and Butterfly rushing toward them, and no words were needed to explain what had happened. The six of them emerged from the palace together, blinking in the noise and light of the Old Palace Yard.

Q and Moneypence were the first to greet them, but Moneypence, seeing the blood on Jane's collar, immediately stepped back. "I'm fine," she assured him.

M elbowed his way through. "Foncé?" he asked.

"Dead," Wolf said. "It's over."

Jane watched as relief flashed on her uncle's face, and she saw something else as well: regret. It would never be over for Melbourne. And it would never be over for her.

"My lord! Lord Smythe," a voice called from outside the circle of the Barbican. Beside her, Wolf raised his head.

"Wallace?" He sounded confused. Jane was confused as well. What was the Smythe's butler doing here?

"My lord, Lady Smythe has sent for you."

"How the devil did you find him here?" Baron asked.

The butler gave him a withering look, as if to say there was no place he could not find his employer. "I have my methods, Lord Keating."

"Sophia," Wolf said, bringing the matter of his wife

back to the forefront. "She sent for me?" He'd gone rather pale, Jane noticed.

"She has begun her labor, my lord."

Wolf's knees gave way, and he would have sat down if Blue had not caught him.

"She requests your presence at her side," Wallace said, as though his master had not all but collapsed.

"Of course," Wolf—who was looking more and more like Adrian Galloway and less like a renowned agent for the Barbican—said and attempted to stand on his own.

"It will all be well, Lord Smythe," Butterfly said, stepping forward. "Winn and I will go with you. Wallace, have you brought the carriage?"

"Yes, my lady."

"Good. Then make haste, Lord Smythe. You will soon be a father."

Baron took one side of the unsteady Lord Smythe, and Butterfly took the other. They began moving toward a carriage sitting on Margaret Street. In the last of the day's light, Jane could just make out the Smythe crest on the door.

Lady Keating looked back at them. "Are you coming?" she asked.

"Ahh…" Blue stammered. "No. I have a prior engagement."

"Coward," Baron called over his shoulder.

"You leave assassins to me," Blue answered, "and I leave babies to you."

"Shall we accompany them on horseback?" Dominic asked. Jane turned, surprised at his words. "That is, if you are feeling well enough." He touched her neck gingerly.

"This? It is just a—"

"Scratch. Yes, I know."

She studied him in the gray dusk. Unlike Blue, his face showed no sign of panic. "You want to go along?"

He shrugged. "Perhaps we should see what is involved in the business of marriage and family. That is, if you still want to marry me."

"Oh, I do. I do."

Hand in hand, they started for their mounts, and it was only when they had arrived at the Smythe's town house on Charles Street that she realized her uncle had not accompanied them, nor had he spoken except to inquire after Foncé. The man who had once been so central to her life had faded into the background. She glanced at Dominic, riding beside her, and found him looking back at her.

All was finally as it should be.

Twenty-one

THEY LAY IN THE CLEAN HAY OF THE STABLES AT Kenham Hall, listening to the sounds of the horses settling down for the night. Jane rested her head on his chest, and he absently stroked her bare shoulder. She still wore her chemise, but little else. He'd yanked his trousers back on because he did not relish the idea of one of his grooms seeing him bare-arsed, although that was exactly what he'd been a few moments before.

It still amazed him that this beautiful woman would soon be his. His wife. What amazed him more was that she loved him. She really did. She'd been patient with him these past few weeks as the last of his rules slipped away. Now he felt only slightly edgy when she touched him, as she did right now, her hand resting on his chest beside her cheek. The feel of her hands on him had become more comforting and arousing than triggers to the past.

He still had nightmares. He had not forgotten the past, but he was learning to separate what he had with Jane from the abuse he'd suffered as a boy.

She shivered, and he pulled her closer to share his

warmth. It was summer now, but the coldest summer he could remember. "Shall we go inside?"

"Yes," she answered, not moving. "In a moment. Tomorrow night you shall have to allow me to come to your rooms."

"And if you're caught?"

She made a sound of derision. "I will not be caught. Besides, now that we have the grain thief, we do not need to meet in the stables any longer."

He smiled. "I think you like the stables. There are no servants to hear you."

She rose on one elbow, her chemise dipping low to reveal the swell of a breast. "I am a perfect lady."

"You are. Even on your back in the straw. Even when you toss me on my back." He was grinning, and she grinned back. She could not stay angry with him, not when they both felt so pleasantly satiated at the moment. Not if she was even slightly as content as he. His grain thief had indeed been caught just a day after they'd retreated from London and come to stay at Kenham Hall. The man had been a disgruntled groom Dominic had let go last season. He'd been sneaking into the stables and stealing the premium grain then selling it. Now the thief sat in the local gaol, awaiting prosecution.

Jane could finally rest easy. Foncé was dead, and the country was safe. He knew her thoughts still turned to the Barbican at times. They had left it in a state of upheaval. He would have stayed in London with her while matters were sorted, but she wanted out of the city, and where better to go than her betrothed's country estate?

"I had a letter today," she said quietly. The tone of her voice alerted him to the seriousness of the contents, and he sat, pulling her up beside him. A lamp burned nearby, and in the dancing flames her hair looked like gold and her face glowed like an angel's.

"From whom?"

"Baron—Lord Keating."

"What does he say?"

"The gist of it is that he is now head of the Barbican group."

Dominic blinked.

"You thought it would go to Wolf?" she asked, noting his surprise.

"I thought Melbourne would remain."

She pushed her hair back from her face. "Then there would be no Barbican. The king would not force Melbourne out, but no agent would work for him. Foncé was one of his, trained by him personally. M failed in his role as a leader."

"Is that what Baron said?"

"It is what my uncle said. Here." She climbed to her knees and reached for her discarded gown. Rifling through it, she found a crumpled envelope. Dominic squinted in the dim light of the lamp but could not make out the words. "Never mind, I have it memorized. The part that matters says, *and so I am retiring. I take full responsibility for my failings. Baron has my support and loyalty, and I hope yours as well.*

"He goes on like that for a page or so, and then he apologizes to me."

"That does not sound like him."

She shrugged. "He says, *I always loved you, but I*

suppose I did not love you enough." Her voice broke on the last, and Dominic gathered her into his lap.

"I'm sorry." He cradled her close, like one might a child. "I love you. It isn't as much as you deserve—"

"It's more than I deserve," she interrupted. "It's everything." She snuggled into his chest, and he held her to him, savoring the feel of her. This was what he had been missing in his life. This closeness, this oneness.

"You once said you would laugh when I told you I loved you," he reminded her.

"I do not feel so jovial at the moment, although there is cause to celebrate."

"What is that?"

"Lady Keating included a note along with Baron's letter. I read it first because I do tire of Baron's directives."

He smiled. "And what did it say?"

"That the Smythes' son is doing very well indeed. She says he has a hearty appetite and a lusty yell, and Lord and Lady Smythe have called him their most difficult mission yet. Lord Keating has taken to trying to steal the weary Wallace away, or at least convince the butler to tutor the Keatings' man."

"So Baron is the type who kicks a man when he is down."

She giggled. "For a chance at a butler like Wallace? I'd kick Wolf too, though I do not believe a mere babe will lay him low for long."

"I, too, trust the Smythes will meet the challenge."

"That's not all."

He stroked her hair. "What else, my love?"

"My love?"

He could hear the smile, the pleasure in her voice.

"Lady Keating writes she hopes to soon share in their joy. Can you imagine?"

He could not. "Are you saying she is breeding?"

"I forgot that I cannot be subtle with you. Yes, she is going to have another baby. Perhaps they will finally have an heir. Baron, the lout, did not mention it. Is that obvious enough?" She poked him.

"Oh, it's subtlety you want, is it?" He pulled her down on the hay, settling his body over hers. "I can be subtle." He nipped at her earlobe, tracing a warm path down the skin of her soft neck until she was moving beneath him, pushing to be closer, to melt her body into his. "Admit it, Jane," he whispered, his hand trailing across her shoulder to caress her warm breast. "You don't like subtle."

"Oh, very well. Throw subtlety to the dogs. Ravish me." She raked her fingers through his hair and closed her legs about his waist. "I want to know I've been ravished."

He bent to take her nipple in his mouth, then paused and sat back. She raised a brow. "Is this more of your subtlety?"

"No. It occurred to me we are to marry in a fortnight, and I have not yet proposed to you."

She rose on her elbows, allowing her chemise to fall off her shoulder. One breast was already visible in the lamplight. He need but tug on the material, and he could have both in his hands. He could have her in his arms.

"You proposed in my uncle's offices at Barbican headquarters."

"A proposal that you called the worst in history, or something to that effect."

"Hmm." She reached for his waistband and pulled him to her. "I don't care about that any longer. Come here."

He stood. "Not until I do this properly."

"No." She shook her head. "You're no proper gentleman. If you're going to propose, do it most improperly."

"Is that what you want?"

"Oh, yes." She tugged him closer, but he resisted, instead falling to one knee before her. She raised a brow.

"We are in a stable, half-naked, and about to make love. I cannot think of anything more improper. This is a story we will not tell the grandchildren."

"Or perhaps we might tell them an edited version."

"And it shall go something like this. Miss Bonde, from the moment I saw you, you stole my heart. I did not give it freely."

"God knows that is the truth."

He ignored her. "And you did not request it. You stole it away, and when I tried to reclaim it, I found I didn't want it anymore. I wanted yours instead."

Her eyes were shining with tears now. "You've thought about this, haven't you?"

"I wanted it to be perfect."

"Oh, Dominic. *You* are perfect." She reached for him.

"I am not finished."

She had the nerve to appear exasperated.

"And when you gave me your heart, I knew there was only one thing to do. Miss Bonde, will you do me the honor of becoming my wife?" He was actually nervous saying the words. He hoped she had not heard his voice waver. She would say yes. Of course she would say yes. The banns had already been called twice.

"Dominic—I mean, Mr. Griffyn—I would like nothing more. Except"—she tugged him to her—"perhaps to be ravished."

Dominic gladly obliged.

SHANA GALEN'S NEW REGENCY ROMANCE SERIES

Covent Garden Cubs

WILL BE INTRODUCED IN EARLY 2015
WITH A NOVELLA

Viscount of Vice

READ ON FOR A SNEAK PEEK

HE WAS GOING TO HELL. SHAME, FLYNN THOUGHT, dangling from the third-floor window of a town house in exclusive Grosvenor Square. It was his birthday tomorrow, too. Actually, given the time of night, he'd already attained his twenty-seventh year.

His hand slipped, and he felt the moisture gathering on his fingers. He could not hold on much longer. Perhaps his death was for the best. It wasn't as though anyone would mourn him. It wasn't as though he had anything to live for.

Still, it seemed harsh even for one such as Beelzebub to claim him when he was hanging naked from the window of one of the most prestigious addresses in Mayfair.

"Flynn!" a woman's voice hissed. His name was Henry Flynn, and he was the new Lord Chesham, but most everyone still called him Flynn—that was, when he wasn't being called something far less complimentary.

"Still here," he answered through teeth clenched with the effort of maintaining his hold.

A cloud of blond hair appeared above him, and he felt her hand on his. "Quick! Climb up before he returns."

He was her husband, a duke of enormous wealth and power. If *he* found Flynn in the duchess's bed-chamber, he'd ruin Flynn and the entire Chesham family. The danger of discovery hadn't deterred Flynn from accepting the duchess's invitation, though. In fact, the more risk, the better. He should simply let go of the ledge and get it over with. Then he could stop looking for death.

Instead, he squeezed his eyes shut and hauled himself upward. His arms shook with the effort, but he managed to gain the leverage he needed, and the duchess made a show of hauling him the rest of the way inside.

"Where are my clothes?" he asked without preamble.

"You cannot think to leave now," she protested. She was dressed in a frilly robe, cut low to display her generous cleavage. In truth, the duchess was beautiful, if a bit past her prime, but their close call had stolen away Flynn's desire for the distraction provided by a dalliance.

"I *do* think to leave now, Your Grace." He looked about for his clothing. It had been scattered about on the floor by her bed, but now it had vanished. He did not want to walk through the ball naked as the day he was born, but he would do so if it became necessary. Let the duchess explain that to her guests. Of course, the *ton* expected nothing less of the man they'd proclaimed the Viscount of Vice.

"But, my lord," the duchess protested, extending

a long finger to stroke his chest. "You have not yet fulfilled your promises. This was to be a night I would not soon forget."

Any lingering desire he might have felt revolted at her touch. "It is a night *I* will not soon forget," he replied. "And one your husband will not soon forget if I'm forced to exit dressed—or rather, undressed—like so."

"That would be unwise, Flynn," she said, raking her gaze over him. "One look at you and the female attendees would swoon. You are an excellent specimen of manhood."

"Thank you. My clothing?"

She folded her arms across her chest. "Certainly. As soon as you fulfill your promises."

Flynn narrowed his eyes. She thought that sort of veiled threat would persuade him? Even if she'd been the queen herself, Flynn was not going to bed a woman he did not desire. He had not sunk that low. "Very well, Your Grace," he said with a nod. She smiled and reached for the tie of her robe. Flynn walked right past her, ignoring her squeal of protest, and stopped to retrieve his beaver hat, which he'd spotted under a side table. From that angle, he spied his trousers under the bed, and one of his boots behind a curtain. Thus attired, Flynn stepped into the corridor outside her bedchamber.

A maid rushing by with an armful of linen shrieked and dropped her load. Flynn tipped his hat and continued on. He was halfway to the main staircase when the duchess appeared in her doorway. "Flynn," she hissed. "Flynn!"

Without looking back, he descended the stairs. The footman stationed at the base of the enormous curving marble staircase looked up at him, blinked, and looked forward again, his expression stoic. The guests in the vestibule were not quite so well trained. Fortunately, there were only a dozen or so men and women in the entryway. Most of the guests were in the ballroom, but there were always guests leaving early or arriving late. Several women shrieked, a man or two cursed, and Flynn kept his head high despite the chuckles and murmurs of appreciation.

An old school chum, whose name Flynn didn't remember, nodded at him. "Nice hat, Flynn."

"Thank you."

"You ought to be ashamed of yourself!" a woman yelled, pointing a finger at him. Her other hand was wrapped around a debutante's head, shielding the girl's eyes. He could see the girl blinking at him through the spaces between her mother's fingers. Flynn winked and kept walking. Finally, he was at the doorway.

"Your carriage, my lord?" the butler asked.

"Yes."

"Shall I have your greatcoat fetched, my lord?"

Flynn glanced at the man and nodded. "Please. I find the breeze a bit nippy this evening."

"Yes, my lord."

And so it was that the Viscount of Vice had to return to his town house for a change of wardrobe before he was able to travel to his club. Of course, by the time he arrived at Brooks, the news had already spread, and he encountered every reaction from slaps on the shoulder to cold stares.

He headed for the Great Subscription Room, intent on gambling and drinking his way into oblivion, but he was stopped at the wide double doors. A bleary-eyed man with disheveled gray hair and a bulbous red nose stepped in front of him.

"Excuse me, my lord."

The man was the earl or marquess of something, but Flynn would be damned if he could remember. He did remember he'd won a great deal from the lord the last time he'd gambled here. Apparently, the man held a grudge.

"You choused me out of three hundred pounds the last time we met."

Flynn raised a brow and observed several heads turned in their direction. The Great Subscription Room had a concave ceiling, which ensured sound carried. "I did not chouse you," Flynn said. "I won fairly."

The lord stumbled forward and pointed a lily-white finger in his face. "You've never lived an honest day in your life. Get out before I have you thrown out."

Several men, presumably the lord's friends, stepped forward in a menacing show of support for the man. Flynn sighed. This was not his night. Hell, it had not been his year or even his decade. He sure as the devil was not going to retreat, which meant he was going to be thrown out, probably quite unceremoniously. At least this time he'd be fully dressed. Flynn stepped forward, mirroring the actions of the men facing him. "I'd like to see you try to throw me out."

"Gentlemen," a genial voice said from behind him. Flynn turned to the Great Subscription Room and watched as the Duke of Ravenscroft ambled toward them. "We are still gentlemen, are we not?" the duke asked, spreading his hands. "I came here to escape the squalls of the new infant in my home, and instead of peace, I find quite the opposite."

The bulbous-nosed lord opened his mouth to issue a retort, but one of his friends pulled him aside and muttered something in his ear. Flynn imagined it was something to the effect that they would all be ejected if this continued. Flynn glanced at Ravenscroft, who motioned to the green-walled room, where rows of tables, each with its own lamp or two, housed games of cards or dice.

Ravenscroft led him to a rectangular table against a wall and seated himself on a red velvet couch. Flynn reached for the cards, but Ravenscroft moved them out of reach. "I would do better to hand you my blunt rather than try to best you. I have not slept in three days. Apparently, the phrase *slept like a babe* means one did not sleep at all, or rather, was woken at half hour intervals by screaming and wailing." The duke lifted a decanter of brandy and poured three fingers into the snifter on the table. He surprised Flynn by pushing the drink toward him. "You look like you need it."

"I do." Flynn downed it and pushed the snifter back for more.

"Do you search out scandal or does it find you?"

"I am a lodestone for it," Flynn said, taking the snifter when Ravenscroft had filled it again. Flynn leaned back in his chair. "Why did you help me just now?"

"Clearly someone has to, old boy."

"If you are my last hope, I have fallen far indeed."

Ravenscroft laughed. "You always did amuse me, Flynn."

"That's because you were generally foxed and easy to amuse." Flynn drank the snifter down, feeling a pleasant sense of warm numbness settle in his bones. When he was numb, he didn't have to think, to remember.

"I had another purpose for coming to your aid just now."

Flynn fingered the snifter and waited. No one, not even old friends, did anything for free.

"Someone is looking for you. I told him I'd keep you here until he could return."

"Does this have to do with—?"

"That *revealing* incident at the ball in Grosvenor Square earlier this evening?"

Flynn winced. "Touché."

The duke smiled. "I do not think the two are related. Do you know Sir Brook Derring?"

"Derring? Is that the family name for the earls of Dane?"

"Flynn, you *do* pay attention."

"Are you trying to goad me into punching you?"

"This is the earl's younger brother. He works for Bow Street."

Flynn rose. "What the hell are you about? An *investigator*? And you claim to be my savior?"

A hand clamped down on Flynn's shoulder from behind. "You'll want to hear what I have to say."

"Derring." Ravenscroft acknowledged the newcomer.

Flynn shrugged the hand off and turned to face the man. "Touch me again, and you're dead."

"And with that," Ravenscroft said, rising, "I will take my leave. Flynn, let's not meet again." He nodded to Derring and walked away.

Derring indicated the table. "Sit."

Flynn glanced about, noting the men who had threatened him earlier still loitered nearby, standing in plain sight under the chandelier. Perhaps now was not the best time to walk out. His gaze slid back to Derring. The man looked as though he'd been up all night. His dark blond hair was in disarray, as though he'd repeatedly run his hands through it. He had not shaved in a day or so, and his eyes were bleary. He had taken the time to dress, however. One did not enter Brooks in anything less than proper attire.

Derring leaned forward. "As you might have gathered, I am an investigator. I was hired to find a missing person. I have not found that individual—yet—but I have found your brother."

Flynn felt his world tilt and spin. He gripped the edge of the table to keep from falling out of his chair, and he closed his eyes against a wave of dizziness. Derring was still talking, saying something about shocks, but all Flynn could hear was the howl of the wind. That was strange, was it not? He was inside.

His hand snaked across the table toward the decanter of brandy Ravenscroft had left behind. The hand looked as though it belonged to someone else, though he recognized the stain on the thumb of the glove as well as the sleeve of the coat. The hand trembled, and Derring finally took pity, lifted the decanter, and filled the snifter to the rim.

Flynn gulped it as a dying man gulps the elixir

of immortality and pushed the snifter back. Derring shook his head. "I need you sober."

"No, you don't." Flynn looked Derring in the eye. "You do not want to see me when I'm sober."

"I will have to take that chance because you are to come with me to Bath. Now. Tonight."

Flynn shook his head. "I'm not going to Bath." Good God, his mother was in Bath, taking the waters or some such nonsense. He did not want to be obliged to call on her. She'd only shake her head at him and look disappointed. He hated it when she looked disappointed.

"Your brother needs you," Derring said. He reached across the table and caught Flynn's hand before he could rise.

"My brother is dead. He died years ago. I killed him." The words echoed in Flynn's mind, taunting him as he'd been taunted his entire life since that day so long ago.

Acknowledgments

Heartfelt appreciation and gratitude go to
   My editor, Deb Werksman;
   My agents, Danielle Egan-Miller and Joanna MacKenzie, and Abby Saul too;
   My assistant Gayle, who takes care of all the administrative stuff so I can write;
   My web mavens, Maddee and Jen at xuni.com;
   Danielle Dresser, my publicist, whom I adore;
   My fellow writers at the Brainstorm Troopers, the PBK Moms, the Jaunty Quills, and the West Houston RWA chapter;
   My friends and supporters, Tina, Sharie, Tera, Laura, Jo Anne, Emily, and Amy;
   The Shananigans;
   My family, especially my husband and daughter;
   And last, but not least, my readers.

About the Author

Shana Galen is the national bestselling author of fast-paced, adventurous Regency historicals, including the RT Reviewers' Choice *The Making of a Gentleman*. She taught English at the middle and high school levels for eleven years. Most of those years were spent working in Houston's inner city. Now she writes full time. She's happily married to a man she calls Ultimate Sportsfan and has a daughter who is most definitely a romance heroine in the making. The family is owned by two cats Baby Galen named Mickey and Maisy. Shana loves to hear from readers: Visit her website at www.shanagalen.com, download her free author app for exclusive content and first looks, or see what she's up to daily on Facebook and Twitter.

The Truth about Leo

by Katie MacAlister

New York Times Bestselling Author

— ❧ —

Can Dagmar flee Denmark

Dagmar Marie Sophie is a poverty-stricken Danish princess whose annoying royal cousin is about to have her stuffed away in a convent. When she finds a wounded man unconscious in her garden, she sees a way out of her desperate situation.

By lying to Leo?

Leopold Ernst George Mortimer, seventh earl of March, and spy in the service of the king, finds himself on the wrong end of a saber and left for dead. He wakes up not remembering what happened…in the care of a beautiful woman who says she is his wife.

Back in London, Leo—with the help of his old friends, the eccentric Britton family—sets out to unravel what he's forgotten… Is Dagmar truly the wonderful, irrepressible woman who makes his heart sing, or is she a dangerous enigma bent on his destruction?

— ❧ —

Praise for Katie MacAlister:

"Delightful…MacAlister's comic genius
really shines!" —*RT Book Reviews*

For more Katie MacAlister, visit:

www.sourcebooks.com

A Midsummer Bride

by Amanda Forester

❧

One unconventional American heiress can be even wilder than the Highlands...

Outspoken American heiress Harriet Redgrave is undeniably bad *ton*. She laughs too much, rides too fast, and tends to start fires pursuing her interest in the new science of chemistry. And despite her grandfather's matchmaking intentions to the contrary, Harriet has no interest in being wooed for her wealth.

Duncan Maclachlan, Earl of Thornton, would never marry to repair the family fortunes. Or would he? When he saves Harriet from a science experiment about to go very, very wrong, all bets are off...

❧

Praise for *A Wedding in Springtime*:

"This entertaining novel is a diamond of the first order... The clever combination of wit, romance, and suspense strikes all the right notes." —*Booklist* Starred Review

"Forester promises her fans a warm, humorous jaunt through Regency England—and she delivers with a cast of engaging characters and delightful intrigue." —*RT Book Reviews*

For more Amanda Forester, visit:

www.sourcebooks.com

To Charm a Naughty Countess

by Theresa Romain

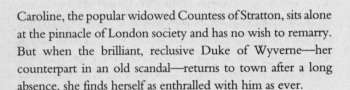

Caroline, the popular widowed Countess of Stratton, sits alone at the pinnacle of London society and has no wish to remarry. But when the brilliant, reclusive Duke of Wyverne—her counterpart in an old scandal—returns to town after a long absence, she finds herself as enthralled with him as ever.

Michael must save his family fortunes by wedding an heiress, but Caroline has vowed never again to sell herself in marriage. She offers him an affair, hoping to master her long-lasting fascination with him—but he remains steadfast, as always, in his dedication to purpose and his dukedom.

The only way she can keep him near is to help him find the wealthy bride he requires. As she guides him through society, Caroline realizes that she's lost her heart again. But if she pursues the only man she's ever loved, she'll lose the life she's built and on which she has pinned her sense of worth. And if Michael—who has everything to lose—ever hopes to win her hand, he must open his long-shuttered heart.

For more Theresa Romain, visit:

www.sourcebooks.com

Once Upon a Kiss

The Book Club Belles Society
by Jayne Fresina

~ტ~

The Perfect Hero

When handsome, mysterious Darius Wainwright strolls into town, the Book Club Belles are instantly smitten with his brooding good looks and prideful demeanor. It's as if he walked out of the pages of their favorite new novel, a scandalous romance called Pride and Prejudice. But Justina Penny can't understand why her fellow Belles are starry-eyed in the newcomer's arrogant presence—surely a wicked Wickham would be infinitely more fun...

An Unlikely Leading Lady

Justina is the opposite of Darius's ideal woman—not that he's looking for romance. But when he discovers her stealing apples from his uncle's orchard, he can't resist his own thieving impulse. A stolen kiss from the mischievous Miss Penny leaves Darius wanting much, much more. If it's a dashing villain she desires, Darius is more than willing to play the part...

~ტ~

Praise for *The Most Improper Miss Sophie Valentine:*

"Eminently witty." —*Publishers Weekly*

"Decidedly humorous, as well as sensual...a true charmer of a read." —*RT Book Reviews*

For more Jayne Fresina, visit:

www.sourcebooks.com

In Bed with a Rogue

Rival Rogues

by Samantha Grace

— ❧ —

He's the talk of the town

The whole town is tittering about Baron Sebastian Thorne having been jilted at the altar. Every move he makes ends up in the gossip columns. Tired of being the butt of everyone's jokes, Sebastian vows to restore his family's reputation no matter what it takes.

She's the toast of the *ton*

Feted by the crème of Society, the beautiful widow Lady Prestwick is a vision of all that is proper. But Helena is no angel, and when Sebastian uncovers her dark secret, he's quick to press his advantage. In order to keep her hard-won good name, Helena will have to make a deal with the devil. But she has some tricks up her sleeves to keep this notorious rogue on his toes…

— ❧ —

Praise for *One Rogue Too Many*:

"Filled with humor and witty repartee… Grace woos readers in true Regency style." —*Publishers Weekly*

"Charming…Grace captures the essence and atmosphere of the era." —*RT Book Reviews*

For more Samantha Grace, visit:

www.sourcebooks.com

How to Lose a Lord in 10 Days or Less

Tricks of the Ton

by Elizabeth Michels

❧

Their love sparks in the stables

After years away from home, Andrew Clifton, Lord Amberstall, is attacked by a hired hit man on his way back to London. But with an injured horse and no shelter, Andrew becomes the unintentional houseguest of the Moore family.

But it's bound to be a bumpy ride

Katie Moore could always be found at the stables—until her riding accident. Now she locks herself away from Society—embarrassed by her injuries. While Katie tends to Andrew's horse, the two are at odds about everything, except their feelings for one another and the danger that they're about to discover on the road ahead…

❧

Praise for *Must Love Dukes:*

"Michels's fast-paced debut is sweet and…accurately depicts the difficulties faced by nineteenth-century aristocratic women." —*Publishers Weekly*

For more Elizabeth Michels, visit:

www.sourcebooks.com

Mischief by Moonlight

Regency Mischief
by Emily Greenwood

❧

Be very, very careful what you wish for…

With the night so full of romance…

Colin Pearce, the Earl of Ivorwood, never dreamed he'd desire another man's fiancée, but when his best friend goes off to war and asks Colin to look after the bewitching Josie Cardworthy, he falls under her sparkling spell.

Who can resist mischief?

Josie can't wait for the return of her long-absent fiancé. If only her beloved sister might find someone, too… someone like the handsome, reserved Colin. A gypsy's love potion gives Josie the chance to matchmake, but the wild results reveal her own rowing passion for the earl. And though fate offers them a chance, a steely honor may force him to reject what her reckless heart is offering…

❧

For more Emily Greenwood, visit:

www.sourcebooks.com